THE
WHITE TREE

ALSO BY EDWARD W. ROBERTSON

THE CYCLE OF ARAWN

The White Tree
The Great Rift
The Black Star

THE CYCLE OF GALAND

The Red Sea
The Silver Thief

THE BREAKERS SERIES

Breakers
Melt Down
Knifepoint
Reapers
Cut Off
Captives
Relapse
Blackout

THE
WHITE TREE

THE CYCLE OF ARAWN, BOOK 1

EDWARD W. ROBERTSON

Copyright © 2011 Edward W. Robertson

All rights reserved.

Cover art by Miguel Coimbra

ISBN: 1470150603
ISBN-13: 978-1470150600

To Caitlin, for letting me get lost in other worlds.

Mallon, Gask, and other lands.

1

It was the dog's fault Dante was about to die. The ruins of the chapel hunched behind him, hiding the man who'd soon kill him. Because of the dog, he was thirty miles from Bressel, ten from the nearest farm, and a world away from help. Despite his isolation, he didn't doubt his body would be found—corpses had gravity, as if the vapors released by death were starkly visible to the mind's eye. If the man who'd attacked him didn't find his body lying in the cold grass and colder wind, a farmer or a pilgrim would.

But they wouldn't know who he was. He'd be a body. A nothing. Another lump on the surface of a world too large to understand.

He sat up in the grass, pain rushing down his side and thigh. The chapel was supposed to be abandoned. Instead, he'd found a guard waiting inside its walls. The man had cut him. Badly. He'd been lucky to escape into the fields with his life.

Blood gleamed dull black beneath the overcast sky. Dante's stomach cramped. He fell back into the grass, panting, tears sliding down his temples into his hair. He caught his breath and shrugged off his cloak. It tore easily. Too easily. Would never have made it through the upcoming winter. He bound his wounds, tying them tight, grimacing against the dizziness and nausea. Wind hissed through the grass and pines.

He tested his leg and found that he could stand.

It would be stupid to go back inside. Dumb like a severed arm is dumb. But the man lurking in the temple wasn't a looter or a squatter. He was a guard. Guards, by definition, guarded. The man wasn't there to protect the chapel itself. That had been torched during the Third Scour. The following century of weather and vandals had ruined the rest of it. Stonework rubbled the field, cracked rocks fuzzy with moss. Holes spotted the pitched roof, darker than the clouds. This temple of Arawn was four generations and a hard day's walk removed from the last time and place anyone had cared about its god. It was a cold night and the sporadic rain was colder still.

And yet there was a guard. Dante was onto something.

He drew his knife and crept toward the chapel, smelling the tall, wet grass as it soaked against his legs. Nothing moved except the wind-stirred trees. He touched the damp stone of the wall. He felt his way forward, fingers trailing the wall. After a few steps, they fell into empty space. He froze, breath catching in his chest. That moment of cowardice saved his life.

A man coughed from so close Dante could smell his breath. The guard emerged from the hole in the wall into the cloud-occluded starlight. His sword hung from his hip. He gazed into the bobbing pines, most likely imagining the boy he'd cut up not five minutes before curled beneath the cold boughs, heat and blood slowly ebbing from his body.

The man wandered into the grass. Dante pressed his back against the wall. He waited for the guard to take another step, then lunged forward and slashed at his hamstrings. The man screamed and fell. He rocked in the grass, clutching the backs of his legs. Dante danced back and wondered what the hell to do next.

"Get back!" the man yelled.

Dante found himself. He pressed his boot against the man's ribs. "Where is the book?"

"What book?"

"I'll cut your throat," Dante said. His voice caught. He swallowed. "You'll be a body in the woods. Eaten by badgers."

"I don't know of any book." The guard pawed a bloody hand at Dante's breeches. "If there was anything here, they took it back north long ago."

"Then why are you here? Your health?"

The man started to speak, then took a long, shuddery breath, squinting at Dante's face. "How old are you?"

"Would you ask death his age?" Dante said, and felt immediately foolish.

"I'd say he looks about fourteen."

"I'm sixteen. My name is Dante Galand. And if you don't tell me where you keep the book, I'm the last man you'll ever see."

"I'm telling you. It's gone. Returned to Narashtovik where men don't want to burn it."

Dante knelt and dug his knife into the guard's smooth-worn leather shirt. The iron tip clicked against the man's breastbone. The guard sucked air between his teeth, eyes white and watery. Dante gulped down a retch, withdrew the knife, and hovered it over the man's heart.

"I hope its secrets are worth your life."

"Stop!" The man wriggled his shoulders, pushing himself into the sodden grass. "It's in the basement. Downstairs."

"I didn't see any stairs."

"Third row of the graveyard. Fourth stone. There's a ladder underneath it. I haven't seen anything down there but candles and prayer books. I drank all the wine. But if there's a book, it's down there."

They stared at each other in the damp autumn air. Dante couldn't leave the man here. It would be like cleaning a deer. Focus on the knife's edge. Keep your fingers out of the way. Work fast, concentrate on the cut. Wash up when you're done.

But deer didn't talk back. They couldn't call you a murderer. Dante steeled himself and poked the blade between the man's ribs.

"You promised!" he gasped.

"And you tried to kill me."

Dante drove down hard on the hilt. The guard bucked, legs thrashing, knocking Dante off balance. He grabbed the knife's handle again and leaned on it with all his weight. The man went as slack as a summer pond. Dante's stomach spasmed. He felt a thousand feet tall. He wanted to die. He was frozen, stunned, waiting to be smited by the man's god. The wind whispered to him through the needles of the pines.

All this for a dog.

He'd seen it just that summer. Its body lay on the bank of the creek miles upstream from his village. Short, skinny trees grew so thick around the stream that you could barely see the sky. One of the dog's paws dangled in the water. Its fur was clumped with blood, its eyes shut, legs rigid. Flies whirled around its nose and lips. A noose trailed from its neck.

Its death was a stain on the face of innocence. Dante shrank behind a birch, gripping its smooth, papery bark. This was his place. There was nothing between it and the village but marshes and ponds. A few hills with grass on their crowns and trees in their folds. A couple of shacks, too, but their roofs were staved in, homes to no one. You could hunt it, perhaps—it was common ground—but it was otherwise useless land. Unless, like Dante, you had a thing for exploring. He spent whole days following the creek, turning stones over in its quiet pools, throwing pebbles at waterstriders, poking at snails to watch them suck into their shells. He was too old for such things. He knew that. He just didn't know where else to go.

Leaves crackled thirty yards upstream from the dog. A man in a bright mail shirt stepped out from the trees and knelt beside the water. He cupped his hand, drank, and flopped back on the bank to pluck burrs from his black cloak. A silver icon clasped it around his throat, the emblem rayed like a tree or a star.

Finished, the man stood, stretched, and started downstream toward Dante. The man's hand whipped for his sword. Dante breathed through his mouth, rooted in place. The man stalked forward and stopped over the dog.

He hunkered down and prodded its throat. The stream splashed along beneath the clouds. The man drew a knife, put it to the dog's throat, and sawed briskly. Dante tasted bile. The man pulled the now-severed noose from the animal's neck and tossed it into the creek.

He then touched his knife to his left hand. Blood winked from his palm. The air blurred around his hands. Small dark things flocked to his fingers, moths or horseflies or bad ideas, black motes that clung to the blood sliding down his wrist. They congealed into something round and semitranslucent. The man lowered his hands to the dog's ribs. The ball of shadows flowed into the motionless body.

He fell back, smirking, and pressed his bleeding palm to his mouth. The dog kicked its legs.

The man in the mail shirt got to his feet. After a faltering, stiff-limbed try, so did the dog. The man scratched its ears; it whined; the man laughed. Still whining, the dog backed up the bank and limped into the trees. The man belted his knife, glanced down creek, and followed it into the woods.

Through all of it, Dante could sense what was happening the way he could smell cold or feel a shadow on his skin. When the dog shivered up to its feet, that was the world showing him just how big it really was, and that if he wanted it—if he wanted to wield what the man in the bright mail had drawn from the air—he would have to come find it.

Half-dazed, Dante ran back to the village. No one there had seen the man come through. When Dante turned and gazed at the creek winding its way out of town, the woods and fields looked pale and common. The snails and waterstriders were just bugs. Dante went to bed and couldn't sleep. When he was a child, his dad had made lights dance in his hands. Told stories of playing bodyguards for dukes. Of hiring on with ships and using his talents as a soldier-doctor. That route was technically illegal—only royals and the church could employ the ether-users—but it wasn't the law that had taken his father away. Nine years ago, the man had sailed west. He'd stayed there. Perhaps he'd died along the way.

In the morning, Dante worked up his nerve and asked the monk who cared for him about living shadows and a silver star or tree. The monk's face grew distant. After a moment, he explained that before anyone now alive in Mallon had been born, shadow-wielding men carried the book of the White Tree and worshiped the old god Arawn. But they'd been burnt out of the land, the men and their books, during the Third Scour. The monk had once read a fragment of the book. The rest was lost to the ruin of the past.

The monk retreated into the monastery in search of his notes on the fragment. Two weeks later, Dante went to Bressel in search of the book itself. There, he spent his pennies buying beer for the capital's archivists and churchmen. One mug at a time, Dante learned the book wasn't a sort of recipe of spells, but the holy text of the

Arawnites, quite comparable to the *Kalavar* of Gashen or the *Silver Thief* of Carvahal. The scholars and priests agreed that all known copies had been burnt, but that if any remained, they could be identified by a cover bearing a white tree.

That had been it. Dante ran out of money. Ran out of ideas. Empty-handed and out of options, he tracked down one of their temples and headed into the woods.

The wind surged through the trees. A strange chain connected him from the dog to this place. Because of it, a man lay dead at his feet.

He wiped his knife and hands in the grass and headed around the back of the chapel. Gravestones dotted the swaying grass. The fourth stone of the third row was flinty and black and flat. Dante nudged it with his toe, then dug his fingers under its lip. He strained against the stone and pivoted it into the weeds.

It revealed a hole hardly wide enough for a man to pass his shoulders. Dante squinted into the gloom. The trapped air smelled musty, faint with the human odor of sweat and skin, the scent of another man's house. He shrank back, fighting a sudden terror for what lay in the darkness below. It wasn't anything as certain as eels or as vague as monsters that slunk through the outlands of his imagination, but something in between: pale things with the tentacles of squid, the intelligence of men, and the cruelty of the stars.

He leaned over and spat, counting two before it spattered. So it had a bottom. The rungs of a time-smoothed ladder descended from the starlight into blackness. Dante dropped his legs over the edge and scrabbled for a rung. The ladder creaked. Hand over hand, he descended, armpits slimy with sweat, until he stood in a circle of faintest light at its bottom.

Dante owned two things worth stealing. The first was his boots. The second was the only thing his father had left him before sailing into death or waters too warm to leave. He took it from his pocket, a torchstone, a small white marble. He held it in his palm and blew. It warmed and glowed. In the soft white light, dust caked the slanted shelves along the walls. Dante pawed through moldy cloth, water-spotted braziers, foul-smelling candles. A patina of age coated everything, greasy and yellow-gray.

There were two shelves of books. Dante's heart leapt, but they were all copies of a common prayer manual he'd seen in the Library of Bressel and the vendors in the binding district. He stuffed the least mildewed in his pack anyway.

He swept through the basement wall to wall. He turned in a circle, hunting for anything he'd missed, then went through it again, piling up the junky relics in the middle of the room and prodding the shelves and drawers for hidden compartments. What he'd taken as a stool turned out to be a scuffed-up chest. He smashed its rusty lock with a brick and was rewarded with three sludgy bottles. With waning patience and waxing despair, he searched the small basement a third time, moving as slowly and carefully as he could make himself go. At the end, he wandered to the circle of starlight and gazed up the ladder. It would be dawn soon. At some point the guard's relief would find the body cooling in the yard. Maybe not for days, but for all Dante knew a second guard had already arrived and was already scouring the grass for the killer of his friend.

Dante was wearing down, too. The scabs of his cuts dribbled blood with every too-quick gesture. He was tired and thirsty and sore. The sphere of light shrank back toward the torchstone. In thickening shadow, Dante sat down on a desk. It was too big to have been lowered down the hole as it was. They must have brought it down in pieces and nailed it together in the cellar.

His hope contracted with the light. The first frost would come any day. He'd used up half his cloak for bandages and didn't have a cent to replace it. If he went back to Bressel, he'd starve and freeze. If he returned to the village, he'd regret it all his life.

The stone flickered, throwing the room into deep shadow, revealing a crease in the shelves near the ceiling. Before Dante could be certain it was there, the light blinked off for good.

He shuffled across the blackened room, candlesticks clattering away from his feet, and bumped into the wooden shelves. He climbed them until he could press his palm against the cobwebbed ceiling. He'd seen the crease just below the top shelf. He scrabbled his fingernails against the coarse wood. They slid into a crack.

Splinters drove under his nails. Bit by bit, he pried the false top away from the shelf. With a high-pitched groan, it fell away and whapped against the floor. He smelled dry paper and earthy leather. Dante reached blind into the crevice, heart beating hard. There couldn't possibly be anything lurking inside; there was no chance he'd feel a sharp tug and pull back one less knuckle than he'd started the day with. His fingers brushed over a flat, pebbled surface. It was the first thing he'd touched down here that wasn't dusty or greasy with neglect. He lifted the object loose. The shelf he stood on snapped in half.

He hit the ground hard. His hip and shoulder roared with hammerblows of pain. He waited for the ache to fade to a dizzy tingle before he tested them for breaks. His limbs moved freely and without fresh hurts. By right, the fall should have left him broke-legged or paralyzed, trapped in the ground beneath the graves. He shouldn't have even made it this far. Except for dumb luck, he should have died two hours ago, struck down by the guard. His body splayed outside the chapel. Wounds long done bleeding. Body held down by the wind and the clouds until it merged with the dirt.

But his bones weren't broken. The guard *hadn't* killed him. He was bruised and weak and leaking blood from his side, but the thing in his hands was a book. He'd held onto it as he fell. After he hit the ground. Now, he stashed it in his pack and climbed back up the ladder.

Up top, he got it out once more, turning it to face the charcoal-clouded starlight. On its cover, a pale tree spread its branches to the darkness.

The White Tree. Barden, the monk had called it. Supposedly, it was as real as the hills and stood in the twilight valley at the north end of the earth. According to the monk—even when they'd talked, Dante had been skeptical; wasn't it convenient that it existed so far away—it had sprouted from a god's own knuckle. Instead of bark and leaves and wood, it had grown of bone and bone alone. Its knotty trunk hewn from thighs and spines. Its long limbs the arcs of ribs and the knobby curls of fleshless fingers. Instead of flowers, it budded teeth.

Book in hand, Dante laughed lowly, spooking himself. Why not just paint a bunch of flames around it, too? Or bind it in skin and ink it in blood? That would be no less ridiculous than the gleaming bones on its cover.

Yet there was something to it. He could feel its weight. Its age. When he closed his eyes, he thought he could feel the power the man in the mail shirt had used to raise the dog from the creek. Goosebumps stood out on Dante's neck and arms. He packed away the book and hauled the heavy gravestone back over the pit into the cellar.

Ragged black mountains hung to the west. To the east, Bressel was a full day's walk for a well-rested man. Dante slunk into the woods, shuffling along the rutted path hidden beneath the grass. As the sun rose, his legs faltered. He balled himself up under a squat tree, shading himself from the itchy light of morning.

Before he slept, he gave himself one last look at the book. Exposed by the daylight, the tree looked less absurd, less melodramatically morbid, and more like something that could be waiting in the wilds, if only the world were a slightly weirder place.

He'd wind up standing beneath it within half a year.

2

The funny thing about robbery, Dante thought as he crouched in the filth of an unlit alley, is how little the concept of property meant to him once he'd started going to bed hungry. So the watch would hang him if they caught him? That didn't mean he was wrong to do it, that just meant he shouldn't under any circumstances get caught. What kind of rule was so weak it had to be backed up by death threats? Who cares about being hanged when the alternative's starving? And if they really didn't want robbers in the city, why did they build their alleys exactly like the fish-pens that funnel careless salmon into waiting nets?

He heard footsteps at the other end of the alley and shrank down further. The moment the man passed Dante clubbed him above the ear with the polished horn of his knife's hilt. The man dropped, voiceless. As Dante stripped the body of its purse and the pair of rings on its right hand he noted the man was still breathing. Good for him. The penalty for Dante, if caught, would be the same whether the victim lived or died. He didn't understand that, either. A man of lesser principles would be tempted to kill the man he robbed so he couldn't be identified to the watch. Dante opened the man's jacket in search of a second purse and saw the taut-laced buckskin badge of the tanner's guild. He frowned. He didn't want trouble with guildsmen. They were too close to running the city these days. He hurried to cover the unconscious body with some shredded rags he found among the other garbage, then left the alley in something less than a jog.

The walk from the chapel had taken three days. He'd managed

about ten stiff-legged miles the first day, then no more than two on the second before he collapsed at a waterway so small it was more puddle than lake. He laid down on its cool banks, moaning and burning, and whenever he closed his eyes the crystal-clear faces of men and women he'd never seen swam in his mind's vision. When the fever broke early next morning he shuffled over the roots and rocks toward the city in the east, stopping frequently for rest and water, but he reached Bressel before sunrise and immediately spent the last of his silver on a room for a week. He haunted the corners of its common room those first couple days, snaking from the safety of the wall to nab meat and bread when their owners' heads hit the table or they swayed off to find the privy. That had worked until the boy who worked the mornings threatened to throw him out if he caught him again. Dante nodded, face stony as he suffered the threats of a kid who couldn't be more than fourteen, then retreated to his room to pass the day throwing his knife at the rats that skittered across the floor. It was a pointless task, though; he knew he'd never work up the courage to spit them and set them over the common room fire.

Robbing, from there, and after what he'd done at the chapel, came easily. His nerves had threatened to give out on him on his initial try, but when he left his first mark in forceful slumber in the shit-caked gutter of an alley, he wondered that it took so little effort to turn things they owned into things he owned. An average purse could feed him for a week—and this was just the money people carried around for luxuries and whims—what did they need it all for? He limited his own expenses to food, room, and candles to read by, but he knew he could have more if his interests had been in things instead of in the book. Whatever authority had given these men their wealth was no more substantial than the power of a rabbit's foot—it felt good to carry, but when things went bad, it turned out all you were carrying to protect you was a lump of meat too nasty to eat and the knowledge that somewhere a bunny had left the warren and never come home.

He walked on. Bootsteps rasped from behind him in the alley and he started. He fingered the knife beneath his doublet, but let it be. Men who showed blades without a landed title or writ of the guild of arms were taught the things a whip could do better than a sword. Dante turned onto an arterial road and huddled in a doorway until the man passed without a glance.

He knew he'd been jumpy lately, but how else should he act after a killing, the possession of a banned book, and multiple acts of armed robbery? It sounded terrible when you said it all at once. Most of the time he carried it lightly, knowing any deed done out of necessity couldn't be wrong, but other times he was struck by an emotion so powerful he wanted to cease existing altogether. At those times he muttered to himself, walking through the streets as if in a dream, drowning in the memory of the short shouts of those he'd robbed, the slackening face of the dead man at the temple, the snore-like expulsion of his last breath. It was clear he couldn't go on like this. It wasn't how he'd meant to live when he'd left the village for Bressel, but it was what circumstances had forced him to. His only hope was with the book. If it could somehow teach him what the man in the mail shirt had known, he'd no longer have to look over his shoulder at every footstep or risk his life in the alleys just to keep from starving. His thoughts on how that power would help him were vague—he could hire himself out at the courts, he supposed—but he knew that once he had it, the opportunities of great men would find him on their own.

The book was dense. Not just in the literal sense of its thick-as-a-brick 800 pages, but dense with dozens of unfamiliar places and names, with warlords and sorcerers and tales he dimly remembered hearing as a child, cluttered with huge but bizarrely precise numbers like 432,000, stuffed with scores of words from a language he didn't recognize. Even its title was gibberish. Dante found some references to the book's people and places in the other book he'd taken, the prayer manual, but three or four hours of careful reading and cross-checking would let him read no more than ten or twenty pages of the book itself. Yet when he tried to read it straight through he found he'd absorbed nothing more than an occasional phrase or, more often, an illustration. He went to bed angry, handling the words in his head for an hour before he could fall asleep.

After three days of sluggish and haphazard reading he understood he didn't know a damn thing and set to copying all the foreign words and names out of the forty-odd pages of the book's first section. He bought a ream of paper and a bottle of ink with a week's price of food and spent a full seven days in the Library at Bressel, the onion-domed, marble-faced structure meant to gather the wisdom of the world. It was well-stocked, he found, for works composed in the fifty years since its founding, and he filled his blank pages with the histories and places in the book of the White Tree's beginning. The foreign words remained obscure: similar to the dialects they spoke up in Gask, he thought, maybe an archaic form, but far enough apart to render the study of Gaskan useless. Many of the book's stories reminded him of Mennok, the mopey old god of grief and blackbirds. Dante had always thought its followers were a joke, the kind of guys who groaned through the streets, whipping their own backs with supple reeds to remind themselves of the agony of the physical world. They just had to shove it in your face. He thought they could learn a thing from the supplicants of Urt, the more fanatical of whom spent 23 hours a day sleeping and meditating in dark rooms with planks hammered over the windows. Its saints had been known to seal themselves in barrels for months at a time. Most faiths, he thought, could stand to learn the virtue of keeping their devotion to themselves.

 He bought the collected cycle of Mennok from a run-down storefront in the book district and then a clean, simple doublet and trousers so he wouldn't be thrown out of the monastery's open archives before his second foot hit the threshold. Then the money was gone, and rather than scavenging at the inn, he robbed again, splurging that night on roasted beef. He woke mortified at his opulence, vowed to skimp through the rest on bread and cheese, and spent the day rereading that first section. At its conclusion he felt closer to his desire, as if this time he could see the shadow of what a wise man was supposed to glean from its contents, and here and there he even felt elevated by a glimpse of a world much wider than the one he'd known. Still he felt helpless with idiocy, like understanding the book was like trying to move a mountain with a bent fork and two broken arms, and he slammed the cover (after marking his place) and pounded to the common room, where four cups of ale floored him. He woke flushed and sweaty, sicker than the day after he'd been at the crumbling chapel, and wasted the day sipping water from the comfort of his bed, amazed that men could spend a life at the drink. After that, when he saw the men drooping over the smoky tables, shambling outside to vomit on the streetstones, he curled his lip, hating whatever weakness caused them to poison themselves that way.

It took another week of eye strain and the glares of white-haired monks to find a match for the words he'd never heard. Narashtovik, an old language, a dead language, indeed from the north, from the kingdom of Gask's earlier age, seen now in little more than the frostlanders' convoluted laws and nonsensical meal-rites. No dictionary, of course (they didn't even have such a thing for the local language of Mallish, other than a few vanity projects by wealthy men with no other diversions), but Dante found enough matching words to know he'd found their source. And there the lore stopped: nobody had books on all that old junk, or if they did, they were clapped away in the private libraries of nobles and the obsessive collectors of the scribe's guild. For now Dante set his search on hiatus and returned to the cribbed script of his stolen book, a book he now knew was named the *Cycle of Arawn*.

The mere act of finding its name shed fresh light on the first section that had so far given him such trouble. That night he read with mounting excitement, beginning to understand that Arawn was a god of death who didn't in any way seek it, a notion that ran heretical to those who'd won the Third Scour and denounced Arawn as a bloodthirsty monster ever since—but was nevertheless the undeniable interpretation of the text. This time when he finished those first forty pages, a chill of something close to ecstasy ran up the base of his neck. He had proof that at least one thing the other sects said was dead wrong. What else had he been taught on the basis of a mistake? How many lies had Dante taken on a faith that would prove unfounded? Did anyone know anything at all, or finding times when the truth didn't suit them, had they all been repeating falsehoods and nonsense for so long they no longer remembered what was fact and what was invention? In his enthusiasm, he nearly brought it up with a monk of Mennok he'd become friendly with, thinking his learning would be greatly hastened by a man who'd spent his life studying such things, but Dante had the sense to ask questions about Arawn would be to invite a slew aimed back at him, and it wouldn't be long after that he'd be locked in the stocks, and the only things aimed his way then would be airborne cabbage and the stroke of the lash.

He already had enough attention. Since the night in the alley when he thought he'd been followed, he often saw a face in the morning when he ducked into the Library and the same face waiting for him when he returned to the street in the afternoon. They'd pretend not to notice him, but when he paused to haggle over pennies on a loaf there they'd be again, gliding up to a stall like one of the flat-bottomed boats taking port in the river. Even in his new clothes Dante couldn't be mistaken for rich; he looked like an apprentice at best, possibly a young scholar out on an errand. He might be easy enough to rob, but he hardly looked worth the effort. Nor did he know a single soul in town, wasn't old or important enough to have earned any enemies, excepting the guard at the ruined chapel, and he was too busy rotting to hold a grudge. But for however little sense it made, people were following him, and every day he spent in the stacks he sweated buckets into his formerly-clean clothes, certain his knife would slip from his waist as he bent for a book and out him to the monks who hovered over their written treasures like robed dragonflies. Yet he didn't dare leave his room without it.

The attack came the night after he translated the title. The blow should have killed him, but he saw the flash of steel and moved with a quickness he hadn't known he possessed to raise the book of Mennok like a shield. It too was thick, bloated with footnotes and appendices and interpretorial digressions, and the attacker's dagger buried itself in the cover and stuck fast. Dante met the attacker's eyes and saw he wasn't a man but a neeling, the sharp face and elongated muzzle meant for cleaving the waters of the marshes and tide flats, the bumpy, translucent, toadlike skin, the thick glaze of a third eyelid over its wide and watery eyes. Web-footed things from the western archipelagos, they made good sailors and decent wharf rats, and though their light bones put the biggest of them in Dante's weight range, when the merchants of Bressel's bursting docks could hire three for every one real man, there were times on the wharfs when those froggish faces outnumbered their captains and mates ten to one. No one asked questions when they ended up dead, either, something that happened more and more the more they crowded the city and found themselves enmeshed in the crimes of the hated and despised.

The thing gave a panicked grunt when it saw what had blocked its blade. Dante had two inches and ten pounds on the neeling, and when he twisted the book the dagger popped from its hands without a fight. He lashed its knee with his boot and put a thumb to its throat as it fell, knife held high in his other hand.

"Wrong book," Dante said. It bared its poky teeth at him, watching his knife. "How did you know?"

Its hairless brows pinched together and Dante felt a pure instinct to cut its throat.

"They told me to follow you."

"How did they know it was me?"

"Dante Galand," it said.

His mind hung. Probably this creature had no idea who "they" were, but they had Dante's name and they knew his rounds through the city. The neeling's half-sphere eyes bulged in the hatchet of its face and a base anger kinked in Dante's guts. He brought his blade across the neeling's throat and a hot fan of blood spat over his hand and he jumped back and squealed. He wiped his hand on the thing's jacket, then wiped his blade, and by the time both were clean it was dead. Steam curled from the gash in its neck, from the pool spreading beneath them on the grimy cobbles.

He picked up his book and stashed the creature's dagger under his shirt. It was late and the streets were empty. He stuck to the broadest ones, the ones with oil lamps dangling on the corners. What few men he passed ignored him. By the time he reached the inn he understood. The error hadn't been telling the chapel guard his name, it was in not making sure the man had stopped breathing before Dante left to find the book.

The common room was stifling, full of braying laughter and clanking earthware. Dante paused at the bar, staring at the casks and cups.

"Your poison?" said the keeper.

"Keep it," Dante said, starting. He tromped up the steps and locked his room and braced a chair against the door, for whatever good that would do. He sat down on his straw pallet, shaking from his shoulders to his toes, and set the two blades out beside him. Twenty minutes later he'd reread five pages of the *Cycle of Arawn* and couldn't remember a word. He spit on his fingers and snuffed his candle and opened his shutters to the street. Men stumbled down the thoroughfare, concentrating hard on keeping themselves upright. None of them raised their eyes to the shadow of his face in the dark window. By morning the men of the chapel would know their agent had failed.

Dante woke with a jolt. The light through the open window was gray, fuzzy. He was freezing. There was something he was supposed to do. He pulled the coarse blanket over his face, then opened his eyes wide, heart galloping. That was it. He was supposed to run away.

He gathered his minor library, shoved the books and bread and dagger into his pack. He took his candles, his coinpurse, and his spare set of clothes, dressing himself in his new ones. Already they were dirt-streaked, sour with old sweat, but at least they had no holes or patches. He wrote an obscenity on a piece of paper and put it on his pallet, then, worried the innkeep might find it before the men of the chapel came here, snatched it up and crumpled it into his pocket. Dante liked the keep, didn't like the thought of the man's jowls drawing up at the kid who'd left his room a mess and insults as his only goodbye.

He left the inn and made a loose spiral around the old quarter, giving himself time to sort out his thoughts and watch for pursuit. The cool air and light morning breeze off the river kept the stink of the city to a tolerable horror. Already men plied oxcarts toward the docks or scurried between districts with wax-stamped letters in their hands like the blades of angels or dragged themselves home to begin sleeping it off. Dante didn't see anyone trailing him, but he knew he couldn't stay in his room. Nor could he leave the city without losing the resources he needed to understand the book. Where else could he go, the village? They were morons. He could count the ones who could read on two hands. The woods would be safer, but the men there lived like animals, preying on foot traffic like wolves, rutting like dogs, and dying, when their short wicks burnt out, like rats.

So he'd stay in the city, try to lose himself in a place where he couldn't carry a proper blade without being arrested within the day. Not that he'd know how to use a sword even were he licensed — he was more likely to cut off his own fingers than fend off the swords of whoever the chapel men sent next — and there would be others, bought with heavier coin than that neeling pawn. Men who knew more about fighting than how to run and how to lay in wait.

He paused at the corner of a broad avenue that led all the way to the docks. If all it took was money, why not hire an armsman of his own? Someone who could wear a blade without the watch hounding him for his papers? Bressel was huge, bulging with trade, and with it foreign merchants with more money than friends. The guild of arms was growing faster than all but the shippers'. If these people wanted their book back so bad, let them try to take it from the kind of security only silver could buy.

The sun hauled itself above the mists of the horizon, stuck behind buildings that sprung from two and three stories to four and five as Dante made his way toward the docks. At the end of the arrow-straight street, the thin pikes of riverboat masts bobbed in the swells. The roads clogged up with people on foot and single riders and the clop of teamed carriages. By the time he reached the vast markets that crowded the shores all the way down to the mudbanks, the roofs of the wares-houses reared to eighty feet above his head. Dante hunched his shoulders, gazing at them as if he could hold the looming walls upright by force of will alone. He turned a corner and the babble of commerce clobbered his ears like thunder after the flash.

Men clustered in loose knots, shaking pages in each other's faces like the paper were no more valuable than leaves scraped from the gutter. Courtiers banged in and out of the doors of shops and warehouses that stood without a foot's room between their undecorated eaves. Mounted retinues jounced through the throngs and the throngs parted without looking up from their business. Dante noted, with no small embarrassment, he appeared to be the only one fazed by the yammering crowds. He wandered around the square, not knowing where he was going but with both eyes out for the crossed swords of the houses of the guild of arms.

He found the first with little trouble. Men lounged at the walls of its mostly-clear court, oiling their swords, occasionally shoving themselves upright to tangle blades for the benefit of the traders, who were easily distinguished by their dress, a bizarre confusion of flower-bright colors and the plain practicality of travel wear. Dante threw back his head as he approached, trying to mask his face with the same professional detachment he saw in the eyes of the merchants.

One armsman stood out at once, a well-built man somewhere around thirty (though to Dante's eye everyone over twenty looked the same), his face and arms scar-crossed but intact, a couple shades duskier than most of the olive-toned Bressel locals, like he'd come up from the Golden Coast. After a moment's indifference, he glanced Dante's way and Dante nodded.

"What's your fee?" Dante said, folding his arms. The man raised a brow and Dante knew he'd made a mistake.

"Two chucks a day," the man said, referring to the silver of the late Charles III that had displaced most of the old coinage, "and board."

"Why don't I just buy a horse and an armada while I'm at it," Dante reeled. He shot a glance at the waist purses of the nearest traders.

"Well, you'll need something to get you around once the nails fall out of those boots." The armsman spat between his teeth. "Maybe you could saddle up a dog."

"Go to hell," Dante blurted. He turned his back on the laughter that followed, eyes stinging. At the next yard, a smaller, louder and more crowded affair, he hung on the edges, watching the exchange of money before he asked any questions. He thought he'd robbed his way to a respectable sum, but the traders tossed purses so bloated they could crush a cat. For a while he just wandered, browsing past a half dozen houses of prohibitive expense. The sun climbed. He began to sweat. Hollow-stomached, he came at last to the freelancers, the few too feeble to represent the name of the guild of arms. Dante'd seen plenty of healthy, battle-hardened men this morning, but if he'd never seen a soldier at all he'd still know at a glance why these men were on their own: they ranged from the doddering old to the beardless young, sixty-year-old men with gray in their hair and weakness in their arms mingling with needle-thin boys who looked like nine-year-old girls. The handful of fit age would have been put down if they were horses—patches over scooped-out eyes, pinned-up sleeves, bouncing limps where their tendons had snapped in a battle and never mended. Where the men of the guild proper had spoken through the clash of their swords, these rejects called to him in phlegmy voices like common marketeers.

A young enough man peeled from their ranks and swiped a few left-handed cuts in the air in front of Dante's face. His right arm stopped just below the elbow. When he gestured the smooth ball of his stump swung as dumbly as the blunt head of a turtle.

"What's your price?" Dante said, skipping the formalities he'd seen the merchants make. Decorum ended the moment you considered hiring an armsman who only had one.

"Two chucks," the man said, and Dante rolled his eyes, "per week. Plus board."

"Is that so." He sighed through his nose. He could actually afford that, so long as he kept up his late-night rounds rolling drunks, but he had the notion he'd be getting exactly what he paid for. He glanced around the freelancers, searching for a stone in the rough—not a diamond, but maybe he could find a decent quartz, a smooth piece of glass. In some way, the presence of a bodyguard was more important than his skill at guarding. If nothing else, it would give Dante a few seconds to run while his man was being stabbed to death.

Still—they were so damned old, so damaged, and the couple who were young and whole didn't look like they'd be any better in a fight than he was, and that wasn't much at all. Risking his life in the alleys for their pay seemed counterproductive if the help he hired were entirely decorative.

"What's crushing your junk? That's a bargain by any measure." Dante turned to the voice and met a pale boy whose face was apple-smooth.

"How old are you?" he said, making no effort to conceal his frown.

"Fifteen and a half," the boy said.

Dante burst out laughing. "And a half? What are you, five?"

"Plus ten and a half."

"A real veteran," Dante said. "You don't look like you'd know the sharp end of a sword if it were stuffed up your ass."

"Yeah, well your mother's still got teethmarks on her tit. And not all of them are yours."

With nothing else going on in their overlooked yard, the other unguilded men chuckled, gazing on Dante with bloodshot eyes. He flushed and gave the boy another look. He had an inch and several pounds on Dante despite being a year younger, though that still left him smaller than most boys his age, but he had a broadness of shoulder that might someday make him a decent soldier if he could grow past his ludicrous wiriness. He had close-cropped blond hair and obviously didn't need to shave. His clothes were time-torn, worse than Dante's old set, thick with the black stitches of mending and too short at his wrists and ankles. With a decent diet and another two-three years he might be in the yard of a real house. But Dante wasn't a horse-broker making investments, he was a kid with a price on his head. If he hired this bodyguard and waited three years for the boy to grow into himself, Dante had the sense he'd spend two years and 364 days of that wait in the grave.

"What's your name?" Dante said, readying himself for something to seize on. An odd gleam entered the blue of the boy's eyes.

"Blays Buckler," he said.

"What?"

"I said it's Blays Buckler."

"Blays Buckler?" Dante said. He'd meant to win the crowd with a big laugh, but found a real one instead. He chortled stupidly. "Did your dad read a lot of the romances, then? When your mom heard that name, how did she not murder him? Just strangle him with your birth cord?"

The kid's hand settled on his hilt. "My dad earned his name with his shield. I'll live up to mine."

"With your belt, maybe. But for that you'll want to head a little farther toward the docks."

Blays' face went red from brow to chin and he pressed his lips together so hard they disappeared. The whisper of steel cut the men's laughter short. Dante stared at the boy's drawn blade. Far too late to call for the watch. They might be out for him anyway.

Blays raised his arm and threw the sword behind him and before Dante had time to look past the hand he'd lifted to protect his face (as if it would help against killing steel) Blays sprung, tackling him to the ground. They rolled in the dust, grappling too closely for their punches to dole out any real hurt. Blays landed a sharp sting to Dante's nose and his mind blanked with rage. He got a grip on Blays' waist, meaning to drive him into the ground, but the boy dropped his knees and turned his hips and flung Dante onto his back. The boy's knees pinned his shoulders to the ground. He wriggled back and forth, kicking his legs and bucking his shoulders, but he couldn't free his weight, could only slap weakly at Blays with arms he couldn't move above the elbows.

Instead he fell limp, breathing hard. Blays jerked his head at Dante's face, as if he meant to batter Dante's brains in with his own skull, then caught himself and leaned back. He got to his feet, brushing dust from his knees and back.

"Do you even realize how stupid it is to try to beat up your clients?" Dante said from the ground. Blays bent to pick up his sword and laughed through his nose.

"Wasn't much trying involved."

"You took me by surprise."

"So take another shot."

"Two weeks," Dante said despite his anger, speaking from an instinct he didn't understand and would have overruled with another moment of thought. "Longer, if you execute your service well."

"I'd hate to disappoint your lordship," Blays said. He scratched his ear and gazed down on Dante as if he were considering whether they were actually bargaining for his dignity, then offered Dante a hand and hauled him to his feet. He followed Blays inside their cramped office and signed a paper, had it stamped, and parted with half his cash. A week's food and lodging in a single room on the edge of the dock slums wiped out the rest. But he had his guard, someone to watch his back while he studied and roamed, and he bent back to his book, alive for a while yet.

He moved from the book's first section to its second, allowing himself one new page of the *Cycle* for every chapter of the background and supplemental works he plowed through so the men and places of the book might make sense. He deciphered a foreign word that cropped up on more pages than it was absent from: "nether." His spelling could be off, and lords knew he had no idea how to pronounce it in the original, but it was the antonym of "ether," at least, the word the priests used when they yakked on about the celestial firmament while everyone else twirled their fingers beside their ears. Now that he had this word, certain passages that had been hopelessly obscure were now just uselessly mystical:

> *The ether stretches to the nail of the sky and meets itself in the dim caverns below the Earth. In the time before time it was the substance of all things, the water that suspended the stars, the air that made the breath of the gods, the same in all the four corners of the world. Men lived without hunger or death. But the ground grew heavy with their teeming number: and when the mill of the heavens cracked from their weight the waters broke forth and dashed them upon the peaks.*
>
> *Arawn took up the mill once more and set it upon the pole in the north, but when he tried to patch the cracks he tore his fingers on the shattered stone. He reset its course, but when he made it grind he found it would grind only nether. When he mingled this dust with the dust of men they rose with murder in their hearts, remembering how they'd doomed the sky.*

On the surface that was just a crazy pile of words, no less arbitrary than any of the other explanations he'd heard through the years for why things were the way they were (bad, usually), but as he read and reread, patient and disciplined in a way he'd never been—taking his time not because some daft instructor insisted he should, but because he knew he'd always been a sloppy reader and this was the only way to penetrate the book's hoary legends and lessons—Dante had the unflagging sense he was moving toward a higher understanding, though he didn't yet know what shape it would take or even exactly how he was getting there. He was taking more from the book than a base memorization of its tangled narrative, that was for certain. It was like the very act of confronting the confusion the book was stirring in his mind was making the view of the world he'd held before he started reading it seem laughably small. However naked it might leave him, he felt ready to leave it behind, to throw it away like a pair of pants that had grown too small.

Dante looked up from its pages and into the mildewed timbers of their room, giving his eyes a moment to rest before he turned back to the beginning and started over again. Blays worked something loose from his throat, spat it from the window, and leaned out to see if he'd hit anyone.

"Boredom doesn't bleed, you know," the boy said.

Dante went on staring at the ceiling, lost in whether the book meant the ether and nether as real things, or if they were more of a metaphor of some sort, and if so, of what. Take their names: was "nether" more important because it encompassed "ether"? Or was it less important because it depended on it? Or were they meant more as antonyms or complements? Already he'd read them so often they'd begun to lose all meaning. He glanced at Blays, realizing he'd said something a minute ago.

"Is that what you needed a bodyguard for? To protect you from dying of boredom? Boredom doesn't have a heart. Well, other than church. But I can't stab boredom's heart, I mean. So if it was all this boredom you were afraid of," Blays went on in the leisurely manner of someone used to long days of sitting around killing time while he waited to be hired, "I don't think I can help you."

"I'm not afraid of anything," Dante said, squinting at him. "And it's not boredom I'm concerned about."

"Maybe you hired me to fight that chair that's sunk its teeth into your ass."

"I'm in danger." Dante dropping his eyes back to the page.

"Of bedsores, maybe." Blays leaned back in the windowframe he used as a recovery nest from the late-night sentry duty he pulled in the common room keeping close eye on the beer. He let out a long breath. "Four days cooped in this room and whispering in libraries. I haven't seen a thing. I think my sword's rusted to its scabbard." He planted his hands on its grip and mimed being unable to pull it free. "Gods no!"

"You're being paid for it, aren't you?"

"Is someone chasing you? That it? From whatever village you

ran off from?"

"No."

"Probably a priest's son," Blays said, tugging at his lower lip. "Nobody cares that much about scripture unless he needs to prove Dad wrong. He's probably trying to drag you back to the chapel and bring you up right."

"I am not a priest's son," Dante said, going back to the beginning of the paragraph he hadn't been able to read through Blays' prattle.

"You're right. A priest would come with lawmen, not daggers in the dark." He squirmed on the sill, staring at Dante through the dusky room. "You stole something."

"Bread, maybe," Dante said, bringing a hand halfway to his chest. He kept his eyes on the text.

"Oh, more precious than bread. No baker's got the time and money to be chasing after some kid. Not that he wouldn't hang you if he had the chance."

"I'm trying to read."

Blays made a thinking noise. "It's just money, isn't it? You've been rolling drunks in the alleys. Everyone's got to eat, I guess, but if you've got the watch after you I think I've got a right to know."

Dante looked up. Blays' face was blanked by the light shining behind him through the window.

"Why do you think that?" Dante said.

"You are! You're stealing. That's rich. No pun."

"How did you know?"

"I guessed," Blays said, prodding the sill with a small knife he kept around for apparently no more than paring his nails. Dante laid a finger in the book to mark his place and swiveled in his chair.

"No you didn't."

"You're right. I followed you."

"You followed me!" The chair banged against the boards of the floor as he stood. Blays regarded him a second, then turned back to his nails.

"The money had to come from somewhere. It's not like you do any work."

"You followed me."

"Isn't that what I said?" Blays stood up and met Dante's eyes. "Gashen's swinging balls, you spend all day in here reading, then the one time I can be any use you're out sneaking around by yourself? What am I protecting you from, papercuts? What am I doing here?"

Dante frowned, his self-righteousness draining away. He hadn't thought about what Blays would think about their arrangement, but he sounded awfully proud for a fifteen-and-a-half-year-old beanpole who Dante knew he could probably beat up in a fair fight.

"It's not just stealing," Dante said instead.

"What else? Robbing? Maybe some larceny?"

"You talk a lot for hired help, you know that? You're not paid by the word."

Blays rolled his eyes and sat back down in the window. "Whatever. It's your money."

"You see this book?" Dante said, not caring he was shouting. He leaned over the windowsill and shoved the image of the white tree in Blays' face.

"No, why don't you bring it a little closer."

"I took this from one of the old temples of Arawn. They want it back."

"Looks spooky enough, doesn't it?" Blays flicked the cover with his nail. "Who's after you, a bunch of ghosts? That would explain why I've never seen them."

Dante glared at him. A dark speck swam over his right eye and he blinked until it went away. He no longer knew what he was trying to prove. Conversation had always felt like a strange art, and in the weeks since he left the village he'd spoken no more than was necessary to buy things—that and the threats he'd made about the book to the guard.

"You're being stupid," he said.

"You're the one talking about getting murdered over a book."

"Just be quiet," Dante said. He righted the chair and sat down and opened the book. He stared blankly at its first page, massaging his temples with one hand.

"So what's so special they'd want to kill you for it?" Blays said at half the volume of their last exchange. He dropped from the sill and craned over Dante's shoulder.

"Get off me."

"I'm not on you."

"Well don't breathe so hard."

"Stop breathing? Have fun dragging my corpse out of here, then."

Dante smirked into the clean white pages. If the book had been there since the Third Scour it had to be a century old or more. Other than a bit of residual dust, it showed no signs of age.

"It wouldn't be the first."

"Oh, sure," Blays said, pulling upright. He wandered back to the window. "And I'm the queen of Gask."

"I killed two people before I hired you," Dante said. He realized he'd meant it as a boast. His hands curled into fists. "Well, one. One of them must not have died when I stabbed him. And the other was a neeling."

"You killed a neeling and stabbed some guy? Why haven't you been knighted?"

Dante half-heard him through a memory of the pain-clenched face of the man he'd left for dead in the grass beneath the clouds. Blays saw his expression and gave him a sharp look.

"What was it like, then?" he said, voice lined with irony in case Dante was kidding.

"I don't know."

"Come on, tough guy."

"They both tried to kill me first."

"That's not what I asked."

"At the end," Dante said, rubbing his finger along the pebbled leather of the book's cover, "there's a kind of gurgle, a bubble of their final breath, and you wonder how they lived so long at all."

"Sick," Blays said. He drew his sword and swooshed it through the air. "Why do people have to die at all?" he said, but he kept swinging his sword, slashing the space between himself and Dante, air whistling over his steel like the wind in the pines.

The sun had dropped into the jaws of the western mountains before the monks kicked them out of their cloisters a few nights later, suggesting if Dante had such interest in their order, he should speak with them rather than poring over old manuscripts that really didn't reflect the modern understanding of Mennok. Dante thanked them and made vague noises about doing so. Crazy old idiots. How could the gods change when they were already perfect?

The door to their room at the inn creaked open while Dante was still trying to insert the key. His breath caught. Blays shouldered him out of the way, side-sword ringing as he wrenched it free. He edged into the room, leading the way with the point of his blade.

The only room Dante could afford was little bigger than one of the monks' cells and even before he lit a candle it was obvious there was no one else inside. Their few possessions were scattered on the floor, the table tipped on it side, books thrown from the shelf, lying face-down with their pages spread like the bodies of birds. The pallets had been gutted, scattered from corner to corner.

"Funny," Blays said, stirring the spilled straw with his sword. "I don't remember wrecking up the place."

"They were here," Dante said.

The kid shuttered the window and turned to face him. "For the book?"

"Do we have anything else worth a pair of pennies?"

"Could have been thieves," Blays said, eyeing him. "I hear you can't walk down an alley in this town without bumping into one."

"Grab your stuff."

"Okay," he said, and stood there. "Done."

Dante ignored him and started scooping up his gear. He smoothed the pages of the tossed-off books and piled them in his pack.

"You're serious," Blays said.

"Very."

"What, some hired thug comes poking around and you light out like a rabbit?"

"If that's what rabbits do, then rabbits are smarter than you are." Dante bundled up his dwindling supply of candles. Senselessly, some appeared to have been struck in half.

"It really could have been vagabonds."

"It wasn't vagabonds."

"Well, if you're so sure it's some shadowy cabal, doesn't running away mean they win?"

"In what sense," Dante said, raking up the last of his notes, "can I be said to win if I'm beheaded in my sleep?"

"Now I don't understand that at all." Blays glanced at the open door, then shut and bolted it. "What about standing your ground? Sword in hand?"

"I don't have a sword."

"Symbolistically."

"That's for idiots. Idiots who don't know anything." Dante stood and looked around for anything he'd missed, dismayed at the sight of his old clothes shredded and mixed up in the straw. He liked wearing them when he could get away with looking like he'd been run over by a herd of pigs. "Let's go."

"I know plenty," Blays said, setting his mouth. He put his sword away but kept it loose in its sheath. They bustled down the stairs. "My dad knew how to read."

"Do you?"

"What's your point?"

They exited the inn and Dante led them up the larger of the roads that crossed outside. The evening had grown brisk and their breath billowed from their mouths in a visible fog. A team of horses rattled past, forcing them into the gutter. The heat of the animals' bodies rushed past them, followed by a flickering wind that grew steady a moment later, like the team was dragging a stormhead behind it.

"We're being followed," Blays murmured a few minutes later. "Don't look back."

"Do you believe me now?"

"Anyone who didn't would be some kind of moron."

After a quarter of an hour of brisk walking Dante began to get winded. Blays seemed fine and Dante tried to keep his breathing quiet. His brain wasn't working well enough to take advantage of the fact they were relatively safe for the moment; the arterials carried decent traffic yet, and would for a few hours more. He stepped over a reeking puddle and was glad for the minimal lighting of corner torches and the half-moon. He had to think. They couldn't just walk forever.

"We can't just walk forever," Blays said.

"Yeah, I'd figured that out."

"They'll follow us wherever we go."

"They've got to sleep, too."

"Even if we somehow gave them the slip tonight, do you really think that's going to stop them?" Blays glanced briefly over his shoulder. "They've found you twice now."

Dante touched the knife in his belt. "Bressel's big enough to get ourselves lost in."

"Oh, that's worked so well so far."

"Well what do you suggest?" he spat, then looked around to see if anyone had heard. The street was quiet, a few brisk footsteps and the occasional clatter of a team or the reeling song of a drunk.

"Stand and fight," Blays said, resting his hand on the pommel of his sword. "Once we don't have anyone right on our ass, we'll have plenty of time to figure out our next step."

"That's crazy."

"Is it? You've killed people before, haven't you? Why run this time?"

Dante shook his head, feeling pale. "You're just a kid and the only thing I know about fighting is it helps to stab them in the back. We'd be slaughtered."

"Then let's do that."

"Getting slaughtered is not a plan."

"Stab them in the back, stupid."

Dante frowned. "I suppose you think we just hide in an alley, then jump out and say boo."

"It beats waiting for them to catch us." Blays glanced behind them again, brows knitting. "At least we'd take them on our own terms."

"How many are there?" Dante pressed a palm against his right eye. The black speck was back. "Two?"

"Three. There's another trailing a block behind the first two."

"Those are not the world's greatest odds."

"Well, make a decision. If we just keep walking, eventually we're going to turn down the wrong street and that will be it."

Dante shook his head. He never should have stayed in Bressel. For all his reading, he still couldn't *do* anything. For all the times the book's authority had made him feel holy, it wasn't like learning about history and creation stories that contradicted what he'd been taught would help him stand against armed men. There weren't any instructions in it, nothing about the proper way to sacrifice a calf to gain a godly blessing, no words of power, no maps for a pilgrimage to sacred lands and artifacts. The mail-shirted man had been real, but Dante's hopes were faint as smoke. There were men after Dante now, men who knew how to kill, and he was nothing more than another kid from the middle of nowhere.

"Shit," he said. "Gods damn son of a bitch."

"That about sums it up."

"I can't keep doing this," Dante said. "My luck's going to run out. Once we get rid of them, I'm running as fast and as far as I can."

Blays crooked up half his mouth. "I've got strong legs."

Dante shook his head again. "Money runs out in a few days."

"I don't think that will stop them from sticking cinders under my toenails and chucking me in the river when I can't tell them where you've gone."

"Gross," Dante said, then shut his mouth. If Blays wanted to throw in his lot with Dante for a while longer, that was his business. "So what's your big plan?"

"You strip down and run at them naked while I circle around behind them."

"Shut up."

"When we get to this corner," Blays grinned, "we make like we just saw them—you know, get all scared and shouty—then we run down this alley and hide. When they run past us, we jump out and stab them."

"That," Dante said, "is a really poor plan."

"You've got better?"

"Not at all," Dante said. They reached the corner a moment later. Blays stopped and turned in a slow circle, gesturing broadly at the landmark of a finger-thin spire in the heart of the city. Dante caught on, shrugging like a stage-actor. Blays glanced back down the street, dropping his jaw when his eyes settled on the men following them, then cried out and darted for the dark mouth of the closest sidestreet. The heels of his boots disappeared into shadow before Dante had the presence of mind to run after him.

The footsteps of pursuit rang out immediately from so close behind him Dante didn't know whether they'd have time to hide. From twenty yards down the alley, Blays looked back, then seemed to blink right out of existence. Dante's mouth went dry—a ruse, he'd run off, left Dante as bait to make his escape—then a hand snaked from a doorway he hadn't seen until he'd gone by it. Blays yanked him from sight and they huddled in the dark, struggling to slow their panting before the men rounded the corner.

"Here," Blays whispered. He handed Dante the little ratsticker he'd been carving the windowsill with a few days ago.

"I've got these." He brandished his knife and the neeling's dagger. They weren't much, but next to Blays' offering they looked lethal enough.

"Throw it at them or something."

Boots echoed down the narrow-windowed walls of the alley. Dante couldn't catch his breath. The gray figures of three men strode by, swords in hand, and he made a rodent-like peep. He felt Blays' hand on his shoulder and then he was being pulled back into the street and his hands were shaking so hard he was sure he'd drop both knives.

Blays lashed his sword from its sheath and raked it across the back of the trailing man. The others spun, points raised, and Dante cocked his arm and hurled the knife. It winked in the moonlight, then somehow hit and stuck in his target's shoulder. The man shouted and yanked it free, hurling it back at Dante, but he threw it like you'd throw a stone and its butt bounced from Dante's chest. The third man closed with Blays and they circled like crabs, trading exploratory strikes. Neither of the other men were exactly giants, but they were full-grown, and as Dante's opponent recovered and menaced him with his two-foot blade he saw how much each inch of reach meant in a fight. Dante pulled the dagger from his belt and waved it in front of him, wondering how it would feel when he lost his hand.

The black mote was back in his eye. He batted at it with his left hand, narrowly avoiding putting out his eye with the point of his knife, and the man across from him laughed and swung. Dante ducked, hearing the sword whine over his head. Blays fell back under a harsh assault and bumped him in the shoulder. His man swung again and when Dante blocked it with the dagger a sting jolted up his arm so hard his eyes fogged over and he couldn't tell whether he still held his weapon. Blackness spread across Dante's eyes, rushing over his vision like ink poured on quiet waters, and he cried out, feeling no pain and not even having seen the man's killing stroke, but knowing he was dying.

He heard cursing, then, which probably wasn't uncommon in hell, but also the oafish shuffles of men who've gone blind suddenly and without reason. Dante dropped to his knees and heard blades whiffing the air. Beneath him the earth felt solid as ever. Steel clanged into a stone wall. As he'd passed from the world of the living to this confusing netherland, Dante'd had the presence of mind to keep Blays' location fixed in the map of his head well enough to know the boots scraping a few feet in front of him weren't the boy's, and, touch returning to his shock-numbed fingers enough to know he still held his dagger, he struck out, blind but no more than everyone else, waving the short blade back and forth somewhere around knee level, stabbing out at every stutter of the man's steps.

The first swipe missed, the second landed and glanced away, and the third dug deep into yielding flesh. He heard a shriek and screamed back as the man folded into a heap, clubbing Dante's outstretched arm with his falling body. Dante launched himself forward, arms held in front of his chest to prevent himself from being gutted if the guy had his weapon ready, but landed on the man's unguarded torso. He stabbed down with both hands, knives tearing through soft things and thudding into bone until the body's blood was sopping from his fingers and dripping down his face.

Not six feet to his left Blays and the last man struggled and he heard the tentative squeal of their swords meeting. The man under Dante's knees was dead enough to stop worrying about. He stabbed him again, tasting bile, then flopped back on his ass. He'd lost track of who was Blays and who was the last enemy standing. Loose gravel grated under his trousers as he scooted back. His eyes grew damp, and then the darkness shimmered in a way he'd only seen light do. Two silhouettes faced each other, blades straining, and then they were whole under the moon and the stars and the torchlight trickling from the main streets. Dante planted a palm on the dirt and buried his dagger in the attacker's side. The man twisted away, flicking him across the chin with the very end of his sword. Blays leaned into his open body and swung sidelong. The sword cut into the softness of the man's side and clicked when it met his spine. The man bent his head, mouth wide. His neck strained into cords, working with some final words he couldn't quite voice, then he slumped over the sword. His weapon banged against the ground, his hands hanging like gutted fish. He fell and didn't rise.

"Screaming, weeping Lyle," Blays said, jerking his sword free. He wiped it on the body and Dante saw a deep red crease over the boy's left arm, a spreading stain on his upper ribs.

"You're bleeding."

"Shut up and take his sword. It's a good one."

"I've never used one before," Dante said, putting away his knives. He looked down the empty length of the alley and shuddered.

"You can learn, dummy." Blays' mouth drew into a long, thin line as he looked down on the bodies. He made a closed-mouth gasp from deep down in his throat and Dante had to turn away to keep from puking. After a few quavering breaths, Dante bent over the man they'd killed together and unbuckled his belt, tightening his throat when his hand brushed the warm body. He sheathed the dropped sword, then bit his lips and pulled open the body's cloak.

"What are you doing?"

"We're going to need money."

"That's sick," Blays said, backing up a step.

"You're the one that just killed him," he said, but Blays made no move to help. Dante hurried through the pockets, fishing for coin, then rifled through the clothing of the two other corpses. It wasn't a fortune, but it would last long enough if they were careful. After a moment of staring he pulled off the least bloody cloak and swung it over his shoulders.

"His cloak, too?" Blays wrinkled his nose. "What are you, a ghoul?"

"We need to leave. Now." Dante stood and headed for the other end of the alley, refusing to let himself run. His legs were shaky and weak beneath him. The whole thing had taken less than two minutes. Ninety-odd seconds for three dead bodies and a wall of darkness he couldn't explain. The looted sword bounced against the side of his left knee and he hoisted his belt over his waist. He tipped his head to the stars, trying to regain his direction. In the weeks he'd lived in Bressel he'd learned no more than a smattering of its streets (he had the sense you could live there all your life without knowing more than a single district) and had never gotten the hang of which way was which. He picked out the seven-starred bow of Mallius pointing the way to Jorus, the north star, and led Blays west at the next intersection, away from the direction of the docks. They moved down a broad street and passed cloaked men, armed men, men on horseback, ragged men missing ears or noses and clutching flasks. The unlicensed sword felt like a beacon on his hip. He put it out of his mind. For now their only worry was putting some distance between themselves and the bodies.

"What are you?" Blays asked, and Dante felt his bones try to leap out of his skin. They crossed Fare Street, Bressel's old outer boundary, and the cobbles gave way to dirt.

"I'm fine."

"Did you hear me?"

"I'm a sixteen-year-old man," Dante said flatly.

"Most men I know can't blot out the stars."

"They're there now, aren't they?" Dante said, waving at the whorls of constellations. Blays grunted and bumped into Dante's shoulder. He gripped Dante's collar, steadying himself, and Dante leaned into the boy's weight. He felt blood seeping through his sleeve. "Shut up and sit down. I can bind those up."

Blays didn't say anything, just seated himself on the dirt road and stared at the wooden walls of the rickety two-story rowhouses that didn't look any older than ten or twenty years. Dante cut strips from the bottom of his new cloak and pulled them tight around the boy's forearm. What he really needed was stitches, but Dante had forgotten his needle and thread back at the room. The gash across Blays' ribs was bleeding more but wasn't so deep. He let a strip of cloth soak up some blood so it would stick to Blays' skin, then wrapped another long piece around it.

"I didn't see him hit you," Dante said.

"Big surprise," Blays said. Dante frowned, knotting the cloth over Blays' shoulder. The kid was off somewhere else, working something over when he should have his eyes out for the watch or other pursuit. Dante didn't think it had anything to do with the shock of battle or Blays' loss of blood. He wanted to say he'd had no control over the darkness, which was true; he wanted to say he had no idea where it had come from, which might not be. The way it blacked out like ink and then flickered away when Dante's emotions had changed reminded him exactly of a passage around the twentieth page of the *Cycle* when Stathus the Wise, facing six armed warriors, had encased them and himself in a lightless sphere and slain five of them one by one. The last of them then struck Stathus and clouded his mind with fear, causing the sphere to fade at once—a coincidence of patent ridiculousness, since it had said nothing about how Stathus had gone about dropping them in darkness in the first place. All Dante'd done was try not to drop a load in his trousers. There was no way the mere act of reading the book had somehow limbered up his mind to the point where he could do things like Stathus.

What had it been, then? Trick of the light? Widespread hysterical blindness, like the kind he'd read afflicted soldiers on the eve of a battle so they couldn't fight? The first signs of a degenerative and apparently infectious ocular condition, or a priest watching from the windows, drunk, using parlor tricks to toy with them? Lunar eclipse? Any of those was about as likely as father Taim strolling down from his constellation and shaking Dante's hand. The one explanation that fit was he'd done something without knowing how he did it and that was no explanation at all; as wrong as Blays was to suspect him, Dante knew he was equally powerless to tell him why.

They passed from the low, half-mud half-fieldstone houses inside the Westgate to the low, half-mud half-fieldstone houses outside the Westgate. This whole range of city looked like it had been built within the last five years. The roofs were mudcaked reeds, the doors flimsy things, firelight visible in the gaps of their frames. Blays' feet swept over the rinds and pebbles in the roadway.

"Tired?" Dante asked.

Blays shrugged. "We can't exactly stop here."

He nodded, conceding the point. "We could rest a minute, though."

"Why?" Blays met Dante's eyes for the first time since the fight. Something dark lingered in his face. His lips curled. "You too worn out to keep going?"

"I'm fine," Dante said, feeling the dullness in his knees, the burn in the backs of his thighs. "It's just a couple miles to the woods. We should be all right there for the night."

"Then we'll stop when it's safe."

He had thought there would be some triumph if they survived their first skirmish, but instead of standing back to back against a shared danger, it had made Blays hate him. The wind kicked up, dragging leaves and trade papers and a few forgotten scraps of cloth past their feet. Graying things he was glad not to recognize moldered in the gutters. Since the time Dante'd left the village of his birth he'd enjoyed his solitude, his total freedom. Other people only intruded on his ability to learn. If Blays was going to part his company because he was as scared as a little girl about whatever Dante'd done when Dante himself didn't know what that thing was, he wouldn't mark it as a loss.

Open fields showed between the houses after another half mile. Within two more minutes the last of what could be said to be the city had been replaced by brittle cornstalks and the puzzled moans of cows. The city fires died away and overhead a thousand stars pricked out from the black curtain. A god was there, if the *Cycle of Arawn* could be believed, turning the stone, milling the substance that changed men's hearts to darkness.

3

They rose with the dawn and ate a cold breakfast in colder silence. They'd slept back to back, Dante's stolen cloak thrown over them both, and when Blays stirred Dante felt him freeze with a jerk before jumping up and jogging some ten yards off. Face buried under the cloak, Dante heard Blays slapping his arms, his face, working up the circulation. Dante sat up, glared at the sunlight filtering through the leaves. His legs hurt. So did his hand, where that merc had nearly torn away his knife and his fingers along with it. Most of the flies had died in the first snap of frost earlier that week, but the ones that remained found the two of them and sizzled fatly in the breezeless morning. He tossed his head when they landed on his neck, waving halfheartedly at their stupid black bodies, imagining every buzz was a bee about to sting him.

Blays wandered off as soon as he saw Dante was up, mumbling something about having seen some mushrooms, and Dante waited till he'd merged with the trees to open his pack and then the book. He thought the words would feel different, that the act of reading them after the night before would fill him with some deep and nameless force, but there it was, the same old clean black hand of a meticulous scribe recounting legends and troubles of succession no one'd cared about since the moment the last man who'd known those heroes and kings had died. Dante found it interesting, in its way, was somewhat mystified to be confronted with hard evidence life had been going on for so many hundreds of years, but none of that vague awe explained how he'd been able to summon the darkness. Leaves crackled and he plopped the book shut and stowed it, watching the treeline.

"Found a few," Blays said, emerging and holding out a double handful of mushrooms with smooth pink-gray caps and pleated black undersides.

Dante twisted his mouth. "You'll die if you eat those."

"Right," Blays said, and when he lifted one to his mouth Dante bolted up and hit his wrist hard enough to sting them both. Mushrooms flew to all sides.

"It's poison." He nudged one with his toe, then crushed it into the dirt. "Probably wouldn't *kill* you, but you'd barf up anything else you put down with it."

"Pardon me for not wanting to starve. We can't all be from the middle of nowhere," Blays said, but he dumped the couple he was still holding into the leaves and kicked them away. He brushed his hands clean on the front of his trousers and looked up at the angle of the sun. "Wasting light."

"I can teach you those things." Dante bent over and slung his cloak and his pack over his shoulders.

"I just want to get the hell out of here." Blays started off and kept a couple steps ahead. For a while they just walked. They'd made about five miles from the city before they'd gone to sleep, Dante figured, though they'd been traveling in the dead of night without a road, so who the hell could tell. Blays kept a quick pace through the sparse grass and falling leaves. Not too smart, Dante thought, not when he'd lost some blood the night before and there was no chance they were still being followed. He kept his mouth shut. He had the impression Blays wasn't in a talking mood.

They broke off for camp before the sun had finished cradling itself in the mountains. Dante gathered up some tinder, meaning to risk a fire. He doubted the temple men would figure out he'd left the city for another few days. They could spend weeks combing Bressel before they could be certain. He and Blays were off the trails in open country; there was no rhyme to their course other than a vague northerly direction so they wouldn't lose total track of the river. Three more days like today and they could be a hundred miles away. Their trail, as he saw it, was cold from the moment they'd left the men dead in the alley.

"Cold again," Blays said, shifting the night-facing side of his body toward the fire. His thick straight nose threw a broad shadow over the far side of his face. He prodded the dirt with a twig, snapping off a couple inches at a time and tossing them into the flames.

"Yeah."

"It hasn't bled since this afternoon," Blays said after a moment, peeling back a half inch of the strip of cloth over his left arm.

"That's good. Does it look red?"

"No." He sniffed. "What about you?"

"I wasn't hurt." Dante watched tiny flakes of ash sail into the smoke and the heat. "Just bruises."

"I see." He broke the twig in two and dropped it into the fire. "Isn't there a bark you can chew to make it hurt less?"

"It's not the bark," Dante said, "you just can't feel pain when you're chewing." Blays waggled his jaw and Dante put a hand over his own mouth. "I can't believe you believed that."

Blays looked away. "Shut up. I'm not a physician."

"There is a tree like that," Dante said, squelching his laughter. "I'll find some tomorrow if you want."

"I'm going to sleep."

Dante watched him stretch out on the ground, back to the fire, and wondered if he should apologize when it was Blays who couldn't appreciate a joke. Before he'd made up his mind, the boy was breathing deep and easy. Dante stayed up a while, letting his eyes drift over the branches of the forest, but for however hard he tried he couldn't make the black speck come back.

Blays stayed silent the next day, but he kept close by, didn't range ahead or disappear into the woods when they sat to eat or rest. The bread ran out at noon. They found a linberry bush, but the berries were fat, wrinkly, an overripe maroon. They took a break at late afternoon, hunkering down in the tall grass of a clearing. Tomorrow they'd head dead east, Dante thought, toward the river. Find a town. From there, Blays could leave and Dante could —do something. Hitch a boat downriver and make for the coast below Bressel, maybe. Sail for Albardin in the Western Territories. It wasn't as big as Bressel, but it would be a port town, lots of weird lore from foreign lands, and plenty far from the eyes of the temple men.

"It's working," Blays said, a hunk of bark sticking from his lips. "Tastes like shit."

"It's bark."

"Animals eat it, don't they? Don't they have tongues?"

"You can't trust animals. They eat their own vomit."

"Dogs, maybe. I've seen dogs eat things from both ends of cats." Blays spat flecks of wood, wiped them from his tongue. "But that's why they're dogs."

"You're eating bark. What does that make you?"

"I'm not *eating* it."

"Chewing it up, then. That's even more like a dog." Dante bit the skin around his thumbnail, tasted blood. "Are you ever going to show me how to use this stupid sword? Or am I just carrying it around to impress all the girls out here?"

"Go stick it in a goose," Blays said, stretching out in the grass. The bark wiggled in his mouth.

"I don't think that would be fun for either of us." Dante leaned back on his elbows. He tried to picture a map of the lands north of Bressel. Whetton was up there somewhere, it was decent-sized. Not that it mattered where they ended up. If they followed the Chanset long enough, they'd find somewhere with some people.

"Hold it while we're walking."

"What does that even—? What would your mother think of you saying that?"

"My mom's dead. And I'm talking about the sword, idiot," Blays said, the bark between his lips jumping with his words. "Carry it in your hand. Swing it around. Get a feel for it. A sword doesn't react like a knife. It's heavy, it takes a while to respond to whatever it is you're trying to get it to do, and you've got to learn to account for that."

Dante gave him a look. "Is that how you learned?"

"It was wooden and I was about ten years younger, but otherwise, yeah."

"And then you'll teach me."

Blays shrugged, hands behind his head. "Why don't you go find us some food."

"Why don't you take a dive down a hill," Dante said, but he got to his feet and walked out of the clearing. The light yellowed as he searched, plucking berries, gathering the bland, low-slung fungus that took more time to clean the dirt from its folds than it did to eat. Orange and red leaves drifted from the boughs and settled to the ground in the windless silence. He spooked a grouse, heart bursting at the thrash of its wings. He could try a few snares, but that would mean setting them up, then remembering where they were and checking them later, then the several centuries it'd take to pluck feathers—hours of work when he'd already gotten no thanks for all the other food he'd found them. On the way back to the clearing he saw the green sprigs of wild carrots and pried them from the soil. They had the end of a rind of cheese left, too. Even if Blays ate like a pig it would be enough for dinner and breakfast. The carrots dangled from his left hand and the sword from his right. He whooshed it over the grass, lopping the heads from burrgrass and the brittle, straw-like elkwood where it grew in the damper dirt.

He'd readied a few choice taunts about how Blays would starve the first five minutes he spent on his own, but returned to find the boy sacked out in the grass. A couple hours of daylight left, he guessed. It would hardly be worth it to wake him up and deal with his nonsense. They could walk by night if they had to. Dante tamped down a patch of grass, plunked down. Got out the book.

His constant urge was to read through without stopping, but he knew whatever was between its covers was too important to treat like a fruit pastry, something to be devoured as quickly as possible. It deserved patience, deliberateness, the kind of disciplined caution Dante'd never managed in any other part of his life. This, though, this was different. He could nearly recite the first dozen pages by memory. Already he remembered the tales of the first hundred pages like the nursery rhymes that stuck in his head whenever he gave them a foot in the door, like the dry-as-sand history of the royal house the churchman had made him read whenever he came late to supper or didn't sweep the corners. He'd separated the proper names from the words of Narashtovik, teased through their context until he had at least a vague concept of their meaning, and in many cases could readily define them. He no longer had to page back to figure out which displaced brother had slain which usurping regent. Its pages were becoming a part of him. With no other leads on an entry into the world of his desire, he read with no less a goal than branding the book's pages on his mind so brightly he'd remember them to the day his eyes went dim.

After half an hour he glanced up and saw a world drenched in shadows. They flowed like water, pooling on the undersides of leaves, drifting through the air as fine as mist, defying the sunlight that still stretched through the branches. He blinked and his head rushed with the warm, tingly delirium he got when he stood up too fast. Like that, the vision was gone.

Blays' snoring snagged so hard his head jerked. He sat up, rubbing his eyes with his fists.

"How long have I been out?"

"I don't know," Dante said. His voice sounded far away. He cleared his throat. "An hour, maybe."

"Why'd you let me do that? I'll have all night to sleep." Blays bounced to his feet while Dante struggled with a reply. "Let's go. Let's move."

The sun slanted through the trees in buttery bands, that thick yellow light Dante'd only seen on cool autumn days, a light that reminded him of the years when he'd been young. An hour left till dusk, maybe less. He could see but not hear knots of tiny flies bobbing around each other. Dustmotes hung in the windless air. Dante wiped his right eye.

"You did that, you know," Blays said, swinging the walking stick he'd picked up before they'd started back out.

"Did what?" Dante said.

"Made it go dark."

He avoided Blays' eyes, suddenly aware that an entire future depended on what he said next. His pause grew too long to pretend he wasn't lying.

"I couldn't do it again," he tried.

Blays whacked a branch in his way, snapping it clean. "Too bad. It probably saved us."

"Saved me, maybe. You had a chance without it."

Blays grunted. They walked on. "What's in that book, anyway?"

"History and a lot of stories," Dante said, gripping the straps of his back. Blays stopped, tapping Dante on the shin with his stick hard enough to welt.

"Bullshit," he said. "That thing you just said is the product of a cow's ass. You wouldn't be risking your life over a bunch of stories. They wouldn't be trying to kill you to get them back, either, whoever they' is." He reached for the pack and Dante drew away. "What's so damned special about it?"

"I don't know."

"Stop it."

"I don't!" Dante worked the muscles of his jaw, reaching for an explanation he couldn't define. "I heard it was supposed to teach you how to do the things the priests say they can do, throw fire and change the weather and whatever other crazy things, but I haven't read anything that tells you how to do that. So far it's just like the *Ban Naden* of Taim."

Blays snorted. "I don't know anyone who read the *Ban Naden* and then made a whole street go dark."

"Oh yeah? You want to read it and see?" Dante slid the pack from one shoulder.

"No way!" Blays said, jumping back. He narrowed his eyes to bright slits. "You know what I think it is?"

"What do you think it is?"

"I think," he said, raising his blond brows, "it's a spellbook."

"Yeah, that's what it is."

Blays raised a palm. "Well, just look at it! It's got a big old bone tree on the cover. What else could it be?"

"If it's a spellbook, it's the worst damn one I've ever read."

"Just how many *have* you read?"

"There's no such thing." Dante closed his eyes and sighed through his nose. "Have you ever heard of the Third Scour?"

Blays kicked a rock at his feet. "No, I'm a halfwit."

"Then what was it?"

"One of those things where all the people kill each other? What do you call those?"

"It *was* a war," Dante said. "A big one." He paused. From his right he heard the chirr of a redwinged blackbird. Pond nearby, then. Fish. He frowned at himself, glanced back at Blays. "It was a little over a century ago. All the sects of the Celeset sort of banded together to wipe another one out."

"I presume their reasons were perfectly noble."

"Most of the histories I've read say the sect was a death cult that served a god named Arawn. You know, sacrificing babies, no respect for human life, whatever." Dante looked away, feeling stupid. Somehow exposing his knowledge of such boring, dusty histories was like admitting he collected pornographic illustrations of centaurs and mermaids, or saved up his coin for the commemorative daggers of the Explorers Clubb. "Supposedly, since the serfs no longer respected the law of the righteous gods, they stopped listening to the rule of the king. You know,'this life is short and the next one is long, so who cares what that guy says.' That sort of thing. There were rebellions. The one in the Collen Basin worked — they hanged the count, burnt his wife. But when the cavalry came the renegades didn't have much more than pitchforks and the bows from the manor's armory. The steps of the house were stained so red they painted them crimson to cover it up. If you believe that stuff. That's why the new count established it as his colors."

"That is truly fascinating," Blays said.

"I thought it was."

"So they splashed a little noble blood around. Peasants do dumb stuff and get killed for it all the time. Why did the whole kingdom have to fight a war?"

"It wasn't just in the Basin," Dante went on. He bit his teeth together. He'd read hundreds of pages on this stuff back in the books in Bressel. How could he distill all that work into something Blays would get? "It was everywhere. It was really popular, probably because its members were saying things that hadn't been said in a long time but used to be really important. You know Carvahal, right?"

Blays made a blasphemous appeal to the sky. "I'm not three years old, Dante."

"I was just asking. So Carvahal took the fire from the north star and brought it to us and was exiled from the Belt of the heavens for it by Taim, right. That's the story you hear when you're a little kid. Well, these Arawn guys, they say Carvahal didn't originally oversee the pole-fire, that his half-brother Arawn was its keeper. He gave Carvahal the fire, but they say Carvahal locked him up behind the wall beyond the stars so he could have the credit. Then he brought the fire to Eric the Draconat, etc., etc."

Blays nodded like he was paying any kind of attention. He planted his staff and lowered himself onto a lichen-fuzzed rock.

"Let's sit down over there." Dante nodded to the trees on the right that looked just like the trees to the left, as well as the trees ahead and behind them. "At the pond."

"What pond?"

"Can't you smell it?"

"No," Blays said, but he stood and waited for Dante to lead the way. He did, ear cocked for the blackbirds, and he had to cut back once but then it was there, barely more than a stone's throw across but maybe five times as long. Blays gave him a look, snapping a reed from its banks.

"The birds," Dante said, after a blackbird had called. "They like the water."

"Right." Blays dropped down on a rock near its edge and wriggled off his boots. He skimmed the tip of the reed over the placid waters. Dante watched the gray missiles of trout drifting near the banks. The flies were thicker here and the surface rippled with the rings of breaching fish. The water did smell good, now that he was on it, damp grass and clean mud, that way stones smell when water's always drying from their smooth faces.

"The important thing is, Arawn was the one who guarded the north star," Dante went on.

"So what?"

"So what? From a theological perspective that's huge! It undermines the legitimacy of Taim and Gashen and all the twelve houses of the heavens! If Arawn was the keeper of its fire, then he was pretty much the big chief. Worse yet, if he meant to hand his secrets down to mankind, that means *he's* the one who deserves our devotion, not Carvahal, and if they got something that big wrong, how can we trust anything they say at all?"

"Yeah, but it's all just stories." Blays moved to his knees and overturned a stone. Pale pink worms wagged their tails in the last of the sunlight before sinking into the murk. "They're not *real*."

"Doesn't their belief in the gods make them real?"

"No," he said, "it makes them stupid."

"I guess everyone in the world's stupid, then." Dante dropped his eyes to the waters around the reeds. Now and then a trout weaved through their stalks, nibbling at the seeds and bugs caught in the net of plants. "It doesn't matter if they're stories. The priests tell the stories that will make the people eat out of their hands and the kings have power because they have the authority to say which priests are right. They don't like it when the stories that give them all this control are threatened."

"You know who you sound like right now?" Blays said, grinning up at him. "The guys back at the arms house I was with after they'd been drinking all night. The kings this, the priests that. Everyone's stupid but them. Then they sleep it off and when they wake up they're back out selling their blades for pennies and getting turned down nine times out of ten even then."

"I'm not saying I thought it up." He threw a pebble at the water near the point of Blays' reed. A shadow of a fish darted into the deep. "I'm just trying to explain why people get so mad when you start talking about this stuff."

"Lyle Almighty, get on with it."

"So Arawn gave us the fire," Dante said.

"You've said that five times," Blays sighed. Dante glared at him. The boy sat three-quarters turned, but when he ducked his chin Dante could see he was smiling.

"The histories of the Third Scour paint him as a bloodthirsty death-god. That's how they explain the revolts, that Arawn ordered the serfs to kill the lords and the guards and the followers of all the other temples to satisfy his own need for blood. But see, I don't think that's right. In the *Cycle*—the book—it mentions Arawn a lot and he never talks about wanting people dead. In fact, he's not very interested in us at all. I mean, everyone dies eventually, right? If you're an immortal god, who cares if a soul finds you in the stars today or twenty years from now? Even if he wanted to build an army, and I don't see anything to support that either, it's not like he's in a hurry to do it before he dies of old age."

Blays plopped a rock into the waters. "I'm going to be seeing Arawn myself pretty fast if you don't quit being so boring."

"Well, does that make sense to you? That a god would be in a rush about a thing like that?"

"Of course not. But we're the image of the gods, aren't we? So obviously they think like us. That must mean they're pricks like us, too. Who wants to wait fifty years when you can snap your fingers and poof, you've got an army of the dead? For that matter," Blays said, tapping Dante's chest as he built up steam, "if they're so high and mighty, how are we supposed to guess what they're thinking? We're probably like ants to them. Can ants understand what *we're* thinking?"

"That's different."

"How is it any different at all?"

"It just is," Dante shrugged. He groped around for his place. "So whatever Arawn was, nobody else liked him anymore, what with the dangerous belief your standing in this brief wick doesn't mean hell-all to the one that comes after, and once things got so crazy in Collen the counter-army practically conscripted itself. They smithied up a few thousand pikes for the rabble and promised the land to the nobles and off they went. Needless to say all the heretics in Collen were killed. That only stirred up the ones everywhere else all the worse, but to make a long story slightly less long, they were all killed too. The traditionalist armies burnt their temples and their books, beheaded the priests who renounced and quartered the ones who didn't. That's where the Fellgate came from."

Blays dropped his jaw. "What, those little black knobs are their *heads*?"

"Yeah," Dante laughed. "Look like old apples, don't they?"

"And they get to spend the rest of their years watching the asses of horses ponce down the street."

"And the thing is, they were wrong. They lied about Arawn, and when his followers objected, some of them were killed, and then when they tried to fight back, all of them were killed. It's like people care more about preserving their power than serving the truth."

Blays bobbed his head. "The powers that be wouldn't be the powers that be if they didn't."

"Yeah." Dante grinned a moment, then realized just what he

was grinning at and made his face go serious. "I took the book from one of the ruined temples of Arawn."

"Ah," Blays said, nodding sagely. "The kind of crime where it's a race to see who can hang you first."

"The best kind."

"You'd better hurry up and become an invincible wizard, then."

"I don't know how," Dante flushed. "I wish I'd had more time in Bressel before they found me."

"And I wish I had a princess in her skivvies. In fact, forget the skivvies." Blays chuffed at himself, then looked down. "Actually, I want to see some damn food, then eat it. What've you got?" He reached again for the pack.

"Let's catch some fish. Before it gets too dark."

"Great idea," he said, standing and contemplating the pond. "Where's the hooks?"

Dante got to his feet. "Can't you sort of stab them?"

"Yeah." Blays whipped out his sword and the metal rang in the quiet. He brandished it at the banks. "Come on, you cowardly fish! Come up on dry land and fight like a man!" He slashed the waters, sending droplets hissing. "I missed!"

"Well maybe if you actually tried."

"I thought you were Nature Boy," Blays said, flipping water at him with the weapon's point. Dante shrank back. "Can't you whittle up some bones or something? Lure them out with the song of the sea?"

"If I catch any you can't eat them," Dante said, unsheathing his own sword. He trailed the bank, eyes on the lurking shadows.

"A challenge!" He heard mud slurping and jumped when the rock Blays had thrown catapulted into the pond. He spat water from his face.

"You ass!" He brushed uselessly at his soaked doublet.

"I'll catch twice your stupid fish," Blays said. He turned on his heel and stalked the opposite way. Dante hurried to a tall stand of reeds some thirty feet down. Within moments his eyes set on a trout hovering in the shallows. He lunged at it with his sword and fell to his knees in the water. He splashed back ashore, checking to see if Blays had seen, but the kid was occupied with his own prey. He scared away a second fish, then a third before he moved further along the shores, and it wasn't until it was so dark he was beginning to see fish where they weren't there that he drew back his sword after a strike and found a trout speared on its tip.

"I hope you enjoy your carrots," he said a few minutes later when he found Blays at the far point of the pond.

"Screw your carrots," Blays said, displaying his sword over a stomped-down basket of grass. In the gloom he saw the silver bodies of three cleaned fish. A wind riffled the waters, stirred the dry leaves of the trees against each other. They retreated into the woods where a fire wouldn't be seen from the clearing at the pond and bit into the crackle-skinned fish while they were still so hot they burned their mouths.

For days they stayed at the pond, content to fish with branch-cut spears in the morning and the evening, scrubbing around for plants in the woods when the noon sun drove the trout into deeper waters, sometimes swimming, sometimes crashing around the undergrowth until their trousers were thick with burrs, running around for the simple sake of running around. Most days Blays went off for an hour or more in his own explorations while Dante plunged into the *Cycle*. Without references and histories and his own footnotes, he feared he couldn't grasp more than the surface of what he read, but the further he pressed the more he understood. His progress was slow as ever; he was often forced to flip back to earlier sections, interrupted by the frequent need to forage for things to fill a stomach that seemed to empty every couple hours at the book, but he was building toward a new peak. He could feel it in the hollows of his bones.

When Blays got back from his solo trips Dante shut the book and came at the boy with sword in hand. He learned the delicate mechanics of the parry and riposte, to watch the hips of his opponent to know where he was going, to use his footwork to create the balance that would be the difference in who died on whose blade. Dante didn't know much, but he could tell Blays was better than he should be at fifteen and a half. He had a natural grace, a quickness to his wrists that never let his blade stray too far to leave himself open. Compared to that, Dante's relative clumsiness with the sticks they used for their full-contact duels was a constant frustration that filled him with a shame he hadn't felt since the night at the temple. He'd carried that feeling for as long as he could remember, that solitude, that sense that whatever he did was being judged by things he couldn't see. Before he'd met Blays he would have given up swordplay the moment he realized he wasn't any good at it. He was aware of his foolishness now, that Blays had to hold back to keep from disarming him the moment they began, but he sparred on until his arms were so noodly he could hardly lift them above his shoulders. The memory of the temple began to fade, lurking beyond the edges of his sight.

"Not great," Blays said, bending over to plant his hands on his knees after one of their sessions, "but maybe you'll keep them from killing you long enough for me to run away."

"Not fair. That's what I hired *you* for.

Dante went to bed exhausted, rose with the dawn and read through the pink filter of sunlight. The days were mild. The frost stayed gone for a week, then reappeared in their sleep without warning, waking Dante a half dozen times. Each time he woke he pulled his knees tighter to his chest or added another tent of branches to the fire. He got up for good a half hour before dawn, cold and tired and sore, and he watched the flames blacken the thin kindling they cut each day, the odd hunks of wood they sometimes found sunk in the dirt, the wet fibers of which crackled like crumpling paper and spat smoldering knots of embers their way. All the wood would be too wet before long. A pre-morning breeze kicked up, bearing the smells of damp leaves and the stark cut of cold. The snows could come at any time. They'd be early if they showed today, and he thought the air would stay warm enough when it was mixed with sunlight and hard work, but it was there, biding behind the mountains, marching from the north.

He'd spent time in the wilds around the village before, but mainly in the summer, and when he tried to think about where they'd go when the snows came his mind turned its face from his worries. Years later, when Blays was gone and so was his youth, he'd look to this time as a beacon, the single span of his life after the warm haze of childhood that he could remember without the twin shadows of doubt and regret. These couple weeks in the woods would hold the weight of entire seasons of the years before and after; when he thought of these days, allowing himself the memory like an old dog getting up to bark at a fox he'd once chased, he thought of the yellow touch of sunlight through the trees, tasted the sweet, clean flesh of lake trout caught that day, heard the twitter of blackbirds and the laughter of two boys, saw Blays' sword flashing before it crashed against his own.

A snake in every garden, the death of every pet. A day when one wakes to find his parents are gone. The bitter tail to those memories, all those years later, after the gray passage of decades, after everything had changed. There would have been a way to make things different, if he'd known enough to make them run to far-off lands and so avoid the treason and bloodshed and heartache to come, but then that would come at the cost of the man he'd become. He'd close the memories like a book, an irrelevant story from a place that no longer existed. There was no room for looking back on what couldn't be undone.

~

> *When they saw what he'd done they clapped Jack Hand (as he came to be known) in thirty pounds of chains and locked him in the lowest level of the oubliette, where he was to be kept until his eldest brother's hourglass ran dry, which was said to be fed by the sands of the endless Mandal Desert. He lived in darkness, fed once a day, nipped by lice and by rats. Before enacting his imprisonment they took the index finger from each hand — one finger for each of his brothers' wives. There had been calls for more drastic justice, but royal blood was royal blood, which was more than could be said for the wives of his brothers, and not lightly spilled.*

Dante looked up and wondered whether it were all right to laugh at history, and more specifically a history of the killing of women. The *Cycle* had taken a strange turn, abandoning the lumbering attempts to explain the skies and the encyclopedic catalogue of names and kings for digressive stories. Not that he'd read many of the Second Classical authors that had prospered in Gask centuries before, but that's what its tone reminded him of. It read with a certain ironic distance, not so stiflingly self-serious as the recent works he'd absorbed back in Bressel. He hadn't known books could be written in anything but the artless blunder of the holy books, the juvenile wit of romances and adventures, or the overelaborate posing of poetry and history—these last of which frustrated him most of all, seemingly written more with the intent of intimidating whoever opened them than to *say* anything—and he read on with half a smile and the small but sharp fear this new tone was an aberration, something that would disappear as soon as the story was over.

> *Jack Hand's cell was as dark as the caves under the earth. They'd intended it as punishment. He recalled the things he'd learned, dwelled on the last few hours with the bodies. He hailed the shadows to slay the rats and plague the lice and sooner than later they no longer swarmed his cell. After a while he likely went mad, though the lack of observers and Jack Hand's own questionable temperament render the status of his mind a matter of philosophy rather than fact. Who knows how we'd act, locked away, locked alone. The mind is a vast place and its hungers far sharper than the body's.*
>
> *The mind is a vast place and the black of his world was vaster. He drew that darkness, shaped it, and when, three years later, they opened his cell because the growing stink, reportedly legendary even by the spongy standards of dungeons, could mean little other than its occupant had died and was rapidly being converted to the kind of brown sludge kept only at bay by the continual intake of breath, his captors were met by a chattering horde of rats.*
>
> *Skinless, fleshless, bloodless, the creeping bones of 72 life-sucked rodents flooding from each of 30 different cracks in the walls, forming into two streams of surging beasts that overwhelmed the guards as saplings before a tsunami. It's been wondered how so great a force could be stowed in his constricting cell, but what is not under debate is how they maimed and murdered every living occupant of the keep. There they ceased, and Jack Hand took his throne; their bodies fed his armies, and he, in turn, was fed by that shadow that lurks behind all things.*

Blays was off trampling grass, but for now Dante marked his page. He'd kept a smile till the final sentence, when at once he knew, in the same way he knew if he jumped he'd come back down, that if he stared hard enough and right enough at the deep morning shadows cast on his knees by the leaves, something would happen. Before the blushing hand of stupidity could grab him by the neck, he blanked his mind and settled his hands in his lap. He felt a pressure, a tangible presence, like water were being squirted into the front of his skull. Somehow it didn't *hurt*—it felt wrong, but not so wrong to tempt him to stop.

Sweat welled from his temples. A hand's span of the nearest shadows stirred as if by the wind. The illusion was so real he didn't register shock until another part of his mind told him his hair wasn't moving and he didn't feel colder like he would if air were moving over his sweat-slick skin. He raised a hand and he had the queasy sensation of going blind as the dark substance swelled, casting him into a darkness as deep as the space between constellations.

His breath came hard but he stood slowly, not wanting to spook it, for as little sense as that made. He still felt nothing against his skin, not like if he were wading through something solid. He took a trial step. It wasn't a disaster. He took another and tripped on a root. Pain shot through his palms and knees when they pounded ground and the delumination weakened till it was more like a gray fog than like he had no eyes. Dante saw the condensed shadow was roughly spherical, highest a few feet behind him—it had stayed put when he started moving.

He emptied his mind and the darkness ate up the light. After five paces in a straight line the world winked on again. When he looked down he saw his body rising from the mass of shadows at an angle across his waist, centaurian, as if his dad had mated with a globby black hemisphere. He wouldn't put it past him.

"Hey! Dante!" Blays' voice reached him in a hissed shout.

"I'm here," he called back, matching the boy's volume, and when he looked down the shadowsphere was gone. He picked up the book and walked toward where he'd heard Blays' cry.

"What were you doing?" Blays peered past him into the trees.

"Reading."

"Not riding horses?"

"Not recently," Dante said, eyeing him.

"Then someone else is here. There were tracks down at the pond."

"Travelers?"

Blays quirked his mouth. "We're miles from any road."

"Maybe it's someone's land. They're out for a bit of fishing."

"And maybe you're about to get an arrow through your neck." Blays rubbed his mouth, then his eyes. "We've got to go."

"All right," Dante said, spooked by the boy's seriousness. They headed for the camp. A stone's throw from it Blays barred an arm across his chest and pressed him down into the bushes. "What is it?" he whispered.

"Maybe nothing, but if it's a damn trap I don't want to walk right into it."

The grounds looked empty. Their fire had gone out during the night and any smoke was hours gone. The stillness of the wood pressed on his ears like he'd dived underwater. Blackbirds chirped at each other. He heard the furtive rustle of small animals tracking through the fallen leaves. A crow cackled and he jerked his arms to his body. A sour tightness took his chest. He'd come to think of themselves as the only two in this place.

"We'll circle around," Blays whispered. "If it looks clear, we'll grab our stuff. If you see or hear *anything*, freeze on the spot."

Dante nodded, glad to follow Blays' steps. The kid hunched down and advanced around their camp, pausing every twenty or thirty feet to cock his head to the silence. When they'd made more than half a circle around it he hunkered down for a minute, lips a white line. Dante culled small comfort in the fact horses were noisy by nature, always snorting and whickering at each other like big hairy idiots. They couldn't take two steps in the dense forest floor without sounding like something falling down a mountain.

Blays tapped him on the shoulder and they stole straight for their gear. He saw no sign the ground here had been disturbed by anyone but themselves. They gathered weapons and vegetables, wordless, wrapping the two half-eaten fish from the night before in fresh-fallen leaves. Dante grabbed a stray book and that was all it took to be ready to move.

They drew back, Blays leading them direct away from the pond sitting a tenth-mile to the east. They moved quickly but without panic, feet crumpling leaves but not crashing them; still, Blays would halt them every couple minutes to crouch beside a trunk and listen to the forest. It was early morning yet, the sun bright without being warm. The season had begun to shorten its track through the sky, but it would be light another eight hours, maybe nine, and the thought of going on like this for hours on end made Dante want to lie down then and there.

"There's no way they tracked us from Bressel," Blays said at one of their halts. "They'd have been on us in two days, not two weeks."

"We don't know it was them," Dante said, looking behind them.

"No one else has any reason to be out here."

"Other people exist, you know."

"Don't be a fool." Blays' voice had jumped and he bugged his eyes and brought it back to a whisper. "It *could* be fox hunters. It *could* be vagabonds, though that would raise the interesting question of how the hell they got their hands on horses. Even if they were those things, it wouldn't make us any safer. There's no law here."

"Just us," Dante said, clenching his teeth. "How does anyone get anywhere when everything's this screwed up?"

"By being so nasty mere sight of them makes everyone else run away. Let's go."

Despite living in the woods for weeks, he hadn't truly noticed how many animals shared the land. Every crunch of leaves or sudden shrill cry made his neck go tight. The air was cool, almost cold, but he was tickled by icy lines of sweat down his ribs. Blays walked with his back bent, leaning forward and hurrying along like his nose weighed two hundred pounds and only constant motion could keep him from toppling. Dante urged the sun on, outraged that something so big could be so slow. Hours passed. His feet got sore but he found he wasn't tired, not after the last few weeks of fake swordfights and stomping around the pathless woods. The back of his mouth tasted like the dry, sour aftertaste of cranberries. His head felt thick, fuzzy and no more substantial than puffwood seeds, and when he took his eyes off the ground and held his hand in front of his face he saw that it was shaking.

Noon. The sun came straight down and lay against his skin without warmth. He kept his eyes on the beat of his feet. There was no wind and when he saw the ripple of the shadows of the leaves his foot almost missed the earth. With a few more days of reading and concentration, he thought he would be able to do more with them than see them. He hadn't had those days, though. All he could depend on, if things fell apart, was his blade and his training. He trusted the steel, at least.

He nudged Blays toward the subdued trickle of a stream and they knelt at its edge and drank away the sweat of the journey. He shrugged his pack from one shoulder, meaning to eat some carrots, then froze and listened to the language of the woods.

"Get back," he whispered.

"What is it?" Blays' hand went to his sword. Dante shook his head and retreated along the route they'd taken, breaking after thirty feet to head away from the stream. He pulled Blays down under a thick bush and closed his eyes, trying to hush his breath. Blays made as if to speak and stopped at the snap of twigs from the direction they'd just left. He pressed himself lower to the dirt.

"They crossed the stream," they heard, a harsh, deep voice that rumbled through the air. Dante raised his head a couple inches, but the trees were too thick to see anything but branches. "What've you got?"

"Not far off. I can feel them." The second voice was high but faint. Dante heard more words but couldn't differentiate them, then: "It's too close to tell."

"Let's take a damn break," said a third man. "Haven't eaten since sunup."

"We can catch them now," the first one said. "They're close."

"We can catch them just as easy without starving to death in the meantime. They're on *foot*."

The discussion dropped to a mutter of details. He strained his ears, made out the words "trail" and "book" and "carry the bodies." They went silent a minute later, and after another minute Blays caught Dante's eye and gestured north, away. Dante raised a finger to his own mouth. A few seconds later a horse blew air past its mouth. He thought he could smell its animal sweat over the gaminess of his own.

Hooves splashed through the stream a few minutes later. Dante waited, eyes closed and mind wide, but he felt nothing. With a prickle to his neck he realized he was disappointed.

"We should head back," he whispered. "Toward the river."

"Could be others searching that way."

"I don't think so. We can cut northeast. Find a town."

"What good will a town do us?" Blays said.

"Keep us from getting killed in the woods like dogs? Come on." He got to his feet with exaggerated care, arms held to either side. He didn't know how long the stream would delay the riders and he led the way this time, setting a pace so fast his trailing foot sometimes left the ground before his first had fallen. The leaves clicked together in the afternoon breeze and he couldn't keep himself from hastening to a jog. They covered three or four miles before his wind gave out and they dragged themselves beneath another umbrella of undergrowth. Not for the first time, he wished one of his books had a close-scale map of the land around them; he knew there would be people around the river, that's what rivers were for, but they could easily cut ten miles of north-south travel if they only knew where they were. He kneaded his back where the pack had bounced against it.

"They were following us," Blays said. His voice was above a whisper but still soft enough not to carry.

"No kidding." Dante pulled his knees to his chest and rested his head against them.

"I mean, they were trailing us. Like hounds. The one who sounded like a fairy said he could *sense* us."

"He can."

"How is that even possible?"

"Don't ask me."

"Come on," Blays said, poking him in the side. "You study these things."

"The key word is 'study,'" Dante said, narrowing his eyes. "I don't know how to *do* anything."

"This is hopeless. If they can pick up a trail that's weeks old, they can follow us to the ends of the earth."

"No they can't. They lost us for a few weeks there. We can walk on rocks instead of dirt. Whenever we find a stream we'll wade down it a ways rather than cutting straight across."

"That'll just slow us down."

"It'll slow their woodsman even more." Dante got to his knees, readied himself to stand. "I don't think the one who said he can sense us can tell any more than that we're near. If he could, we'd already be dead."

"But we can't hide when they've got him and a tracker," Blays said, wrapping his fingers around the hilt of his sword. "That leaves running and fighting. I'm getting sick of my legs having all the say. My arms are getting restless, they're asking 'When do I get to do my part?'"

"Tell your arms to stow it."

"We can ambush them. Like in the alley."

"No," Dante said, then felt foolish at his own authority. "We're not prepared. These ones are more dangerous than the others."

"This is cowardly," Blays said, but he stood.

Dante's face went hot. "Better yellow than red."

Branches lashed their faces. Mud sucked at their boots. Roots reached up with gnarled fingers, scrabbling for their toes. Their feet were stubbed and sore and sweaty. Their packs chafed their shoulders. Dante did all he could think to make his passage look weird—walking on just his toes for a hundred yards until his calves gave out; striding longer with one leg than the other; sometimes, when Blays was ahead and distracted with making the trail, he'd hop on one foot for eight or ten bounces before he was afraid Blays would hear the odd rhythm and look back. He had no idea whether it would help. He doubted it would do more than make the hunter laugh. What else could he do? Turn their blood to fire inside their veins? Conjure a demon to drag them down to hell? Maybe he could just make the entire world blow up while he was at it. He trudged on.

A few miles further another stream blocked their way and they waded till the waters sluiced by just under the tops of their boots. They followed it upstream a couple hundred yards until it bent back toward the west, then clambered up the bank. Dante's feet felt like stones. They couldn't do another crossing, he thought.

Their boots wouldn't dry before dark.

Their time in the woods had taught them to walk it with minimal noise and they halted together when they heard the slow but steady steps among the leaves. Something heavy, many-legged. They ducked behind an ivy-wrapped stone and listened to the steps grow nearer. When he saw the branches approaching Dante thought, for one crazy moment, the trees had taken life and were walking around on their roots, and then the tan sweep of the buck's head cleared the brush and he ached for a bow. But they'd have no time to clean it, no strength to carry all that meat, and they let out their breath and hurried on. They continued through the afternoon, rested in the twilight, then walked a couple hours in the weak moonlight, guided by the bright northern wink of Jorus, which he'd come to think of as the Millstar. Just as he thought his legs would give out beneath him Blays stopped short, squatting down and planting his hands on his knees.

"That's all I've got in me. One more step and I'm going to fall on my face."

"We've made good time," Dante said, plopping down beside him. "Should find a town tomorrow."

"How far off from the river?"

"Fifteen miles? Twenty? I've never been this far north."

"Me neither." Blays laughed for the first time that day. "I'd never left Bressel."

"You never saw the sea?" Dante said, tucking his cloak around him.

"Well yeah. Never any further than that, though."

They thought their private thoughts. Dante's heart thudded when Blays reached for the pack, but he emerged with the leaf-wrapped fish and a handful of withering mushrooms. He passed Dante one of the fish. "May as well eat these. Won't need to save anything if we'll hit town tomorrow."

"Yeah." They ate their largest meal in days and sipped from the water skins. Exhaustion hit him before he was full. He could feel the puffiness in his eyelids, the discontent in his muscles that would mean full-fledged aches in the morning. Without speaking they both knew the insanity of lighting a fire, and instead pawed leaves over their legs and torsos, to hide and to insulate.

"It's the book," Blays said, and Dante realized he'd been asleep.

"Huh?"

"They're following the book."

Dante opened his eyes. He reached into the folds of his cloak, felt the leathery cover of the book where he kept it wrapped beside his face.

"Leave it, if you like," he said around the lump in his throat. "I won't."

Blays didn't respond. Dante lifted his head to see if the boy had been talking in his sleep.

"I don't run from my problems," Blays said at last. "Well. Not if I can help it."

"We'll outrun them to town. When they get there, they won't find us, we'll find them."

"That's a different tune than you were singing earlier," the boy said. "I can't tell if that's the kind of optimism that's like to take them by surprise or the kind that gets us killed."

"If you die," Dante said, closing his eyes, "what's it matter anyway?"

"I assume it will hurt," Blays said. Dante didn't know whether to laugh or curse or learn to pray. How had it all ended so suddenly? How did this violence keep finding him? If the nether drove them to it, and if the nether lurked behind all things, where in the wide realms of man could he go where it couldn't follow?

4

He woke up. That was a good thing. It meant he hadn't been killed in his sleep.

He stood and wished he had. Leaves fell from the folds of his cloak, rustling like distant water, and Blays stirred. Dante's calves and lower back felt like someone had been tugging on both ends of them all night. He stretched out, gingerly, closing his eyes. After the initial shock, and as long as he didn't move, the ache was almost pleasant. The sun hadn't yet lumbered over the fields of the east but the stars on that side of the sky were growing faint in the deep blue. Through a gap in the trees the six stars of Taim's hourglass were just above the horizon. Autumn was slipping away. He sat back down, shivering a bit, giving Blays a little longer before they picked up where they'd left off.

The world was shadow. In the moment of that thought his senses seemed to fade—the hesitant predawn birdsong became muffled, the fuzzy shapes of the last of the night grew darker, less distinct. His own breath galed in his ears. He reached out for those shadows, extending both his hand and his mind. They didn't come and somehow he knew that was right. He tried again, slitting his eyes until he saw more eyelash than forest, counting the seconds between his deep and steady inhalations. Somehow he expected the slivers of darkness to be cold but the only way he knew they were sinking into his skin was through sight and a dull, far-off feel for its travel, the way you can finally see the sun move when it hits the horizon, or how the moon and fixed stars seem to have jumped whenever you look to the skies of the night. The pain faded from his limbs then; a bright red bramble scratch on his left hand went pink and then to the rusty brown of an old scab. He picked it away with his thumbnail and beneath it the skin was fresh. He closed his eyes and thought if the opposite desire of his mind would cause the opposite change to his flesh.

"What time is it?" Blays asked, rousing him. The nether—naming it for what it was—shuddered back into normal shadow.

"Just before dawn."

"Time for unreasonable men to be on their way," Blays muttered.

They packed up and lit out. Leaves spun to the forest floor. Dante let Blays lead. He wouldn't know how fast to travel if his legs still burned like they had when he'd woken. Birds chirruped in the treetops like nothing were different. He walked with a stillness of thought, feeling light, feeling holy, the calm in the center of a storm of all this life.

He'd stopped pretending like he didn't understand what was happening to him. He'd imagined it would take longer, in fact. That he'd need a teacher or a guide. That he'd need to meditate or pray to be handed the way. He didn't know how the book was showing him the way, only that it was. Dante watched the back of Blays' head bob as he stepped over fallen branches or ducked under live ones. He'd learn faster if he didn't have to watch himself, to keep what he was learning hidden. He needed practice, but couldn't get it when proof of his ability would turn the boy to silence and sidelong glances when he thought Dante wasn't looking. Blays had become something like a friend since the days in the woods had shown him Dante was nothing but an average kid. He didn't want to lose that. He'd had friends before, but not many, and he'd left them all behind the day he'd left the village. He missed them, in an abstract way, knowing they were gone to him and he would never see them again.

He began to forget himself. Little tricks as he walked. Concentrating on the shadows until they curled around his finger. Putting a dark globe on the toe of his boot and seeing how long he could make it keep up with his steps. Thinking on the men he'd read about in the *Cycle* and the thrill they must have felt when they reached out with their hand and made the world change. They were no longer so unimaginable, so distant and alien; Stathus the Wise and Linagan, Jack Hand and Kerry Cooper—he wished he could meet them and hear their words for himself.

"Stream up ahead," Blays murmured, and Dante jumped.

"Okay."

"It should turn into the river."

"That's what streams do, become rivers," Dante said, tucking his chin against his chest and peering into the crossed boughs of the trees to the east, as if looking hard enough would summon up the gray waters of the Chanset.

"We could follow it, I mean," he said, shrugging off Dante's tone.

"That's an idea. Can't follow our tracks if there aren't any."

"Let's cross it, head upstream a bit, and double back."

A couple hundred yards on the other side they turned around, retracing their path as closely as they could. The stream was shallow, fast, and strong, widening abruptly from ten feet across to twenty or thirty of ankle-deep flow, then constricting again, just as quickly, at the next elbow in its path. Its banks were dug deep—if they ducked they couldn't be seen unless someone were watching right from the lip—and its bed was a carpet of rocks, as smooth as if they'd been sanded, some as small as robins' eggs, others sturdy and immobile as the heads of bulls. Big floods in the spring carved it deep, no doubt. They walked on dry rocks at its edge for a while, throwing out their arms for balance, stones thocking together under their weight. The rush of water washed away the sounds of the woods and they spoke, when at all, in raised tones that would have carried like seeds on a breeze if they'd been above the banks. At the bends in its path the banks narrowed on them until the stony beds were buried in cold water that yanked at their ankles with the strength of a man. They slowed at these times, keeping a hand on the wall of dirt to their right or the shoulder of whoever was leading the way.

"This is not a civilized way to live," Blays said after the third or fourth such passage, raising one soggy boot while he balanced himself against the slope of the bank. The waters were getting deeper, reaching their knees when they took a wrong step.

"Want some food?" Dante said. His feet had begun to ache

again. He wiggled his toes, fighting back the numbness. The water felt like it came from close snows.

"I want a fire." Blays stomped his feet, squirting water over the pale gray rocks, darkening them with dampness.

"And I want a pony. That breathes fire. And craps strawberries."

"You'd probably eat them," Blays said. He sat down and let out a long breath.

"You wouldn't?"

"Out of a pony's ass?" Blays hawked and spat into the swirling current. "I don't even want to know where you think the cream would come from."

Dante shrugged. "More for me, then."

He found a few mushrooms wrapped up in his pack, squashed by the books as they'd shifted on the walk, moist and drooping in their own fluids. He handed Blays the bigger share and the boy set them on his lap and stared at them a moment.

"This is what I mean." Blays popped one in his mouth, chewed, paused, then swallowed. He dipped a hand in the water and drank. "This is how animals live."

"It's just for a few days, you baby."

"You're the baby."

"Why am I the baby?"

"Because you're always scared like one. No one's going to save us. We've got to deal with this ourselves." Blays ate slowly, chewing each off-white cap for a long time. Dante had to still his arm to keep from punching him. He blinked, looked away. This whining.

"I'm starting to learn," he said when he could trust his voice.

"Good. I'm tired of running this show by myself."

"Not that." Dante pulled his lips from his teeth and put his hand on Blays' wrist. The boy met his eyes, then looked down, saw the gray trailing from Dante's fingers like wisps of smoke.

"What are you doing?"

He called to it, brought the dark places under the rocks like he'd brought the black images of the leaves that morning. He felt a click in his chest, like something there had turned on its side, but he kept the summons, his mind an empty tunnel.

"Stop it!"

"Shut up." The words didn't break his command. Then it was done and he sucked air and freed his hand, shaking it. The tips of his fingers felt as cold as his waterlogged feet.

"What did you do?" Blays said, sharp as his weapon.

"Stand up. Walk around."

"Go to hell," he said, then got to his feet and bounced in place. He walked a circle around Dante and Dante saw the knots fade from his face.

"I'm not tired."

"Neither am I," Dante said, sticking out his jaw. He let the silence linger, let Blays think his thoughts.

"Can you do anything else?" Blays said, gazing into the woods.

"Not really. Not yet."

Blays folded his arms. "No. It's not right."

"Why? Because you can't hold it in your hand?" Dante picked up a rock and chucked it into the stream. Its splash was too soft to hear over the ceaseless whorl of water. "It's like you just woke up, isn't it? Like you haven't been walking at all."

Blays rubbed the faint blond hair on his upper lip. "My dad used to say if you build your life around nothing more than swinging a sword, you'll start to think all things come down to who can swing it better."

And he's dead, Dante thought. "You're a swordsman!" he said instead.

"That's not the point."

"I'm being careful," he said. "I'm not about to mess with things I don't understand."

"It's not enough to save us," Blays said, dropping his eyes.

"It's just a start." He tightened the drawstring on his bag, jerking the knots so they wouldn't slip. He got his feet under him and walked on down the stream bed. Blays kicked pebbles behind him. The only trees that could cling to the steep sides of the banks were small things, deep-rooted gnarls with close-clustered branches, and they walked in the full light of day. They hadn't seen sign of their pursuers since they'd heard their talk the day before. For all they knew the three riders had headed west, lost their trail, and been turning in circles ever since. They were being chased by shadows. With a week to himself, with a month of study, Dante knew he could learn things to put a stop to all this. His eyes stung. Why didn't they just leave him alone? If the book was so special, why had they left it abandoned in a ruined temple? He slipped on a moss-coated stone and Blays grabbed his arm.

"Thanks," he said, brushing his sleeve where Blays had touched it. The stream turned again and the walls grew tight. Overhead, trees leaned over them, casting them into shadow. A gap no wider than an armspan separated the leaves on one side from those on the other, a blue and ragged line of sky so small he thought it could close completely if they faltered. He planted his feet in the water, each step deliberate as a chess move, thwarting the pull of the current. His legs were soaked past the knees. He walked on, eyes split between the treacherous stones under his feet and that thin blue band up above, one step, then another, cold but not tired, alone but leading his friend.

It was hours before the banks leveled out and the trees pressed them to the water's edge. Dante'd cleansed himself of his weariness again but hadn't touched Blays since. If he wanted to ache and struggle to lift his feet that was his business. The stream doubled in width and when he looked to its middle Dante could no longer see the bottom. The voice of the waters moved from the thin nattering of gossips to a deeper, thoughtful hum. Sometimes he wondered where the speed of the stream had gone, then he'd catch sight of a leafy branch on its surface, hurtling past them at twice their swiftest walk, and he'd remember clear waters didn't mean still waters.

He didn't speak up, but it wasn't long before he thought he could smell it, that faint tang of fresh water. Not so stagnant as the pond, less of the earthy musk of dead, wet plants and more that of a moving body, the crisper scent of pebbles being ground into mud and dry dirt taking on water. A final elbow and the forest disappeared in front of them, giving way to the flat gray depths of the Chanset River, half a mile wide if a foot, the same river Bressel straddled eighty or a hundred miles downstream.

There they rested long enough to catch their breath and wring out their stockings, which steamed on the broad rocks where the stream funneled into the river. They crunched down on the last of their carrots, tossing the limp green tails into the water. They felt the sun on their faces.

"Which way?" Blays said, jabbing between his teeth with a stiff sprig of grass.

"North? Put more distance between us and Bressel?"

"Makes sense. Five more minutes, say."

Dante nodded. He cupped his hands to the stream, made sure his water skin was full. He wriggled the feeling back into his wrinkled toes, drying them for the first time since they'd been following the waterway. It might be days before his boots dried.

"What's funny?" Blays asked.

"I don't know why I bother," he said, nodding to the damp on the rocks where his feet had dripped.

"So moss doesn't grow between your toes," Blays said with an air of authority.

"You can't grow moss on your feet," Dante said. A small string of carrot dislodged from his teeth and he spat it out.

"I suppose you've soldiered in the fields where such things are common."

"You have?"

"No," Blays said, scratching his nose, "but my dad told me. Moss on your feet like the hair on the knuckles of grown men's toes."

"Moss only grows on things that don't move," Dante said, but he no longer knew if that were true. He'd passed plenty of days with wet feet, but couldn't remember any that hadn't ended around a fire.

"Be quiet."

"Like trees and—"

"*Be quiet*," Blays commanded. Dante glared at him and saw he was peering down the riverbank. It was a moment before the horseman moved into view a couple hundred yards distant. Dante pressed himself against the rocks next to Blays.

"Do you think he heard us?"

"No," Blays murmured, then wiped his eyes. "Too much other noise. Do you see any others?"

"No. Could be in the woods."

"What's he doing?"

"Looking for sign," Dante said. "See how he zigzags? How slow it is?"

"No wonder they haven't caught us," Blays said, and then his smile went away. "Yet."

A minute went by, another. The man kept to his search, looking up every twenty or thirty seconds to scan the area. The first time he did so Dante pulled his head down so fast he barked his chin on the rock and almost cried out.

"What do you think?"

"I think," Dante breathed, "he's alone."

Blays nodded. "There's two of us."

"Think so?"

"Better now than when the odds are back in their favor."

"I don't know."

Blays touched the hilt of his sword. "We can get him if we sneak up on him."

"He's on horseback," Dante said, swallowing against the dryness of his throat. "He'll ride away. Or ride out of range, then turn around and trample us."

"What if we went down a little closer, then ran out on the banks screaming and running away?"

"Like scared little kids?" Dante said, giving him a look.

"Exactly like that," Blays grinned.

"But we're not little kids."

"What do you bet he *thinks* we are? If you're strong, you're supposed to fake being weak. It's like the first rule of the field."

"Um," Dante said, wrapping his head around that. "He's still on horseback. He'll murder us."

"That's where you come in." Blays lifted himself a couple inches and started backing on elbows and hips into the protection of the trees. Dante did the same. When they could no longer see the rider and the river showed in faint flashes behind the wall of reddening leaves, they got up and drew closer, placing their feet in the forest carpet like the first steps onto the uncertain ice of a pond. After what felt longer than an hour's march, Blays put a hand on Dante's shoulder and snuck forward to where the trees thinned, peeking around a bole.

"Still there," he breathed when he got back. "Grab a couple

rocks."

"Rocks aren't going to make any difference."

"Every little advantage," Blays said, then bit down hard to stop a laugh when he saw the look on Dante's face. "You never know. Might get lucky."

"I bet." Dante rolled his eyes and scooped up two smooth stones, heavy for how well they fit his palm. He followed Blays toward the river. Insane, he thought. All this chasing had driven them insane. Knowing this was the smart play did nothing to slow his charging heart, to dry the dampness under his arms.

"Ready?"

"I guess."

"Go," Blays whispered, then ran out on the bank and began shrieking for his mother. Dante followed him, body tight with panic when he saw the rider not a hundred feet downstream. He heard him actually laugh, then ran harder at the thunder of hooves in the grass. Within moments the rider had halved the distance between them. He whipped his sword from his back and crouched in the saddle, lining the two boys in his sights. Dante tripped, flailing his arms for balance, and his screams were real.

"Now!" Blays yelled, but the stumble had stolen Dante's focus on the nether. He reached out again, the edges of his mind roaring like the wind. "Now, you son of a bitch!"

The rider raised his sword. Light flashed over Dante's eyes. He could see the sod leaping from the horse's strides. He stopped and turned, laughing in horror, and when he imagined he could feel the horse's hot breath he flung out his hand and the beast's head disappeared in a ball of blackness. A stone hurled past his shoulder and the rider swiped at it as his mount locked its legs and skidded on the damp grass. One of its front legs buckled and then it was down, sliding and rolling in the grass, the snap of its bones and the suddenly scared curses of its rider as he leapt free and collapsed to the ground. The boys charged then: Dante threw both rocks with all his strength, missing the first and clipping the man's shoulder with the second; Blays' blade bobbed beside him and Dante tore loose his own and they were on the downed man before he'd found his feet.

"You tricky shits!" he screamed. He struck from his knees, a fierce blow Dante blocked but which sent him staggering. The man's eyes were bright with some feral emotion when Blays' counter cut off his left hand. He swung wildly, forcing the boy to fall back, then reeled to his feet. Dante stepped forward and swung his weapon with both hands. The man deflected it, but his motion threw off an already poor balance and Blays' stroke broke his ribs like the staves of a barrel. He fell to his knees, propping himself up with his bleeding stump. He opened his mouth and spit hung in strands. His elbow quivered as he raised the point of his blade at the two boys. Dante's backhand strike knocked it from his hand. Blays aimed a final blow at the soft stretch of his neck. It didn't fall cleanly, but when he pulled back his sword the body dropped and didn't move.

Blays laughed, a hollow thing. Dante didn't join him.

"The others can't be far," Blays said.

"We can hide his body." Dante slid his sword into its sheath. The man's wide wounds steamed in the chill air.

"Not the *horse*."

"Then we'll run," Dante said. He found a small coinpurse and added it to his pocket. The horse was thrashing on the earth, legs shaking each time it tried to rise and the bones wouldn't hold. Its great glassy eyes rolled in its skull. Dante looked to Blays.

"I can't," Blays stated.

"There's a bow," Dante said, pointing. "Take it."

"What if it kicks me?"

"It couldn't kick through a broken board," he said, and when he went for more words he found half-digested carrots instead. He leaned over and spat them into the grass.

"He was looking for us to have gone south," Blays said, turning away from Dante's gurgles. He shouldered the bow and a half-full quiver. "There must be a town that way."

"Whetton," Dante said, the sour taste of his stomach on his tongue. He spat again. "We can go faster on the bank."

"Can't risk it." Blays headed back up the bank. "Let's stick to the forest's edge."

Dante disagreed but found himself light on the guts to speak up. They broke back into the trill of birdsong and the rattle of wind-shaken leaves and made a brisk trot south. Within seconds

Dante was shivering without stop.

"That wasn't how I'd imagined it would be," he said once his blood had calmed.

"You think about killing people a lot?" Blays said, smiling faintly.

"Sometimes," he smiled back. It didn't last. "On his knees like that."

"Don't feel sorry for him. He was all set to trample us into the grass."

"But it was so...savage," Dante said, and Blays shrugged. It was worse than the other times. It felt like a regression, like an act of a man he didn't know. He had no illusions fights were supposed to be fair. If the one with the tracker had been even, he without his horse and them without surprise, he expected it would have ended with a few pounds of steel through his heart. Yet he couldn't shake the feeling what they'd done had been unnatural, that somewhere the gods were watching them and their judgment would be harsh.

"We'd be dead except that spell," Blays said softly a moment later.

"Yeah."

"Were you scared?"

"No," he said, running faster. "A little. When I tripped."

"I just about dropped a pile in my breeches," Blays said, chortling so hard he had to sputter out the words. "Then the look on his face when you blinded his horse! Gods!"

Dante chuckled weakly. It had looked otherworldly, the black ball where there should have been a head, the rider throwing his hands over his head like a man falling through the false floor of a wildcat trap.

"You have a strange sense of humor."

"He'd have laughed too if he could see it." Blays giggled. Dante joined him, feeling outside himself. Their nervous energy gave out after a mile or so and they slowed to a stroll to catch their breath. Dante clasped his hands behind his head to ward off the stitch in his side.

"They're not going to miss our tracks after that," he said, gazing into the woods. "Not even with their woodsman dead."

"I figured that's why we were running away," Blays said.

"The nearest town could be twenty miles from here. They're on horseback."

"So what?"

"So what? So they'll find us and kill us!"

Blays rolled his eyes. "So what do you want to do about it?"

"I don't know!" Dante said, startled at the pitch of his own voice. He thought he was angry with Blays for being so cavalier, but after a quarter mile of silent seething he'd reached the same conclusion as the boy. They couldn't hide. They had no horses. Returning to the woods would do no good when the temple men had already found them once. All they could do was run and hope. The trees thinned and he saw a stream of smoke rising from a fraction of a mile down the bank. For a moment he let himself think their luck had turned, that it would be the outskirts of a town, maybe even Whetton, but it was a single house on the river's edge. The land rolled empty beyond it.

"Wait," he said. "That smoke."

"What about it?" Blays yawned.

"There'll be a boat."

"Smoke means *fire*."

"At the house where they have the fire, you dunce. You don't live in a river and not have a boat."

"Oh," Blays said. "Sure. If we cross over, they'd have to waste time finding a ferry."

"The current's fast," Dante said, frowning, picking at this new thread. "If we row hard, they'd have to be riding pell-mell to keep up. We can reach town ahead of them."

They looked at each other. "Ambush," Blays said.

"Nater," Dante agreed, one of those words you repeat without a clue where it came from.

"Yeah," the boy said, licking his lips. "That's it. We take them out of the mix and that gives us time to think up what the hell we do next. If we can't figure out what to do before they send the next guys, maybe we deserve to eat it."

Dante crouched in the bushes of the forest's fringe. Nothing but open grass north and south.

"Can you run?"

"Let's do this thing."

They cut right down the shallow slope of the grassy band and then the steep rocky banks until their boots touched water. The house lay straight ahead. It was a small thing, clearly no more than a couple rooms, and as they got closer Dante grew afraid they'd found the one fisherman in the wide world who didn't own a boat. They drew to a quick walk at a couple hundred yards off, ears sharp for footsteps, for shouts, any sign of its owners other than the white wisps of smoke. At a hundred yards he could smell it strongly, the sweet smoky scent of dry heat and crisp winter. His eyes locked to the hut as they fell into its shadow. The bank stretched out in a tiny spit right before the hut and as they crested the moist earth he heard the hollow slap of water on a hull.

"Nice deduction, Sage Pratus," Blays muttered, regarding the rowboat moored in the miniature bay beneath the house. A light wind blew in from the north. It smelled like the weather were turning.

"Think it's safe?"

"Does it matter?" Blays said, tromping down to the two-person skiff. Its timbers were bleached with the wear of water and sunshine, and above the waterline the wood was fuzzy to the touch. Blays knocked near the top of its hull and one of the beams actually rattled. "What's holding it together? The power of prayer?"

"They take this thing out?" Dante hissed, glancing at the river. "I wouldn't trust it in a puddle."

"River looks okay," Blays said, grabbing hold of the unraveling rope at its fore and following it to a stake a few feet up the bank. "Get in."

"Lyle's balls," he swore, then edged up through the water and rolled himself inside. It was decently broad and didn't threaten to show its belly at the addition of his weight, but he didn't like the way it rolled on the current. Blays freed the rope and swung the boat up sidelong to the shore, then wiggled his rear like a cat before it makes a leap and hurled himself in behind Dante. The boat flapped around like a man who's just stubbed his toe and Dante threw himself flat against its bottom. "You ass!"

"I'm no sailor," Blays said. "Now I'm the captain here. Grab a damn oar."

"Are you sure you wouldn't rather finish drowning me?"

"I think I hear someone coming," Blays said, cocking his ear and shoving them off.

"Where?" Dante whispered, ducking down and taking up an oar. He dipped it smoothly into the water.

"Well, that got you rowing." He smiled at himself and picked up the other oar. Dante glared at him over his shoulder, then pressed his fingers to his temples.

"Row on the other side, you idiot."

"I said I'm not a sailor," Blays spat back. "Doesn't sound really carry on the water?"

"One reason among many you should shut the hell up."

Blays muttered to himself. They pointed the nose downstream and paddled out into the current. From forty or fifty feet off, the bank rushed by like they were running on the water. The blade of Dante's oar spun whirlpools and clouds of bubbles into the light chop of the gray waters. Each time he lifted it clear a stream of water spattered away from the oar. Blacks and blues shimmered beneath the silvery surface, a hint at the vastness of its depths.

"Whose idea was this?" Blays asked. In five minutes of travel the hut was already little more than a dark blot upstream, further than the opposite shore. "It was a good one."

"You sound surprised," Dante said. He let his paddle skim the surface for a moment, arching his back to flex the kinks from his shoulders. He thought about calling to the nether, soothing his muscles, but let it be. Rowing wouldn't kill him.

The breeze was very faint, buffering him around the ears with only the occasional gust, but back in the woods the heads of the trees were swaying. Brown leaves tore loose and fluttered south, hanging nearly motionless with regards to the boat. For perhaps the first time in his life Dante wished he knew more about mathematics.

Waves beat gently on the sides of the boat in glorps and burbles. The two paddles swished rhythmically. The trees on the banks fell away, replaced by fields of black-brown dirt and old yellow wheat stalks shorn of their heads. Now and then a house stood up alone in the farmland. After a while Dante's knees cramped under him and he squirmed into a cross-legged stance.

When he grew hot he shed his cloak. A few miles down, the Chanset bent to their left. Following its curve, they saw it widen further yet, and beyond the broad gray bulge of waters, no more than three miles away—twenty minutes, he figured, if they kept to their strokes—the welcome smoke and low-slung spires of what had to be Whetton. Dante looked back and laughed at Blays.

"Let's pull up before we hit town," Blays said. "It'll look weird, paddling right up to the docks in this thing."

"I'm sure we could come up with something," Dante said, but a mile upstream they angled it into shore on a sandy beach and disembarked into the shallows. He picked up the rope from inside the bow (as far as the rowboat could be said to have one) and carried it to shore. "There's nowhere to tie it up."

"Who cares?"

"We should at least drag it aground," he said, holding the rope in both hands. "Maybe it will treat someone else as well."

"Fine," Blays said, and blew air past his lips. They grabbed hold of its slippery sides and leaned forward, pulling it up the sand until it was clear of the waves lapping up the beach. "Good enough, master?"

"It'll have to do," Dante said, looking away.

"Well. Forward ho?" Blays took the lead. The land north of the city had been cleared for farms and firewood, coverless, so they took to the road. The hard, rutted dirt felt odd beneath Dante's boots. It had been weeks and many miles since he'd walked on anything but forest floors and the beds of creeks. He looked down on himself, at the mud stuck to the bottom of his cloak, the knots in his bootlaces where they'd snapped and been retied, the grime coating his hands, the black crescents of his fingernails. He looked filthy even by city standards. He realized, with a small shock that made him feel old, he wanted a bath.

The north wind kept Whetton's stink of smoke and sewage and tanneries and manure and sweat from their noses until they were within a bowshot of its gates. It hit them all at once and they looked at each other, noses wrinkled, then laughed quietly.

"Haven't missed that," Blays said.

"We're probably no better," Dante said, nudging his nose against his shoulder. He was right.

"At least we came by it honest." The boy stopped before the gates and put his hand on his sword. "Um."

"Whetton's a free city," Dante said, then frowned. "I think."

Blays glanced among the modest traffic passing through the crossroads behind the gate. Men and women on foot, a lot of ox- and mule-teams bearing wagons filled with the harvest of corn and wheat and potatoes and beans. A good number were armed. Not all, not even a majority, but in a minute's watching they saw more men (and a couple women!) with swords at their belt than anywhere in Bressel but the arms yards and the barracks of the town watch.

"I'm thinking it's okay," Blays said.

"I suppose we could just act natural."

"I don't know about that. For you,'natural' seems to involve getting wrapped up in death cults and murderous intrigue."

"They're not a death cult," Dante said, falling in behind. Among other minor miracles he'd learned to walk without knocking his sheath against his knee, and he allowed himself a small swagger as they rejoined civilization. The shadow of the gate swallowed them up and spat them back into the sunshine of the interior crossroads. A few blocks passed without purpose, lost in the vision of houses of timber and stone, the pillowy white smoke of smithies, the simple presence of other people. Dante found himself watching every man who walked their way. Sometimes, sensing his gaze, their faces darkened with the half-felt emotion of troubled dreams. Sometimes he thought he saw fear.

The shadows grew long and longer yet. Size-wise, Whetton was no contest to Bressel, but it was large enough to hide them, if they wished, and it soon became clear it was far too big for them to keep watch on every road.

"We should get the nearest inn to that north gate," Dante said, stopping at an intersection. He stepped back from an oncoming carriage. Horse sweat ruffled his nostrils and he tasted bile.

"I was thinking about that. They might cut through the forest. We should hire a beggar to watch the western gate, too."

"Make it a kid," Dante said. "That way we can threaten to beat him up."

"The docks, then. That's where the scum always floats up."

Dante nodded, deciding not to remind Blays where he'd first found him. They made a left for the river and descended into the noise and clutter of trade, the stink of old fish and things rotting in the water, the tall blank walls of wares-houses. Down near the docks swarms of mudders and the kind of boy who's always bumping over bread stands tore through the streets like skinny, reeking flies. None of them looked older than ten. One such group shrieked past and Blays hauled one in by the collar.

"What's your name, kid?"

"Whatever you want it to be," the boy said, eyes held fast on their belted swords. He looked about seven, but his clothes flapped loose around his body and his arms were straight and thin, knobby at the elbows and hands.

"Smart," Blays said. "We've a job for you. Come on."

"Can't I stay here?" The boy's round eyes stood out from his cinder-smudged face.

"There's money in it," Dante said, bouncing a chuck off his chest. The kid seemed to rematerialize at ground level to snatch it up, then stood and stared up at them, head cocked.

"George," he said. "What's yours?"

"We need you to watch the west gate," Blays said.

"Don't the guards do that?"

"The guards would want more money," Blays said, smiling tightly. "Come with us or cough it up."

"Let me go get Barnes," George said. "That way he can watch if I fall asleep."

He darted away before they could object. They hustled behind, tight on the heels of their investment.

"He'll betray us in a second," Dante said.

"We'll promise him more if he doesn't. And a thrashing if he does."

"You'd make a good magistrate," Dante snorted. George pried another dirty-haired youth from the crowd around an impromptu wrestling match and they padded back to the older two.

"He's my brother," George said.

"We need you to watch the west gate," Dante said, bending down to put his face level with theirs. "We're looking for two riders. They look like—" He stopped. They'd never *seen* the men, other than the one they'd killed by the river. Doubtlessly pairs of riders filtered into the city a score an hour. "What do they look like, Blays?"

"How the hell should I know? One sounded nasty and one sounded like a princess."

"One's going to look weak and the other will look strong," Dante said. He rubbed his face. How could he have made an oversight like that? How had they planned to ambush them when they had no idea what they looked like? "The weak one should look like a priest. Wearing a robe or something."

Blays scratched his neck. "At least the nasty one will have a sword."

"And they'll be on horseback," Dante added lamely. "Only two of them."

"Okay," George said. "What do we do when we see them?"

"What's the closest inn to the north gate?" Dante asked.

"The Foaming Keg," Barnes put in. He was a few inches shorter than his brother, bore the same moppish dark-brown hair, a year or two younger. "It's the one with the picture of the foamy keg over the door."

"Right," Dante said, squeezing his eyes shut. "If you see them, one of you comes and tells us right away. The other one follows them and sees where they go. Another chuck's in it for you if you do."

"And the fist if you run off," Blays put in, shaking his under their noses.

"Ask the innkeep for Dante."

"Or Blays."

"Okay," George said. "When do we start?"

"Now," Blays said. The brothers looked at each other and trotted off toward the west. They weren't wearing shoes. "That may have been very stupid."

They made haste for the Foaming Keg and spent ten minutes arguing with the keeper about the vacancy of windowed rooms on the second or third story facing the north gate. Back in Bressel, Dante would have given in at the keeper's first sob story or breakdown of expenses, but after the last few weeks, facing limited silver and an uncertain future, he accepted no terms until he was paying only half again what he thought fair. Both parties left angry, which struck him as the mark of true sophistication in the intercourse of society.

Blays installed himself in the window to watch the streets. His tanned face grew murky in the twilight. Dante lit a candle and holed up in the corner, spreading the *Cycle* over his knees.

"There's a couple riders," Blays said, leaning forward. "No, wait, that one's a woman. A woman riding outside a carriage? What kind of a town is this?"

"Couldn't say."

"There's a couple...but that guy looks like he's a billion years old. He looks like he died about five miles back." Blays laughed and clapped his knee. Dante scowled at his pages. "And those two look like they've bathed in the last month. Can't be them." A couple minutes dragged by. "Oh, there's a—"

"Enough," Dante said.

"Hey, at least I'm doing something here."

"Do it quietly."

"There's a couple," he stage-whispered, then laughed at Dante's glare. "All right. Fine. Read your damn book."

"I will."

"Good."

"It is good," Dante said, and found he'd lost his place. The skies grew dark. With fading frequency Blays would crane his face out the window to meet the clatter of hooves. Dante lost himself in the book, flipping between sections to make certain he was matching names to lineage and king to kingdom. A knock banged against the door and he bit his tongue.

Blays pointed at him, mouthed "You." He lowered himself from the sill and stepped to the side of the thin door. Noiselessly, he drew his blade.

"Uh, who is it?" Dante called, giving Blays the eye.

"Barnes, sir," a small voice said from the other side. Blays let out his breath and Dante unbarred the door.

"Did you see them?"

"George says to say we saw the two people you wanted us to see," Barnes said.

"Where's George now?" Dante asked.

"Following them."

"Where'd they go?" Blays said.

"I dunno," Barnes shrugged.

Dante looked at Blays over Barnes' greasy head. "Shit."

"It's okay," Blays said, eyes darting. "Uh. We should have at least a couple hours until they'd go to sleep. Barnes, do you think you can find George before midnight?"

"Yeah. He's my brother!"

"Then go find him. You two keep following until they go inside an inn. Then George stays there while you come back here. You got that?"

"I think," Barnes said, twisting his hips and swinging his arms.

"What'd I say?"

"You said go find George, then when they go to sleep come tell you."

"That is what I said," Blays said, giving Dante an impressed look. "Well, go do it, damn it!"

The boy disappeared without a word. Dante stared through the open doorway, wondering how many of them died before they reached his own age. His older brother'd been among them. Sending Barnes and his brother to spy on killers for a chuck apiece. But they were willing to take it. To them it must feel like the wealth of dragons.

He rebarred the door and yawned. The dawn in the woods felt like ages ago. He slumped back in the corner, massaging the back of his head. The rears of his eyes felt like someone were pressing against them with a thumb.

"I'm going to nap," he told Blays.

"Switch you in a couple hours."

He settled down on the pallet, wrapping up in his cloak. Some time later a knock stirred him from sleep and he drew a deep breath. There was the tick of a lock, a muted conversation, but in his half sleep he couldn't make out a word.

"Get up, dummy," Blays said. "Barnes is back."

Dante sat up straight. His brain felt like it had been left in the thoroughfare for a season. He blinked at Blays' wiry height, at the squirming Barnes who didn't rise past his rib cage.

"Hello," Dante said, scratchy.

"Hi," Barnes waved. "The two men went to their room a while ago."

"How'd you find George?"

"I asked the other boys if they'd seen him until one of them said yes."

"Oh." Dante got up. He emptied his pack of everything but the book and a knife and relooped his sword belt around his waist. He had no idea what time it was. He felt worse than when he'd gone to sleep. "What's everybody standing around for?"

"Lead on," Blays said, shoving Barnes lightly between the shoulders. They tramped down the streets. The night was cold. Wind channeled down the empty streets. Overhead the stars watched with blank eyes. For ten minutes Barnes led them through an impossible tangle of alleys, stopping briefly to greet other small boys who looked up at Dante and his sword with round and gleaming eyes. Barnes stopped in the mouth of a sidestreet and pointed across an avenue to a wooden building with a painting of a frog's head above the door.

"They're the third room on the second story," said a voice behind them. They whirled, swords out, and saw George. "Don't hurt me!"

"Sorry," Dante said. "Get up already."

"Do we get our other chuck now?" George said, scooting toward them, ignoring the fresh dust on his breeches.

"How long ago did they go to their room?" Blays said.

"A while," George said. "First they had some drinks. I got thrown out but I sneaked back in."

Dante handed him a blackened piece of silver. "Go buy yourself some bread."

"Don't tell me what to do," George said. He jogged into the depths of the alley. Barnes waved at them and ran to catch up to his brother.

"Did you hear what he said to me?"

"You'll get over it," Blays said. He put away his sword. "Sounds like they're drunk. Couldn't ask for more."

"You ready?"

"Are you?"

"It's the only way to get them off our backs," Dante said.

The common room was stifling, rank with smoke and the sweat of men and the vinegary odor of vomited wine. The innkeep glanced up and they kept their eyes front and beelined for the stairs. At the second floor Blays brought out his blade and Dante followed suit. Blays counted off the doors, pointed to the third. Dante nodded. Blays squared himself in front of it, paced back. He waited till loud laughter pealed up from the first floor, then barreled forward, leveling his shoulder against the wood. It splintered to chunks and he hurled right through into the darkness. Dante yelped and leaped over the wreckage of the door, whacking at the first figure that wasn't Blays, who was busy extricating his sword from the chest of the same man Dante'd just stabbed. The dying man gurgled and a candle flared from the far end of the room. They paused, wrists flexing when the dying man slumped forward on their blades.

"Dante Galand," the remaining man said, and they heard the high, reedy voice from the stream two mornings before. He had a long, pale face, black hair queued at the base of his neck and falling past his shoulders. He was wearing nothing but a dirty gray set of underclothes which sagged at the ass and elbows.

"Some son of a bitch who won't leave us alone," Blays said back at him, twisting his sword in the other man's body and hauling it free. Blood sprayed over his hand and the corpse dropped onto Dante's feet, pulling his sword from his grasp. The man splayed his fingers at them and Dante saw the air go dark. By instinct he punched back and a black gout rippled like flame from his hand. The two forces met and became nothing.

The man curled his lip, gestured with index and middle fingers. Dante felt the nether enfolding him like a cloak. He swung his arm from the elbow as if to say "Behold!" and again negated the man's power.

"Stop that," the man said.

"Burn in hell!" Blays shot, chopping the air and spraying the man with blood. He stepped forward.

"Don't move," Dante warned.

"They didn't tell me you shared the talent," the black-haired man said, fists held out from his sides. A temporary stillness stood between them.

"What *did* they tell you?"

"You'd stolen the *Cycle*." He smiled with half his mouth. "I can see that much is true."

"Can you?"

"It's cleared your mind," the man said, eyes and voice pinched with suspicion. "Opened the paths to the nether."

"I see," Dante lied.

"Indeed," the man nodded, glancing between Dante and Blays' blood-slick sword. "This may change things."

"How's that?" Blays said.

"They may welcome another into the fold, that's how."

Blays laughed. "The only fold's going to be the one I cleave into your forehead."

"Then it's a good thing it's not your decision to make, because I'd crush you like a bean."

"You've been trying to kill me for weeks," Dante said.

"That was then," the man said, drawing back his shoulders. "What you need now is proper training."

"I've stopped you well enough without it."

"If kicking down a door should impress me, then I'm impressed," the man said, brushing the shoulder of his underwear. "But I'm not much, really. Nothing compared to the ones who'd teach you, or the ones who'd come after you if you deny me."

Dante said nothing. To accept would be to part with Blays. He knew there were parts of the book that would take years to untangle, that its pages held knowledge he'd never learn in isolated scholarship—the powers he saw when he slept. He didn't even know how it had caused him to come in tune with the nether in the first place. He did know he didn't like this man and didn't trust the sect he represented. They may not be the amoral, bloodthirsty force the histories tried to paint them as, but Dante suspected a force as primal as the nether couldn't be tapped without a certain recklessness of spirit that must taint their entire order.

"Who are these others?"

"The holy of Arawn," the man replied, as if he'd asked which direction the sun rose.

"And what is it they want?"

"Open worship of our lord. An equal place among the houses of the Belt."

"Their temples are smashed," Dante said. "Their people are slain."

"The gods can't be killed! And neither can the ones who'd praise them. As for temples, we have ours within Mennok's, with Carvahal's. Even the houses of Gashen count priests of a deeper alliance."

Dante drew back his chin. "What? You've been seeding them with your own people?"

The man snorted. "Am I supposed to think it's dishonorable? What's the honor in getting slaughtered in the open field? What's the glory in a Fourth Scour when you're the one getting scoured?"

"I don't understand," Dante said, trying to remember all the men of cloth he'd met in the temples and cloisters and cathedrals of Bressel. How many of them served a second god in secret? The very one whose knowledge Dante had been seeking? "How long has this been going on?"

"That's enough." The man held up his hand, palm out. From the corner of his eye Dante saw Blays' arms tense up. "Come with me back to Bressel and we'll sail to Narashtovik. There, you'll learn whatever you want. Things you don't yet even know to ask about."

Agreement ached in Dante's chest so hard he'd almost said yes before he could think. He glanced at Blays and the blood sliding down the boy's sword. Say Dante left now with this man for Bressel, for this Narashtovik. Say Dante had thirty or fifty years left to his life: three to five decades to spend forging a name so bright he'd rival the stars. And every day of which he'd spend regretting the moment he'd left Blays to whatever mean fate awaited him.

"I won't be bound to anybody," Dante said, knowing there would be other ways. "Not even the gods."

"I thought the same thing when I was your age," the man chuckled. "Have faith in those above and some day you'll be the one looking down."

"I'm not much for waiting," Dante said, and when he flung out his hand he sent the opposite edge of the shadows that would heal. The man jerked his hands up to his chest, but before he could speak his stomach spilled open like a sword had torn across it. His hands plunged to catch the intestines that slithered to the floor. Blays screamed.

The man hunched, clutching at his belly, gaping at Dante. The man raised shaking fingers thick with the blackish blood of the body. Dante reached for more shadows to meet the man's summons and found only a flicker. Blays' arm blurred and his sword spun across the room, pinning through the man's neck. The black-haired man made a choked gasp, tongue jutting from his mouth. He rolled his eyes, as if exasperated it had come to this, killed in his underwear in a foreign town by two dirt-caked boys. Then he went limp, hanging from the sword embedded in the wall.

"What in the name of whoever you hold holy was that?" Blays said, planting his foot against the wall and clearing his sword. The body thumped. He wiped it clean and sheathed it.

"I healed him," Dante said.

"No you didn't!"

"I mean, I did it backwards." Dante lowered himself and groped for his own sword beneath the body of the first man they'd killed. He touched the warm stick of blood and drew back. "I didn't know it would do that."

"I don't think he did either!" Blays kicked the corpse, then shuddered so hard he fumbled his sword. He turned to Dante, face white and misted up with sweat. "Did you mean what you said? About not being bound to anyone?"

"I'll find my own way. I don't need them or anyone else to find what I'm searching for."

Blays nodded and looked away. His face soured. "This place stinks like a slaughterhouse."

They left down the stairs. For whatever racket their disturbance may have raised, there was no sign the drunk keepers and drunker patrons of the common room had heard a thing. The two of them took to the streets, hunting their way back in the bath of the moon till their eyes found the painting of the Foaming Keg. Dante pushed down his nausea. His shoulders felt as broad as a bear's. There was no power in the world that could stop him and Blays, he thought. They'd bend the world to its knee.

5

"They arrested your friend."

Dante spun for the high-pitched, sexless source of that news. He backed in a circle, then saw the dark head of one of the two brothers. Now that they weren't standing next to each other he couldn't tell which was which.

"Arrested? For what? How do you know?"

"I saw them go in after you left," the kid said. "There were a whole lot of watchmen. They carried him out on their shoulders." He tipped his head till his ear touched his shoulder. "He said lots of nasty words."

Dante grabbed the boy by the collar and hauled him into the alley he'd just come out of. If they'd been after Blays, they'd be after him. It was only blind chance the kid had found him on his way back from the market before he'd returned to the Keg.

"Where are they keeping him?"

"They keep them all at the old bailey. They have the trial on the Saturday, and then if they're guilty they hang them the next Saturday."

"How do they tell who's guilty?"

"I don't know," the boy said, sweeping the dirt with his toe. "I guess they all are,'cause they're all at the hanging."

"Go see what you can see, kid. I'll reward you beyond your dreams."

"I can count to a hundred," he said, then spun off down the streets.

Dante rested his hand on his sword, glancing down both ends

of the alley. He double- then triple-checked his pack to make sure the book was still there. Anything at the Keg was lost. Going back would mean arrest. His prayer books, his histories, his candles and his notes and spare paper, all that was replaceable. It hurt to leave it, but he had no choice.

His first instinct was to skip town. His second was to hunker down in the woods until the Saturday after and make a one-man assault on the city when they brought Blays down to the gallows. He saw several flaws in this plan, however, not least of which was he'd have no chance of surviving and Blays would be killed anyway. The gesture would be nice, noble even, and if there were a bard in the crowd maybe Dante would have a song written about him everyone could sing and forget in a season or two, but that would make him no less dead, except possibly in a metaphorical way that would do nothing to stop the worms from eating his skin.

He picked up a shard of cobble and hurled it against the alley wall. He took a breath and looked around again. What did he have? Time, in some small measure. He had time. He should juice that for all its worth before getting sucked into anything rash. The trial was two days off, the hanging a week from then. The first order of business was to find a place to hide so he couldn't be caught before he had a chance to try anything tremendously stupid.

He drew his cowl over his head. Rule out the docks. The boys were too easily bought if any of the watch were canny enough to throw a little coin their way. Plenty of other inns in town, but inns attracted traffic, and traffic attracted do-gooders and bounty-vultures. Even if he holed up in his room, coming and going by cover of darkness, *someone* would see him. He needed isolation. The kind of place no one went without being dragged. An abandoned building could work, if he could trust himself to differentiate between the truly abandoned and the merely decrepit, but that could be little better than an inn—abandoned buildings attracted vagabonds and vagabonds attracted lawmen. The basement beneath a slaughterhouse would be avoided by anyone with a working nose, but he'd have to do an awful lot of sneaking to avoid the laborers, and anyway it was a place of trade. A churchyard, maybe. No one went to graves except on the anniversaries of the faithful departed, but he'd feel too foolish skulking around the tombstones. Leaving for the woods would cut him off from the clockwork of the city. He had to stay close. If for some reason the courts changed their schedule, Blays could be killed before Dante'd heard word one.

The graveyard, then. He set his mouth. At least his shame would be private.

Dante fake-limped through the foot traffic, coughing wetly like a man on his way out and enthusiastic about sharing his imbalanced humors. The first man he stopped drew his sleeve over his mouth and waved Dante to the south. Not knowing local landmarks or much other than what Bressel had taught him of how cities worked, he kept to the main streets, trusting his hood and his cough to deflect wandering eyes. Twice he crossed paths with officious men in cleanish brown uniforms. They walked without hurry, sweeping the crowds. Dante steeled up and strolled past them. If they had his description, he'd either run, fight, or die.

Finding the churchyard wasn't hard. He just kept heading south until he saw a steeple surrounded by green lawns and gnarled old trees. Its lower stretch was coated in simple wooden poles, flat stones, fieldstone piles, and the dicklike obelisks of Simm, Lia's wayward husband who made sure to come back her way every spring. Just as often there were no markers at all, just scruffy grasses on an ankle-high mound. The yard was big and quiet and empty. The shouts and hooves of the city faded behind him, blending into birdsong and the rustle of the wind. He made for the towering markers and mausoleums that clustered at the crest of the short hill a ways inside the yard.

The first mausoleum door he tried didn't budge. The second swung with a sound of grating stone, but before he'd taken two steps inside he was floored by the meaty stink of the recently deceased. He backed out, tenting the collar of his cloak over his nose. The fifth vault he tried opened reluctantly and he eased inside, breathing through his mouth.

All he smelled was dust and things turning into dust. Old flowers rested on the shelves with the urns of the cremated, but they were gray things, and when he touched them they crumbled away, paffing against the stone floor. With the door propped part open, there was enough light to read by if he squinted.

He sat down on a cool stone shelf at the back of the room. He could bribe the bailey guards, maybe. He didn't have much, but the collected purses of all the men they'd put down between Bressel and here would make a decent temptation to spring a nobody like Blays. Just as likely they'd see right through him and lock him up and take the money. He could use George and Barnes as a go-between, but that was no better; they'd be beaten or killed if they showed up with that much silver, and them showing up at all after he'd handed them that much coin was no sure thing. He could try getting Blays a note, notes were simple enough and maybe Blays could tell him something that would help Dante break him out, but Blays couldn't read. Dante covered his eyes with one hand. He'd relished his solitude not a month ago. Now it felt empty, powerless as a childless old woman.

Blays had been arrested for the crime of being caught keeping himself alive. Those were the facts, but Dante had the sense the arrest itself would be proof enough of his guilt. He grabbed a vase and hurled it across the vault. The lacquered pottery exploded, shards tinkling on the stone. Ashes billowed low on the floor like a fog. Where had the law been when they'd been hunted like foxes? The watch had only shown their fat faces after the blood had been spilled, the blades put away. Blays had been sleeping when he'd left. No doubt they'd crept up on him that way, catching him in his bed. They wouldn't have the decency to meet him with a sword in his hand. Whatever his fate, Dante resolved to slit as many of their throats as he could reach before it was over.

He spent the daylight with the *Cycle*, groping for answers that would bring him the strength to find a solution. Jack Hand kept showing up:

> *Jack Hand's kingdom grew to hold the two rivers at its north and the golden forge at its south; he married the maiden of the west and saw the sun rise over two hatches of cicadas, but as with all growths it began to take forms he could neither guess nor control. He wiled the days in the Tower of Venge and brooded on the new powers he could feel stirring within his lands. Shadows played in the hands of men he'd never met, men who owed him no homage. In the time-honored right of a king to own*

the hearts and minds of those who live by his grace in his lands, he dispersed the army of rats to train their eyeless sockets on the men who practiced in secret. He called his advisers to the Tower, trading tactics over maps and oaths over ale.

At the end of seven days he knew the names of the 54 conspirators and the homes of their families. Wise to the ways untreaten roots will bear poison fruit even when the trunk and its branches are hacked and burnt, he dispatched his bluecloaks to reach every manor within an hour's span, and in that way he cut short that threat in a single long-armed stroke; the wails of the doomed had no time to reach the ears of the next in line, and they perished before they could take to the road and plant the seeds of retribution.

He'd meant to send a signal of fire that night to all who watched, but when he gazed from his tower at the fresh green folds of land and the fine white houses of the dead, he puzzled on the balance of destruction and creation. Instead of burning the houses of the traitors, he washed them clean of treachery and bequeathed them to the priests of his patron, and they sang the miracle of the man who'd turned crippling poison into the strength of blood.

He napped through the twilight and first hours of night, then cut out for the docks. Boys shrieked and punched and threw dice. He lingered in the shelter of doorways, wasting half an hour before he spotted the kid who'd told him of Blays' arrest.

"Hey. Barnes."

"I'm George," the boy said, separating from his group.

"Did you find anything?"

"No," George said, waggling his head. "They won't let me into the bailey."

Dante swore. "Doesn't it have windows?"

"Why would a bailey have windows?"

"There has to be some way in."

George shook his head more. "Vance tried to go in when he wasn't supposed to last year and we never saw him since."

"You're smarter than him, aren't you?" Dante said. The boy shrugged and anger flashed through his veins. "I'm beginning to doubt your value."

"You smell," George said, and before Dante could strike him he'd retreated to a pack of eight or ten other boys. Dante took a step toward them and their eyes glittered like animals beyond the light of a fire. They moved forward as one, faces and hands tight. He spat in the dirt and turned away. Once he left their sight he ran and didn't stop until he reached the churchyard. He called out for the nether, released it, called again, convincing himself it was his to command.

The next day gave him nothing. He read through the morning, leaving long enough to buy some bread and salted meat and ask the grocer where and what time they held the trials, then returned to his tomb and read and ate and slept. Like that the hours were gone.

He woke that Saturday and it was some time before he remembered enough to be afraid. He didn't intend to do anything more than go down to the trial and see what turned out, but even that modest plan shook him like a boy shakes a lightning bug in a bottle. He ate a bite of bread, chewing long after it was soft enough to swallow, then put the rest away. He'd puke if he tried any more.

For a while he walked among the tombstones, reading names, feeling his boots in the grass and the dirt between him and the bodies of the forgotten. The stones bore names and titles and families, lands and holdings and glories, cracks and crooked bases and vandalism. A bent-backed figure trudged slowly through the flat part of the yard a couple hundred feet from the hill. Dante crouched behind a tombstone and waited for the man to go away. He reminded himself he was just going to observe, to see if maybe they'd just give Blays the lash and then the two could be back on their way. He scooped up dirt and rubbed it on his cheeks and neck, mussed his black hair, combing it through his fingers to stretch it over his ears and down his forehead. Let them recognize him through that.

The crowds weren't too bad. A few hundred people had found the time to loiter around the square to laugh and jeer the accused. Others formed a lopsided ring around a red belt of flagstones kept clear by a passel of watchmen in rich brown cloaks. The red stones were divided into twelve sections and looped around an inner circle of white stone. At its center a magistrate held court on a raised dais. Before him, attending his words with dirt-streaked faces, three men dressed in rags and chains awaited sentence. Dante's heart shuddered. Had he missed Blays' hearing? He threaded among the crowd, trading elbows and shoulders. The magistrate murmured something and the mob ruffled with laughter. Dante got about four people deep from the belt of red stones and found he could go no further. He stood on his toes, scanning the faces of the accused, and after several long moments he found Blays. The boy's cheeks looked puffy. A number of lumps and cuts stood redly on his nose and chin, but his eyes were hard and bright.

The three men were dragged off for various beatings and imprisonments and the next man in line was brought to stand before the court and be accused of attacking a tailor. For the next two minutes the magistrate heard arguments of witness and defendant. The crowd cheered his sentence.

"See you next Saturday!" some wag called as he was hauled off. The bailiff stepped up beside the magistrate and thinned his eyes at his parchment.

"Next to stand before this court, Blays Buckler," he said. The people exchanged glances, laughing as the name circulated through the crowd. Dante clamped his jaw together as Blays waddled into the open circle, chains clanking.

"Blays Buckler," the magistrate said, and bulged his lower lip with his tongue. He had a fine, delicate-boned face, and he stroked the saggy skin of his neck while he considered Blays. "The charges against you are of two murders in a public house. What say you of your guilt?"

"Not," Blays said.

"Very well. The witness?"

A man stepped forward and Dante recognized the innkeep they'd seen in the common room of the Frog's Head. He was a fat man, the kind of man who spent more time in his own kitchen than fetching drinks.

"That would be me, sir."

"What did you see that night?" the magistrate said, leaning forward.

"I saw the two boys come in," he said, looking around the

craned faces of the crowd. "They looked like rough boys. I've seen too many like them to be fooled by youth."

"To the point?"

"Right. They went upstairs. After a bit we heard some crashing around like the end of the world and a bit after that they walk down cool as the nor'wind. I go upstairs and see the two slain. They had their guts hanging out like does."

"Sickening."

"Yes, sir. I'd never seen human intestines before. Were a sort of pinkish gray, with these funny blue bands around them. Ghastly."

"Indeed," the magistrate said, pursing his lips. "As concerns your earlier statement, is that to say you didn't actually see the murders take place?"

"Well I wasn't about to go upstairs," the innkeep said. "It sounded like people were being killed up there!"

The crowd groused with laughter. The magistrate quirked his mouth, then beckoned Blays forward.

"What do you have to say in your defense?"

"They were tracking me and Dante for days," Blays said. His voice lost its waver as he went along. "They're cultists. They tried to kill us before we turned the tables on them."

"So you admit killing them," the magistrate said, raising a gray brow. He met the eyes of the audience and they laughed.

"It was them or us," Blays said, standing straight in his chains.

"So you say. Can anyone corroborate your story?"

"Co-what-o-wait?"

The magistrate steepled his hands. "Were there any other witnesses?"

"Well, Dante was there," he said. "If he was here he'd tell you the same thing."

"Wouldn't he tell me anything to save his neck from rope burn?"

Blays cocked his head. "Is your majesty calling me a liar?"

The magistrate lifted his eyes to the overcast sky and waited for the nattering of the crowd to die down. He chuckled once they were reasonably silent, scratching his upper lip.

"I'm no king," he said, "and I'd say your motivations cast some aspersions on your words."

"What? Well, how do you know *he's* not lying?" Blays said, pointing at the innkeep.

"Because he'd be hanged for it. He's run the Frog's Head for two decades, and his father before him. Do *you* have family here? Property?"

"I'm a registered armsman of Bressel."

"Your papers," the magistrate said. Blays said something Dante couldn't catch. The bailiff approached him and fumbled through the pockets of Blays' grimy doublet. From here and there the men of the crowd started hissing. The blank-faced bailiff removed a greenish crust of bread from Blays' shirt, then scowled and cast it away. In another pocket he found the papers and carried them to the magistrate. "You're not of the arms *guild*," he said after a moment's examination. "Perhaps you gave them some trouble."

"They said I was too young!" Blays cried.

"A likely story."

"Look, you old crow, those guys were trying to kill us! What else were we supposed to do?"

"Peace, peace," the magistrate said, raising his palms. "The court has other business today and you're not the first nor the last to hold himself above the law. That's all this matter is, isn't it? Your defense, so far as it can be believed, is the law of the wilds. The laws of man are derived from the gods of the Belt itself. We believe in justice on this earth and mercy in the heavens." He parted his lips and gazed up at the clouds. "You're to be executed one week hence."

"Well eat shit!" Blays shouted. The bailiff punched him in the eye and he dropped out of sight. Dante shoved the man in front of him out of his way, bouncing up and down to get a glimpse of Blays before they wrangled him back to his cell, but the boy stumbled on his chains, pelted by hard bread and softer, less savory things, and was swallowed by the rabble. The next prisoner was brought forth and the mob forgot about Blays as the process began again.

Dante turned and forced himself away from the white stone circle and its red band. He bumped someone and they responded with a fist to his ribs. Dante's hand clutched at his sword. The man's life was saved by Dante's dim understanding he would only have the chance for one big scene in this town and this wasn't the time for it. He walked on. He walked back to the tomb. He walked in a fugue of scarred faces and screeching voices that echoed from the city walls like the whole thing was shaking apart. Nothing but a show. A dance. An act for the men of Whetton to pat themselves on the back and feel great about having sent a trumped-up monster to his grave. Their laws were as hollow as the black between the stars. He'd see them swing from their own nooses next Saturday.

He felt grass beneath his feet and stopped to get his bearings. Rain was falling, pocking against his hood. Back in the churchyard. Back among the dead. The rest of the town could learn a thing from the way they laid there without screwing anything up. He closed his eyes, shook his head. His chest quaked as he sucked air.

"See the show today?"

Dante didn't turn. He cleared his mind, as best he could, and gathered up the shadows.

"You were there, I'm sure."

"Ah. Already I begin to see how you survived." The voice was nasal, accented with the clipped, burnished words of the kind of man who rode around in knee breeches. Dante faced him then, expecting a strong-chinned, empty-eyed lord, and meeting instead a skinny, dirty, two-steps-from-sackcloth graybeard with stringy hair and an air of patient amusement.

"What do you want?"

"It isn't what I want. It's what *you* want, Dante."

"Now that's downright profound," Dante said. He froze, tightening his grip on the nether. "How did you know my name?"

"Lucky guess," the old man said. "My name's Cally."

"Pretty nice beard for a Cally."

"I think I've been hearing that joke for longer than I've been alive." Cally smiled at Dante, letting him stew. "It's short for something obnoxiously longer."

"I'm sorry," he said, unsure why.

"Don't be." The old man folded his hands behind his back and gazed up into the churchyard. A drop of rain hit him in the eye and he blinked. "Anyone would be angry after what they did to your friend."

"It was like a punchline without a joke," Dante said. "It's not fair. He was telling the truth."

"What are you going to do about it?"

"Wait a week and find out."

"I know your name," Cally said, looking on him with fever-bright blue eyes, a green corona around their pupils, "because I'm one of them."

Dante jerked back and lashed out with all the nether he could hold. The old man should have ruptured like a sack of oats, spilled his guts like the devotee in the inn. Instead nothing, a slight pressure in Dante's ears. Cally pinched his upper lip, chuckling.

"I didn't say I was trying to kill you."

"Oh, I suppose you're just here for a friendly chat about the glory of Arawn."

"That would be boring for us both," the old man said, beetling his brows. "I've got far more interesting things to teach you."

"Like what?" Dante said. His hand drifted toward his sword.

"Like how they wanted you to find the book."

"Right. That explains why they've been trying to kill me to get it back ever since."

"And sending a single neeling to fetch a copy of a priceless relic makes sense!" Cally whooped, slapping his knee with his shapeless black hat. "I always told them that would be transparent as a window pane, but it always works. It always works!"

Dante rolled his eyes. "So logically, they wanted me to have it."

"Well, they did and they didn't. It's a large organization. It isn't like a single body, where all organs work in harmony. There are many cross-purposes. Contradictions. Disagreements in methodology."

"Are you expecting me to believe or understand any of this?"

"Think about the gods for a moment," Cally said, then glanced behind him. He leaned in and touched Dante's elbow. "Walk with me. We shouldn't do this here. Good. Where was I: the gods. It always comes back to them, doesn't it? How is it they're able to make everything so clear?"

"Perhaps it's the advantage of their heavenly perspective," Dante muttered. Cally chuckled at that, a noise surprisingly like heh-heh, and led Dante further into the churchyard. Once a few trees stood between them and the eyes of the city the old man stopped and mused a moment, listening to the patter of the rain on the leaves.

"We speak of the houses of the Belt of the Celeset as if the gods were all one mind. Yet all the stories are about how they squabble and shift alliances whenever it's expedient. And who could blame them? Their brothers and sisters and fathers and daughters are all bitches or the sons thereof. In similar fashion, the admirers of Arawn are fractured in their methods. The underlings who don't know what's going on see a book's been stolen and are ordered to sprint off and plant you in your grave. Others, notably the ones who give the orders, put the book there for it to be stolen."

"Why the hell would they want to do that?"

"Because it suits their purposes, obviously."

"And what's your purpose in telling me all this?" Dante said.

Cally just laughed. "A good question. Listen. Do you want to save your friend?"

"Of course."

"Do you think you can do it alone?"

"I think a lot of them will die," Dante said. A crow cawed from among the graves. Cally's own mouth stayed shut. "No," Dante admitted. "There's too many of them."

"It turns out true justice can always be made up for with numbers," Cally agreed, clenching his fists and cracking his knuckles. "It's enough to make a man wonder if there's any such thing. On the other hand, a pure state of justice wouldn't be sullied just because—"

"Can you help me or not?" Dante grabbed the old man's arm. A cold shock ran from his fingers to his shoulder and he pulled away. "What are you?"

"You know what I am," Cally said, deadly soft, and the whole world went dark. Dante staggered back, hands shielding his face until he saw the overcast light of mid-afternoon, the silent flight of birds, the fall of rain, the row on row of long-buried bones. When he looked back at Cally, he looked old and skinny as ever.

"Will you help me?"

"Teach you," Cally corrected, holding up a finger. "'Enhance your knowledge' may be a more accurate phrase. I trust all that running hasn't left much time for reading."

"Right again," Dante said slowly. "How do you know all this?"

"Simple deduction," the old man said, "and having lived an awful many years in the company of men too given to scheming."

"So why do they *want* people to steal the *Cycle*?"

Cally sucked his teeth, smacked his lips. "You should know that already."

"Until a few minutes ago I was under the impression its theft was a capital crime."

"Who is Arawn?"

"Is this a trick?"

"Humor me."

"The god of death," Dante said. His face flushed, but he let his simplification stand.

"More like the god who greets the dead and transfers them to what comes next. What else?"

"I don't know. He's Carvahal's brother."

A gleam took Cally's eye. "And the history between the two?"

"Not very good." Dante frowned. "He gave Carvahal the secret of fire, then Carvahal walled him up so he'd get all the credit."

Cally raised his eyebrows. Dante thought he had the answer, but it was too wild, too conspiratorial. The old man sighed and dropped his eyes.

"And you seemed so promising."

"They want to release Arawn from his prison," Dante blurted. "And they want someone to steal the book because — they can't do it themselves?"

"You'd make a decent rhetorician," Cally said, applauding.

"*I* can't do that! I don't even know what I'm doing!"

"Oh, indeed. It's more complicated than that. Much more complicated. But the book is bait for the kind of person who might be able to help them. Running you through all the rigamarole like that—"

"What?" He drew back. "To weed out the ones who can't help?"

Cally bit his lip and wagged his head, weighing the statement. "Something like that."

"Isn't trying to kill me a little extreme? Couldn't they just have me read a few pages and then have a go? Or, you know, ask whether I've ever seen a shadow slithering around like a snake? Wouldn't that be easier than some big charade where either I die or a lot of them do?"

"First off, the minions who've been chasing you don't know anything more than that you stole the book. They really do just want you dead." Cally scowled. "I told you, it's complicated."

"Is that your word for insane?"

"Lower your voice, for the gods' sakes," the old man winced, patting the air with his hands. "It's one of those things that's worked, no matter how crazy it sounds, so it's hardly worth getting into *why* it works. It has a lot to do with the fact everyone else thinks they're dead in these lands, so if they don't want to spill the beans they have to be elaborately sneaky about these things. The rest of it's one of those webs of politics where understanding it would take a lifetime of history and then another lifetime of theology. If it turns out you've got two lifetimes to spare we'll hash it out in front of a hearth some day, but for now, stop asking stupid questions and just believe what I'm telling you."

"And what's your role in this web?" Dante said, ignoring the bevy of suspicions that popped up whenever anyone talked about taking something on faith. "Why are we even talking right now?"

"Because I happen to think my brother believers are full of shit." He looked around himself, as if noticing their surroundings for the first time. "What are you doing staying in a cemetery, anyway?"

"No one comes to a graveyard if they can help it."

"Smart. Smart enough to ask your damned question a third time." Cally sighed, wrinkling his nose, then laughed just as suddenly. It was supposed to be charming, Dante saw, but he found the man's shifts of mood jarring, a sign of a mind more fractured than fanciful. "I am not a fanatic of their ends-over-means philosophy. That's what caused all this trouble in the first place." He tugged his beard, far away. "So. I'm cast out. Meanwhile, they've found a way to tell people about the power of the book and the truth of Arawn without exposing themselves, then recruit the few who can actually make any use of it. But you know what happens to tools that don't get the job done, right? Or tools that ask too many questions?"

"What?"

"They're thrown away, you idiot." Cally huffed. His breath curled in the moist air. "But I know the same things they do." He narrowed his eyes, sly. "The things that can't be learned by reading the *Cycle*. I can turn raw men into great men, and in so doing steal them away from the hands of my foes."

He smiled and with his gray beard and bright eyes Dante thought he looked like a grandfather who'd spoil a boy hardened by the father's tough love. He shifted his feet.

"Every man of Arawn I've met so far's wanted to make my head a separate entity from my body."

"Indeed. And when you tried to throw that little trifle at me, what did you feel?"

"You barely had to think to deflect it," Dante replied. "You could have smashed me to bits."

"Tiny ones! But then I'd have blood and bone all over my cloak." Cally cracked with laughter as he stroked his grime-streaked rags. Dante shut his eyes. He'd resigned himself to flinging himself at the men who held Blays in chains and dying in the attempt. Ever since he'd run out on the village he'd felt hemmed in, a minor part in an infinite play, casting out blindly for a force that could never be his. Three months since he'd left them behind. He could still see the grasses turning yellow in the heat of high summer as he ran down the path that led to Bressel, still smell the dairy-like stink of his feet when he'd unbooted them after that first day's travel. Before he left he'd been taught nothing more than what the monk of Taim who'd housed him had seen fit: the stories of the gods, how they'd created man and then been betrayed by men's foolish arrogance, how we wouldn't know peace until we learned to return to them on our knees and seek forgiveness—a weak-minded lie the monk told himself so he could accept his meager place. Dante owed nothing to anyone. And so he'd left, chasing the story of the book, but when he'd found it the monk's threat of a mediocre existence had been replaced at once by the mortal threat of the men of Arawn. Never in his life had Dante been left alone to find his own way.

"I want to learn," Dante said, gazing into Cally's mirth-wrinkled face. "I'll burn the whole city if they stand in my way."

6

The vault was as good a place as any for their work, Cally had declared, if a little dramatic, so there they went. Cally swung the door shut behind them, closing them in darkness. Dante reached into his pocket and his torchstone bathed them in a pale light.

"Where'd you get that?" Cally said, seating himself on the pedestal near the front of the room.

"I've always had it."

"I may have made it, for all I know."

Dante lowered himself to the cold stone floor and tried not to sigh too loud.

"Made a lot of them, did you?"

"I did, actually, so stop making that face. We all need money." Cally puffed out his cheeks and looked around himself. "So. Let's see about tying some terminology to these vague things you've taught yourself so far. We'll start at the beginning."

"Oh good."

"Modern understanding says the ether is the force that illuminates the firmament and bestows motility to man and beast. Some schools take this a step further, equating this original force with jurisprudential order, explaining that just as the laws of our courts are derived from the reflection of the perfection of the revolution of the heavens, so are the laws of man's nature a reflection of the animatory power of the Belt of the Celeset. So. Personally, I feel these schools are unnecessarily harmonious, establishing a false dichotomy of order meant to reinforce the position of the elite in the minds of the blank-slate boys they're supposedly educating.

Any idiot can see this school is an artificial imposition of the human mind. As if the mishmash of vengeance and despotism we witnessed this afternoon bears any resemblance to the unabridged consistency of the stars. Do *you* think the ether's responsible for poor Blays' fate?"

"No," Dante said, face stony. Cally barely noticed, launching into the next phase of his lecture with the intensity of a man who's spent decades thinking without an audience to relieve the pressure of his head.

"Tell me what I just said," he said some ten minutes later.

Dante turned his hands in his lap.

"You said the nether—"

"The ether."

"You said the ether," Dante said, pausing until he was certain there'd be no interruption, "lurks behind all things, and that's where we draw our power."

"That's *not* what I said." Cally snatched his cap from his head and twisted it in his bony hands. "You're just parroting the book. Treating the ether like a mirror image of the nether. Is gold the opposite of silver? Is the sun the opposite of the moon? You've got it all backwards."

"Backwards?"

"First the ether, then the nether. How can you define the primary when your view of the secondary's all warped up? You don't even have the grounding to understand the words 'primary' and 'secondary' are themselves gross assumptions of a Taim-based perspective!" Cally scowled, combing out his beard with his fingers. "Listen, I've got some things to go do."

"But I haven't learned anything," Dante said, rising to his feet.

"I'm beginning to understand how true that is. I'll be back by dark." Cally pushed his frail back against the door. It grated open and he wormed into the gap. "Meditate on what it means to be a duck," he called back into the tomb.

"A duck?" Dante said, but the old man was gone. Dante wandered from the door and propped himself on a shelf. Somewhere across town Blays was in a room like this. Probably it was smaller, darker, had been home to more of the dead than this mausoleum. Dante punched the stone shelf, then sucked his bleeding knuckles.

A duck? What the hell was that supposed to mean? If this was a game, why didn't Cally just spell out what he wanted? If Dante was supposed to do all the work without any guidance, what was Cally doing there in the first place?

He took a long breath. There was a chance Cally knew what he was doing. He was very old, after all. If he wanted ducks, Dante would give him ducks. He'd give him so many ducks the old man would be ashamed he'd ever given him such a juvenile exercise.

Okay. A duck had wings. It had webbed feet, like the neeling, but that couldn't be important. A duck had a bill. Feathers. Liked water. Could travel by land, sea, and air. Was that it? That its home was everywhere and thus nowhere? That sounded like the kind of shallow paradox that would send Cally twittering. What else? What made a duck a duck? Was it the feet, the bill, the feathers? The sum of its physical features? If you chopped all the duck-like parts from different animals and sewed them into one new animal, would you then find yourself holding a duck? Or was the opposite true—a duck was created with an inherent element of duckiness that informed its growth from the egg itself? Dante glanced at his torchstone as its light grew dim and found he was no longer angry. He dug a hunk of bread from his pack and chewed.

It wasn't a chicken or a goose or a swan; it was close, but the differences were enough to earn it a separate name. It walked on two legs, but it wasn't a man. It swam, but it wasn't a fish. Dante traced a mallard in the dust on the shelf. He didn't think Cally intended him to define it by what it wasn't. In the end, a duck was very few things. There was a whole world it wasn't.

Was a duck its quack? Nothing else he knew of quacked. Geese honked, but that was different. Hens clucked and roosters crowed and chicks peeped; meadowlarks sang and starlings chirped and crows cawed; a duck, it seemed, was the only thing that quacked. That must be a part of it. If a duck walked up to him and asked him about the weather, that would make it, in some sense, a man. Still a duck, but less duckish. He bounced his heels against the stone wall beneath his seat. How long could you spend sitting around thinking about ducks? Was there a point where you'd know everything there was to know? He decided to go back to basics. Ducks lived in pairs, but sometimes they lived in flocks. Ducks laid eggs. Ducks also hatched from eggs, which he thought might be a slightly different thing from laying them. A duck ate water-weeds and bugs, he thought, though he wasn't certain of that. He realized he was just listing their traits without conclusions. Duckiness was something more than what it ate or how it looked or lived or quacked. All those things were true, but if he told someone who'd never seen a duck all the things he'd just thought, they might be able to visualize one, but they wouldn't really know what made a duck a duck, would they? How could he explain the nature of duck-kind so an outsider would understand?

Footsteps jarred him from his maze. How long had it been? The sun was all but set. Dante stuck his head out the door, hand on sword, and saw Cally's bent-backed figure trudging up the hill through the drizzle.

"Have you dwelt on the nature of duckhood?" he said as he entered.

"I have."

"What have you learned?"

"A duck is a duck," Dante said.

Cally pinched the bridge of his nose. "Go on."

"It's not a chicken or a goose or any other bird, though if you told someone that's what a duck is like they'd start to be able to see one. It's got a bill and feathers and wings. It swims, flies, and walks; so what element can be said to be its home?" He stuck his tongue between his teeth and waited for a cue. Cally screwed up one eye, shrugged. "It quacks," he tried. "Nothing else quacks."

"Except a duck call."

Dante went pale. He hadn't thought of that. "I don't think you can ever define a duck," he said slowly. "If you could, you'd have created one. I think all you can do is describe it, piece by piece, until you've got an animal like nothing else."

"An interesting theory," the old man said.

"Well? Am I right?"

Cally pulled back his chin and snorted. "How the hell should I know?"

"Well why did you make me do all that thinking about ducks if you don't know what one is yourself?" Dante said, pounding his fists against his thighs.

"You weren't doing well with the discursive approach. What else do you want?"

"Why ducks?"

"To hear you quack," Cally shot.

"That doesn't—" Dante snapped his jaw shut. He walked to the back of the room and glared at the inscriptions on the wall. His face felt hot as a branding iron. "Making sport of one's students doesn't strike me as enlightened instruction."

Cally laughed brightly. "Were you so petulant with whoever taught you to talk like that?"

"Do you always expect the ones you teach to read your mind?"

"Youth," Cally spat, a grunt so hateful Dante's scalp tingled. He spun around and Cally's pinched face opened with laughter. "You take yourself too seriously, do you know that?" He rubbed his hands together and got the look of a man who's just had his first puff on a pipe. "I suppose you want to get down to business."

"That had crossed my mind."

"Double-crossed it, maybe," Cally said, looking worried. His eyes flicked to Dante and he smiled tightly. "Think about the nether the same way you taught yourself to think about the duck."

"That's it?" Dante's mind flashed with the notion this had all been a mistake, that he was wasting what short time he had left. "What about this ether stuff?"

Cally waggled a hand. "Forget it. We're taking a new approach. Dwell long on the nether and we'll see where you are in the morning."

"But the night's just started. You haven't shown me anything!"

"Patience!" he thundered. "It's a week from now till your destiny becomes known. That's as long as it took the gods to build the world. Do you really think this will be harder than the creation of everything in existence?" Dante worked his throat and Cally stepped forward, craning his thin neck. "You know what happens to apprentices who try to work gold before they've hammered iron, don't you?"

"They're commended for their initiative?"

"Their masters stuff them into the forge." Cally patted his palms against his stomach. "If you unravel all the secrets of the nether tonight, read your damn book. Lyle's wrinkly, sweaty sack, boy, haven't you ever heard the tale of the tortoise and the hare?"

He spun on his heel and left the tomb. Dante closed the door and lit a candle. He yawned, tired as he'd been after a full day's march through the woods. He didn't think the shadows would help. He sat down on the cool stone floor and let his mind unspool. What was Blays doing at that moment? Sleeping? Staring at the ceiling? He had no doubt the boy was alive, at least. If the condemned died before they could be killed the whole process was thwarted.

The man they'd killed to get them in this mess, the long-haired man at the inn, had said the priests of Arawn had infiltrated the shrines of the other gods. Somehow this inclined Dante to believe Cally's ludicrous assertion that they wanted people to find the book. There was a strange intuitiveness to it all, a compelling alternate logic in sacrificing a few pawns to expose the people like Dante and draw them into the fold. What were they after? Rebellion? Build influence in the temples while they scared up talented men to—he still didn't know if he believed it—to release Arawn from his starry prison? How would they do that, exactly? Build a really tall ladder? Or better, hold a fake olympics to find who could jump the highest and then launch him into the heavens. He tried to laugh. They were going to take a shot, though, no matter how stupid their plans sounded. Where did they get that kind of power?

It would come from the nether, he knew that much. What was it? He stretched out on the floor and plumped his pack under his head. He closed his eyes and tried to picture what it looked like when he called the darkness to his hand. It was darkness, yes. Intangible, but it moved less like light and shadow than like water. Flowing where resistance was least, pooling in the low places, filling the gaps between things like water filling up a box of pebbles. But it wasn't water. It moved with a mind of its own. What was it? When he drained his thoughts and let the black tide take their place, what was it he held inside his head?

"Get up! It's the guards!" Fists pounded on the door. Dante's heart jump-started itself right off a cliff. He couldn't see a damn thing, just the faint light wriggling through the chinks in the wall and the narrow line that traced the door. Pretend he wasn't here. They might be dumb enough to believe it. More likely they'd force their way inside and chop him into geometry. He'd need to think fast. Act fast. He cleared his mind and let the nether come. He rose then, drawing his sword with a steely hiss, left hand wrapped in darkness, and swung open the door.

"No, it's just me," Cally said in his normal nasal pitch. "Be proud. You looked like you could have scared someone."

"I suppose this is a lesson on the virtue of vigilance," Dante mumbled, sheathing his sword. He stepped out into the yard.

"I just thought it would be funny." Cally blew into his cupped hands and stood in the feeble sunlight. "Make any progress with the *Cycle*?"

"I fell asleep."

"Good. Sleep's more important than history, as evidenced by the fact the latter puts you to the former." Cally spent a minute gazing over the graves. The morning was foggy, the grasses bent with dew. Their breath roiled from their mouths and hung in the air. One of the yard's many crows cawed out, waited, then cawed again, as if it were asking if anyone was home. "Did you think on the nature of the nether?"

"It's like the ocean at night," Dante said. His face bunched in thought. He shook his head. "I feel like the moon, in a way. When I look on the dark water with the fullness of my face, it rises and heaves to meet me."

"Poetic," Cally judged, "but ultimately as inaccurate as all poetry."

"What do *you* think it's like?"

"Were you listening at all yesterday? What do you think all that talking was for, my health?"

"Maybe it's not the subjects that are slippery," Dante said, a thrill in his skin, "but the manner of their instruction."

Cally frowned at him. His gray eyebrows were so thick Dante worried they'd pull his brow right over his nose. The old man looked away, letting it pass.

"It's not the answers, it's that you remember to seek them. Each definition you find brings you one step closer to an unreachable ideal. Don't take that to mean you shouldn't try just because you can never reach it, of course. That's what babies do. Are you a baby?"

"No," Dante said through his teeth.

"Of course not! Who said you were a baby?" He sighed like all hope had faded from the world. "Don't think of it as hopeless. If you had no name for it, would that mean it doesn't exist? We have no single word for this pre-winter breeze that teases you into thinking it might snow although it's not really that cold and which kind of buffets against your face rather than streaming or lashing," he took a breath, "but does that mean you don't feel it, and in a different way than you'd feel a dozen other kinds of wind'? Defining the nether's the work of a lifetime. The only way to keep reaching closer to its central duckiness is to know you'll never be done."

Dante waited to see if there was more. "So you'd define the nether as semantics."

Cally shook his head. "Just—keep trying to think about it in new ways, but don't get so wrapped up in trying to understand what it is you stop learning how to use it. That's all I'm saying." He blinked, chuckled. "Well, not really. But let's pretend that's what I said."

Dante thought, and not the first time, taking the man as a teacher might have been a blunder. So the old man had thoughts so deep he couldn't capture them with words. Cally whistled something mournful and keening, ignoring him for the moment. Dante's eyelids fluttered. He clumped the shadows in his hands and unleashed them on the old man, just a sort of probe, and before it reached Cally it disappeared like spit on a summer flagstone.

Cally stopped whistling. "What was that?"

"Just how much do you know?"

"Enough to know how little you do."

Again Dante gathered the nether. This time it boiled off his hands before he could unleash it.

"I said stop that." Cally's voice echoed against the walls of the vault.

"What's your mind like, when you call out to it?" Dante asked, clasping a coin-sized pool of the stuff between his palms.

"You're not used to it yet. That's why you have to think so hard." Cally regarded him with one eye closed. "To me it's like scratching my ass, my hand's there before I have to tell myself I'm itchy."

"That's beautiful." Dante opened his hand and blew the shadows at Cally in a puff of tiny motes. Cally flinched, scowled.

"You could punch me in the stomach and it wouldn't make a difference," the old man said, tossing his head. "You could probably stick a sword through my heart and I'd still strike you down, though that must remain a regrettable hypothetical."

"Do something," Dante said. "I want to see how someone else does it."

"Could be useful," Cally said. His face kept its vaguely bored expression. Dante was about to ask when he was going to start when he felt Cally's summons looming in front of him like the empty space beyond a cliff. Dante laughed and punched the old man in the stomach.

He woke up some time later. The world was fuzzy and gray. A toe nudged his side and he realized it had been doing so for some seconds.

"What happened."

"You expressed a sudden urge to cease existing," said a blurry, Cally-shaped object. The object helped Dante to his feet and the boy faltered and leaned against the old man. "See what you wanted to see?"

"I'd had enough talk," he said when he trusted himself to speak. His nose tickled. He wiped it, saw blood.

"We'll start there," Cally said. "The nether will come once the mind is ready to receive it, but it's the nether's nature to thirst for the water of life. And I'm not talking about whiskey."

"Blood?" Dante said, wiping his fingers in his palm. Except for that last part, Cally had sounded like something from the *Cycle*.

"Blood."

"I'd wondered about all those scars on your arms."

"Most of them are actually the product of an oversized mouth." Cally smirked, then pressed a knuckle between his eyes and peered at Dante. "Call to it. It's going to look like it's eating you. It's not, so don't be afraid."

"It can sense fear?"

"What? It's not a bear. Being scared just makes you do stupid things."

Dante counted his exhalations for most of a minute, then unlimbered his mind. They came at once, swirling in his outstretched palm, minnow-like wraiths that seemed to flash black.

"So far you've worked the nether in its most basic state," Cally said. "Blood amplifies its strength, allows it to truly alter what it touches."

Dante waited, watching them circle one another. Others came without being called. The ball expanded from a large marble to the size of his closed fist, but mostly it grew denser until he thought he could feel an icy weight denting his skin.

"It's a fragile thing in this state. It burns as violently as Souman's oil."

Little pricks and tingles rippled across the flesh of his palm, as if the leechish things were nibbling with razor teeth. He no longer felt the dull throb from when Cally knocked him out. His vision flickered, then returned brighter than before. The scent of grass stuffed his nostrils. It would snow that night, he knew, he could feel it in the breeze. The muscles of his arm began to twitch.

"This is when it wants to create or destroy. This is the nether in its most potent state. Release it now."

The thing was so dark he could barely bring himself to look at it. The individual motes had stopped following each other's tails and the ball pulsed slowly, almost as if it were breathing. A note as high as the clouds sounded between his ears. His hand had gone numb. He thought he could crack the tomb with a punch. Raze it with a look. Nothing seemed beyond him.

"Release it! For the sake of the gods, let it go!"

Dante turned his hand palm down and jabbed it at the trunk of an acorn tree thirty feet away. Its bole was a foot and a half across. It crumpled like paper. Splinters of bark shot into the air. A great crack thundered past him; he staggered, stripped of all strength and senses with the departure of the nether. He wanted it back. He wanted the shadowy outlines he'd seen around all things to retake their shape, for his eyes and ears and hands to once more feel like the world's own will. He mewled, and as the tree's wide head boomed into the grass he fell to his knees, paused there, then slumped in a heap.

"We should probably hide somewhere for a while," some part of him heard Cally muse. "Oh. Right." He grabbed Dante's wrists and dragged the half-conscious boy into the sanctuary of the vault.

Dante squinted against the candlelight. He tried to sit up and the blood rushed from his head.

"They're all going to die," he said, and his laugh twisted into a cough. He slapped the stony floor, fighting for air.

"Always good for a boy to have ambitions," Cally said. "For your next trick try something a trifle less flashy. Think of yourself as a channel through which the nether may flow. Like the narrow banks of a creek. If a meandering little stream suddenly finds itself engorged by a few hundred thousand cubic tons of water, it tends to no longer resemble itself once the flood has gone away." He got to his feet, eyes glinting down at Dante. "A stream doesn't really capture my meaning, however. Swollen streams aren't all bloody and shrieking and flopping around until they die."

"I'll be careful."

"I doubt that. And for gods' sakes, eat something. Stop making me sound like your father. These things will burn you up before you know it."

Dante managed to sit up. Nausea and hunger battled for his stomach. He had a headache. He touched his face. It was still there. That was good.

"If you were my father I'd make patricide popular again."

"Oh, shut up," Cally said with no real annoyance. He furrowed his brow. "What were you thinking? Were you trying to destroy the city with your first attempt?"

"I just wanted to see what would happen."

Cally rubbed his chin, whiskers rustling. "Frankly, you shouldn't have been able to do that first try. Be more cautious next time."

"I am learning fast, aren't I?" Dante said. He squared his shoulders, daring himself to press for praise. "I mean, have you seen other people learn as fast?"

"Probably," Cally said through a yawn. "Some take faster to it than others. Like a duck to water, you might say."

"Ha ha. Why do they pick it up so fast?"

"Why do some students learn to read quicker than others?"

"What? No lecture on the nature of the talent?"

"A physician named Kamrates once theorized a correlation between the width of one's veins and one's ability to channel the nether," Cally began, considering the ceiling. "Obviously bunk. The notion of channeling is only a metaphor. That didn't stop him, however, from dicing up a dozen corpses in his search for proof, including a couple that may not have been corpses for another few years if he wasn't so dead-set on proving an anatomical connection. No pun." Dante opened his mouth and Cally immediately cut him off. "What's your birthday?"

"February 12. Why?"

"Duset. The two rivers. Ruled by Arawn in the old design, you know. The Belt's first link."

"You think your birthsign influences it?"

"No," Cally said, sighing heavily. "That's what *some* people think."

Dante bit his teeth tight. "You don't have any idea, do you."

"I think the answer is a boring variation of 'all things in moderation': it's likely there's some inherent quality that gives one man more facility with the nether or the ether than his fellow, but the strength of one's will probably has a great deal to do with it as well."

"That is boring."

"Would it be more interesting if I told you there was a gland in your skull that's probably twice the size of a normal man's?"

"Did Kamrates discover that?" Dante's face went guarded. "No, wait."

Cally chuffed with laughter. "Listen, there's a lot of theories, but none of them are very good. Would you believe you're chosen by Arawn? Or maybe you're the offspring of an imp and a woman? Be practical."

"One could well argue it's nothing but practical to try to find out why you're good at the things you do well."

"Well, then one would probably be slaughtered by the town watch in a few days when he should have been learning to kill them instead." He clapped his hands on his thighs. "You've got work to do. Book to read. Do it."

"You're leaving?"

Cally turned and went for the door. "Good night. You've got a lot to do. I'll be back in a couple days."

"You're always running off just when I'm beginning to learn."

"Shut up and accept your progress for once."

"I could hurt myself," Dante mocked, but Cally was already on his way. Beyond the doorway the land was dark. Flakes of snow drifted into the grass. Cally had stayed for hours while he slept. He fished out the rest of his bread and chewed it in the dark. He wanted meat. A beef stew of a haunch of lamb. Something so big he'd feel silly taking bites out of it. He clinked the coins in his purse. What use was money if you didn't spend it? Who wanted to save when you could be dead the next Saturday?

The following days were quiet. He ventured out for food and lingered around the market, eyes sharp for members of the watch. No one mentioned the executions. They talked about whether the snow would stick next time and the work they still needed to do on their homes, about the new viceroy appointed for Whetton and its farmland, the recent turmoil so intense in the streets of Bressel a member of the council had been killed and another had stepped down. The retiring man said he meant to focus on his work at the guild of arms, but the talk was he'd been exiled for a secret incompetence even rumor couldn't unravel. Dante edged closer to the four men who spoke of this, daring himself to ask questions about violence he'd seen no hint of when he'd lived there, whether it had anything to do with the city's temples. Strangely, he was concerned for the city. He'd only lived there a few months, but he'd heard so many stories about it as a boy it had felt like a home from the start. He still considered himself a Bresselman, could speak with more authority than these bumpkins on its onion-domed Library, Tenterman Palace, the fiery eyes of the statue of Phannon planted centuries ago where the sandbar had once regularly grounded the dumber, drunker, or unluckier captains of the merchant fleets. He'd live there again, he resolved.

He knew better than to ask about the riots, though. They'd want to know his name, whether he was from the great city and if he had news of his own, might even want to know his position on the struggle. He was an adept liar, as all boys learned to do to avoid chores and beatings and, once they were old enough, public whippings, but he had no room to chance it. His tongue didn't always listen to his brain. He wouldn't have the freedom to join such talk until Blays was out from under the law.

Instead he went back to the mausoleum, intending to ask Cally next time he saw him. Of the *Cycle*'s 800-odd pages, he'd consumed no more than a quarter, and he set on the remainder with the same futureless abandon he spent his money. When he stopped to rest his eyes or stretch his legs he messed around with the nether, forming a shadowsphere inside the tomb, or sweeping it along the ground to stir the leaves or send a small rock rolling. He fed it no blood. No matter how badly he wanted himself at the center of all things once more, he was dogged by the memory of how crushingly small he'd felt after he released it and destroyed the tree.

"So, how's it been? Transcended this mortal existence yet?" the old man said when he appeared some time later, tugging his cloak tight around his shoulders.

Dante closed the book and looked up. "Who wrote the *Cycle*?"

"Many people," Cally said, fixing him with a look. "The first part was assembled, according to the few scholars who've done credible research on the time, in something like a half dozen sources over a span of sixty-odd years. The second part is actually much older. Some of them go back as far as we have records. A Gaskan scholar named Nettigen once claimed to have found a tablet in the ice north of Narashtovik with an Arawn story dated at 9,000 years ago by its description of the locations of the stars."

"No one was alive back then!"

"How do you know that? Were you there?"

"No doubt *you* were." Dante cocked his head. "If it's got so many authors, how do we know we can trust it?"

"It's not like it's the word of the gods themselves," Cally scoffed. He tugged his fingers through his beard. "I think the many authors are a stroke of its genius. They're all collected under the umbrella of authority that is the *Cycle*, yet it's possible, if you read closely, to read the writings of men with distinctly opposed states of mind.

Who's right, then? Neither? Both? Maybe the answer lies not in the words of the men but in what emerges from their implied dialogue." He stuck out his lower lip, conceding. "Or maybe one of them is just wrong. This is dangerous, in a sense, since his inclusion in the *Cycle* would seem to make his words infallible, yet a learned man will know they're clearly false. Is this intentional on the part of whoever finalized its structure? Is it a deliberate maze meant to guide us not so much to a certain set of facts as to an enlightened flexibility of mind? Well? Is it?"

Dante started. "I didn't realize those questions were anything but rhetorical."

"They weren't, but let's pretend."

"We can't know the answers to any of your questions without digging up the authors and shouting interrogatives at their bones," Dante said, not entirely meaning to make fun with his aping of Cally's mode of speech.

"But—"

"Yeah, yeah, that doesn't mean they're not worth asking. But it does mean there's no way to know for sure. Besides, wouldn't a much simpler explanation be there was no plan, they just scooped up all the legends and poured them between two covers?"

"I suppose," Cally said. He huffed. "It's possible they didn't write the *Cycle* with the express purpose of refining our mode of thought. But I don't see how else we're supposed to reconcile all the disconnects."

"I don't know about that. When I read the stories of Jack Hand, I see justice in his vengeance. I admire his courage, that he can just seize things and reorder them how he sees right. Isn't that a truth that's always true? It's the story of every age, isn't it?"

"Ah. The time-honored absolutism of youth."

"I'm young, so that means I'm wrong?"

"No," Cally said. He sighed. "Age muddles things, that's all. You'll see what I mean if you thwart all decency and live another couple decades."

"Ah," Dante said. "The time-honored condescension of age."

"Mind yourself," the old man warned, but his voice was warm. "I suppose you'd even try to make sense of all those numbers the *Cycle* is so fond of repeating. Anyway. I didn't come here for sophistry. Frankly, it bores me." He scratched his ear, face clouded with thought. "What's the name of your reprobate friend?"

Dante looked up. "Blays."

"I've found a way to contact him."

"When can I see him?"

"You can't," Cally said, silencing him with a look. "What I can do is pass him a message."

"Tell him I'm coming," Dante said, pressing his hands together. "Tell him not to worry. I won't let them get away with it."

Cally smiled beneath the thatch of his beard. "That'll show em."

"What? Then tell him to start figuring out how he's going to repay me. Is that better?"

"Much." Cally yawned and went for the door.

"That's it? Aren't you supposed to be teaching me things?"

"You've already got too much to digest and not enough time to do it in. Practice. Think on what you've learned. Read the damn book. I've got better things to do than mope around a graveyard like a widow pining for her husband's yard."

"Fine." Dante turned away. "Go lecture at someone else for a while."

"Choke on your ingratitude," Cally spat. He flipped his hands. "Bah."

Wind gusted through the open door. Dante watched him go, then turned his eyes to the walls, to the drawers full of corpses. Like Jack Hand and the bones of the rats in his prison. He'd been one man against a keep full of defenders—and he'd taken it and made it his.

When Dante'd first settled into the tomb he'd found other things dead than men: the leathery bodies and dry skeletons of rats and rabbits that had found their way in but not out, pigeons and crows that had taken shelter from the weather and battered themselves dead at the cracks of daylight in the walls. Seven or eight tidy piles of bones. Maybe the *Cycle* was a past meant to be borrowed by the ages to come after. Was that why its authors had written it, however many hundreds of years ago? To let later men stand on their shoulders? To preserve themselves through the actions of people they could never hope to meet?

Something rustled in the shadows of the vault. He doubted

that, whoever'd written the book, whatever they'd had in mind, they could have seen what he had planned. He hoped it would be enough.

7

A holy day, a joyous day, the midpoint between autumnal equinox and winter solstice when Lia left the land and Mennok reluctantly took up its reign. The day, by coincidence, of the execution.

Dante watched the sun spark up over the roofs of the east. He'd loved this day when he was younger. The night before was Falmac's Eve, the Night of Fire, the night Carvahal flew down from exile to take arms against white-bearded Taim who'd thrown him out for bringing the fire to man; the night when head-high stacks of wood were burnt in the squares and boys wore masks and "robbed" men of apples and tin pennies in the street, "slaying" any man who bore a beard. The theater dressed in yellows and reds and bright-burning gems and played out Carvahal's original betrayal, how he lit a torch from the Millstar of the northern heavens and descended with it from the skies to the earth. Taim saw the blaze of its fall and gathered his children and his children's children to destroy whoever'd defied him, but Carvahal brought the torch to Eric the Draconat, he who ate dragons' hearts, and Eric climbed the ladder of the heavens to duel winged, scale-backed Daris and so win his northern army to face the forces of Taim. They met on the snowfields of the north and the snow churned and boiled under the heat of their blood. There Taim slew Daris, and confusion shouted across the land. Eric's rebellion of men and the half-gods and Daris' drakes were smashed, but in the final moment when Eric struck deep at Taim's heart with Anzode—the sword tempered in the hearts of 108 dragons—he actually spilled the god's blood upon the ground, forcing the father of the skies to retreat to his seat in their heights.

Carvahal fled then too, bearing Eric's unconscious body to the hole in the north sky where Mallius' bow had punctured it long ago, and every year on Falmac's Eve Carvahal seduced the blackbirds of Mennok to bear him down to earth and drag the punishing fires of Barrod's sun away so he could wreak his rebellion by cover of dark and the earth could rest and heal. The next morning the farmers set down their scythes and plows and flails and drank to the cycle of the gods. They toasted Lia for her faithful bounty, praised Simm for making their wheat and oats and barley grow tall, thanked Barrod for the life of his yellow rays; they gave a cry for Carvahal's daring that would keep them warm through the winter, for the saturnine locking of the time of Mennok that would make the return of the gods of light and life all the sweeter. Many of them ended up passed out before the sun had gone down. Dante thought he could already hear the earliest revelers singing out in the city. The watchmen would partake too, he knew. There would be few better days for the confusion he meant to sow.

"All set?" Cally said when he showed up twenty minutes later.

"Yes."

"Good. Overconfidence is a strong ally. People are always surprised when you try to do things you can't." He started at the soft skitterings in the dark corners of the tomb, then snorted. "You've been reading too much."

Dante flushed despite the cold. "I haven't had anyone around to teach me different."

"It'll probably make them think they're crazy. That should be fun." Cally wiped his nose. His ears and cheeks were pink. "Auspicious day."

"Does the nether run stronger on Falmac's Day?"

"Don't be daft," Cally said, rolling his eyes. "As if the forces of nature change because a kingdom throws a party."

"I just thought—"

"Ridiculous."

"I walked out to their tree a couple days ago," Dante said after some silence. "It's in a clearing south of town. Not much in the way of cover."

"I'm sure there'll be plenty of meatshields," Cally shrugged.

"When do you think we should leave?"

"Sometime before they hang him, I imagine."

Dante pursed his lips. "I want to be there an hour early. I haven't exactly been able to find out how many guards they'll have, or how they'll bring him in. I won't know what I'm doing till I see that."

"Fine."

"Are you coming with me?" Dante said, heart jumping up a tick.

"I'll be there," Cally allowed after a moment of hemming. "You realize I can't just wave my hand and bring peace unto the world."

"Why not? What can they do to you? We can be so quick they won't know what's going on."

"I haven't lived as long as I have," the old man said, tossing back his chin, "through vulgar displays of power."

Dante glared at him through the dawn. "Why have it if you won't use it? What can you possibly be afraid of?"

"There's a difference between fear and prudence. And even if there isn't," Cally said, sticking his finger at Dante, "fear's a good thing to have. You might live longer if you had more."

"Sounds like a pretty crummy life to me." Cally looked away from him, like the matter were too stupid to discuss. Dante folded his arms. "Just do what you can, then. I won't be holding back."

"That's the spirit." The old man rubbed his jaw. "It's probably best if you hone your plans under the assumption I'll give no help at all. That way if I drop dead between then and now you won't be left in the lurch."

They killed time speaking of the meaning of the figures in the *Cycle* and then about where they might meet when the two boys escaped. Cally suggested running (or riding, if circumstances allowed stealing a horse) into the southern woods, saying he could find Dante easily enough; he'd found him in the first place, hadn't he? The old man bitched for a while about the weather, made threats about sailing for the islands of the south. They watched the sun shed clouds and fog, resolving from red to orange to yellow, and then Cally once more took his leave.

Dante couldn't quite understand how the day had come so

quickly when the last week had dragged like a broken leg. He paced away the morning in the tomb, trying a couple times to sit down and meditate on the nether, but every time he tried he'd get five seconds of clear thought followed by five minutes of noodly worries about what if the watch carried bows which they probably would and what if the innkeep was there and recognized him before he made his move and what if he made it there and they were just too fast and turned Blays off before Dante could wade his way through. What would Cally tell him? Some paradox about allowing his worries but rising with them like an eagle on a storm. In other words, something useless under any practical circumstances.

He took up the pen and ink he used to make his notes on the *Cycle* (though never within the book itself) and sat down in that late autumn daylight that always looked to him like the pure light of nostalgia: fuzzy, faintly yellow, hardly warm but not quite cold. He didn't care if no one would ever find his letter, or if it was only read when they tore down this tomb to build something living people could use. He didn't care if it had as little impact as if he'd written it in water, he just wanted something to leave behind. He had no kids, no lands, no books written by or about him, and if he failed his only notable friend would be every bit as dead. He spent an hour alternately scribbling on and shredding up his dwindling supply of paper. He tried to elevate his speech with the grand aphorisms of the men in plays, but that just sounded dumb. He tried to match the happy irony of the *Cycle*, but it sounded hollow. He tried to tell his story, at least the part where Blays had been unfairly condemned, but that ended up sounding whiny. He should have thought about this yesterday, let himself sleep on it. Now it was too late.

He listened to the crows jabbering at each other and found them no help. The sporadic bells and shouts from the city weren't any better. He listened to the light wind whistling in the bare branches. No dice.

At last, exasperated with himself, doublet damp under the arms, worn down by the jitters he'd had since waking, he set his pen going:

> *If this note is found, it will mean my uncertain fate has been clarified, and to my detriment. I leave now to fight. I'd like to think the cause is just, but don't all men do what they think right? Let's leave the issue for once. Know only I laid my life at the door of a cause I felt worth it. I hope, if there is some final judge of these things, he will look on me with more mercy than he's shown so far.*

He signed his name and closed his eyes a while. At least it was less foolish than his other tries. He tucked it under an urn. Who knew, maybe he'd be able to come back and rip it up before anyone could see it. If not, he'd have far more pressing worries than what some idiot thought of his final words.

The bells of Whetton's many temples and pair of proper cathedrals tolled across the damp air. Two hours till that time. The walk to the Crooked Tree wouldn't take more than fifteen minutes. He meant to arrive an hour early, size things up. He figured the minimal chance of being recognized in that span would be outweighed by having the time to conceive a more detailed plan than "show up and start killing everyone."

Where was Blays? Still clapped in his cell? On his way? Eating his final bread? Swearing at everyone within range? He'd forgotten to ask Cally whether he'd passed along his message, and now that too was too late. At once he felt himself on the brink of tears. Deeper than the chance he might never speak to Blays again, he felt ruptured by the knowledge that even if they survived this day, one would come when they didn't. Dante was sixteen years old. He quite possibly wouldn't live to twice that. At the outside, he had four times as long to go. What he'd lived so far felt like no more than a blink. He could barely remember anything beyond the last three years. Was that all life was? A brief bubble of memory that slid through the years until the sudden stop? If Blays died and he didn't, would he still think of Blays when he was twenty? Thirty? If he died and Blays didn't and Blays forgot him, would Dante then be gone for all time?

Dante opened the *Cycle of Arawn* and flipped through from beginning to end. After about 600 pages his blood went cold. He stopped, pawed back through the pages one at a time. Narashtovik. The final third was written entirely in the dead language of Narashtovik. How had he missed that? How had he dragged it around for a month without knowing he had no way of reading over 250 pages of it? He'd glanced at the last page or two before, but he'd assumed they were an appendix or a glossary, and since he couldn't read any of it he'd just put it out of mind. Foreign words always drove him mad. Besides, he'd been a little preoccupied with running for his life to spare much curiosity for what the next section would hold. This was, in no small terms, a disaster.

In all of Bressel he'd found no works that would offer any significant inroads into deciphering the dead language. Were there any translations of the *Cycle*? Supposedly the fires of the books they'd burnt in the Third Scour rivaled the rising sun—well, that's what the priests of Taim and Gashen and all the others said, and he'd certainly never seen any evidence to prove them wrong. Most of the references he'd found to the old texts came in the form of warnings that owning them would result in your beheading, or after the initial post-Scour excitement had wound down, behanding. The *Cycle* wasn't strictly linear, which muddied the matter of the importance of the part he wouldn't be able to read, but surely there was something of value in the last hundreds of pages. Nobody would just throw together a pile of nonsense and build a faith around it. Cally would have something to help him, perhaps. At least point him in the right direction.

The half-hour bell rang out and he remembered this was one more worry he could delay for now. Dante laughed nervously, feeling light as a gnat. Perhaps he should risk his life every day.

Departing places without leaving anything behind was getting to be a habit. He double-checked the nooks and corners, then cycled down the list. The book in his bag on his back. His sword at his belt under his cloak. A knife on his other side. Bread and meat and waterskin in his bag along with the couple of candles and the tools of writing. Torchstone in his pocket, of course, and a few other necessities, his silver and flint and needles and salt and a couple neat rocks and those small objects he'd found in the tomb. Why was everyone else so eager to tie themselves down with things? They were idiots, that was why. A man should own no more than he can carry.

By the time he'd gone a block from the churchyard he knew the crowd was going to be huge. The streets were stuffed with red-faced farmers and squads of young boys running around with a hand pressed over their left eye like the one Carvahal had lost in the battle in the snowfields. Carriages crept through the mob, unable to build up the momentum to give the pedestrians the choice of clearing a path or being stomped into the dirt. Impossibly, even more filth than normal clogged the gutters and spilled in the roads. Shattered mugs and the busted slats of barrels lay everywhere. Pigeons dunked their beaks in soggy hunks of bread and the stems and seeds of a dozen different vegetables. From all sides he heard laughter, whoops, the cheery hails of men and women who haven't seen each other in whatever they think's been too long. He kept his hood on his shoulders. Unless the followers of Arawn had already dispatched more men to rub him out and reacquire his copy of the *Cycle*, the only one in town at all likely to recognize him would be the keeper of the Frog's Head, and between the twin crowds of holiday and hanging he was no doubt more than a little tied up with his work. Dante running around with his face bundled up like a criminal would only have the watch asking why he was running around with his face bundled up like a criminal.

The standing water in the streets wasn't frozen, but it wasn't far off, either. His breath whirled away from his mouth, just barely visible. It felt good to be moving. He strode with purpose, weaving his slight body though the blathering clusters of people. He watched their faces, how they laughed and told jokes and found common ground bitching about the boys running wild (with special emphasis on how things had been different in their day) and the unreasonable tithing practices of the churches and the signs of degradation in the criminal element of Bressel. One of them opined that men emanated a mischievous vapor which, when mingled with the same vapor of others in the level of density and proximity you can find only in such overpopulated hives as Bressel, resulted in a much more malicious strain, the kind that led to the careless robbing and killing of drunks and, eventually, widespread anarchy. Dante slowed to hear the man expound his theory, but the hundreds of other voices drowned him out; within seconds he was no more than a single note in the symphony.

There was no one direction to the flow of people—there were public houses on every street in Whetton—but the general movement tended toward the south. No hurry, what with the executions over an hour away, and probably lots of boring proclamations and condemnations to kick it off, but wait too long and you'd get a place too far back to see their feet kick when they were turned off. A hanging wasn't a hanging when for all you could see it may as well be a sack of potatoes strung up on the branch.

Even in the cold the people stunk. Dante tucked his nose into the collar of his cloak and was reminded he hadn't bathed since their stay at the pond. At least his ripeness was his own. A dark-haired boy brushed past him. Of course. They'd be drawn to the hanging like flies to a cow's ass. Dante pulled up his hood then and tugged it low enough to shade his eyes. George and Barnes would be out there somewhere. They knew enough about him to turn him in if there were any price on his head.

Single-story houses began to outnumber those with two or three floors. Sometimes they even had strips of dirt or grass between them. Another couple minutes and he reached the trampled-down field that never quite recovered from the monthly crowds. Copses of trees fringed its edges, but the only tree of note stood planted at its center, casting a shadow over the path that cut across the grasses. A light crowd milled about, talking and drinking, buying meat pastries and finger vegetables from the stalls that no doubt materialized overnight here every four weeks like clockwork mushrooms. Dante stopped a short way into the commons to take stock, wishing he had a pipe to light or any other way to immediately look casual.

Obviously the wain would come in down the path. Already people were mostly keeping clear of the rutted dirt. The tree spoke for itself. The prisoners on the wagon would be bound, but their heavy chains would probably be replaced with rope so hoisting them up and down wouldn't hurt anybody's back. Besides, with five extra pounds of iron on their wrists and another ten clamped tight around their ankles, the hangman might misjudge their weight and pop their heads off when they fell.

A few guards would walk ahead of the wagon, he imagined. A

second wagon would bear the hangman and his understudy and their armed entourage. No officials, most likely, other than a bailiff or some other nobody with a loud voice. At minimum six men of the watch. Probably twice that, with the potential for more. They'd likely be in varying states of the inebriation that was impossible to avoid on Falmac's Day, but that wasn't going to be as big an advantage for Dante as it should. Their minds would want to be off raising tankards and groping paired deposits of fat like every other man, but their captains would want them martial, swords ready. Between a troop of armsman and the Crooked Tree, the crowds couldn't help remembering their place.

People kept filing in in twos and threes and boisterous beer-sodden throngs. He figured the guards would cluster up on the way in, give themselves some protection from the revelers. That would be the worst time to try to take them. Ideally there would be a few self-important speeches to give the men of the watch time to disperse and get distracted by the fights and taunts of an intoxicated, high-spirited crowd; if he were really lucky a few guards would use the confusion to slip off for a pub. Dante would bide his time, then, and hope they wouldn't try to string Blays up first as an hors d'oeuvre. What about the other prisoners? Instant allies if he could free them. The watch wouldn't know which escapee needed to be killed first. That was it. He'd have to act fast, but he could make that happen. Then what? He headed for a copse of trees and thought that over as he searched for a walking stick suitable for staving in skulls—the men he released might have the fighting spirit, but they'd have a serious want for weapons.

And that, he thought, was as far as he could take it. Let them get ready to strangle a few men, then set those men free and go from there. There would be at least a little fighting and a lot of running. Other than that, it was all up in the air. Maybe he'd be able to steal a horse, maybe not. Maybe Cally would strike down with a word everyone who looked at Dante cockeyed, but almost definitely not. He clenched his teeth, stomach twisting. He didn't like depending on all these contingencies. He wasn't sure he could trust himself to act smoothly in the confusion of battle. He considered himself a deliberate man, the kind of man who didn't make a choice until he'd thought it all the way through. That's what you did when you wouldn't tolerate mistakes, least of all from yourself. But this, this was chance, chaos, the toss of a die, the blindfolded plunge.

He should have hired the boys to make a scene. He should have taken the offer three years ago to sail from Bressel to Portsmouth and back; it wouldn't have taken more than two weeks, and he'd never sailed. He should have enticed a couple bodyguards to aid him with careful lies and the reckless expenditure of silver. He should have read more, not just *the* book, but books, all the books of the Library of Bressel. He should have practiced more with the blood—he'd done so one time more, lighting the shadows into a small fire one afternoon outside the tomb, but he'd quickly stamped it out, afraid someone would see the flames and the smoke. He should have found a way to speak to Blays himself, just one last time. He should have written a letter to the monk back in the village. His life there hadn't been so bad. Boring, but not bad. After the stark and brutal lessons of the last month, he'd come to appreciate the strength of the monk's quiet methods, the lessons he taught more often with a well-turned sentence than with an open hand or a bark-stripped branch.

The low-key panic he'd felt since waking up had left his mind reasonably flexible, fast, if a little flighty, but as the minutes rushed on he found it harder to keep a rein on his thoughts. Sweat oozed down his sides. He maneuvered up to within a stone's throw of the tree. The crowds had swelled quickly, filling the field, spilling into the path and jostling each other for lines of sight before there was anything to see. The bells of one o'clock pealed from Whetton proper. He squeezed his eyes shut. Within moments, his ears filled with the cheers and whoops of those at the edge of the field nearest the city. The wains were rolling in.

A hush preceded the wagons as the people looked on the faces of the condemned and for an instant imagined themselves seated with the prisoners. Once they'd lumbered past, the catcalls and laughter started up again, louder than before, and in that way Dante followed the progress of the watch. His stomach felt like something were pushing up on it from below. There were too many tall men between him and the path to catch a glimpse of the wagons, but underneath the crowd's babble he thought he could make out the rumble of two separate sets of wheels. Bad sign. He wanted to get close enough to see Blays, but if he moved now he'd never get back his place some twenty yards from the clearing around the Crooked Tree. Half of Whetton must be here. With Falmac's Day, along with the farmers and peasants who tended to show up in direct proportion to the scarcity and brutality of the method of execution—though hangings were enough to do the trick—there could be twice as many men in Whetton today than was normal.

The wave of silence and the shouts that followed on its heels came nearer. Whips cracked from the direction of the path. He gagged, swallowed. He still had time to leave. No one would know he'd been here but Cally, and Cally would understand. Dante's death, when it came, wouldn't mean anything, wouldn't strike any blow against injustice and the corrupt law of man. He'd just be a body. But as much as his legs were ready to run—and they were shaking so hard he thought he might drive himself into the earth—he knew, if he left now, he would hate himself for all his days. He'd carry a mark so deep it may as well be branded on his forehead. He'd filter all his actions thereafter through the memory of the day he'd let them kill Blays, and in that sense his life would already be told, worthless for however many more years it may last.

Besides, as Cally might say, just because killing the watch wouldn't do any good didn't mean it wasn't worth doing.

The quiet took the crowd around him. Wheels creaked in the cold. He heard the snorts of the draft horses, saw a blip of their driver through the shoulders of the men in front of him. The driver's bass voice carried past his ears as all the people thought on the day they'd take their own ride on the wain to the tree at the end of the path; and then they were shouting, jeering, and Dante was shouting too, eyes clenched shut, head thrown back, a wordless cry of defiance. He was ready.

He pushed up further into the crowd. If these idiots were still in his way when the time came he'd yank out his sword and give it a taste of their blood before it bit into the watchmen. He shoved his way onward, matching glares, refusing to yield, and made his way within ten feet of the inner rim of the masses. Close enough for now. Close enough to crane his head and see the wagons break from the walls of people and into the clear circle around the tree. He started counting men. Six at point in front of the wagons, brown cloaks flapping behind them. Three more to either side. Five more trailing, one bearing the banner of the city, the eagle's black talons clutching the golden shock of wheat. And three—no, make it four—crouched down in the bed of the second wain, hands resting on their hilts, scanning the crowd for anyone with any funny designs on the black-hooded man sitting cross-legged at its center.

Dante's eyes flicked to the first wagon to count the condemned. Seven. Somehow there were always seven. There among them, blond hair a mat of grease, face smeared with dirt and soot and dried blood, sat Blays.

Dante stretched on his toes and pulled his cowl a couple inches back from his face, but he didn't dare cry out or wave his hands and the boy didn't look his way. He didn't appear to be seeing anything at all, in fact. Dante'd never seen that look on his face: eyes downcast, face tranquil as a slack sail, body swaying loosely at the jolts and jounces of the wain. He hadn't looked that way when they'd been chased through the forest by three grown men on horseback. He hadn't even looked that way in those days after he'd seen Dante call the shadowsphere in the alley in Bressel—he'd pouted and brooded and kept to himself, but beneath all that he'd kept a spark, an air of confusion and betrayal that lent some moment to his moods. Now, he looked like he were already dead. Dante's knuckles whitened on his staff. Sure, a veritable army of men drawn for honor guard. For their sake he hoped they said a prayer before it began.

Time blurred. Men jumped off the wagon and hauled the doomed men to their feet. The black-hooded man lowered himself and took down a couple stools. He set them beneath the Crooked Tree and slung two of the nooses draped over his shoulder onto the tree's one straight and level branch. Dante turned his shoulders and wiggled closer. The watch picked out two filthy men whose age he couldn't guess and made them step up on the stools. The hangman fitted the ropes around their necks, setting the knot at the back, behind their heads. With a jerk to his gut, Dante realized these men weren't going to be kicked off a platform so their necks broke like had been the practice of Bressel's most recent hangman, they were going to be turned right off the stools. They looked like they'd have no more than a foot to fall, two at the utmost; Jack Gray, executioner of Bressel, averaged his ropes at eight feet and, so he boasted, varied their length to the build and weight of his client just enough to make sure the spine snapped without yanking the head clean off.

These men would hang till they strangled. Some of the older men he'd known, men who could remember the hanger before Gray, said it could be five or ten minutes before the legs stopped kicking, that some of the condemned had dangled for a full half hour and been found to have their hearts yet beating. Before they'd made it law that all who hanged must be kept on the line for a full hour after their initial turn, Half-Hanged Kurt had been cut down after forty minutes, buried, then been dug up filthy but breathing when a traveler had heard his cries beneath the dirt. So Jack Gray had brought new methods with his contract.

Dante was amazed the two men who stood before the crowds offered no resistance as the ropes closed around their throats and and tied them to their fates. Why so spiritless? What could they lose? Now was the time for rage, to exact some minor measure of control in choosing the moments of their deaths. Not this farce, this resigned obeisance. Maybe they deserved what they were about to get. Was that it? Did they feel the same way? Had the fact some fancy-man on a podium had deemed them guilty of their crimes convinced them it was their time to move on? The hooded man finished his preparations and stepped back. A watchman with silver pins flashing on the collar of his cloak took center.

"You have been tried and condemned in the courts of this land. Any final words or requests?"

"I ask the mercy of the family of the man I did kill," one man said. "I only wanted food." The crowd booed.

"Another slug of whiskey!" the second man shouted through his thick brown beard. The crowd laughed, raised flagons and flasks.

"So it ends," the watchman said. The hangman stepped forward, draped a white cap over the first man's face, then the second. Dante's heart shuddered as he reached into the deep folds of his pockets and gathered up his burden. The captain of the watch reeled off some speech about justice and the obligations of civilization.

"We take no joy in meting out the fate you've earned yourself," the captain smiled at last. "A moment of silence, please. Pray to the gods. They have been known to grant mercy, even to the wretched."

He held up a hand and the crowds went quiet. Dante's fingers slid over the fragile bones he'd taken from his pockets. He set Jack Hand's inspirations on what little open ground he found at his feet. The six fleshless rodents raised their eyeless heads at him, clicking their teeth. No going back now. He held his hand close to his chest and gestured toward the tree. They skittered through the clustered legs of the audience, unheard, unseen. For whatever extra insanity it would add he popped the torchstone into his mouth. Someone cried out at the sight of the bleached-bone animals streaking toward the bound men. It would have been more dramatic to wait till Blays' turn had come beneath the judging branch, but he wanted as many men turned loose as he could manage, as much chaos as he could muster to conceal his true intent. More shrieks rose up on the tail of the first. The watchmen glanced around. A couple loosened their swords. Within seconds the dead rats had leapt on the hands and ankles of the criminals. This was it, the plunge, the toss of the die.

A cold anger stole over Dante's bones as he watched the rats' teeth clashing through the ropes of the condemned. The hangman cried out and bumped one of the men off his stool. His bare feet kicked at the air. One of the rats jumped on his feet and scrabbled up his legs to the noose. It chomped down and within three heartbeats the rope snapped and the man thumped against the ground. Everything began to move at once and Dante whooped like a savage and plowed through the men between him and the clearing. With a terrible thrill he wouldn't unlive for all the world he burst into the open ground. The dead rats were running out of ropes to gnaw through and with a thought he sent them to assault the first guard who'd figured out Something Bad was going down. Blood leapt away from the man's leg as the rats ripped in with tiny claws. He smashed the bones of one with the pommel of his sword, then fell screaming to his knees. The rats swarmed up his body.

Dante rushed into the field, staff in his left hand and sword held high in his right, torchstone gleaming from his open mouth.

"The judgment of the gods has come!" he screamed around the stone at the men who'd be hanged. "Kill them all! Fight for your lives!"

Heads turned his way. The cannier men seized the confusion for their own. One of the guards cut down a distracted prisoner while one of the prisoners punched out a guard and snatched up his sword. Like a school of fish every man moved at once. The watch clustered up and began an advance on the tight circle of condemned men. The vast crowds wailed like a roof-stripping gale as some fell back and others pushed forward for a glimpse of this new chaos.

"Fight, you bastard sons! Fight for your lives! Don't you dare give them up to these dogs cloaked in law!"

Dante closed on their ranks. He threw the staff at the first prisoner to look his way. One of the watch broke rank to intercept him and Dante stretched out his free hand and the man's ribs popped, dropping him mid-step. Blays' shocked laughter bubbled over the shouts and the roar and Dante met the boy's eyes and tossed him his sword. Its point speared the earth and Blays snatched it up and met the first wedge of watchmen, lashing out with the full strength of his arm. Dante spat out the torchstone and dropped it in his pocket. He took his knife from his belt and laid open the palm of his left hand, flashing his teeth at the hot rush of pain. Blood wicked up the lines of his palm and he closed his fist.

He looked up, meaning to join the skirmish beginning in earnest between law and outlaw, and met eyes with a watchman not three feet in front of him. The man's sword whooshed through the air in a downstroke that would cleave his skull. Dante shouted out to the nether, but there was no time. His eyes and nostrils went wide. He thought: so there's nothing up there looking out for us. Perhaps it wasn't all in vain. Blays still lived. Blays could still make it out.

Steel flashed as the stroke fell. Dante heard a hiss like a doused torch and then a gurgle and a wet boom and his face was showered with stinging blood as the guard's sword exploded in what had been his hands. Dante fell back, swiping gunk from his eyes, and the guard raised his spurting stumps and keeled over like a cut tree.

Cally. Hope flared back up in his chest. He rushed to the main battle, feeling sure and invincible as a panther. A line of bodies from both sides marked the border of the struggle. Small, crushed bones lay in disordered piles, but a pair of his rats fought on, digging into the stomach of one of the watchmen. The man doubled over, crushing one of the vermin as it squirmed through the other side of his body. Blays whirled, knocking back their attacks to right and left, but the guard's sheer numbers gave him no room to strike back. Three of the other convicts still survived, one with Dante's staff, one with a guard's sword, the last with just his own bleeding knuckles; before Dante could make a move a watchman lunged in and ran the unarmed man through. He felt as if it were someone else's hands grasping the nether and sending it in a black bolt that squirted the guard's brains from his ear. A knife flipped through the air and into Dante's left biceps and he screamed and went numb to the fingertips. He yanked it free and flung it at a watchman closing on Blays. The man flinched back and Blays swept out and sprayed blood into the air. At least a dozen of the guard left, though, to their mere four, and already he could feel his control of the shadows growing tenuous, threatening to burst from the channel of his body. He risked a backwards glance, saw some of the crowd had fled to the city while others had fallen back to the safer perspective of another dozen steps away. He thought he saw a brown-garbed group pushing their way forward. Their progress was hampered by the countercurrent of the mob, but they couldn't be more than a minute or two away. They'd come fast once they reached the clear ground around the tree. The watchmen facing them noticed it as well and fell back to reform their ranks. The prisoners panted, glancing around themselves, beginning to understand the reprieve Dante'd given them was coming to an end.

"I hope the brilliance of your plan doesn't stop here," Blays said, edging up to him.

"There's more of them on the way. We're not going to be able to fight them all."

"That's a no, then," Blays said, crestfallen.

"Affirmative," Dante said.

"Do the thing on them where it goes dark," he whispered. One of the watch tightened his mouth, cursed, then stepped forward and raised his sword against Blays. Steel met steel and both sides stood transfixed, as if waiting for a cue. The watchman made a series of tightly controlled thrusts, forcing Blays back. Blays tried a counter and the man brushed it aside and responded with a stroke that, were Dante in Blays' place, would have taken off his head; Blays leaned back, swiveling his hips to speed his sword enough to meet it, and the man's blade scraped down his and into his arm. As if the sight of the boy's blood were a command, the rest of the watch started forward, points of their swords held in front of them, and Dante coaxed the shadows to plunge them into total darkness. They shrieked blindly. The watchman's attack on Blays had left his stance open, just a hair, and when he heard the cries behind him he hesitated long enough for Blays to wheel his sword down in a three-quarter angle and lay open the man's chest. The watchman staggered back into the pitch.

"Charge!" Blays bellowed, shaking his sword high over his head, then turned and ran away for the wagons. The two other prisoners took a step forward, shouting battle cries, then caught on and swerved to follow Blays' retreat. Thrown by the feint, clearly terrified that their eyes had suddenly stopped working at the command of an archmage who'd come to them in the form of a boy slinging death and destruction over their ranks, the first of the guards didn't emerge from the shadowsphere until the band of rebels had cut the beefy horses free from the wagons. Blays heaved himself up onto the bare back of a black horse and swirled his blade.

"I can't ride!" Dante shouted from the ground.

"Neither can I!" Blays said, face blended in terror and exhilaration. He hugged his body to the neck of the horse and reached a hand down to Dante. Dante grabbed it and they wrestled his weight up on the animal's back. By the time he was set the guards were pouring down the hill toward them. Behind them, another squad rolled out from the road, moving to cut them off.

"This is bullshit!" Blays shouted. He kicked the horse in the ribs and was almost thrown off its back as it galloped straight at the men coming down the hill. He caught his balance just as the first came into striking distance. Blays laid out with his blade, meaning to decapitate the closest man in one clean stroke, and instead his sword caught in the man's skull and yanked back Blays' arm, nearly dismounting him for a second time. "This is hard!"

"Just don't get us killed," Dante said, gripping the horse for dear life. He'd put away his knife and had no other weapons than the shadows. A faintness in his head and chest told him he needed at least a moment's rest before he went to them again. To their rear he saw the two other prisoners trotting their way. The one with the staff was clenching himself against his horse's neck and rapidly falling behind the one who'd picked up a sword. That man kicked his heels, holding the weapon wide away from the horse's heaving flanks like he'd been born armed and in the saddle. Within seconds he closed on them and matched Blays' speed.

"What's next?" he called over.

"What's the hurry?" Blays said, swiping and missing at a ducking watchman. He cursed and started their mount in an awkward circle.

"Horses are faster than they are," Dante suggested loudly in Blays' ear.

"That just means I've got plenty of time to kill a few more first," he said, righting the horse for another pass.

The two groups of guards had merged and were making a slow turn to try to drive them toward the city. Blays set a course for the stragglers and rode one down beneath the horse's thundering hooves. A second watchman turned and raised his sword and Blays cut his arm off at the elbow. He drew the horse up short by the makeshift reins left over from its ties to the wagon and the animal reared back. Dante flattened himself, clamping his legs so hard against its sides he felt sure he or the horse would break. Blays crouched down but lifted his fist and carved a tight arc through the air with the point of his sword.

"Cower then, you sons of bitches!" he yelled, spit flying from his mouth. "I'd kill you all, but you stamp one roach and twenty others take its place!" The horse's front hooves landed and a shock ran up Dante's spine. Blays turned it to the south, where the staff-wielding criminal was spurring his horse through the thin remnants of the crowd. "Rot in hell! Did you hear that? You can all just die!"

He charged forward. The guy with the sword hurried to their front. Dante laughed as the remaining peasants parted like flocks of quail. Young men and women in ragged clothes waved their hands and cheered them on. Blays tipped an imaginary cap and the girls cheered harder.

"What's your name?" one called after him.

"Blays Buckler!" he shouted over his shoulder. "And my friend Dante, greatest sorcerer to walk the earth!"

"That's not very wise," Dante said.

"Ah, we'll never see them again. This way they can write some songs about us. Make the watch feel like jackasses for years to come."

They neared the forest fringe at the edge of the field. Blays laughed and cursed a few gods for good measure. As if they'd taken personal interest, Dante saw a spearpoint of men on horseback break from the crowd and angle to intercept them before the woods.

"Oh, come on!" Blays said, slapping the horse's sweating side. "I didn't mean it!"

Dante whistled to the other two prisoners galloping ahead. The swordsman glanced back, saw the pursuers, then slowed to let Blays fall in beside him.

"Can't outrun them," the man panted, and Dante saw it was true. The horses they'd stolen were so bulky they were practically plowhorses. Next to the saber-thin bodies of the watchmen's horses, the ones they rode were like the jewel-fattened swords kings used to ennoble their bravest and richest knights. The watch would be on them before they reached the woods. And once again, they were outnumbered.

"Don't these people have anything better to do?" Dante muttered.

"Can't you make the earth swallow them up or something?"

"Can't you stab them all in the heart wearing a blindfold and women's drawers?"

"You've got women's drawers?" Blays gave Dante an intensely interested look, eyes going wide when he saw the riders behind them. "Hey, they're really getting close!"

One rider spurred himself ahead of the pack, intent on Dante's undefended back. If they slowed down to fight, the others would catch them. If they rode straight on, the one would run him through. His eyes felt moist. He blanked his mind and touched the nether. It leapt up easily, ready to return. There was no holding back now. Dante shouted at the swordsman on their flank.

"Can you hold that one off?"

"The one, sure," the prisoner said, straightening his arm and slanting his sword at the ground.

"I just need a few seconds." Dante turned his face from the wind trying to tear the breath from his mouth. The man dropped a couple lengths behind them and blocked the path of the lone watchman. They crossed blades and the other five pulled side-by-side with each other and hurried to his aid. Dante's palm had mostly scabbed up and he sucked in air and cut an X across his hand. Shadows flocked to his blood at once, wriggling around his fingers, coating his skin halfway to the elbow. His body went cold. He could see the individual beads of sweat rolling down the faces of the watch, could smell the horse's sweat and the earthy mulch of rotting leaves. He felt as if he could drop down and outrun their horse on his own two legs. Why hadn't he been doing this more? What was there to be afraid of? Lightning in his veins and vision so sharp it was like he could see into time itself. This was everything he'd ever wanted.

"Watch this, Blays. I'm going to do something neat."

He splayed his fingers and released the nether, shaping it to the image in his mind. For a second nothing happened. He looked at his empty hand, expecting sparks or smoke. Nothing. They were going to die, then.

In the gap between the battling pair and the five galloping watchmen a wall of flames erupted from the earth. It roared twenty feet high, then collapsed to half that, a fire so hot it was white. The five men screamed as one. Their horses bleated, reared back, trying to stop the wild rush of their bodies. One man and mount tried to leap through and the fires scorched the skin from its belly.

They tumbled apart. Dante saw the silhouette of another man flying forward, thrown by his horse. By the time he cleared the fire he was a corpse.

Dante tried to swallow, but none of his muscles wanted to work. Behind them, before his sight started going gray, he saw the sword-wielding prisoner swing forehand, knocking aside the watchman's blade, then backhand, slicing off his hand, and finally swung his shoulders in a second forehand, sending the man's head spinning into the grass. A low branch rushed past Dante's face.

"Someone kill me while I'm happy!" Blays shouted. "I can't believe you came back, Dante. I didn't know what to think when I saw your face back at the tree. If I'd had a real meal in the last week I probably would've filled my trousers."

"Unggh," Dante said, meaning something about how he couldn't think either. His vision tunneled. His legs loosened their grip on the horse's flanks. Blays had escaped, he thought, and then the darkness took him.

8

Pain woke him. This didn't surprise him—some animal part of his brain had been registering hurt even as he slept—but rather than the all-body throb Dante'd slumbered through for however many hours or years since he'd collapsed mid-ride on their escape from Whetton, this pain was in his face: light and stinging, and with it a flat smack.

"What did I tell you," a nasally voice said, "about streams that want to be rivers? Don't you remember the part about the dying?"

"Stop it," Dante slurred, pawing at whatever was hitting him. He blinked a few times. "Cally?"

"No, bearded Gashen himself. I'm here to recruit you as my chief general in the war for the heavens." The old man scowled down on him. "Were you *trying* to get yourself killed?"

"Kind of the opposite," Dante said, and before he could say more his lungs spasmed. Cally threw a handkerchief in his face. Dante dabbed at his lips and the mess came away bloody. "Where are we?"

"Somewhere safe from Whetton's watch and the Arawnites' hounds."

Dante blinked again, gazed dumbly at the musty stone walls. "It looks like a dump."

"It's my temple," Cally said. "Show some respect."

"You blew up that man's sword when I was charging them," Dante remembered. He laughed, quickly clutched his sides. "Ow."

"At that moment, you weren't looking very capable of not dying."

"Dante!" Blays shouted, head stuck through the doorway. He poured into the room and shot Cally a black look. "I told you he wouldn't die."

"Technically it was a bet."

"You should have seen yourself running onto that field," Blays said, grabbing Dante's shoulder and shaking him like a crying child. "Those rats stampeding in front of you like hell's own army, staff in one hand, sword in the other, face all lit up with light—you looked like a demon come down to earth, or one of those old wizards that used to obliterate a battalion just by pointing at them."

"Those stories are all exaggerated," Cally said.

"You're old enough to know."

"So you admit you're wrong."

"What happened to the others?" Dante said. "Did they make it?"

"They're out in the yard somewhere," Cally said, flipping a hand. "Eating up my food and drinking down my wine, no doubt. Why couldn't you have saved a 16-year-old girl?"

"I wasn't trying to save anyone but Blays," Dante said. He eased himself upright. The blood left his head and he felt as if he were floating in a warm sea. He waited till his eyes weren't full of specks. "I was just using the others to make a mess."

"I don't think mess' quite covers it," Cally said. He frowned through the snarl of his beard for a moment, then couldn't help chuckling. "All right, it did look ridiculous. They'll be talking about it for generations. Ten years from now, all the people who'll claim to have witnessed the Execution That Wasn't could fill an ocean."

"How long was I out?"

"A whole damn day," Blays said. He bounced on his heels. "I'll go grab the others. They've been waiting to thank you."

"What?" Dante said once Blays had run off. "What do they think, I was trying to save them?"

"That's exactly what they think," Cally said, running his fingers through his beard and laughing to himself. "They think you have a special purpose for them."

"That's crazy! In what way is 'dying so I don't have to' a special purpose?"

"Try to get them to swear you a life-debt. Never know when

that might come in handy."

"Will you be serious for a minute?" Dante doubled over in another coughing fit. He brushed water from his eyes. "What am I going to tell them?"

"Obviously not the truth. That would crush them." Cally explored a gap in his teeth with his pinky nail. "In a minute, they're going to bound in here and slobber all over you trying to convince themselves you really do have a meaning for them. The polite thing would be to play along."

"Well, I'm not going to lie to them. Not about something like that."

"Oh yes, it would be far more ethical to strip them of their illusions and leave them to fend for themselves philosophically naked."

"You talk like they're little babies. I think they can do all right for themselves."

Cally rolled his eyes. "The first time you saw them they were about to be *hanged*."

"That doesn't mean anything," Dante said, wriggling upright in his bed. "Those people hang anyone they don't like. The whole thing's a sham. They were going to kill Blays for looking like a scumhole and not having any friends there."

"And for killing all those people."

"Those people were trying to—" Dante started, then bolted upright, scanning the room. Cally looked puzzled, then his face wrinkled up in a smirk. Dante turned back to him. "Where's the book?"

"Your pack's on that peg over there," the old man said, tipping his chin past Dante's shoulder. "You wouldn't let go of it even after you'd been knocked out."

"Praise the gods," Dante said, sinking back into the bedclothes, then glanced in fresh panic at the door as Blays burst back into the room, followed by the bearded swordsman, who Dante now recognized as the noosed-up man who'd asked for more whiskey before they turned him off, and the staff-wielding man who'd made a poor horseman and, Dante noted with a strange thrill, was still carrying the staff, as though Dante's touch had made it into something more than a snapped-off branch. The two ex-prisoners exchanged a smile, then looked back at Dante.

"Was some talk of whether you'd pull through," the bearded man said, glancing at Blays and jingling some coins in his pocket. "My name's Robert Hobble."

"I'm Dante."

"No, I mean, I'm Robert *Hobble*."

"And well met," Dante said.

"Guess I'm not as well known as I thought," Robert smiled. "Thought I was a corpse for sure up there. I had this half-assed notion the mob, once they saw it was me, would rush right up and uproot the Crooked Tree for now and for ever, but I guess they thought I deserved it after all." His face went blank, just a light crinkle around his eyes like he was trying to fight off a headache. "Don't know what to make of getting rescued by you."

"Think nothing of it," Dante said quickly. The man with the staff stepped forward.

"They don't tell stories about me like they do for Robert," he said, ducking his head, "but I appreciate what you've done just as much. It's like I've been given a second chance."

"Then spend it well," Dante said, avoiding Blays and Cally's eyes. "What's your name?"

"Edwin Powell, sir."

"We might not have made it if you weren't fighting alongside us, Edwin."

"Might be," Edwin said. He leaned on the stick and nodded at the far wall. "But I'd be strangled and buried if you hadn't led the charge."

"I'd planned to die there," Dante said. "I think I would have if you two hadn't discharged yourselves so well." To his ear, his words didn't sound entirely his own. He had the sense he was repeating sentiments he'd once heard from someone else, and while he meant what he was saying, there was something platitudinal in it, a blandness that made him feel as if he were lying. He flushed, and before he could find a way to thank them that felt real he coughed so hard he sat up straight, eyes watering.

"The young lord needs his rest," Cally said, restraining his smile till the two men had turned back to Dante. "In other words, get the hell out."

"I pledge to spend my second chance better than I did my first,"

Edwin said. He tapped the staff against the stone floor. "I won't make you regret what you did for me." He looked down. "My family's worried, no doubt. With your leave, I'd like to go back to them now."

"Of course," Dante said.

"No one's eager to see me back," Robert said, scratching the stubble on his throat. "Would probably be best if I stayed out of sight for a while, in fact. Maybe I can pay you two back by teaching Blays all the ways he's embarrassing himself when he waves around that sword of his."

"My dad taught me how to fight," Blays said, hands gripping his belt.

Robert held up his palms. "I just mean no education worth its salt ends at twelve."

"I'm fifteen and a half."

"My mistake. I try not to pay attention to anyone under twenty. They have the habit of dying right around the time you start to like them."

"Maybe you've got a habit of boring them to death," Blays said.

"Enough," Cally said, tugging at sleeves and shoving at backs. "Go yammer at each other out in the yard." He overruled their objections and ushered them out of the room, then closed the door and pressed his back to it. "Country hens. The real crime was not letting the watch turn them off when they had the chance."

"I couldn't find a way to thank them," Dante said.

"You sounded fine to me. I once heard a duke say the same thing after a successful siege."

"That's exactly the problem."

"You want to be you and you alone," Cally said knowingly. "The key is to be less civilized."

"What does that mean?" Dante said. The old man just stared at him through the gray halo of his beard and ruffled hair.

"What are you going to do now?"

"Sleep," Dante said, stretching his arms over his head and sliding back beneath his blanket.

"Yes, but I presume at some point, hours or even days from now, you'll wake up and be wanting for something to do."

"Finish the part of the *Cycle* I can read. Then learn how to read the part I can't."

"I see," Cally said. His eyes flickered wide with something that looked bizarrely like hunger. Then he nodded, inscrutable as ever, and went for the door. "First, rest. Once you're done coughing up blood, then you can think about what comes next."

Dante could stand after the first day and walk around after the second. When he felt well enough to hobble outside his room he found the building really had been a temple. A poor one, most certainly, more of a shrine, given that it had only four rooms and the largest of these wouldn't have held a congregation of more than forty. It was a sturdy edifice, though, all mortared stone, with high arched ceilings that stole up the heat even when the main hearth was blazing. The walls were covered in bas relief from Dante's knees to a foot above his eyes, filled with hand-sized figures of bearded men in crowns and robes with stars flaring from their hands and a number of smaller figures who appeared to be getting killed by those stars. Concealed among the kingly shapes was a frame of a man standing in a cell. Rags hung from his shoulders in abstract tatters. At his feet, three rats stood on their hind legs, front paws dangling. His outstretched hand bore four fingers.

He saw Blays no more than two or three times a day, at meals or when the boy came in from hours of traipsing around the open wood as he'd done when they lived by the pond. In the mornings and late afternoons of the shortening days Dante heard the crash of swords out in the yard mingled with the phlegmy laughter of Robert Hobble as he doled out some new lesson. Cally all but quarantined himself to his room, as if he couldn't stand sharing the same space with other bodies for more than a few minutes a day. Dante sat by the fire reading the last sections of the *Cycle* that were still in the Mallish tongue and tried to shut his ears to the shouts and play of blades outside.

By the fourth day he could have joined them, he thought, in that he felt physically well enough to spar. It wouldn't hurt to improve his training; his current worth with a sword was about one notch above being able to take a swing without chopping off his own face. Instead he stayed indoors. He didn't want to slow Blays down. Robert had skill, that much was clear from how he'd acquitted himself in the field. Blays must know that, unencumbered by Dante's clumsy swipes and plodding advancement, he could learn something that might end up saving his life—probably Dante's as well. If they thought it would do any good for Dante to be out there, they'd have asked him.

So he read and reread, scribbling notes, flipping forward and backward, doing his best to place the fractured chronology in some kind of order, borrowing from Cally's bountiful stacks of blank paper to compose small essays on the *Cycle*'s curious symbolism and authorial shifts and veiled concerns. He wrote these not because he intended to amend or refute in the public arena the other scholars he'd read (though he hoped, with a desperation he could never wholly admit to, Cally would some day read them and confirm he was on the right track), but from a compulsion that felt as elemental as the stone walls and wood chairs that surrounded him. It was trying work, but it wasn't tiring; it was slow and uneven and he was constantly frustrated by how little the words on his pages matched the ideas in his head, but he was propelled by the momentum of a boy's first-found love in the subjects of men. By the end of a week he reached the final page of the Mallish chapters before it shifted to the dead language, and in the last light of afternoon finished what he'd started an age ago in Bressel.

> *The final times will come as they began, blinded by the white blanket of the northern snows, settled at the foot of the Tree of Bone where the Draconat spilled the Father of the Heavens' heartblood on the snow and planted his knuckle within the soil. The skies will be black, though it be full day, the winds will howl with the laments of the slain as the starry vault is shattered and all things thought passed once more come forth. A scaled beast will arise with three tails and four wings and lay waste to the land.*
>
> *Rivers will reverse their direction and graves will spit the dead to mingle with the living. Fire will consume the cities of man: the gift never meant to be given turned in hot cleansing against those who tainted its power. The beast will make himself known, lashing out with his tails to smash the false temples of men who have forgotten the true faces of the Belt of the Celeset.*

> *Eric the Draconat is dead, though he lived long, and in this twilight time he alone will not return. The beast will hold its judgment, and its judgment will be that of the scythe to the wheat.*

He knew some priests put great stock in apocalyptic prophecies, but Dante couldn't escape the sense whoever'd written this hadn't meant a literal three-tailed dragon was going to show up in the end days and bring a physical end to the world. It was like this story was an ancient cathedral buried up to its steeple—men could see the spire's tip, but few could guess there was something grand beneath it, and no one could imagine what shape that cathedral might take. An understanding had been lost. Possibly, the man who'd written it hadn't even understood exactly what he was passing along. This story, though, was a thousand years old at the least, possibly many times that, told and retold until it had been embedded in the *Cycle*; how could Dante unearth its true shape when the men who'd first conceived it had been dead for so long none of their names survived? Where on earth would he even start to look?

"Finished?" Cally said, startling him from this tangle of thoughts, as garbled as the web of a whirlpool-spider.

"As far as I can get."

"Good. Then start thinking about where you're going next, because you can't stay here."

Dante's head snapped up. "You want us to leave?"

"I've got my own business to get back to," Cally said, frowning at him. "What did you think was going to happen?"

"I thought you were going to teach me how to read the rest," Dante said, finding his hopes sounded much less ridiculous now that Cally had dashed them. "The nether, too."

"Well, you were wrong."

"Surely you know as much as anyone about these things."

"Miles more." Cally sighed when Dante started in on another objection. He waved his hands in front of his face, brushing it away. "Even if I had the time, which I don't, I'm not an instructor. I was bad at it when I was young and now that I'm old I'm as likely to kill you as tutor you. Things are muddled. I know how to navigate my own coasts, but trying to explain it to fit someone else's mind is worse than impossible."

"Where can I go, then?" Dante said, grasping the cover of the book. "Even the Library of Bressel doesn't have the rest of it. It's like the whole world's forgotten."

"Not the whole world."

"Where, then?"

Cally's blue eyes flinched. "The dead city. Narashtovik itself."

"That's where the Arawnites wanted to take me once they saw I knew the nether," Dante said. He stared hard at Cally. "You think I should go to them now? Why? I thought you hated them."

"No doubt you heard some news in Whetton. About the skirmishes in the plains of Collen. The riots down in Bressel."

"What does that have to do with anything?"

"They stem from the same source as the language of the *Cycle*'s last section."

"The dead city," Dante said, ignoring the embarrassment that came with using its nickname. He shuffled the pieces of what he'd learned and what Cally had told him of their motives around in the workshop of his mind. "They mean to start a war, then. How does that help them release Arawn?"

"It doesn't," Cally said, squinting at him, "but they have this idea it would be somewhat disrespectful to restore Arawn to his seat when barbarians like us still beat people to death for having the audacity to praise him."

"Have you ever seen Arawn?"

"Of course not. He's imprisoned."

"Okay," Dante said. He worried his lip for a moment. "Have you ever seen *any* of the gods? One of their stellar messengers, even? Anything at all that stands as hard proof of the divine?" Cally shrugged at him and Dante bulled on. "So who cares what the Arawnites are up to, then? They're just a bunch of dopes in robes. They're going to sacrifice a few goats, turn their eyes to the heavens, and see nothing but the stars. Arawn's not going to ride down on a flaming chariot and lay ruin to the earth."

"But they will in his place!" Cally thundered, striding forward till his face was no more than a foot from Dante's. "Blaspheme all you like. Maybe Arawn exists and maybe he doesn't. Maybe he's nothing but foofaraw. Fine! They still believe he does and they're still going to war for it. Thousands are going to die for it, including a few who don't deserve to."

Dante drew back, silent until the anger worked its way from Cally's face. He had a long time to wait.

"So why bring this up?" Dante said at last. "What does that have to do with me going to Narashtovik?"

"Two fish, one spear."

"Will you drop the oracular nonsense and talk like a person for once?"

Cally snorted as if making himself clear would be beneath his dignity. Dante maintained his silence and Cally snorted again, tugging at his sleeves.

"What I'm saying, since during your escape you evidently sustained a blow to the head, is it may be within your power to abbreviate the coming bloodshed."

"That's a load of it, isn't it? Why don't *you* stop it?"

"I know, it's hardly in your nature to prevent people from bleeding," Cally returned. "You're much more comfortable rupturing organs and spewing people's brains out their ears. That seemed especially unnecessary, by the way." The old man tapped a finger against his teeth. "It's my very power that prevents me from going there and doing something myself."

"Now that's just stupid," Dante said.

"It's of equal probability that you're the one being stupid. I was known in the dead city, once. They'd no sooner let me through their walls than they would a horde of hooting savages. As soon as I got within a hundred miles they'd strike me down with a pike, then chop me into fragments, stick me on any number of other pikes, and dance around a bonfire. You, on the other hand, appear completely unremarkable, and would stand out no more than any other foreigner."

"Probably because I'm not any more dangerous than a pilgrim."

Cally chortled at that. "I'm not about to fawn on you like those peasants you saved. In fact, if you actually believe the words you just said, I should crush your skull as a service to the collective human race. The truth is, you're a sharp young knife, and so's Blays, in his way. There's a reason sharp knives are the favored arms of assassins."

"Even so," Dante said, flushing a little. Caught off guard—these were the first kind words he could recall Cally saying—it was a second before he understood those words weren't purely poetical. "Assassins?"

"Well yes. If I thought we'd have to kill every citizen of the dead city I'd send an army, not two boys. As it is, I believe we can stave off war with the death of a single priest."

"There are people in the dead city?"

Cally gave him a look. "You thought it was full of talking corpses, maybe? Walking skeletons?"

"Of course not," Dante lied.

"They just call it that to keep out the pilgrims." Cally looked blankly at the carvings on the wall behind Dante's chair. "It was sacked a few times. More than a few. After the fourth or fifth time they'd rebuilt it and plotted out all the new cemeteries someone got wise and moved the palace inland a few hundred miles. Now Narashtovik is sort of a kingdom within the wider kingdom of Gask. A few stubborn dunces who equated their land with their identity stuck around and have continued getting sacked ever since. It's become an isolated place. Weird in a bad way. No one goes there on purpose, and over the years it's become a shell of its former self, but there are those who still live there. Including an awful lot of Arawn's chosen, since in that city they could worship a stuffed donkey for all anyone from civilization would care." He wiped his nose, sniffed. "Some do claim it gets its nickname from the regional practice the people have—suspicious of outsiders, as I hope you see why—of stringing up strangers from the city walls, but I believe it's just those little differences that makes the world special."

Dante ignored him. "Whenever the *Cycle* mentioned it it talked about a place as big as Bressel. Not some horrid backwater."

"Bigger," Cally said. "But the *Cycle*'s a thousand years old, and that's just the young parts. When a text becomes sacred you can't just run around updating it for the modern era. It would throw the whole thing into suspicion."

"So what about this priest?"

"How did we—?" Cally sighed. "Right. It's difficult to tell what kind of idiocy might be in the heads of the council, but I think if its leader were rendered persona non grata, by which I mean dead, the forces of reason may be able to cajole and flatter the dogs of war back from their madness. Her name is—"

"*Her* name? They take orders from a woman?"

"Death doesn't discriminate, does he? Why should his followers? I'm beginning to think you should travel to Narashtovik just to broaden your horizons."

"I just didn't know a woman was their leader," Dante said. He resolved to stop interrupting.

"Samarand," Cally said. "She's not terribly old, though all you young people look alike to me. She's a wretched firebrand. Always going on about how Arawn's faithful have let themselves be pushed from their proper place at the table. I think if she were to stop rushing around exhorting violence and mayhem, the moderate elements would snap out of their collective nightmare and go back to grinding the radicals beneath their heels, as is just and proper."

"Fascinating," Dante said. "I won't do it."

Cally's eyebrows shot up. "What?"

"I'm not a dog of war, either. I'm not going to travel ten thousand miles to kill some woman on your say-so. Do you have any idea how insane this sounds? You don't, do you? This sounds reasonable to you. No way."

"First off, it's barely a thousand miles. Second, you must have killed a dozen men by now."

"That was completely different."

"Was it? It seems to me a dead man's a dead man no matter why he's dead."

"We were defending our lives," Dante said. He clutched his copy of the *Cycle* to his chest. "I shouldn't have to apologize for that."

"Will you apologize when this war kills thousands, then?" Cally said, leaning in again. The old man looked like he should stink like a dock, but Dante was constantly surprised to find he had no odor at all, even when he was practically spitting in his face. "If Samarand lives, thousands will die. How will you split that hair to wash your hands of guilt? What if she was going to kill a million people instead? The entire world? Would you do something then?"

"Stop it," Dante said. He stood up and faced Cally, meeting the man's age-honed glare with his own raw outrage. "Find someone else. This mess is none of my concern."

He started back for his room. He didn't know where he would go if not Narashtovik, but he'd begun to understand just how large the world was once you'd learned to face the fear of leaving everything you knew behind. There were way too many kingdoms, baronies, chiefdoms, and rogue cities out there for all knowledge of the *Cycle* to be confined to Narashtovik. He was only sixteen. It galled him to have to wait a single day to read the rest, let alone however many months or years it would take him to track down a Mallish translation on his own (or, he supposed with an inward groan, to learn whatever foreign language it might have been translated into), but if nothing else, a period of far-flung wandering would give the Arawnites some time to forget him, to stop hunting him through the towns and the wilds and go back to their own business.

"Barden is real," Cally said from behind him. Dante closed his eyes, hand on the handle to his room.

"A huge tree grown out of bone is real."

"Yes."

"Sprouted from Taim's severed knuckle and watered from his gushing heart."

"I'm a few eons too young to know that," Cally said. "Nor do I know whether 'its limbs bear the waters above the world while its roots rest in the waters beneath the world,' as the book would have it. But I have looked on it."

Dante turned, then, knowing it for a ploy, but unable to stop his pulse from thumping till he could feel it in his chest and in his ears.

"What was it like?"

Cally started to speak, then shook his head. "Looking on it was like living in a world without light and air." His eyes drifted from Dante's, lids wrinkled so hard his eyelashes fluttered. The old man pulled his lips back from his teeth. He suddenly looked immeasurably older than his 60-odd years, as old as a wind-scoured mountainside, ages older than all the years of man. "I've seen many things I'd call miracles if I didn't have the training to know how to do them myself. But if the gods left a single fingerprint on our world, it was in the White Tree."

"The book says it's north of Narashtovik."

"Just over a hundred miles." Cally stood there, arms dangling down his sides, hands coarse and spotty and useless, as if nothing existed beyond the walls of his skull.

"Is that supposed to make me agree to kill a woman I hadn't heard of till two minutes ago?"

"That's for you to decide." Cally's eyes snapped to his, some of their former light restored. "If you won't, maybe I'll find another way. Maybe I won't. But if you want to see the White Tree for yourself, the road leads through Narashtovik."

Dante caught Blays before he disappeared the following morning and arranged to have lunch with him down by the clearing with the stream that ran a couple hundred yards from Cally's forgotten old shrine. Hours later, they sat down in the tall grass in that cool November light, listening to the stream gurgle through the rocks. It was the first time since their arrival they'd been by themselves, free of Cally and Robert bossing them around and making jokes and story references Dante almost but couldn't quite understand. As he and Blays swore and laughed at each other's insults, Dante realized he always acted differently when he was around the adults, as if he had to be his smartest and most sophisticated or else they'd stop listening to him altogether, and it was some time before he could make himself interrupt their breezy mood with what he'd come here to say to Blays in the first place.

"Something's going on out there," Dante said after a short lull following the laughter that had followed an unbelievably obscene joke from Blays.

Blays cocked his head. "I don't hear anything."

"I mean, out *there*," Dante said, gesturing his palms up away from each other to take in the woods and the sky. "Something violent."

"If you're talking about life," Blays said with light annoyance, "that started a long time ago." He bit into the leg of a rabbit he and Robert had caught the day before. Dante shook his head and tried to look serious.

"There's going to be a Fourth Scour or something. Cally says we might be able to help him stop it."

"And you trust Cally?"

"You don't?" Dante said with honest surprise. Blays shrugged at him. "It's not just him," Dante went on. "I don't know what you heard while you were in the clink, but it was all over the streets. There's riots down in Bressel. Other places, too. People are getting hurt."

"City people riot over everything," Blays said. He plucked some grass and tossed it at Dante one blade at a time. "One day they're rioting over how it's too hot. The next day they're back in the streets about how it's not too hot enough."

"We'd have to go to Narashtovik. It's on the north coast of Gask."

"That far?" Blays examined him. "Do you want to go?"

"I don't know," Dante said, and found that though those words hid a sea of desires and doubt, they were nonetheless true. "Do you?"

Blays took a last bite from his drumstick and lobbed it into the fast, shallow waters of the stream.

"Whatever you want," he said. "If you think we need to go, we'll go."

Dante nodded. "If we're going, we should leave tomorrow. Waiting will just make things worse."

"I'll tell Robert."

"Think he'll take it okay?"

"I think he'll come with us," Blays said, and Dante could only nod again, silenced by an emotion he couldn't grasp and wouldn't want to put into words. Blays popped up, brushed grass from his legs and dirt from his seat. "Don't tell him I told you, but he thinks you're on to something." He laughed, ruffling his own hair. "He wants to hop onboard your wagon before it rolls off for the land of mead and honey-haired women."

"This needs to stop," Dante said, then laughed too. "I'm serious."

He went back to the shrine and started packing. With little else to do and possessing the brand of spirit that couldn't devote a whole day to any one thing, Blays and Robert had hunted more meat than the four of them had been able to keep up with. Most of it was salting in the cellar, the rest was hanging from a lattice of branches they'd arranged to soak up the smoke from the outdoor firepit and that so far hadn't been molested by a passing bear. Dante gathered up as much as he thought wouldn't spoil on the trip (the nights had been flirting with freezing, giving his guess a lot of leeway) and stuffed into a sack the meat and some of the breads and vegetables Cally had smuggled in from the city twice a month. He gathered his things, his candles and books and papers and knives, and leaned them inside his bedroom door. In the morning, he'd be able to leave as soon as they'd eaten. Cally bumped into him as he was making a final scan of the temple, sized him up, and offered him a slight, solemn nod.

At dinner they ate a great haunch of the boar Robert had brought in days before and drank stream water so cold it stung Dante's teeth. The other three shared a bottle of wine Cally dredged up from the cellar, then a second, then Robert slugged down most of a third. Dante sipped from the same glass all night, rising only when Blays and Robert staggered off to their respective rooms to sleep it off.

"This is the right choice," Cally said then.

"So you say."

"I won't pretend to know how to measure the value of one life against another. But there are times when it's easier than others."

"A few weeks ago I didn't know about any of this," Dante said. He rubbed his eyes. "It still doesn't feel real."

"The legends make it sound grand to be swept into causes you have no part in, but in truth it's grim and it's unfair and it wears you down." Cally stood and moved around the table to put a hand on Dante's shoulder. The skin of his fingers was a lusterless white, flaky from the dry air. Dante didn't move. "Take comfort you won't be alone out there. And that, whatever happens, you're doing something that will keep all these people down here safe."

Though he didn't expect to find any rest in his immediate future, Dante managed to fall asleep in little more than an hour after he laid down. They rose shortly after dawn, gathered up the sacks Dante'd packed, slung them over the three draft horses they'd stolen the day of the Execution That Wasn't and since bought saddles for through the anonymous agents Cally used as go-betweens for his needs. They took up their weapons and their trinkets and their charms. Cally took an old sword from the shrine's walls and gave it to Dante, deflecting his protests with the advice there's nothing more dependable than a sharp hunk of metal. They ate a light, quick meal, then sat in the saddle in the cold morning light outside the shrine, saying their thanks and goodbyes to the old man.

"One last thing," Cally said when they'd hit that final silence between when they'd said everything they needed and when they were ready to ride off. He fumbled in his robes, then produced a wax-sealed letter. "It's for an old friend of mine. He's a monk by name of Gabe. You'll find him in the monastery of Mennok in the town of Shay. It's pretty much on your route."

Dante took it from him and tucked it under his doublet. His gloom from the previous night had evaporated with the daylight and the knowledge they were on their way to somewhere he'd never imagined he'd see. There was a big horse underneath him. The air smelled like damp earth and was lightly cold from a rain during the night, but he knew he'd warm up once they started moving. He was glad, for the moment, to be who and where he was.

"Can't you just fly it to him on the wings of a talking crow?" he said down to the old man.

"Good gods. Just get him the damn letter."

"I'm beginning to doubt you can do anything at all."

"Shut up," Cally mused. He scratched the thick gray beard on his cheek. "Don't leave town before he's read it. He may be some help. He used to be a fairly useful man." He bit his lip. "If he hasn't died, of course. It's been a while."

"We'll die of old age ourselves if we don't head out soon," Blays said. Robert chuckled.

"Then get the hell out," Cally said. "I'll finally be able to read in peace without it sounding like a war outside my window."

"We'll miss you too, old goat," Blays called over his shoulder as they started into the woods. Dante turned in the saddle and waved to the old man. Cally held up his time-gnarled palm and watched them go. A cloud passed over the sun, throwing him into shadow. Dante cupped his hands to his mouth and quacked.

9

Twelve hundred miles, Dante figured. Between winding roads and the detour to Shay, they could count on twelve hundred miles of travel. Honestly, it sounded insane. It sounded like the kind of trip you started off expecting to lose a third of your men along the way. He shifted his seat, trying to get used to the horse beneath him. The way it bumped, the way its muscles rose with more strength than his entire body. Twelve hundred miles of getting jostled around by this monster. Pilgrims and caravans would take a season to cover that much ground. Robert had looked at the horses and the route and projected they could do it in six weeks of steady travel — not counting snow.

Snow could change everything. None had stuck around Whetton yet, meaning they could count on the first two hundred miles to be clear at that moment. The slow rise of the plains could be completely different; so could the weather in the valley in the five-odd days it would take to reach those plains. The valley almost always saw snow at some point, though some years the Lower Chanset didn't get dusted until the full thrall of January. Already it was late November. Unless they could gallop so fast they turned back time, there would be snow by the time they reached the north. In that sense, it wasn't worth thinking about: it wasn't a matter of if, but when, and whether they walked or rode hell for leather, they would see snow before it was through. All they had to worry about was reaching the pass through the Dunden Mountains before it got snowed in.

Cally's shrine was about twenty miles west of Whetton. They

traveled northeast, meaning to intercept the northern road a safe distance above town and follow it as far as they could into the mountains. They rode with no particular hurry, both to give Dante and to a lesser extent Blays the chance to learn how their horses reacted to their commands before trying anything fancy (like moving faster than a walk). Dante had done some riding back at Cally's, but by and large the ways of a horse were as foreign to him as those of the neeling.

Twelve hundred miles. Plenty of time to figure out just how crazy all this was.

He pulled his cloak around his shoulders. It had grown thinner and more ragged since the night he'd stolen it off the body in Bressel, poorly mended and open to the wind. They'd need sturdier clothes. Take care of it all in Shay: Cally's friend, nice thick cloaks and blankets, fresh food, maybe even a night in a real bed.

Blackbirds and robins and crows twittered and coughed. Squirrels and rabbits and larger things crackled among the fallen leaves. The sun swung up into the sky and pierced through the bare branches, warming their bodies. They didn't talk much. No sense throwing out their voices on the first day.

"Good to be out of that place, huh?" Robert said after an hour or so.

"I was starting to get the stir-crazies," Blays said.

"Something off about the old man." Robert let the sunlight fall on his upturned face. "Appreciate his help, but I won't miss him."

"He helped more than you know," Dante said.

"No doubt about that. Just not my sort of company."

A stream crossed their path two-odd miles on and they dropped down to drink and let their horses do the same. Dante watched Robert walk up to the stream and stoop to scoop water into his mouth.

"You don't walk funny," he said. Blays and Robert exchanged a look and a laugh. Fine. Dante drank, flexing his fingers against the cold.

"It's just a name," Robert said.

"Pretty weird one."

They stretched their legs, then got back in the saddle. Robert spent a few minutes rubbing his beard.

"I'm thirty-some years old now," he said to no apparent cue. "Couldn't say for sure. Split the difference and call it 35. Back when I was a young man, a couple years your elder, I'd been at the pub long enough to be feeling right when I stood up to go tap my private keg and found my right leg was completely numb. Been sitting on it a while, I guess, and when I tried to walk it just dragged along behind me. Couldn't feel a damn thing." He chuckled, running his fingers through his beard. "Earlier that night I'd thrown some lip at a man I'd just met. One of those loud, boastful men who's always watching to make sure everyone's watching him as he goes on about the strength of his arm and the speed of his blade and how big the tits on the last one he banged. The kind you want to stave in their head just to shut them up. I'd just offered my opinion on the likelihood of a canine presence in his maternal lineage, but him being that kind of man and all, he didn't see the restraint I'd employed to keep our differences purely verbal.

"Well, fellow sees me stand up, or more rightly *hobble* up, between the booze and my leg, and then limp around the room trying to get back the feeling. He sees his chance: not only am I drunk, but evidently I'm lame. Chance to take back his honor without sticking out his neck. Even a man fundamentally scared inside as him thinks he can best a lamed drunk.

"He comes up and at once I see the murder in his eyes. Spend enough time at pub and you develop an eye for that pretty quick. Anyway, without a word I've drawn my sword and he's drawn his and we're squaring off. He's dancing this way and that, right and left, taking pokes at me, trying to get me off my balance. I've got half a mind to what he's up to by then and bide my time, letting my leg wake back up. Drunk as I was I knew I wasn't in any real danger. He was decent at best, but I was good. Damn good.

"Doesn't take long before my leg's tingling and just a few seconds after that it's hurting a bit but I knew I could move it just fine. I kept up the act, shuffling around the same spot, letting him build his spirit, and soon enough he's taking this big swing meant to open my defense for his backstroke. I jump aside like quicksilver on a griddle and strike for his heart."

The man chuckled some more, gazing back through the years.

It was clear he'd told this story often. Dante guessed this pause was part of the telling.

"Well, for however clear my thinking, however swift my sword, I was still about half a mug short of stinking, and my blade just went through a lung and a few other parts that will kill you but not exactly clean like a good whack through the ticker. I kicked the oaf off my sword and he fell down and gave me a look like I'd cheated him at cards.'You're no cripple!' he gasped.'And you're no swordsman!' I roared back.

"The crowd cheered and rolled him out in the street to die somewhere else. They bought me so many rounds I don't remember much else. Just when I woke up the next afternoon and slouched back in all scared for the watch the crowd cheered again and hailed out'Robert Hobble!'"

Dante joined their laughter. Robert hadn't meant what he'd said about Cally, he'd decided. He'd just been talking.

"Tried that trick a few times after that," Robert added after they'd settled down. "Every time I realized I'd caused some serious trouble, which wasn't half so often as when I'd actually gotten in the stew. Then I'd catch that look in their eyes and I'd start limping around like a man without a foot. Men are like dogs when they see a man's got something wrong. They'll tear him apart just for being broken. If you can get them to come at you thinking you're somehow less of a man, you'll live a very long time."

"Didn't they catch on after a while?" Dante said.

"Sure did," Robert said. He winked at Dante. "Every man in every pub in Whetton knows my name now. These days when I insult them, they just laugh it off. Imagine that, I have to leave my home town just to get in a fight!"

"It's a cruel world," Dante said.

It wasn't hard going, but it was slow going. The horses were used to clear fields and plowed dirt and hadn't yet loosened up to the disorderly rubble of a forest floor. Dante kept his eyes sharp for sign of the road. Once they reached it they would be nearly 2% done with their trip. Fifty times as long as that and they'd be in Narashtovik. They'd hardly been in the saddle for any time at all. Fifty times nothing was still nothing, wasn't it?

Robert stopped them for lunch a little after noon. They tore at strips of salted rabbit, gnawed on lumps of bread that still had some give to them. Dante wandered off a ways to urinate. On the way back he saw a gleam of white within the grass. He knelt beside it. Bones. Sharp teeth. Something small, a cat or a ferret. Just a little dirty black fur sticking to the delicate sweep of ribs. He reached down and brushed away the fur. It was dry as old hay.

He could see one of the horses nibbling a tuft of grass back where they'd stopped but couldn't see Blays or Robert. He got out his knife, wondered what he was doing, and dimpled his left thumb until a tiny blot of blood sprung up on its end. He wiped it along that knobbly white spine. Black flecks leached from the earth and onto the skeleton. The bones shifted as if in a stiff wind and then the thing was on its feet, narrow skull pointing its sockets at his. He grasped it under the ribs (tendonless, fleshless, how did the legs and paws stay stuck to the body?) and stuffed it in the deepest pocket of his cloak. It hung against his body with a cold weight. Dante brushed off his knees and rejoined the others. They were waiting for him, already mounted.

"Find anything interesting?" Blays called down from his horse.

"That's gross." Dante pulled himself up, careful not to crush the slender construct against his body. He ducked the low claws of branches. The trees were getting shorter, he thought. Younger. Within a mile they could see the road. A hundred yards out, a grassy gap in the midst of the woods.

"You boys see anything odd down there?" Robert murmured, lowering his head to peer through the skein of branches.

"Yeah," Blays said. "Traffic."

"It's a *road*," Dante said.

"It's ten, fifteen miles from Whetton," Robert said, tracing the road as it arced to the south. "How many people you seen pass in the last thirty seconds?"

"I don't know. Ten?"

"Where were they going?"

Dante inhaled. What did that mean? Was he supposed to be able to read their thoughts? What had Blays been telling them? He was right about to say something nasty about the nature of roads when he saw it.

"North," he said. "They're all going north."

"Funny, isn't it?"

They watched a while longer. The traffic didn't slow. Dante stopped counting after fifty. Robert raised his eyebrows at them and nudged his horse forward. They cleared the last line of trees and angled their horses down the shallow bank leading to the wide, well-packed road. A few of the people looked up with dirty, sooty faces. Dante glanced north. They speckled the road like rabbit droppings, going on until the path curved and was swallowed by forest.

"Maybe we should keep overland," he said. "There were an awful lot of witnesses at the hanging." He gave Blays a look. "They might even know our names."

"I think they've got worse worries than fugitives," Robert said. He nodded south toward Whetton. Great gray columns of smoke billowed into the air, forming a hazy cloud in the clear skies.

"Perhaps the chimneysweeps are getting a late start," Blays said.

Dante nudged his horse forward and flagged down one of the men on foot.

"What's going on down there?"

"A party," the man said without looking up. "The kind with fire and burning instead of wine and gifts." He continued right on by.

"It seems," Dante said, glancing significantly between the other two, "the city is on fire."

"Hey!" Blays called, moving his horse to block the path of an angry-looking man with a sword. "What happened?"

"Oh, that?" the man said, turning to the mountains of smoke as if he'd just noticed. "Someone smoking a pipe in bed again."

"Have I gone insane?" Dante said.

Blays bit his tongue. "Let's pretend it's them for now."

"We're on horses, you dummies," Robert said. "That makes us look rich." He hopped out of the saddle and waved at a pair of men coughing and leaning on each other's shoulders. "Damn city torched up, did it? Viceroy catch someone squeezing his daughter's ass and go on the rampage?"

"That would have been worth it," one of the men grinned. The pair stopped and swayed in the road, wiping grime from their faces.

"Some riders showed up at dawn, way I heard it," the second

man said. "They couldn't have done all that, though."

"Are you forgetting that enormous mob?" the first said. "I haven't seen one like that since the False Succession."

"Hear what they were up in arms about?" Robert said.

"I've *heard* plenty of things."

"Anything you believe?"

"No," the second put in. "Just the trumpets of swift-wing'd rumor—they're upset about the viceroy's cut of the grain, or all the Colleners been moving in, or their wives' ankles are too fat. Maybe the end is finally nigh and it's time for the guilty to pay for their crimes."

"Can't be that," Robert said. "We're still running free, aren't we?"

"Taim kind of dropped the stick on that one, huh?" the first man said.

"Well, nobody's perfect," the second shrugged. The three men chuckled.

"I'll tell you what I saw," the first one said, squaring his shoulders. "I was walking down Balshag Street when all these people started boiling out of the temples. I can understand coming out of church angry, but they had weapons, right? Swords and torches and flails. There was no one sect, it was all of them. It looked like they were fighting each other—a priest of Gashen was punching another man in a red robe, anyway. That's when I started running. I don't know what's going on, but it started in the temples."

"What's new," Robert muttered. They exchanged agreements and spent a silent moment gazing at the smoke hovering above the southern forest. "Well, we'd best be on our way."

"Say, what's your name, friend?" the first man asked.

Robert leaned in. "Robert Hobble," he said from behind his hand.

"And I'm Lyle's no-account brother," the first said.

"The one who still lived with their mom while Lyle was out talking to the gods," the second added.

Robert began to walk in a stiff-legged circle, mumbling curses like a confused drunk. He stumbled, waving his arms.

"I thought they'd hanged you," the first man said, folding his arms.

"Never underestimate the power of bureaucratic incompetence," Robert said. He reached into a pocket of his cloak and shook out a couple time-tarnished chucks. "Here, friends. Don't let that trouble catch up with you."

They doffed their caps. The second bit his lip and grinned.

"You off to clear it all up, then?"

"Naw," Robert said, raising a doubting brow. "Too much anarchy that way lies. People with no respect for the law scare me."

They laughed again, then clasped Robert's hand and started back down the road. Robert grinned and pulled himself up on his horse.

"Well, as usual, it's the clergy's fault," he said.

"That's what we're going to stop," Dante said. "We're 2% of the way there."

"Sounds horrible when you put it like that." Robert sighed, then brushed off the mood like dirt on his sleeve. "I suppose that means we ought to hurry."

"Indeed," Dante said, looking north on the hundreds of miles of mountains and rivers and snowfields between them and the dead city. "Let's haul ass."

Night came quickly. They'd made another twenty miles along the road, then spent the twilight penetrating far enough into the woods to where they could light a fire without drawing the attention of the bedraggled masses that kept coming out of Whetton. The sun disappeared behind the trees and hills of the west and they brought in the kindling and roasted some of the uncured meat they'd taken along. Considering all they'd done was ride, Dante was shockingly tired, saddle-raw aching. More than a month of this to go. Whetton was already burning. He had no idea whether the local militias would be enough to quash this thing, whatever it was. This unrest and whatever they were trying to accomplish with it had roots as long as a river. They'd hidden for years, keeping their memory alive in the minds of the people, and finally, for reasons he couldn't guess, they'd taken this thing back to the open. They were ready. Dante had no delusions they'd ride into Narashtovik in a few weeks to find Samarand and all her people had fled to exile or been executed for their perfidy against the southlands. The fight would only get bloodier before order showed its sheepish face.

Dante hadn't told the others the full nature of their mission, that they were traveling a thousand miles to kill some old woman. He'd just said they had to get to Narashtovik and go from there. Neither Blays nor Robert were the kind to get too worried for details or complicate things with their own plans; he had the impression they thought of life as something like the act of riding backwards on a pell-mell horse—they could guess where they were likely to head next by the things they saw whipping past their heads, but who could say for sure, and in any event they'd certainly be there soon, so what was the point of turning around and taking up the reins? The horse had done well enough so far. Why mess with a good thing?

They made low talk around the fire. Robert thought they'd made good time despite the slower trek through the woods and the careful path they'd had to weave around the foot traffic on the road. He looked up to the flat sheet of clouds that had rolled in during the evening and grunted.

"Daylight's a little scarce this time of year," he said. "So long as we've got a road to follow, we ought to get our start before dawn."

Dante watched the subdued fire burn against the darkness. "If you think it's safe."

"What? Marching before dawn?" Blays crooked the corner of his mouth. "Growing boys need rest. If not for me, think of the horses."

"Sun sets by six," Robert said. "There's no reason to stay up past eight. That should give you plenty of time to rest your weary bones."

"Eight o'clock? Even Cally burned the candle later than that. And he'd make a dead log look spry."

"Every second you spend yapping's one more second you don't spent sleeping," Robert said. He wiggled down next to the fire and pulled his cloak over his face. "Goodnight."

Dante followed suit, settling down upon the dirt and rocks. Hard to believe he'd been in a bed the night before.

"What a terrible thing, when what's right is overruled by what's popular," Blays said.

"I said goodnight. Third time comes stamped on my knuckles."

He heard Blays mumble something impolite, then the scratch of leaves and the fwoop of cloth being thrown over his head. Six weeks of this, Dante thought. Nothing to it.

He woke to something nibbling on the ends of his fingers. He brushed at it feebly, three-quarters asleep. It ceased for a blessed second, then bit down hard. Dante drew his hand to his chest, inhaling sharply. Before his eyes snapped open he thought he could see his own face. He gasped and bolted upright and pulled the cloak off his head. By the faint moonlight escaping the net of clouds and the fire's red embers he saw the skeleton of the small predator reared on its hind legs, front paws bent at the wrist. Its pale head bobbed. He rubbed his eyes, caught another glimpse of himself, this time from the perspective of something looking up at the puzzled oval of his face. He thought he heard two separate winds whispering back and forth. Again he closed his eyes and again he saw through something else's.

The *Cycle* had not mentioned that.

The thing scampered off a couple feet, then turned and ducked its head. It spun away and disappeared into the undergrowth. If Dante was meant to follow it, the thing didn't have a brain in its skull. Instead he closed his eyes, planting his palms firm against the intense vertigo of what the little beast saw as it rushed along six inches above the dirt. It parted the grass and scrabbled over roots and rocks, fast as a man at a run and quiet as a bird on the breeze. He could hear no more than the most minor rustles of its claws—and through its own ears, he realized, though it didn't have any. For just a second he opened his eyes and heard nothing at all.

It streaked along through the brush. After no more than a minute it stopped short, creeping forward until the fuzzy impression Dante received from its eyeless sockets fell upon a circle of six men in hushed conversation. It was too dark to make out faces or even tell one from another.

"Are you sure it's him?" he heard through the predator's ears.

"I can feel it. Can't be anyone else."

"There's three sets of tracks."

"What, are you scared? They're asleep."

"We were told there'd be two. The Unlocking must have driven ten thousand men into these woods. It might not be them."

"And if it's not, what's three more bodies? We need that book. The book is the key. We can't let them slip away. Larrimore would kill us. I'm not joking. If we come back without it he'll rip out our guts and laugh. He won't even bind our hands because he thinks it's funny when you try to stuff them back in."

"Weeping Lyle."

"You said it, man. Get yourselves together. Not a word until they're dead."

Dante heard steel rasp from leather. He popped open his eyes, breaking the contact, and shook the shoulders of the others.

"Go'way," Blays mumbled.

"*Shut up!*" Dante whispered. Robert awoke soundlessly, sword appearing in his hand. "Six men," Dante said. "They're coming for us. They think we're asleep."

"Then let's not burst their illusion," Robert whispered. "Don't make a move till it's too late for them to fall back."

"But there's six of them."

"What are we going to do, run? Only hope now's to surprise them instead."

Dante nodded, throat dry as sand. He eased out the old, no-frills sword Cally'd given him and pulled his cloak up to his eyes. The fire was nothing but glowing embers. He waited in the darkness, eyes slitted, ears straining. What if he'd been wrong? He dropped his left palm to his blade and slid it along its edge, cheek twitching against the sharp bite of cold steel. Blood seeped into his closed fist, warm and wet, and with it came the shadows.

Leaves crunched softly as the men filtered into the camp. From between his eyelashes Dante saw their swords glinting in the emberlight. They fanned out, splitting between the three prone forms, two on each. How close could he let them get? Fifteen feet, then ten, boots ruffling the dirt, eyes bright in the shadows of their faces. His throat tensed against a scream. They were standing over him then, looking down on him, processing how they'd turn him into a lump of lifeless meat. One of them raised his blade and Robert's voice roared up then and Dante leapt to his feet. Robert rolled away from the downward slice of a sword and in the same motion lashed his own across the calf of the attacker. The man dropped with a shout of shock and pain.

The two men on Dante cried out, then pressed forward. Dante leveled his sword in front of him and flicked the blood pooled in his left hand at the nearer of the two. Where it landed the shadows followed, sizzling against the man's skin and sinking to his innards. The man sunk without a word. The remaining attacker made a quick thrust and Dante fell back, offering a weak counter. The man deflected it, eyes grim in the starlight.

From the corner of his eye he saw Blays retreat to Robert's side as Robert curled past a thrust and laid open the man's back. A flicker from Dante's front and he jerked up his sword to prevent his head from being struck from his shoulders. Someone screamed and a gorge of fire opened up at the spot he'd last seen Blays and Robert. Steel clashed in a staccato smack of swings and backswings. Dante dropped to a knee to dodge another blow. His attacker hefted his blade, then grimaced and screamed as the skeletal predator sank its razor teeth into his hamstring. Dante gripped his hilt with both hands and slashed out as short and fast as he could manage. The first hit cut open the man's forearm and he dropped his sword. The next three put him down.

He turned. He didn't see Robert. Blays faced off against a tall, long-limbed man dressed in the plain black uniform of the others and a caped figure draped in chainmail and trimmed in silver thread. Except for a dancing white flare on Dante's eyes, the fire that had flashed up moments before was gone. He saw Robert then, stretched out on top of the two men he'd slain. He wasn't moving. Blays unleashed a flood of obscenities and charged toward the mailed man, bowling back the one remaining swordsman. Dante felt a cold pulse of nether from the mailed man. The man pointed at Blays and Dante planted his feet and struck the attacker with a column of shadow. The small dark sphere in the man's hand evaporated with an angry hiss and he yanked his hand back, shaking it, glaring at Dante with eyes full of unfairness.

Blays and the last swordsman had squared off, trading blow for blow, but the swordsman's size and range fell back in the face of Blays' rage. He swung heedlessly, sword whipping through the air with the full strength of his arm, and just as Dante thought the boy had overextended he drew his sword level with his ear, muscling the swordsman's downward counter behind his head, then stabbed straight forward into the man's neck. The man gurgled blood and fell face first into the embers.

"How did you know we were coming?" the man in chainmail asked in a tone of open surprise. Dante answered with a spike of nether that would have split the body of any other man. This man's face creased as he cupped his hands as if to catch a ball and split the shadows to either side of his body. His nostrils flared. "Who taught you that?"

"You learn fast when someone's trying to kill you every week," Dante said. He saw Blays advancing, sword angled from his body.

"Rest easy then. This will be the last attempt we need."

He swung his arms at Blays as if he were heaving a sack of wheat and it was all Dante could do to divert the fires to boil away into the sky. Blays bent like a sapling in a gale but somehow kept his balance enough to swing a swift, light backhand that clipped off the last knuckle of the man's middle finger. For the first time in the battle Dante saw fear cross the man's face.

"What was that?" he cried, skipping back a couple steps to try another strike. Blays stepped forward, wary as a cat. Dante held his breath and focused on a point six feet above the man's head. If the man went for Blays now, he could do nothing to stop it. Blays jabbed like a fencer and the man dropped back again. The two were too close for Dante to release the thing above him. The tendril of energy between himself and the summons felt tight as a string tied around his heart. Blays chopped at the man and he actually held out his arm. The sword struck it below the wrist and the metal of the blade and the tight rings of the armor flashed like a storm. Blays yelped and slung away his sword, stumbling back. The man smiled, curled his bloody fingers to finish off the boy, and that was when Dante released it, pouring on the nether till the sheer drain forced him to his knees.

A swirling pillar of white fire leapt down from the point of his focus. An all-consuming crackle roared through the camp like the sky-high bonfires the people lit on Alden's Eve to remind the sun of its strength. In that instant the man's eyes flicked up and his brow wrinkled like he'd splashed mud on a fresh robe. He bellowed and clenched his fists and the pillar faltered but kept on coming, smashing him into the ground. It disappeared as quickly as it had come, wisps of smoke trailing up from a half dozen tiny fires on the man's cloak. Dante took a hesitant step, flinching when the man raised his head.

"Well, now you've done it," the man said, skin sloughing from the left side of his face. "You've gone and killed Will Palomar."

His eyes widened and his breath rattled away. The body relaxed, flopped back against the dirt.

"You've got to help him! Quick!" Blays said.

"He was trying to kill me!"

"Robert, you dunderhead!"

Dante took a woozy step. Not again, he thought, but he clenched his jaw and forced away the gray stealing over his eyes. He crossed to Robert's limp body. Blood wicked through the man's cloak. Dante couldn't tell if it was his or from the two men dead beneath him.

His head pounded like the last time he'd been drunk, both the daze of the during and the misery of the after. He balled his fists and rubbed his eyes. He lowered his ear to Robert's nose and heard shallow, uneven breathing. Half his cloak was singed; bright white blisters stood out on his cheek. Dante pulled back Robert's cloak and saw a deep gash along his ribs leaking blood down his side. Some of the hair had been burned from his chest. Dante wiped his nose.

"What happened?" he said.

"What does it look like? They damn well stabbed him!"

"How bad did he get burnt?"

"Can't you tell?" Blays said, crouching down beside him and clasping his hands together.

"I don't know what I'm doing! I'm not a physician!"

"Well help him, damn it!"

"Okay!" Dante roared. He flexed his fingers and called the shadows. He sensed a reluctance in their substance—a reticent anger, even, for whatever sense that made—but he pressed back until they folded to his will. Remembering how he'd shucked off their weariness in the chase through the woods, he concentrated on the source of Robert's bleeding. For a gross moment he thought he could see beneath the skin to red muscle and white bone. As if it were his own, he could feel the sick tickle of flesh knitting back together. His eyelids fluttered. He forced himself to keep going, arms quaking, chest heaving, then felt himself fading and fell back on his ass, gasping for breath.

"Is he fixed?" Blays said, ripping the shirt off a dead man and daubing it over the blood that had washed down Robert's ribs. Dante tried to say "Kind of" but choked instead. He bent forward, coughing into a closed fist. Robert started coughing too, spitting blackish blood past his lips. He groaned, but his eyes stayed shut.

"Is he going to make it?" Blays said.

"How should I know?" Dante battled down an inappropriate yawn. "I am so tired right now."

"He's moaning. Good sign or bad?"

"I think ideally there should be neither bleeding nor moaning." Dante pressed his palms against his eyes. "What are we going to do here?"

Blays' eyes snapped to his face. "What are you suggesting?"

"I'm *asking*."

"I don't know," Blays said. He laced his hands together and huffed into them. "He can't travel like this."

Dante lowered himself to his elbows. "What if they've got someone else?"

"Then we fight them, too. How did you know they were coming?"

"I heard one of them cough," Dante said. He glanced around the fire, shut his eyes. The skeletal animal was gone.

Blays' eyes drifted toward Dante's pack. "How did they find us?"

"I crept up on them while they were talking. One of them said they'd tracked us. They were confused we were on horseback."

"How would they know?" Blays scratched the top of his head. "Maybe someone recognized us on the road. Passed the word."

"Gods know there were enough eyes out there."

"I think he's doing better," Blays said cautiously. "His breathing isn't all ragged any more. That was scary."

"That's good."

"Were you just asleep?"

"No," Dante blinked. He struggled to sit up. "If we try to ride, we could kill him. I don't think I could ride right now, either. That's not a lot of options."

Blays nodded, gazing into the low fire. "Risk it?"

"I think we've got to."

"I guess I'll take first watch."

"Okay."

"I'm going to wake you up if he looks any worse," Blays warned.

"Okay."

"Dante's a stupid idiot."

"Okay. What?"

"I said go to sleep already," Blays said. He shredded another shirt and pressed it to Robert's wound.

"Okay," Dante said, and sleep folded over him like a glove.

Dante sat in the dark and waited for the dawn. Long stretches of silence were broken by the night-noises of the woods, hoots and screeches and the furtive shuffling of small animals. At least there was no wind. He couldn't have taken the wind in the trees.

Blays had dragged off the bodies while he'd been asleep. There was that, too. The ground was thick with the shine of dried blood. Clouds obscured the moon and stars. He had no idea how long he'd been asleep. It felt like fifteen minutes, twenty, but Blays had assured him it had been three or four hours. Robert remained asleep. His breathing and pulse sounded...well, they existed. He didn't know what should sound good for a man who should probably be dead. Blays had stoked up the fire, but he didn't think that was causing Robert's sweaty brow or flushed face. Dante ate from the saddlebags and drank a full skin of water, frowning over the unconscious man. He meant to give the nether another shot once he'd absorbed a little food.

He didn't know how to feel about the lie he'd told Blays. For all he knew the attackers had followed their tracks. To find them in the first place, though, the mailed man who'd called himself Will Palomar had followed their feel. The book's feel. Dante's feel. He didn't know which; maybe it was both. He did know their mission was too important to threaten by telling Blays the truth. He needed Blays, needed Robert, needed their eyes and their arms if he was going to get to Narashtovik. They needed him, too, didn't they? Robert would be dead now without his aid. They'd all be dead if he hadn't seen the men plotting their attack. If he hadn't sprung them from the gallows. Not that that should buy their loyalty, exactly, but there was a give and a take here, he wasn't keeping them around for his own ends alone. In any event, they were big boys. They'd made their decision to stick with him. If they thought things were getting too dangerous, they could make the decision to leave.

A couple birds started chirping. A few bugs whirred and thrummed, but most had already died in the frosts. The survivors wouldn't last much longer.

At the first touch of dawn Dante rose, walked around the fire, worked his blood back into his limbs. He still felt tired, but no longer painfully so. He knelt over Robert's unconscious body and closed his eyes and emptied his mind. When he sent the shadows to the long brown scab on his chest he felt nothing. He saw no change in the flesh. He closed his eyes again, reached out to the wound again, but it was as if the nether were passing under a bridge and disappearing before it reached the other side. He set his mouth and tried at least to assuage the fever. He touched Robert's brow. It still felt hot. He sighed.

Dawn broke, gray and gradual. He let Blays sleep. It was clear they wouldn't be going anywhere until Robert had woken or croaked. Maybe it was the false hope of the daylight, but he doubted the temple men would even know their latest agents had failed for at least a few days. There was no use punishing Blays with sitting around waiting for something to happen when he could hold things down for himself. For once Dante didn't feel like reading. He watched the fire burn and thought about the summers in the village.

"What's going on? Why does hell look exactly the same as earth?"

Dante jerked his head. Robert's eyes were open, crinkled in pain.

"You're awake."

"You're brilliant." Robert lifted his head and looked over his bandaged body. "How'd you get the wizard?"

"I smote him with fire," Dante said.

Robert frowned at him. "Can never tell if the youth of today are being serious. A weakness of character, I think."

"You're right. I played dead until he ran away."

Robert's arms shook as he tried to sit up. He lifted his shoulders clear of the ground, then fell back, squeezing his eyes shut for a moment after the impact.

"That was unwise," he said.

Dante bit his teeth together. "Stop making things worse. We're already losing time."

"You've always got more time," Robert said. He chewed his beard. "Well, until you don't."

"Indeed," Dante said. He decided against waking Blays. It would help if at least one of them kept in fighting condition. Dante felt like he'd been sewn up in a sack and beaten for three days straight. He could probably ride, but if at that moment a one-armed eight-year-old challenged him to a fight, he'd either run or cheat.

"How's Blays?" Robert asked, as if reading his thoughts.

"Unhurt."

"Is that right." He chuckled. The sound was like gravel grinding together. "Robert Hobble himself gets flambeed by a sorcerer and stabbed by a bumbling bodyguard who only knows to grab the handle of his sword because it's the part that sticks out when it's put away, and that kid comes out without a scratch." He wiped sweat off his forehead and smiled with half his mouth. "There's something wrong with that."

Dante shrugged. "He does seem preternaturally lucky."

"Maybe he's just got good taste in friends." Robert stared at him with pain-hooded eyes. Dante kept quiet. "So what are you, exactly?"

"Why do people keep asking me that?"

"Oh, please."

"I'm a young man! That's all."

"I've known plenty of young men," Robert said, turning his head to face the sky, "and none of them can do anything like what I've seen you do."

Dante hunched up his shoulders. "That's why I'm learning all this. I don't want to be like everyone else."

"Lots of people say that, then ten years later you couldn't pick them out in a crowd." Robert shifted his hips to resettle his weight and stopped at once. He bared his teeth and let out a long breath. "I don't suppose you've got anything for curing sword whacks."

"I already tried," Dante said. Inexplicably, shame stole over his face.

"Ah. Guess the dominion of steel still holds sway, then."

"For now."

Robert chuckled, then clutched himself. "Lyle's holy bastard, that hurts."

"Then don't do it."

"What's cracking *your* acorns?"

"This is just the second day," Dante said. He clenched a handful of leaves, flung them into the fire. "This is supposed to be the easy part."

"And I suppose this is the part where I tell you nothing's easy, as if that's supposed to help." Robert sighed and gingerly folded his hands under his head.

"It just doesn't seem fair."

Robert laughed some more. "Could be worse. You could be me."

Dante nodded, glancing up a moment later. "You doing okay?"

"I've had worse."

"I bet this feels like a joke to you," Dante said, uncertain what he meant by "this."

"For about the last ten years, everything's felt that way."

While Dante was busy trying to gauge if he was serious Blays stirred beneath the folds of his cloak. The boy emerged into the daylight, red-eyed, hair sprung out like a dandelion. He gave the world a sour look and belched.

"You're disgusting," Dante said.

"Shut up." Blays draped his cloak over his head and shoulders and clutched it under his chin so he resembled a clothy mountain or a sack with a face. "What time is it?"

"Time to make me some breakfast," Robert said.

"You're up!"

"In a manner of speaking," he said from his place on the dirt.

Blays swung his face at Dante. "Why didn't you wake me up?"

"You're up now, aren't you?"

"I'd have gotten *you* up."

"And I'd have punched you for it."

Blays jumped up, flapping his cloak against the cold, and wandered around the fire to lean over Robert.

"Does it hurt much?"

"Only always," Robert said.

"I thought you were going to die! You should have seen all the blood! It looked like someone dumped a spittoon on your chest."

Robert closed his eyes and made a noise through his nose. "You know what, forget about breakfast."

"Well, it did," Blays said. He straightened up and his eyes drifted to the tethered horses. "They've settled down a bit."

"Yeah," Dante said. "Moving the bodies may have helped."

"I think they got a little spooked when I was chopping them up." Blays folded his arms at the sudden silence. "What? One of them was moving."

"Well done," Robert said. "Now will you stop recounting the recent horrors and get me some gods damn food?"

"I'm not your maid," Blays said, opening up one of the packs and rummaging around. "How's some bread?"

"Marvelous."

He brought it to Robert, who spent a minute propping himself up before trying a couple bites.

"Bread's a dry substance, you know," Robert said, spitting crumbs.

"Will water sate His Majesty?"

Robert pursed his lips. "If you don't have anything stronger."

"You know we don't," Blays said. He gave Dante a look. "You could get off your ass at some point."

"I'm plotting our next move," he said, twisting a blade of grass between his fingers. "While you're up, grab me a bite?"

"I'm going to spit in it."

"Oh no, don't trouble yourself on my account," Dante said. Robert laughed through his nose and winced. He'd live, but it would be three days before he felt well enough to ride. Three days waiting in the woods while the world moved on and Narashtovik drew three days closer to war. Dante spent each one training with the nether till he was close to passing out, vowing they wouldn't be delayed again. Sooner or later—sooner, according to Cally, and if anyone outside the dead city itself would know, it was him—it would take more than two boys and a drunk to stop what was marching out of the north. It would take an army, if it could be stopped at all. A kingdom could be lost for the wounds to Robert's body and the want of three days. If he hadn't been frustrated enough to punch down a tree, Dante might have laughed.

10

Robert had to stop within a couple hours the day their path resumed and for the first few days their march was broken by an equal time spent resting away from the road. Dante and Blays kept a guard at all times, switching between watch and sleep while Robert slumbered or merely stretched out and waited for the throbbing ache to subside. Dante preferred to eat up the hours with sleep, but sometimes it took an hour or more to slip away. Things would go faster once Robert was better, he told himself. They would lose a few days, but it wouldn't always be these stuttery steps of six or eight stops a day. They would make it in time.

The woods gave way to open grassland peppered with trees in the creases in the land. The road held out. The grass rose to their waists on either side of the rutted dirt, swirling in the winds that swept unbroken from the north, carrying with it the promise of winter. Traffic was heavier than normal, or so Robert said, but nothing like what they'd seen the day Whetton burned. The Chanset forked after three days and they curved along its tributary. The plains rose so imperceptibly they couldn't feel it in their steps, but then the grass gave way to soft, rolling hills blanketed in stubby yellow and gray grasses that shot long-tailed seeds into the air when they led the horses off the road to graze or rest or camp. They lit no fires in the open land; there was talk on the road of a wider struggle, of bands of pike-wielding men marching through the fields. Rumor had the king's legions assembling in a counter on Whetton and encamping outside Bressel. But, according to the few travelers they spoke with, the enemy had no strongholds, no apparent homeland whatsoever, and the militia spent more time leaning on their own pikes than carrying them; the cavalry combed out the glens and ponds around the cities, but found nothing more than the miserable camps of refugees from the cities.

After a week's travel the dirt seemed to crackle under their feet and they saw snow streaking the hills ahead. It was no more than a dusting, two or three days old, and it melted in the sun that stayed strong through the day. As dusk fell the sunlight caught the chimney-smoke of a town. They had passed plenty of villages on the way, dropping in a couple times to purchase food but mostly skirting them entirely, cutting through the open lands until they could reconnect with the road. None seemed under siege. Nor were any more than a few hundred strong resident-wise—dots along the river where two roads crossed or traders found deep water moorings and docked their cargo of grain or hemp or hay or wood. The town they looked on in the buttery sunlight could properly be called a town. It could only be Shay. When they encamped Dante took Cally's letter from his pocket and rubbed his thumb over the sigil-sealed lump of black wax. What did it say? An introduction of Dante to his long friend Gabe? A warning? A plea for aid? He put it back away and dreamed of a city built of the hollowed bones of giants.

They woke early and tramped through the stiff dirt of the road, breath fogging from their noses. Dante pressed his fist against a knot in his lower back. A night in an actual bed or even a thick lump of straw would be a nice thing. A fire, hot food. He liked to think he was too hardy to need such things, and in a way he was already used to the sparer ways of the road, but if they popped up he wasn't about to turn them down. The town grew nearer, resolving itself into individual buildings lining the river. He bared his teeth, realizing he still hadn't told Blays and Robert the full nature of their travel. He meant to go to Narashtovik, they knew, and somehow that could stem the tide of whatever was taking the cities of the south. They didn't know its end would be the killing of a woman. They didn't know he sought a knowledge of the *Cycle* only the dead city might reveal. How did Cally know Gabe? How big a role did he intend the monk to play toward them? If they were old friends, and Dante believed they were, perhaps it would all be spelled out in the letter, and when Gabe questioned him or gave him advice or whatever Cally expected from him, the two he traveled with couldn't help having questions of their own. Dante watched the town grow nearer. He should tell them. Give them the story on his own terms. Act as if he had nothing to hide. But the day wore on, and soon they were too close to stop without looking foolish, and then they rode past huts and the small, squatty homes of full families, and it was too late. They'd meant to reach Shay in six days from Cally's shrine, perhaps a week if they hit a delay. Instead it had taken them till the afternoon of the twelfth day.

Ten thousand people, if he had to guess, and most of the ones they rode by on the way into town gave them looks. Not dirty looks, exactly, but the kind with questions behind their eyes. Rumor had reached them, then, but not battle. They killed a few minutes wandering, turning down progressively broader streets, reminding themselves what housing and other people looked like.

"Fun though this is," Robert said, head following an eaveside painting of a stag's head dipping its tongue into a mug, "it's neither enlightening nor intoxicating, and thus must be said to be beside the point."

"It's probably near a churchyard or some of the other temples," Dante said, glancing down the street. He thought he saw the clean lines of Gashen's red shield a few blocks down.

"Probably," Robert said. He pulled up beside a heap of rags containing a man and eased himself down from his horse. "Well met, good man."

The pile grunted at him. Robert smiled at it, then turned to the saddlebags and extracted a hunk of bread.

"We're looking for the monastery of Mennok," he said, "but all this food's weighing us down. Afraid we'll never make it unless we get rid of it."

"Got anything of a more fluid nature?" the man in the rags said, pulling himself to a sitting position and squinting up at them.

"Ah," Robert said, favoring the cobbles with a wry smile. "That lack is one of the many tragedies we wish to unburden on Mennok's ears."

The ragged man accepted the hunk of bread and snapped it in

half. He munched down a couple bites, glancing between the three of them.

"Been on the road a while?" he said, crumbs flecking from his mouth.

"A fortnight or so," Robert said, taking a bite of the bread he'd kept.

He nodded. "Did you travel through Whetton?"

Dante tensed. Robert bit his lip, as if trying to remember, then jerked up his chin.

"We passed around it about a week ago."

"Is it true? That they burned it to the ground?"

"They?" Dante said.

"The rebels," the man said, frowning. "The black-cloaks."

"It was on fire," Robert granted, "but not to the ground, as such. You'd still recognize the city if you saw it."

The man's whiskered face twisted up. He set his eyes on Dante. "You mean you haven't heard of the rebels? From what I hear all the southland's awash in blood."

"We've been on the road a while," Robert said, cutting Dante off.

"Weren't there others on the roads with you?"

"We're men of the cloth," Robert said, surreptitiously pulling his cloak over his sword. "Our vows allow us to pass words only from necessity."

"Hell's bells! And I've been flying off with the questions," the man said. He forked his fingers in the sign of the Owl of Mennok, gaze drifting between the swords at Dante and Blays' backs. "These must truly be trying days if the monks of the gray god won't travel without steel at their side."

"You have no idea how trying," Blays said, glaring down the causeway.

"The monastery?" Robert said. He placed an arm over the bandages under the mailed vest he'd taken from the body of the sorcerer Dante'd killed.

"Of course," the man said. He pointed them down the street and described a couple turns. "My apologies for delaying you, sirs. Might I ask you to make a prayer for me of Mennok?"

"We'd be some damned awful monks if we wouldn't!" Blays

said.

"Thank you, my son," Robert said, working his way back into the saddle in a careful series of limb-maneuverings meant to minimize stress to the vast scab on his chest. "Your aid will not go unrewarded."

He took the lead, leaving the other two to catch up. Dante spurred on his horse, sending a cluster of men wrapped in debate scattering from his mount's heavy hooves.

"Over the years I've worked out a sort of system of classification for the kinds of questions one may need to ask or hear while on the road," Robert began once they'd made their first turn. "There's the rhetorical and philosophical questions, i.e. the ones you can ignore or maybe nod at if the asker's giving you a look like you should have been paying attention. There's the immediate, practical, and useful questions, i.e.'Where is a good pub?' and'For the love of the gods, man, where's the nearest pub?' And then," he said, raising a finger, "there are the stupid, why-did-I-just-open-my-mouth questions, the kinds that are a fancy way of saying'I'm too dumb to see my next birthday,' such as'Please sir, I'm too drunk to make it to the goldsmith's with all these heavy bags, do you know a safe place I might lie down for an hour?' or'*Who's* been burning all the known world?'" He shot Dante a daggerly gaze. "Guess which one yours was?"

"He won't remember it by tomorrow," Dante said, face prickling with heat.

"You won't either if you wake up with an axe in your brain."

"Am I supposed to be able to understand that?"

"I suppose not. Since evidently you don't even know asking stupid questions tends to get a damn sight more thrown back at you."

"I know that. I was trying to find out if he knew anything about them we didn't," Dante said. His face lit up. "Look, there it is."

The monastery was a tall, narrow structure of dark stone. Its upper windows bore shadowcut glass of what Dante presumed were important scenes from the god's life. Its entrance receded from the street, giving way to a well-tended garden of small shrubs and dead flowers. At the garden's center was the boulder of Mennok, meant to represent his imperturbability, his gravity, the solidity of his pensive presence next to mercurial Carvahal or many-faced Silidus or the crimson rages of Gashen.

"What do we do with our horses?" Blays said. "Hide them under that rock?"

Robert winced as he got down. Dante didn't think it was for his wound. He tied the reins to the open gate at the street entrance and rolled his hands at the boys to hurry it up. They tied their horses and scampered after Robert up to the thick wooden door of the monastery. By the time they got there someone had already opened the door to his knock.

"May I help you?" said a skinny, sallow man little older than Dante.

"We're here to see Gabe," Dante said.

"Brother Gabe is deep in meditation."

"Then he's probably bored," Blays said. "Let us in."

The man smiled. "Focused meditation is the closest we men may come to understanding the wisdom of Mennok."

"How long's he going to be?" Dante asked.

"As long as it takes," the man said, tipping back his head. "Even a meditation on the worms and the dirt may take days to unravel. Especially those kinds, since in thinking we know so much about them in truth we know so little."

Robert squinched up his eyes. "Is there somewhere we might wait? We were sent by an old friend."

"All friends are old," the man said, "for all of us are made of dirt, and what's older than dirt?"

"Rocks?" Blays said.

"But rocks turn into dirt when they're old enough."

"Dirt dust?"

The man opened his mouth, then closed it and raised his brows. "Have you ever considered our order?"

"Can't say I have," Blays said. He wriggled his back. "Got anywhere to sit down? All that riding's put a pain in my ass."

"You can wait in the parlor." The man glanced over their shoulders toward the gates. "I'll have a boy see to your horses."

"Thanks," Robert said. "You just let us know when Gabe wakes up."

"Meditation's the opposite of sleeping."

"Sounds awful," Robert said. He snagged Blays and Dante by the sleeves before the conversation could go on and drew them toward the room the man had indicated. The floor was of slate, the walls painted a steely gray. A statue of a droop-eyed dog sat vigilant in the corner. For all the room's simplicity, it was furnished with padded benches, and they plunked down and stared at each other.

"Doubt Gabe will be like that," Robert said to the look on Dante's face. "Mostly it's you young ones who want to preach at you."

"I don't preach at you," Dante said.

"I meant monks and things," Robert said, waving a hand. "Suppose it can be applied to all youth, now that you mention it."

"*You're* the one always explaining things for hours."

"Because you're too dumb to know things for yourself."

Dante set his mouth and tried to think of a reply.

"You sure Mennok's not the god of death?" Blays said, raising a brow at all the gray and black.

"He was originally just this guy who sits around and mopes," Dante said, examining the walls. "When Arawn was expunged, people did start to look to Mennok about death. But it's not the same."

"Arawn?" Robert asked, face suddenly drawn.

Dante unlatched his teeth from the thumbnail he'd been biting. "You know about Arawn?"

"Enough to be suspicious of the fact you do."

They sat with their thoughts. Maybe a quarter hour went by before the man who'd met them at the door stuck his head around the corner.

"Gabe will see you shortly."

"Good to know the universe has been solved," Blays said. He kicked his legs against the base of the bench and waited some more. "Next time, suppose we can go to Simm's temple instead? Get some apples? Fresh pears? Some—ahh!" He bolted upright as a massive, fur-covered beast lumbered through the door on two legs. Blays fumbled out his sword and held it before him. "Get out! I'll hold it off!"

"Put that away," Robert hissed, barring his arm over Blays'. The thing in the doorway blinked at them. Dante saw human-like eyes in its face, that it wasn't furred but deeply bearded, that the man's whiskers climbed so far up his cheeks they nearly met his eyelashes. "He's a norren, you sack of rocks."

"Boo," the man said. His voice rumbled like the gurgles of the earth. He'd had to duck when he walked through the doorway—six and a half feet, Dante guessed, if not taller, and at least three hundred pounds, though it was hard to tell beneath his loose black cassock. For a moment he couldn't see his ears, then noticed they were just small and round as fresh-cut coins and pressed flat against his densely-haired head.

"A norren?" Blays said.

"From the north," Robert said, smiling with embarrassment at the monk. "Usually."

"Was too cold for my blood," the man said. He smiled, showing broad, flat teeth that looked like they could grind Dante's bones. "You're here to see me?"

"You're Gabe?" Dante said.

"That's right," the norren said.

"We're friends of Cally's. He sent us to you."

"Cally?" Gabe blinked at them.

"The old man," Dante said, biting back further words. He had the notion, reinforced somewhat by the fact he was a hermit, Cally's popularity wasn't great. What if, in a slip of his twilight years, he'd sent them to an enemy instead? Or a friend he'd forgotten he'd quarreled with? Or someone he didn't know in the slightest?

"You know," Blays said. "Lectures a lot. Thinks he's quite funny."

Gabe chewed on his mustache, nodding blankly. Dante reached in his pocket and took out the letter.

"He sent you this."

Gabe's hand reached out. It was large as a plucked chicken.

"Oh," he said, scratching the wax seal. "Cally. It's been a while."

"So you know him," Dante said.

"Yes," Gabe said, showing his teeth and looming forward till he seemed to take up all the room, "and now your fates are sealed."

Blays gasped and went for his blade. Its bright snap cut over

Gabe's barking chuckles.

"I see he's up to no good again, then," the norren muttered. He considered them a moment. "Come with me."

They followed him deeper into the monastery. He glanced balefully at a cell that would barely have room for his shoulders, let alone all of them, then led them up a set of spiral stairs and down a hall into a kind of sitting room or library. A great many books lined the walls, at least, though who knew with pious types. Gabe settled onto a mat, sitting on his heels, and nodded the others into some normal-sized chairs next to the window. An odd, dreary light cut through the smoke-stained figures worked into the glass. Gabe slid his thumb under the seal with a dry crack and unfolded the papers onto his lap. Dante examined the window while Gabe examined the letter. The figures were impressionistic, shadows of men, but he thought the window depicted the scene of Mennok soothing Gashen's anger before he could blast the land with sunfire after he discovered his priest Ennan had lain with his daughter.

"You didn't read this, did you?" Gabe asked once he'd finished a couple minutes later.

"Did the seal look tweaked to you?" Dante said.

"I assume you're a clever lad, if Cally took you up."

"That may be," he said, meeting Gabe's stare, "but however much I may have wished, I didn't read that letter."

Gabe frowned, then nodded. "So you're off to kill Samarand."

"Kill *who*?" Blays said.

Gabe glanced at Dante, then laughed, a bubbling thing that may have been called a giggle if it hadn't sounded like a bull choking to death.

"He thinks it will stop all the things that've started in the last few weeks," Dante said, staring at his hands. "The fighting. The burning of Whetton. He says Samarand's driving it all."

Gabe scratched the beard on his neck. "I think he overestimates her."

Blays gaped. "*Her*?"

"Quit shouting," Robert said, touching his temple.

Dante twisted his hands around. "Cally thinks she's a firebrand, that she's whipping up the radical elements of the order of Arawn and leading them into open battle. He thinks with her death, they might fall back from the brink to a more reasonable course."

"What do you think?" Robert said to Gabe.

He shrugged. "I think someone else will step into her place."

"So it's a fool's errand."

"I didn't say that," Gabe grumbled. He frowned at the filtered light in the murky window. "I've renounced all violence as an abomination against the brotherhood of man, but if I could I'd pop that bitch's throat with my bare hands."

"I'm getting mixed messages," Blays said.

"From a moral standpoint, I condemn all sides," Gabe said. "From a practical standpoint, killing her would be grand. I just doubt whether that would put a stop to anything."

"What's so bad about her?" Dante asked.

"How long are you here for?"

"Long enough to learn a little about the woman you all so dearly want dead."

"Samarand's a priestess," Gabe began in a soft voice. "For a long time, the god she serves has been worshiped only in secret. Do you know what they do to anyone caught with a copy of the book you carry?"

"Cut off the hand that turns its pages," Dante said.

Gabe pushed up his lower lip. "They used to kill you. The march of progress." His mouth twitched down as he remembered more. "When she was young, she'd give speeches about how believing in secret was living in slavery. She resented that we'd be persecuted for following a god they want us to forget but was integral to the forging of the world and its people. We all resented it, of course, but some of us recalled the lessons of the Third Scour, and thought it best to continue to live in the fringes than to provoke the war that would obviously follow the path she advocated. There had always been extremists who considered their freedoms a worthy cause of all our lives."

"You saying they're wrong?" Robert said.

"Arawn's glory isn't lessened if his supplicants can only bow to him in the shadows. He's a god, not a king. In truth he doesn't need our prayers and sacrifices at all—he helped forge the fixed stars themselves, for the sake of the gods, he doesn't need me telling him 'Arawn is great' to know it's true—but it does help keep us focused on matters celestial rather than earthly."

"Anyway, we'd have been crushed like a beetle," Gabe said. He paused a moment, glancing from Dante to the others, then back, as if rearranging long-abandoned furniture of his mind. He cleared his throat. A shadow crossed his face. "Samarand. She became de facto voice of the dissenters. Over the years she swelled their numbers to a full third of our ranks. She herself rose to the council, though the continued unpopularity of her views, combined with the insistence of how she expressed them, prevented her from reaching the direct line of succession. She was charismatic. Fiery. Plain-faced, but when she spoke a light took her eyes and men sworn to celibacy hoped Arawn might forgive them for their thoughts. The surprise would have been if she *didn't* attract a following. Nor were the things she rallied behind wrong, exactly—just impractical. The Belt of the Celeset is broad, splintered to its own interests, but there are those things that may reunite them, however temporarily, and the resurgence of the faithful of Arawn is one of them."

Gabe fell silent, staring at the creases of his massive hands.

"How did she come to power, then?" Dante said to break the silence. Gabe looked surprised to see others in the room.

"The usual way," he said, looking out the window. He brooded for a long moment. Distracted, Dante thought, perhaps by old memories. The norren closed his eyes, as if reaching some thorny decision, then went on. "The head of the order dies suddenly and unexpectedly, and she takes advantage of the vacuum to reassemble the hierarchy in the manner she considers proper."

"Did she kill him?" Blays said, perking up.

"Cally thought so. It's why he left, along with the fact those of us who'd been content to stay hidden no longer had much role in the order, and left Narashtovik, where it was safe."

Dante licked his lips. "You disagree with Cally?"

"Who said that?" Gabe clasped his face with his palms, running his fingers through his thick beard. "Always putting words in my mouth. He's probably right. The old man was old, but not that old. When he left—well, his death *was* unexpected. Convenient enough to render an accident unlikely. Samarand's power had grown stagnant. Did she do it? Probably. Even if she didn't, the way she strongarmed the council was reprehensible." He gave Dante a strange look. "She's the one who revived the idea of using the *Cycle* as bait for powerful recruits. That should give you some idea of her methods."

"In other words," Robert said, gathering his words and parsing them out one at a time, "menace she may be, but there are plenty of others who'd take her place easy enough if she were to wake up with a knife in her face."

"More or less," the norren rumbled.

Robert glanced between the boys. "What do you think?"

"What I think is I don't know what the hell's going on," Blays said. He tried to catch Dante's eyes. "This sounds like the kind of thing that gets you hanged. Remember that? Hangings?"

Gabe itched his nose. "Well, only if you're caught."

"Know what I think? I think this thing's a runaway boulder," Robert declared. "Difficult to pry out of a slope, but once the descent's begun, the only way to stop its momentum is to throw a bunch of bodies in its way until it's bashed itself to a halt." He glanced between the boys. "We can either fling our own bodies beneath it in the hopes of slowing it some tiny fraction," he said, shaking his head, "or let lots of other people waste themselves on it while we go get drunk," he concluded, nodding emphatically.

"That's the most cowardly thing I've ever heard," Dante said. He stood and gazed out the window into the filth and decay of the street. "Cally thinks it will work, that we'd be enough to stop it. We have to reach Narashtovik. We have to try."

"Can't promise to follow you there," Robert said, shaking his head. "Sounds virtuous enough, sure. But also like I'd end up six feet under."

"I'll go." Blays rose and joined Dante at the window. "I don't know why. It sounds dangerous and stupid. But I'll go."

Dante nodded. He listened to the muted shouts and whip-pops of the city streets, thinking how to say thanks.

"Well enough," Gabe said. "Cally told you about the dead city's views toward foreigners?"

"He said they're a little aloof," Dante said.

"I've got something that should keep them from killing you on sight. A token the traders use to prove they've been there before without causing problems. It's why Cally sent you here."

"Ah," Robert said, ticking his nails on the pommel of his sword. "Only if it's no trouble."

"No more than anything else."

"Right then. Got any food?"

"Preferably something you don't have to eat with a hammer?" Blays said.

"There is a kitchen downstairs. I'll have a boy fetch the token. You'll stay the night?"

"Wouldn't turn it down for a full keg," Robert said. He patted his stomach. "Well, I wouldn't turn it down, leastwise."

"Well enough," Gabe said. "I'll see to your quarters." Dante turned to go and felt a heavy hand weighing on his shoulder. "A word, young master?"

Dante nodded and watched the others go. Blays waved on his way out the door. Dante took up a chair and scratched the wispy hair on his chin. He needed to learn how to shave.

"How do you know Cally, Gabe?"

"The order. And before that we fought in a war together."

Dante tried to imagine Cally swinging a sword or charging a line of armsmen. He couldn't even see him without the gray beard or bent back.

"Which one?"

Gabe sniffed. "The one twenty or thirty years after the one before it. When a new group of eager young men had had time to grow up without its memory and decided it was time to leave their own mark on the world."

"Oh," Dante said. "That one."

"I left when he did. It was clear the place we'd called home had become something different. Something we no longer felt right to support."

"Thus why you came to lie low in the receptive arms of Mennok?"

"No," Gabe said. He painted Dante with a scornful gaze. "I came to Mennok because of a philosophical understanding with the god. We *should* spend our lives brooding by ourselves. It makes more sense than the egoistic struggles for supremacy of every other sect, including the one whose tome you carry." Dante didn't reply. Gabe let loose a long, slow exhalation and removed some of the edge from his voice. "Tell me how you came here."

"We followed the road from Whetton."

"I'm speaking in a broader, less literal sense."

"Ah." Dante cleared his throat. He thought a second, then, in abbreviated detail, told the monk how he'd heard of the book hidden in the temple outside Bressel, of the men that had come after him once he'd taken it, how they'd chased him and Blays to Whetton, how he'd met Cally when preparing to rescue Blays from execution, how he'd sprung Blays and the other prisoners and fled to Cally's shrine to hide and recover, how Cally'd told him the secrets and menace of Narashtovik and why he had to go. The whole tale took less than ten minutes. When he concluded he thought how unfair it was, that everything that had happened to him since the fall could be summed up so readily. So much got lost in the telling.

"Let me see the book," Gabe said at its end.

"All right," Dante said. He picked up his pack where he'd set it by his feet and held it to his chest. Gabe raised his eyebrows, then Dante opened it and drew out the *Cycle*. He handed it over.

"I see," Gabe said, tracing the cover-image of Barden with one thick finger. He opened it. "I see." He flipped a few pages, then leaned his nose toward the text. Dante saw his eyes scanning lines. His mouth opened a little, showing those big flat teeth. He turned to the back, to the sections written in Narashtovik, and Dante tried to read the emotions that roiled across the stolid flesh of his face: surprise, amusement, wariness, urgency, at last back to guarded brooding. "I see."

"What?"

"I see," he said, "why they want it back so bad."

"You said they use it to discover recruits. Cally, too."

"Yes, but they use copies. Things they can afford to lose if the trail goes cold or the thief goes down with a ship."

Dante actually blinked. "This—?"

Gabe ruffled his beard and tucked in his chin, chuckling in a way that wasn't entirely happy.

"I once knew a man who hated Samarand's idea of how to use the book. Thought it manipulative, dangerous to the order. He once joked about switching out the copy for the original. See how smart they felt without their special book."

"I think I've met that sense of humor," Dante said. "How can you tell it's the one?"

"You know who's conscripted to transcribe these things?" Gabe said, offering Dante a rare smile. "Men like me. Bored with bad eyesight. The mind wanders, you misspell a word. Transpose things. Maybe you editorialize a little. Every copy has errors." He lifted the book. "This one's clean."

"Oh," Dante said. Gabe tapped his fingers together. "Meaning?"

"Objects collect power through age and use. That one's different from its copies."

"I can't tell if you're speaking literally."

"Me neither." Gabe twiddled with one of the black cords around his neck that dangled from the cassock. "You should tell Blays to name that sword he used when you freed him from the law of Whetton."

"Will that make it..." he trailed off, not wanting to sound stupid. "Special?"

"If not, it might make him think it is. These things can't exactly be measured."

"The book," Dante said, taking it back from Gabe and running his fingers over its cover. "Does that mean—"

A high ring of shattering glass sounded from the street. Angry shouts followed at its heels. Dante waited for them to settle up who owed whom a bottle before going on.

"Do you think—"

The door burst open. Robert half-collapsed through it, sword in hand, face bearing that tight, flat expression he'd held the night of the fight around the campfire.

"Something's going on downstairs," he said.

"Just a couple drunks," Dante said.

"No. Downstairs in the monastery."

"What's going on?" Gabe said, getting to his feet in a way cassocked hills shouldn't be able to do.

"One of the monks killed one of the other monks," Robert said. He leaned into the hall and a moment later Blays swung back into the room, sword out, breathing heavily.

"*Killed?*" Gabe said.

"A bunch of them have swords and staffs and things," Blays reported. "It looked like a few of them came in from the street."

"None of the monks would kill anyone."

"It's happening," Dante said, the back of his neck tingling the way it did when he heard an animal creeping through woods by dark, or when he finished a book that read like it had been inspired by the gods themselves. "The fighting starts in the temples. That's what they said." Yells and crashes of wood and steel came up from the first floor, underlining his point.

"Shit," Gabe took a long breath through his nose and nodded at the doorway. "You should leave. You've got other troubles to see to."

"A compelling argument," Robert said.

"No," Dante said, drawing his sword. "We can stop this, here. They won't take this one place."

"Going to save the whole town, too?" Gabe said.

Dante stuck the point of his blade into the wooden floor. It came to him all at once: the idea that he was more than an arrow shot from another man's bow, unable to deviate his course once he'd been set in motion. He'd known Gabe less than an hour, but already he liked him. By nature he had no patience for the self-important mysticism of the men of the gods, but something about this monastery and the quiet conviction of its men was too important to hand over to the Arawnites. Cally might say their passage to Narashtovik was too important to risk their lives in this place, but he was almost three hundred miles away, was too wrapped up in his own dealings to venture out into all this strife. Dante was here now, and here, he thought, was a place worth saving.

"We can't defend the whole town," Dante said. "But we will fight them off here before we run like rabbits. At least you'll have time to prepare for whatever comes next."

"Besides," Blays said, "we still need that token. I'd rather die here than get eaten by barbarians a thousand miles from here."

"Idiots," Gabe said, with neither a smile nor a scowl. He lifted a sturdy, dark-wooded chair and snapped off a leg. He swung it through the air. "Well. Let's go see what the fuss is about."

"Yes," Dante said, neck tingling again. He pulled at his sword and found it was stuck in the floorboards. He yanked again and stumbled into Blays' back.

"What's your hurry?" Blays muttered. He put an arm in front of Robert before they left the door. "Me first. You're unsound."

"Physically, perhaps."

"Tell me who not to kill before I do it," Blays called back to Gabe. They pounded down the stairs. At its base lay the still, bleeding body of the young man who'd answered the door. Blays and Robert flanked out, facing the two doors in. Gabe's face went slack and he knelt beside the body. Dante stood over him, beginning a call to the nether.

"Don't," Gabe said. "He's dead."

"I'm sorry."

"Grieve later." Gabe surged to his feet, chair leg in hand, and took them through the parlor and to the outer entrance of the monastery. Drops of blood shined on the slate flooring. Fresh gashes marred the table in the parlor; dusty old fabric spilled from a slash in one of the benches. The rooms were empty. Gabe cracked open the front door and peered into the gardens. From deeper inside the monastery they heard raised voices.

"Follow me," Gabe said. Blays tried to stay at his side but the hallway was too narrow for any more than Gabe's bearish shoulders. Dante and Robert jogged at their heels. The norren took a right turn and they emerged into a relatively open room of simple chairs and round, roughhewn tables, a dining area or meeting hall. At its far end, some forty feet away, a group of men were pounding on a closed door.

"What's going on here?" Gabe shouted.

"We've trapped the usurpers in the kitchen!" a bald man in a cassock cried back.

"You have swords in your hands," Gabe said, stopping after he'd crossed half the room. "And who are those men with you?"

"They're the gardeners I was telling you about," the monk said, glancing to the men at his sides, dirt-faced men wearing black cloaks and naked swords, one of which streaked blood down its length and tacked against the floor.

"Hansteen," Gabe said in a quiet voice, "lay down your arms. This can end now."

"I thought you were one of us," Hansteen said.

"I thought you were one of *us*!" Gabe cried. "You killed Roger! He was a boy!"

"There was confusion." Hansteen pinched the bridge of his nose. "Help us out and he'll be the only one."

"Have you ever even read the *Ganneget*? Do you remember that second rule? Where you may willingly harm no man?"

"Oddly, it mentions nothing of our conduct toward norren." Hansteen smiled, briefly. "I know what you used to be. It's time, Gabe. We will no longer let ourselves be hunted and killed for serving the first among the gods."

"Then go serve them in the street," Gabe said, taking a step forward, "and get the hell out of my monastery."

"Why don't *you* leave?"

"Because this is the house of Mennok!" Gabe roared, shoulders bunching. The men at Hansteen's side fell back a step, then tightened their grasp on their swords.

"Then let it be reconsecrated in the name of Arawn," Hansteen said. He glared at his swordsmen. "With their blood."

They eased forward, leading the way with their blades. Hansteen flung out a hand. Nothing happened.

"I thought you knew who I was," Gabe said.

The men walked forward, leaning into aggressive crouches. Blays leapt at the lead man then skipped back, drawing him into Robert's waiting blade. Blood splashed against the slate. Dante swung out his sword, blocking a strike at Gabe, whose hands shook as he absorbed the stream of nether Hansteen had slung at him. Dante screamed and opened a wound across his attacker's forearm. His blade clattered against the ground and Gabe laid out a pounding backhand with his chair leg. The wood snapped in half on the man's skull, dropping him. Blades clashed to Dante's left where Blays and Robert fended off two men. The remaining one on Dante's side feinted, knocking aside the tip of his sword, and Dante spun to dodge the following thrust. It ripped over the thin flesh over his sternum and he felt the woozy scrape of steel dragging over his bones. He stumbled back.

Wrapped in his invisible tussle with the other monk, Gabe stepped forward, leaving Dante behind. Dante scrambled backwards, scooting on his ass. The swordsman swung down and he rolled away. He tried a swipe at the man's ankles and his sword was knocked wide. The man leaned forward for a crosswise sweep meant to open Dante's guts and his sword bounced from Robert's. Robert followed up with a quick poke that drew blood from the man's left side. Dante found his footing and rose next to Blays, who was falling back under the wolf-like jabs of a pair of attackers.

"Set my blade on fire!" he hissed at Dante when their shoulders bumped. For once Dante asked no questions, instead shutting off his mind and gathering the shadows. He wiped his hand in the blood dripping down his chest and flipped a few red drops Blays' way. His sword foomped with fire the length of the blade.

"I'll drink your souls!" Blays shouted, waving his flaming weapon in their faces. They actually dropped back and Dante touched his own sword, shrouding it in a shifting mist of darkness. He fell in beside Blays.

"I'm going to get the others," Hansteen said, and from the corner of his vision Dante saw him run across the room to an open door. Gabe picked up a chair and threw it at his retreating back. It shattered on the wall beside the doorway and dropped into a splintery heap. Blays and Dante lowered their shoulders and advanced on the remaining two men. A shout sounded to their right, then a flurry of metal strikes too quick to count and the thunk of a sword burying itself in flesh. Another sword rattled on the ground. Dante glanced back in time to see a man's head spinning over the tiles. Robert staggered back, soaked in blood.

Dante turned back to his own fight and saw a sword headed for his face. He batted it aside and slashed down, cutting open the man's boot and bloodying his toes. The man hopped back, yelping. From the front of the room, Gabe was disappearing after Hansteen.

"I'm going to help him," Dante said, sidling away from his attacker. Robert was red-faced and breathing heavily but his mouth was twisted in angry joy. Dante sprinted after Gabe, banging his hip on the rim of a table, hearing swords meeting behind him. He plunged into the room on Gabe's heels and the battle in the dining room immediately grew muffled.

Hansteen stood in the middle of a dark hallway. Maroon

drapes and pious paintings hung from the walls. Dante reached Gabe's side. Hansteen did something with his hand and Dante's ankles and knees locked and he skidded over the stone flooring. Then his elbows were tight, mid-swing, his wrists and fingers frozen. He couldn't turn his head. Every breath felt like a massive hand was squeezing back against his chest. He tried to blink and his eyelids fluttered. Hansteen snapped his fingers and a gout of flame whooshed down the hall. Gabe grunted and tamped it down with an angled strike of his hand like a cougar stretching out its claws for the rump of a buck. He took a step forward and so did Hansteen. They both raised their arms at each other and for a few long moments they looked to be trying to carry a 15-foot invisible table between them: shoulders shifting, wrists bending over their heads, muscles shaking, Gabe's columnar body bulging like a boulder and Hansteen's spindly limbs twitching beneath the drooping folds of his cassock. Dante watched, literally paralyzed. He felt hot blood slipping down his doublet, a faint breeze where the cloth had been opened by the attacker's sword. The two men huffed and grunted and spat curses between their teeth. He could feel the tingle of power in the air, the way his arm hairs stood when clean clothes rubbed dry skin, or the way the air felt during a storm, but moreso, as if they stood within the thunderhead itself. An audible crackle started between the two men, cutting over a droning hum that twisted Dante's stomach. Sweat dripped from the norren's broad brow. He could see the veins on Hansteen's temples. Gabe's lips opened, showing those flat teeth clenched tight. He growled, an animal noise that started low and suddenly burst into a guttural howl.

"To hell with this!"

He waded forward, one foot then another, as ponderous as if he were walking underwater. A step at a time he closed the distance between himself and the other monk. Too late Hansteen deciphered his plan. The thin man bent back and Gabe reached forward with a hand as thick and knotty as the bole of a pine. He closed his fingers around the other man's neck and lifted him into the air. They grimaced at each other, the nether flipping between them in swift streaking shadows, and then Gabe slammed Hansteen against the wall. His head and hands flopped. Howling again, Gabe lifted him higher, wrapping the trunks of his arms around Hansteen's back and hugging him to the barrel of his body. Dante wanted to close his eyes, but whatever Hansteen had set on him held fast. He watched as Gabe's shoulders flexed and elbows tightened, heard the dreadful snap, saw Hansteen's body bend like a broken fish. Gabe raised the corpse and flung it down the hall. He stared after it, shoulders heaving, breath whistling through his wide nostrils. He turned, then, and Dante was glad his bladder seemed as frozen as the rest.

"Cally never taught you about rooting?" Gabe rasped. Dante tried to shake his head. He tried to speak, managed little more than the weak moan of a sleeper caught in nightmare. Gabe closed his eyes and folded his hands and Dante flopped to the floor. He'd been mid-stride when the thing had caught him. Gabe cleared his throat and spat toward the body. "You'd have died long before you met Samarand."

"Show me once this is over?"

"Of course."

Dante nodded, gazed down the hallway at the pile of robes that looked like a man but bent in a way men didn't.

"I thought you had vows against things like that."

Gabe pushed out one of his bearded cheeks with his tongue. "What is it with you heathens? Always searching for a contradiction. The laws of Mennok aren't like the laws of man—you don't break one and whoops, it's time to pop your neck. Mennok, in his wisdom, knows there are times his holiest laws must be broken." He gazed at the corpse he'd made. "He'll judge me fair."

"Robert's hurt!" Blays shouted from around the corner. They started, then turned back to the room they'd left. The floor was awash in blood. Stretched out by the last of the armsmen, Robert lay prone, rolling back and forth on his stomach. Gabe knelt beside him, turning him to his back and pinning his shoulder to the ground to stop his mindless rocking. He pulled back cloak and chainmail. The wound on his chest had reopened, and below it another gaped on his belly where a few of the links had been split. Narrow but deep. Dante saw something slimy and purplish winking beneath the welling blood. He put his hand over his mouth.

"Stay sharp," Gabe said, pressing his unbloodied fist to his mouth. "I'm going to be out of it for a minute."

"You can put that out at any time," Blays whispered, nodding to his sword laying on the ground, its flames licking at the stone. Dante waved a distracted hand, wiping them away.

Gabe mumbled to himself, planting his hands on Robert's shallow-rising chest. Dante glanced down from the door he'd been watching and saw motes of light and darkness swathing Gabe's fingers. They left him in a murky curtain, the way rain looks falling from a distant cloud, soaking into Robert's body. Robert tensed, arching his spine, teeth bared, the cut skin folding together, pushing out blood and small meaty things that made the back of Dante's mouth taste bitter. Gabe wiped it away with Robert's cloak. The skin was red, welted, as disturbed as a fresh burn, but it was whole. Robert went limp. He blinked as the others looked on. Gabe slumped back, resting on his elbows, chin touching his chest.

"The problem with getting stabbed," Robert started, then turned his head and spat blood. "Is you can only kill the man who did it once."

"I got him," Blays said, shaking Robert's shoulder so hard the man's head wobbled. "His sword got caught in your chain and I stuck mine through his heart."

Robert sat up, closing his eyes. He rubbed the side of his head.

"Surprised they hung around at all after your sword literally caught fire."

"I know!" Blays said. "It looked great, didn't it? Like a demon come to take them away?"

"Yeah," Robert admitted. "You fought like one, too." He cracked open one eye. "What's all that pounding? Or is that in my skull, too?"

Dante realized he'd been hearing it, too. Behind the locked kitchen door. He crossed to it, put his ear to the wood. The pounding started again and he jerked back, rubbing his ear. He cupped his hands to the door, shouted into them.

"Stop that!"

The hammering ceased. "What?"

"I said stop that!"

"No."

"Open up. We're friends of Gabe's."

"That's a rather old trick, don't you think?" said the voice on the other side of the door.

"It's true!"

"I think we'll take our chances in here. It's worked so far."

"Look," Dante said, glancing back over his shoulder to where Gabe still rested, "if you don't open up, I'm going to get Gabe over here and he'll break it down."

He heard murmurs on the other side. Someone cleared his throat.

"We're armed!"

"Good! Then if I'm lying you can cut me down!"

More murmurs, longer this time.

"Just a minute," the voice said. "We'd just about had these bars all set."

Dante heard squeaks and the scrabble of tools against the door. Something clinked mutely on the other side. The process repeated. Behind him, Gabe got to his feet, followed by Robert and Blays, and they came to Dante's side.

"What was that thing you did to Robert?" Dante said to the norren.

Gabe raised an eyebrow. "Fixed him."

"With the specks of light."

"Ether," Gabe said, giving him a look like he'd just said breakfast was his favorite meal of the day. "It's better at building than the shadows. Restoring and creating is all it can do, in fact. Didn't Cally teach you this stuff, either? This is elementary."

"His methods are a little unorthodox," Dante said.

Wood jangled against the floor on the other side and then a lock clicked. The door swung back, revealing four men in cassocks crouching back, kitchen knives held ready in their hands.

"Gabe!" cried a short, elderly monk. The norren stepped forward and they embraced. The monk gazed past him to the wreckage of the dining room. "Brother Hansteen and a couple of the others let in some black-caped men. They told us to join them or leave. When Roger told them this was a house of peace, one of the men struck him down."

"I saw," Gabe said. He hunched his shoulders. "Brother Hansteen is dead."

"I'm sorry," the old man said.

"I don't understand why he did this." The others nodded, saying nothing for a time.

"Who are these with you?" one of the monks said to break the silence.

"Friends," Gabe said, gesturing to them in turn. "Dante, Blays, and Robert Hobble. They helped put down this treason."

"There's going to be more," Dante said. "Where did the other turncoats go?"

"Hard to say," the old monk said, knitting his brow. "We put a lot of wood between us and them. We weren't prepared."

"Better than being put to the sword, Brother." Gabe curled his arm and massaged the hamhock of his biceps. "Find yourselves some real weapons. We'll be ready for whatever comes next."

"We'll secure the place," Robert said. His face was pale but his voice was steady. "Get some arms and then bar everything but the front door. We don't know what's going on out there."

Gabe led them into the hallway where Hansteen had died. They stepped over his twisted body and one by one flung open the doors to the cells. Every third or fourth held a black-cassocked monk clutching a book or a fireplace poker or a brass candlestick. Gabe clapped them on the back and sent them to the dining room to meet the others. They locked the door leading to the inner gardens and Mennok's shrine and moved to the second floor. More of the same: quiet rooms, hunkering monks, whom Gabe calmed with soft words and the boys encouraged with grins and whoops. The small, cramped rooms of the two spires held no one. In the top room of the second spire, a dome-roofed space so small Gabe could have stood at its center and touched both walls at once, he took a dull white object from above the wide window and pocketed it. He gestured to the stairway.

"I don't get this big plan of theirs," Blays said as they headed downstairs. "Three monks and a few guys with swords? Take a monastery, which wouldn't happen in the first place if there were four good men here able to defend it, no offense to you, Gabe, then hang around till the law comes by to pry them out? How is this thing taking hold?"

"Confusion and exploitation," Robert said. "Start up a religious squabble the watchmen want no part of, start rallying the commoners, go from there. All they need's a toehold." He shrugged, playing off his guess. "That's what I'd do, anyway."

By the time they got back to the dining room the monks were abuzz with work. A few carried ceremonial swords and other relics in the rope belts around their waists. Others bore wood axes and hoes and iron-banded walking staffs. A pile of pokers and knives and other fallback weapons lay beyond the kitchen door.

"No sign of the others," Gabe said to Nolan. "Who else was with Hansteen?"

"Allan and Romsey."

"Allan?" Gabe said, face crumpling. Nolan nodded, eyes downcast. Gabe sucked a deep breath and clenched his fist. "How did that happen? I'd imagine him cutting off his own nose before he betrayed his brothers."

"Most of the order remains loyal," Nolan said, gesturing to the monks and hired boys scurrying off with hammers and nails and planks of wood. "Don't be tainted by the poison in a few men's hearts."

"I'll meditate when there's time. I have to see these men off," he said, nodding to Dante and the others. "Don't let anyone in the door. Steadfast."

"We'll give'em a taste of hell if they try," Nolan said, shaking a gardening spade in his fist.

Gabe led them to the front door where they'd arrived little more than an hour earlier. He stuck his head through, looking on the oddly quiet street beyond the gates, then stepped into the yard. The sun had fallen during the fight. Dante sucked down deep breaths of the cold night, suddenly certain they could retake the rest of the town if only they had the time.

"We had horses," Robert said.

"They'll be around the side."

The three muscly horses munched on spilled oats, oblivious to the racket inside the walls of the monastery. Gabe patted one on the shoulder. His eyes were nearly level with its own.

"Dante, the rooting is a simple thing," he said, stroking the horse's brown mane. "You'll feel its tendrils between your feet and the ground. Cut out those roots, and you'll cut out its hold."

"It's common, among the priests?"

"Not common, but deadly when used right. More subtle than that gruesome thing you did back there and not half as sapping to your strength. Quick, call to the nether."

Dante took three quick breaths and held his hands an inch apart. The same stiffness as Hansteen's summons took his joints. He fought to move his hands.

"Ignore it," Gabe said. "Focus on the tension at your soles."

He did feel it then, as if the bottoms of his feet had extended down into the dirt, locking him in place with a hundred wiry roots. Fingers quivering, he guided the nether to the pressure in his boots. The roots withered. His knee twitched. At once the whole thing snapped and he stepped forward, wild-eyed.

"Good. Don't panic if they sneak it past your guard. Clear it away like brambles in your path."

"Easy enough," Dante said. "Don't see why Cally never mentioned it."

"He's always been more of a theorist," Gabe said, shrugging. He smiled a little, his first since before the fighting. "Here." He reached into his pocket, revealed the object he'd taken from the spire. A set of spiraling horns, bound in the middle by a flat section of skull, neither prong longer than a man's middle finger. "Wear it around your neck. It should get you into the city."

"Should?" Robert said.

"They're the horns of a nasty little thing called a kapper that lives in the snows of the north. Should prove you're a native, or at least you're a frequent visitor." He bit his lip. "Of course, they are a wary people. And it's been a while since I've been there."

"Would be nice to shrug off a little trouble," Robert said, shaking his head. "Seems to follow on our heels."

Gabe cocked his head. "Does trouble follow you? Or is it trouble's found all corners of the world?"

"Afraid it's a combination of the two," Robert said, favoring Blays and Dante with an unflattering glance.

"I see what you mean."

"Come with us," Blays said, stepping forward and tilting back his head to meet Gabe's deep-set brown eyes. "We need you."

"They need me here. I'm not a warrior."

"But there's only going to be more of this. If this won't convince you to hit back, what can?"

Gabe drew himself up to his full height and breadth and stared Blays down. The boy's eyes danced away.

"I knew the horror they brought before they touched this temple," the norren said. "I'm supposed to reverse my beliefs because men I'd called friends betrayed me? How petty do you think I am?"

"I didn't mean that," Blays said, dropping back a step.

"I know," Gabe said in a softer tone. He looked over the black outlines of the roofs visible above the willows of the yard. "I couldn't live with myself if I went with you and found out the monastery had fallen. Who knows. Perhaps we can keep Shay from falling to what's taking the south."

"Perhaps," Robert said. He kicked the dirt. "Good luck to you."

"What way will you take through the mountains?"

"The pass, I thought."

"It'll be snowed. The Riverway should be open yet."

"Yeah, and add a week to the journey," Robert said.

Gabe nodded. "You'll see more norren on the other side. Leave them be and they ought to extend the same to you. We look more beastly than we are." He pursed his mouth. "No more beastly than any of you, at least."

"We're not beastly," Blays said.

"If they do come at you with suspicious intent, say 'Hannan,'" Gabe said. "It means 'peace,' more or less. Draw it out, though. Briefer vowels mean something more anatomical."

"Hannan," Dante tried.

"Longer."

"Haaannaaaan."

"Better to err with caution, I suppose." He nodded at Robert. "Wounds should be fine. You'll need sleep soon, though. And food."

"Anything else, mum?" Robert said.

"That's it." Gabe drew up his brows at Dante and opened his mouth as if to say more, then shook his head and looked off toward the street. "You're good men. Don't go dying up there."

Robert nodded and swung himself into the saddle, registering surprise when he felt no pain.

"Good work," he said down to the norren. The boys saddled up and Gabe untied their leads. They exchanged goodbyes and they walked the horses to the gates.

"One last thing!" Gabe called from the steps of the monastery. "When you see Samarand, put a stake through her heart!"

Dante twisted in the saddle. "What? Is she a vampire?"

"No," Gabe yelled, "but I imagine it will hurt a lot."

Robert wrinkled his nose. "Mennok's men are strange ones."

They turned into the street, leading the horses past shattered glass and the strewn refuse and fallen knives of a recent struggle. Further up the street they saw blades flashing in the torchlight.

"What do you think?" Blays said.

"I think," Robert said, hand drifting toward his sword, "if we stop to fight everyone's fights for them we'll have no time left to reach the end of the world."

"Yeah," Dante said, touching the scabbing wound on his sternum. "No more delays."

They cut down a side street. The sounds of skirmish peaked and faded in the still air. Robert kicked his horse up to a trot. They had done something good, Dante thought. When other man spoke of winning a battle, they simply meant they'd survived and stood their ground while the other side had fled and died. In Shay, they'd preserved a spark of thought that would have been blown out by the winds of upheaval if they hadn't risked themselves to save it, and as he rode it was with a centered pride that he'd chosen to act and had chosen well. By the time he remembered he'd forgotten to ask Gabe what it meant that he held the true *Cycle* the town of Shay was nothing but points of light behind them.

11

Cold, Dante thought, and then he thought it some more. He toed the inch of snow on the ground until he could see dead yellow burrgrass. Cold and hills. With the promise of more hills ahead. He scowled at the blue mounds of mountains on the northern horizon. A couple days away. He tucked his chin into the collar of his second shirt and wondered why anyone bothered to do anything.

They'd stopped at a farmhouse the day after they left Shay, where the owner had waved a pitchfork in their faces until Robert used the fact they hadn't already ridden down and slaughtered the man to convince him they weren't bandits. This established, the man accepted a decent chunk of their remaining coin for extra clothes and blankets and bread and cheeses and meats from his cellar. The clothes were rough-spun things, thick with the scent of sweat and dirt, and scratchy as falling into a barrel of drunk cats, but Dante figured it was better than dying of the cold that seemed to grow deeper with every step toward the mountains. They passed a few more fields and farmhouses that afternoon, but had seen nothing but wind-scabbed hills in the day and a half since. Just enough snow to get their boots wet whenever they dismounted. Just enough damp to let them hope they'd find some dry wood down in the draws, but when they settled down for the night they couldn't get a spark to catch. Dante cupped the nether in his hands and set a white burst among their tinder and got nothing but thick plumes of pale smoke. They huddled together, breath steaming, shivering until sleep overtook them.

The road roughened, narrowed. The ruts disappeared. Ostensibly others took this way, and Dante knew entire caravans crossed it in the half the year they could count on the pass to be clear, but they saw no specks of other riders, saw no sign of the campfires and gutted game and other spoor of travelers. The mountains hung huge as ground-hugging clouds, blue with pines and white with snow, distant and implacable as the fixed stars. The wind seemed to grow colder by the hour.

Robert sang crass drinking songs. A couple times, Blays told stories about the battles his dad had seen. Mostly he'd rolled around Bressel as a merchant's bodyguard, but in his early years, when he was just a couple years older than Blays, he'd been a swordsman of the young king's army during the annexation of the southwest coasts. None of the dirty brawls Blays and Dante had seen, Blays said. Formations. Ranks. Thousands of men and scores of wagons and when the battle was over a far greater army of magpies and crows and kites. Blood so thick you could smell it for miles. Blays told these things with a faint smile, a flicker of envy in his eyes. Robert tutted about how those things really weren't so grand, and besides, if Blays liked them so much, there was always another war and the need for men to die in it. Blays rebutted with the belief he'd make a fine soldier. Earn himself a knighthood. Robert just laughed. Kind words from the king, maybe, but he'd never eat at the same table. Men were born into such things, he said, not made.

Dante told them of half-mad Jack Hand. How he'd sacrificed his brothers' wives to see if he could bring them back, how his brothers had mutilated him for it and his long imprisonment, his insurrection and how he'd bested the rebellion meant to replace him. He'd lived 180 years, Dante said, and had 12 sons whose own sons staked out an empire from the far eastern shores all the way to the wide fields of Collen. Robert dubbed them good stories, if the incestuous intrigue of royalty was what tightened your drawers, but the oldest man he'd met had claimed 87 years, and that man had looked like something left in the ground a season too long. Dante shrugged. Things were different then, he said. Jack Hand was a sorcerer. Before he could die, he was taken to the right wrist of the constellation of Arawn, the sign whose crown had burst countless years ago into a pink cloud you could see during the day's full light. The book said its light had lasted for a complete year and rivaled the moon in the night. After it had faded from sight, when people looked up at that headless alignment of stars, they'd seen not the body of Arawn but the currents of twin rivers flowing across the heavens.

The clouds bulged blackly above their heads and tiny flakes of snow twinkled like dust in an autumn sun. Within another hour it was falling as thickly as a burst pillow, paffing against their faces. Dante pulled his collar over his nose and his hood over his brow. He looked out on the whitening world through a slit of fabric, breath warming his nose, and tried to imagine what the world would look like on the other side of the mountains.

"Let's camp up now," Robert said a couple hours before nightfall. "I want to have a full day to tackle the pass."

"How does it look?" Blays said, peering up at the deep fold between two sky-scraping peaks.

Robert shrugged. "It looks like a pass."

"And you look like you're stupid, but that doesn't give me any idea just *how* stupid."

"Well, it's got snow, see? That white stuff?" Robert pointed to a barely visible squiggle along the flank of the left-hand mountain. "Guessing just a foot or two so far, other than the drifts."

"What if it's deeper?" Dante said.

"Start praying it isn't." Robert patted his horse's shoulder. "Shouldn't take more than two days, unless one of you does something especially dumb. Not that it's very far mile-wise. Just takes a lot longer."

Dante woke three times that night to shake snow from his blanket. They'd bedded down in a gulley right off the road, which this close to the mountains was little more than a scraped path of rock and dirt, but the scrubby little pines weren't enough to stop the winds from pouring down the slopes and pelting them with small powdery flakes. He tried without success to wring his blanket dry that morning. He stuffed it in a sack. Maybe when it froze he could just beat the ice away.

"Careful where you lead your horses," Robert told them as they started up a steep incline after a predawn breakfast. "They can't tell a ten-foot drift from solid ground. Try to stick close to the slope and away from any really smooth-looking snow."

"I think I'll just follow you," Blays said.

"Probably a better idea."

The snow stopped falling shortly after the morning broke but what was already underfoot got thicker with every hour of travel. By midmorning Dante turned in the saddle and saw the last of the hills sprawled beneath them like frozen whitecaps. Pines clung to the slopes to their left; chunky black rocks fell away to their right, crusted with ice and snow. Dante had imagined the pass would be an impossibly narrow line carved out of the mountain face, but it averaged about thirty feet wide, sometimes opening into an expanse that might be a meadow in summer weather. They rode single file, slowing to a crawl the couple times the pass closed to the width of two horses abreast. At those times Dante tried to keep his eyes from the way the snow tumbled down for a couple hundred feet before ending in a valley bottom broken by the black bodies of snow-dusted boulders. Winds knifed through the peaks, throwing fine, stinging snow in their faces. Dante's clothing grew stiff. Tiny drifts formed in its folds. The horses plowed through foot-deep snow, sometimes plunging past their knees. The beasts stepped high, snorting, tossing their heads. Robert spoke softly, clucking his tongue, letting his mount hug the rising slope. Just after noon his horse swooped to its chest in the snow and bounded forward, its whinnies carrying on the wind. Once it scrambled clear to snow below its knees Robert halted, panting in the cold.

"How much further?" Dante said, drawing up behind him.

"Can't see too well," Robert said. He hunched his shoulders and gazed uphill into the mists of the clouds. More than half their daylight was gone. Dante blew into his hands. They were stiff, inflexible, as if their motions lagged a second behind his thoughts.

"It's still going up."

"I can see that much." Robert brushed snow from his cloak. He folded down his collar and wiped ice from his eyebrows and mustache. "Should be close to the crest. Dark's going to come fast up here. Won't want to press the horses once it does."

"I don't exactly want to stay here overnight," Dante said.

"And I don't want to get old," Robert said, "but I'm afraid it's my best alternative."

"Can we get back to somewhere less freezing already?" Blays said. "I need to take a piss and I don't want it snapping off."

They waited around to eat a handful of bread and drink from skins filled with melted snow, then got the horses going again. Dante watched steam rise from the shoulders of Robert's mount. He was tired. Cold. He glared across the snow-crusted slopes. They had hundreds of miles of travel after this. A wrong step, a hidden drift, and his voyage would be over. The places where men lived were full of people who wanted him dead and the places where men didn't live were hellholes of ice and snakes and sudden cliffs. How did anyone get as old as Cally? Pure stubbornness? Luck? Hanging around a forgotten temple while he sent the young men out to tramp around the wilds? That was a part of it, he'd wager. He'd further wager it had something to do with the book in his pack and the things it represented. Cally could make him explode by looking at him. Gabe could scrape up his chunks and patch them back together. That monk Hansteen could lock Dante in his tracks, could have killed him at his leisure if Gabe hadn't been there to snap his spine. Even Will Palomar, the man he'd slain with the bolt of fire in the woods outside Whetton, could have struck him down, he thought, if not for the man's arrogance and the blind chance of Dante's sentry. Sometime, he *would* die: if not during this journey to head off the war coming for the southlands, then in another two or three decades. One moment he'd be alive, the thing that made him him embedded firmly in the fortress of his skull, and then the next instant, perhaps before he understood what was happening, he'd be separated from his body —and if his body held a part of whatever it meant to be Dante, he'd never be the same again. Maybe he wouldn't remember anything once he'd gone from earth to the space beyond the stars. Maybe he wouldn't be able to think at all. Why did people have to die? Why couldn't they know what happened once your body died and rotted to waste?

Crags climbed on all sides. He felt like he was walking in the bottom of a bowl. The clouds had lifted from the pass itself, but still streaked by so low Gabe probably could have stretched up and touched them. It started snowing again and he blinked against the freezing bite of the flakes against his face. His eyes grew watery; beneath his collar his nose was running.

Robert called something over his shoulder and the wind snatched it away. Dante cupped a hand to his ear and shook his head. Robert drew up and leaned over.

"I said that's the crest up ahead!"

It all looked the same to Dante. Snowy and rocky and cold. Obscured by walls of wind-driven snow. The shallower drifts were back down to a mere foot deep, he saw. They rode on.

He thought reaching the top of the pass would be inspiring, triumphant, but when they got there all he saw was more snow and a carpet of clouds in the valley to the right. The dark lump of Robert's horse leading the way looked like an anonymous stranger lost in the nowhere. Snow continued to batter his face. He'd always thought it fell out of the bottoms of the clouds, but here he was inside one and the snow was still falling. He tipped back his head to try to get a glimpse at the clouds above but all he saw was close-pressed gray.

Dante's horse slipped then and he grabbed wildly for a hold on the saddle. Hundreds of pounds of bones and guts and flesh struggled beneath him. The horse bucked its front shoulders and Dante heard Blays cry out as the world tumbled on its head and he threw out his arms and crumped facefirst into a snowbank. He kicked his legs and fell back on his ass.

"You all right?" Blays shouted.

"It's cold!" he said, shaking snow from his chest and arms, wiping his hood over the slush melting on his nose and cheeks. His gloves were soaked and his hands stung like they'd been struck. He put a foot in the stirrup and the horse took a step forward and he had to hop along and hang onto the saddle to keep from falling again. Dante patted the beast, mumbling baby words he hoped the others couldn't hear, then hauled himself up.

"Soft landing," he shouted into the wind. Robert's hood whipped around his face as he considered Dante. Then the man turned and continued on.

Robert slackened his pace, letting his horse feel its way through the drifts and the slippery descent. Dante had been gripped by a slow kind of terror on the way up the pass, but as the day drew on he found himself increasingly distracted from the imminence of his death on these rocks. What would Narashtovik look like? Would it be one big fortress to ward off the constant sieges? Would its buildings look like monstrous tombs? How would he find Samarand? Would she be like its queen, gazing down on the snow-wrapped city from the safety of her towers, or would she be like Cally, an underground figure, emerging from hiding only to meet with the others of her order? When he found her, how would he kill her—leaping from the secret of a dark alley to slip a knife in her spine, or meeting her in open single combat, like all the stories of two foes meeting in all the legends of the world? He realized he didn't know a thing about the dead city other than it wasn't really peopled by the dead. Why hadn't he asked Cally more? Would it have helped? Was there any sense in trying to plan before he was there to see Narashtovik with his own two eyes?

His horse slipped again, leg jolting, and without thinking Dante yanked the reins close to his body. The horse stopped short. He took a deep breath, fighting the rushing wind that wanted to tear it from his mouth. He turned his head away from the gales. Stay in the moment. There were hundreds of miles ahead of them yet. There would be time to brood when a misstep wouldn't send him plummeting into a frozen abyss.

He hurried to catch the couple steps he'd lost to Robert, face flushed with a vein-flooding rage. What was wrong with him? Why was he so afraid of the cold and the heights? Robert was managing just fine. Blays wasn't complaining. Either he'd die or he wouldn't. There was no in-between and either way he wouldn't have to worry. He was so sick of the mantle of panic he let himself feel whenever he faced the slightest trouble. It was disgusting. It was commonplace and it was weak. He spit into the swirling snow. It was time to become something more than the sum of his emotions.

Robert slogged along and Dante slogged behind him. He made his mind go quiet and endured. It was impossible to tell how much time was passing. Light continued to fight its way through the mist and the snow, but who knew how much was left. He hummed to himself, having heard you couldn't feel fear when you were humming. Blays didn't seem to notice. He made himself recall from memory entire passages from the *Cycle of Arawn*: the opening verse, "The stars shimmered on the waters and for thirty years Arawn took their measure. As he held the nail of the north, Taim jostled his shoulder and all came loose: and down came the waters to drown out the land"; near the end of the first chapter, "And Arawn said to Van, father of Eric Draconat,'Make no sacrifice, for it shall all be mine in time'"; much later, when Arawn had disappeared as an active force and the tome turned to kings and priests, "Gil Gal-El rode seven times around the keep, shaking his sword and naming the seven bodies of the heavens, and at the seventh circle the keep fell and the king was no more." Fragments, half-remembered stories, scores of names. Again he forgot the trail.

It had stopped snowing at some point. The stuff on the ground was deeper than it had been at the wind-scoured gap at the peak of the pass, now swallowing the horses to their knees, but it no longer lashed Dante's face. The mists began to lift; sometimes he could see the green smears of snow-bent pines a couple hundred yards away. And then it was gone and he could see the entire trail twisting its way along the side of the mountain, and the skies rose until the clouds hung not on his face but a thousand feet above, and to his right, in the valley between the bodies of the mountains, he could see a long, silent lake, its waters cobalt and shining sapphire and at times a creamy, scintillating green he'd never seen in all the world. His breath caught.

"What kind of sorcery are we heading into?" he said to Robert. The wind had dropped to a strong breeze and he no longer had to shout to compete with its moaning grief.

"That's just glacier water, you ninny," Robert said, but his gaze fixed on it while his shoulders stayed in swing with the rhythm of his horse. "It's nothing special."

"Do you see that?" Blays said behind him.

"Yeah."

"It looks like burning glass."

Dante nodded, eyes clinging to the shelf of ice above the lake, ice that was white at its cap, blue as a frozen summer sky in its middle, that same otherworldly green at its feet. The wind hushed and all he could hear was the snow as it crumpled and squeaked under the horses' hooves. The air was cold and clean in his lungs. They followed a curve in the trail and a wedge of rock and pines occluded the aching blue lake. Dante kept glancing back, glancing to where the valley should be, wanting one more glimpse of the hidden waters.

Robert pushed them on till the light ceased gleaming from all that white snow to be stolen by the westerly peaks. They were still in the mountains proper, as far as Dante could tell, but the cold was less stunning, the wind less biting. Robert spied a broad, flat break in the pass a few minutes downhill and took them there, tying the horses to the pines that would offer them some shelter. He started to scoop away the knee-deep snow with his gloved hands, just enough space to lie down in; when they did, Dante saw, their bodies would be hidden from sight and wind. He and Blays pitched in, sweeping away the snow with their boots, grateful for an excuse to flex their numb, sodden toes. It was nearly dark by the time they finished. Robert straightened his back and considered their work.

"There, that wasn't so bad, was it?" he said. "Nobody died? Fell off a cliff? Froze to death?"

"There's still time," Blays said, wiping his nose.

"Hard part's over. Tomorrow we'll get back down in the hills. Might not even be snowy."

"It's the north," Dante said.

"So what?" Robert clapped his hands together. "It's just the north, not another world. You boys need to get out more. Besides, mountains make the weather act screwy, you never know what it's like back in reasonable elevations."

"Couldn't these people have started their little rebellion in the summer?" Blays mumbled. "Would that be too much to ask?" He rummaged through the saddlebags, picking out some food. He tossed the heavy wad of Dante's blanket at his chest. "Catch."

Dante caught it and almost fell back into the snow. It had frozen or something. Thick to begin with, it now weighed ten or fifteen pounds. He stretched up his arms and tried to roll it open, frowning when it drooped to but a slightly less creased position, then shook it hard, sending ice particles flying into the last of the light.

"This stinks," he said.

"Ah, it's not that bad," Robert said through a mouthful of cheese. "At least we've got blankets. Think how bad it would be if we were up here naked."

"Why would we be up here naked?" Blays said.

"But just think if we were."

"There's no possible reason we would ever be up here naked."

Robert shrugged and took another bite. "I'm just saying. Some years it's snowed in six weeks ago. We've been lucky."

"Huzzah," Blays said. He wrapped himself in a couple blankets and stared out on the snowfields, on the black of the trees and the gray of the unlit snow. The clouds parted and a three-quarter moon washed over the valley with pale rays.

"Doesn't that make it all worthwhile?" Robert said, scratching his beard and smiling.

"No," Blays said.

"I'm cold," Dante said.

"Lyle on the rack. Then go to sleep. You may hate this day, but you'll be able to remember the story twenty years from now. Assuming the gods suffer a collective collapse of reason and decide to extend your whining lives that long."

Robert got up and stamped around the campsite, patting the horses, touching the pine needles. Dante hugged his blankets around him and wiggled his fingers and toes. After a while they stopped hurting.

By noon the next day they'd dropped out of the mountains and into an endless sea of white-coated hills. The snow was shallow, though, no more than three inches, sometimes disappearing entirely in the places where the sun shined unshadowed for most of the day. Compared to the trudge through the pass, the horses all but flew as they walked. They saw no one before the sun had set and they took shelter in the hollow of a draw. No riders, no farmers, no trails of smoke and civilization. The day after was just as empty. It was as if the snows had wiped away the world. They crossed a ridge and to their right a circle of great gray stone blocks stood like the grave markers of all things. Dante pulled his cloak tighter around his shoulders. After that moment he couldn't shake the sense they were being watched, that there were eyes in the trees or the dark creases between hills, but he knew that was foolish, people had better things to do than spy on them all day, things like keeping themselves alive or getting the hell out of these wastelands. Still, it stuck with him. That uneasy creep of a presence among the isolation. He didn't mention it, not wanting to look like a scared little child, and so he just walked on, one more hour, one more day, that much closer to the dead city.

"Ever get the sense we're being watched?" Robert asked the next afternoon. They'd crested the saddle of a hill and paused to gaze out on all the ones yet ahead of them. Blays took the break to scare some food from his packs.

"Sometimes," Dante blurted, then waited for Robert to volunteer more.

"Me too. But this time I think we really are."

"Oh?"

"Can't be, though. There's nowhere to move without being seen." Robert gestured to the open rises of snow. Trees lined the folds of the hills and sometimes sat in clusters at their base, but mostly it was empty, easy travel and easier sight.

"Have you seen anyone?" Dante craned his neck. It looked as barren as ever. He pushed back his hood, felt the cold breeze on his cheeks and nose and ears.

"Maybe." He pushed his brows together. "Ah, who knows. Been so long since I've seen anyone but you two winguses I'm probably imagining things."

Robert motioned them on. Somehow Dante had stopped feeling the cold. He recognized its presence, knew if he'd appeared here after a week in the relatively balmy offshore breezes of Bressel he'd be shaking like an epileptic, but for now the chill no longer hurt. They rode downhill and were enfolded in the soft swell of the land. They rode uphill and were bracketed by mountains to the west and south, huge things of blue and white beneath the tight tarp of gray clouds. When Dante dismounted he imagined his shoulders were still rocking to the gentle bounce of his horse. There was no proper road, as such, nothing paved or even rutted, just any number of dirt trails that joined and forked every few hours, but Robert checked Cally's map often, squinting at the course of the sun and, at night, at the particular dial of the stars. A river glinted to their west and over the course of a day it swung to intersect their path. The ground angled down to meet it and they cut through the snowy grass to drink fresh water and fill their skins with the cold mountain runoff. Dante spotted a bulge in the bank that created an eddy where fish might rest, but they had no poles, couldn't spear them from the shallows like he and Blays had done at the pond. They'd made good time on the day and Robert suggested they set up here and enjoy the rest of the afternoon. Dante and Blays shrugged off their second shirts (it was still cold, but between the sunshine and the running around they doubted they'd need them) and ranged down the river's banks, eyes sharp for the deep purple of janberries. Dante judged they had about an hour of sunlight left. It was the first honest free time they'd had since they'd left Gabe and his defense of Shay, the first time they'd had that wasn't spent riding or throwing together a shelter or hugging themselves and trying to remember what a fire felt like, and they ran beside the river, tagging each other with pine cones, cutting reedy branches and dueling in the late afternoon. Blays twirled his branch beneath Dante's with a smooth turn of his wrist and pressed its springy tip against Dante's heart.

"Yield, you menace!"

"Never!" Dante said, cocking his elbow to strike at Blays' neck, and Blays rammed his stick forward. It bent against cloak and doublet, then snapped two-thirds down its length. Dante waggled his weapon. "Ah ha! You're unarmed!"

"And you're minus one heart," Blays said, throwing what was left of his stick at Dante's feet. Dante turned toward the river and slung his like a spear. It disappeared into the waters, then bobbed back to the surface, straightening in the current. Blays jogged up the bank a ways and called Dante over to a janberry bush crouched against the foot of a pine. The purple berries were small and hard and sour, never truly in season, but it was good to taste anything fresh. All the food in their saddlebags was as dry as licking paper. They ate all they picked, then gathered a handful each for Robert, popping a few in their mouths as they backtracked toward the camp.

They climbed a short ridge and saw Robert on his hands and knees in the grassy snow peering across the waters. The boys froze and leaned into the nearest tree, following Robert's gaze. All Dante saw on the other banks was a few squat pines surrounded by bushes. He had a word half-formed when one of the bushes moved.

Norren. Four, make that five of them, swords at their belts, bows slung over their massive shoulders. Staring right back at them. Robert motioned for them to get down. Blays made a long face at Dante and Dante shrugged. The river washed between the two groups. Not quite a bowshot across, and the weapons the norren carried looked as tall and potent as the men who wore them. Blays crammed the rest of his janberries into his mouth, then hesitantly raised a juice-stained hand.

The norren stood as stolid as the hills behind them. Dante reached out for the nether, awaiting their move. One of them lifted a hand and waved back. Another dropped its eyes to whatever he'd been examining in the dirt and poked at it with a long staff. Their voices rumbled over the water. They talked a while, gesturing upriver, then turned as one and walked on.

"What was that all about?" Blays said. He spit out a stem.

"Looked like hunters," Dante said. They started toward Robert, who was already striding their way down the shore.

"Next time try not to bumble right into the war party," he said, glaring between them.

"Well you could have said something," Blays said.

"Yes, I really should have just shouted 'Watch out! There's some men over there that could probably kill and rob you if they wanted to bother!' Would that have done it?"

"What about a signal? Whistling like a bird?" Dante said.

"What about you look around once in a while?" Robert said, poking him in the chest. "We're five hundred miles from home. You've never stepped foot here and I've only been here twice, neither of which was recent. Things are different now. If you don't keep your eyes open, you could be killed, you can't just be goofing around. Have some gods-damned sense."

There was a long silence. "I brought you some janberries," Dante said. He held out his berry-stuffed hand. "Blays ate all his."

Robert closed his eyes and sighed. He grabbed a few from Dante's palm and lobbed them into his mouth.

"Sour," he said.

"They're janberries."

"I know janberries are sour. I was just saying." Robert ate a few more, face slackening as he munched. "May as well follow the river for now. Should be the Lagaganset, if I'm reading the map right. Find a town eventually, pick up some fresh food, then find a road straight to Narashtovik."

"Plus plenty of janberries on the way," Blays said, tipping his chin at another bush a short ways down the bank.

"Just keep your stupid eyes open," Robert said, shaking his head. "Those norren were tracking deer, looked like. Water attracts all kinds of men and beasts. Probably see more of them before we see any chimney smoke."

Blays gazed into the current. "Laga...Lagagaga...what the hell was it?"

"The river. Call it the river."

"Right."

The norren-sightings increased their frequency the further they penetrated into the territories of the north. Blocky silhouettes on dawn ridges. Silent hunters crouched along streambeds, eyes gleaming from the thicket of their beards, tracking deer and elk through the snow. Sometimes Dante saw tracks so big it looked like two drunk children had been falling down every four feet. He tied the set of horns Gabe had given him to a length of leather string and draped it over his neck. They saw men, too: a single-sailed boat coasting down the river one afternoon, the twists of farmhouse smoke out on the flat expanse of the basin, a pair of raggedy travelers on foot who gave them one look before cutting away from the river into open land. It snowed one noon, adding a couple inches to the two or three already on the ground, going mushy and soggy once the sun broke back through the clouds.

Villages began sprouting up every ten-odd miles. Farming, fishing, the smoke of smithies. They'd pass two or three a day. Not yet wanting for food, desiring no contact with the locals, they toured around, cutting through the lightly-treed fields and fallow farmlands. The ground got lower and the snow got thinner until one day it gave out altogether. For the first time in two weeks they were able to light a fire. The boys leaned so close their damp clothes and blankets steamed. Dante doused his bread in water and let it warm until it wouldn't crunch between his teeth for once. In the mountains and the hills they'd sometimes slept without keeping a watch, but in these lowlands, with the spark of their camp visible for miles in the night, they split shifts between watch and sleep. The nights were coming on the longest of the year and even with three hours of guard duty spent sitting with their backs to the fire or pacing around the rim of light they'd wake before dawn, fixing breakfast, chatting idly, waiting for the ground to grow gray enough for the horses to see.

"That spire there," Robert said the day they saw their first real town in these lands, pointing to the tall, dark finger of a temple sprouting from the middle of the city. "I've been there. Almost twenty years ago, but I was there."

"Does that mean we should go around?" Blays said, giving Dante a smirk.

"What? Of course not. Anyone who'd remember that's probably dead by now." Robert rubbed his beard. "Or wouldn't recognize my face, at least. I'm sure they've forgotten."

"Oh," Blays said.

From a few miles out it looked the same as the cities of the south. From half again as close it smelled the same. Once they drew near enough for the buildings to resolve from grayish lumps to individual structures, Dante could see some of the outlying houses seemed to be roofed with sod. Not even the poorest houses were thatched, like he'd always seen in the outer ring of Bressel or down by the docks; these homes were roofed with steeply piled dirt or tight-set planks or overlapped tiles of shale. The nobler manors and wares-houses were set from firm, chunky, mortared stone. It looked like a city that would last a thousand years after its last occupant had died.

"Looks all right to me," Dante said.

"Wait a minute, I'm sure it will get horrible soon enough." Robert took the lead toward the town.

"I mean, no fires. No fighting. No hordes of armed men. Where are Arawn's faithful?"

"Maybe it's already over," Blays said.

Robert rubbed his mouth. "Could be it hasn't started."

"But this is much closer to Narashtovik," Dante said. "That's where Samarand and her council lives. Things should be ten times as crazy up here. What's going on?"

Robert shrugged, then gave him a sharp look. "Don't go asking any questions."

"They'll know we're foreigners anyway."

"But they don't know we're *stupid* foreigners."

"They won't think I'm stupid!"

"I do," Blays said.

"Yes, they will." Robert ticked the numbers off on his fingers. "First they'll think you're stupid because your accent's bad or you can't even speak the language and you dress funny. Smell, too. Second they'll think you're stupid because you don't know the things that everyone knows.'Why isn't your city burning to the ground?' you'll ask, and they'll look at you like you just tried to eat a loaf of bread through your asshole."

"That's what's stupid," Dante said. "They'd be stupid to think that."

"Well, why don't you just educate them as to the error of their ways, because that's how people think everywhere. Go on. You're not in any hurry, are you?"

"Fine."

"I thought we were in a hurry," Blays said.

"We are," Dante said. "Quit dawdling."

They rode into town. Other than the sturdier buildings, the occasional presence of norren rather than neeling, and the foreign language—Gaskan, Dante presumed, since for the last few hundred miles they'd been in Gask and its territories, as far as anyone could be said to rule over the worthless lands around the Dunden Mountains—it didn't feel that much different. He'd never really paid attention to the traders and travelers who'd spoke Gaskan back in Bressel, but with an ear cocked toward the tongue he started to think he was going mad. It was a thicker, more imperative-sounding tongue, but it sounded just enough like Mallish to make him think he could catch about every tenth word, if only they wouldn't speak so maddeningly fast. With a jolt, he realized he understood one of their words, and not from his native tongue, but from the *Cycle*: to release or unlock.

"*They* dress funny," Blays said, nodding to a couple men wearing long, open-bottomed clothes that struck Dante as some kind of fur-lined dress. Robert sighed. He took the lead and headed for the market, where they wandered around until they found a merchant who spoke enough Mallish to sell them some fresh bread and dried meats and could barter with Robert over a couple bottles of wine. Eventually they reached some kind of agreement and Robert cradled his bottles and smiled out on the bustle of the market, the cries of the sellers and the guarded eyes of the buyers. Not all the smells here were bad, either. For every whiff of old fish there was one of cinnamon, for every sulfurous blast of hide-tanning there was the sweet, sagey lilt of lan leaves.

"Don't suppose we can spare a day or two here," Robert said.

"No," Dante said.

"That's why I said 'don't.'" Robert kept lingering, though, arguing with tradesmen in a broken combination of the two languages, sometimes resorting to exaggerated gestures and repeating himself very loudly. He bought some salt, some fresh-cooked crayfish which he sucked from the shell, a bag of strong, bitter-smelling leaves.

"We'd better get moving," Dante said, checking the light. Good for another ten miles, maybe.

"One last thing while we're here."

"Robert."

"Dante."

Dante squeezed his teeth together. "We're not here to stuff ourselves with treats or take a wife. We need to go."

Robert bit his lip and took one last long look at the flash of coins changing hands, the laughter of men sharing a bottle, the wry faces of women sweeping doorways or naming the price of their vegetables. He nodded. Dante mounted up and led them on. Robert lagged at their tail, head turned over his shoulder, watching all those people fade into the waning light.

The river unspooled across the land, bowing east and then back north, and they followed it across the days. From the berth of a few miles' distance they saw the steeply pitched black roofs of another town dotted with snow. Three days from the dead city, Dante reckoned. He tried to imagine what Narashtovik would look like, but all he could see was the twisting alleys of Bressel, the damp-rotted docks, the overgrown clusters of houses ringing the city on three sides to the river; half the city was fresh-cut wood, houses and halls that hadn't existed fifty years ago, to hear the old men talk. He couldn't picture a city that had been Bressel's rival when the last pages of the *Cycle* had been penned a thousand years ago. And once he was there? How would he complete his two tasks? Who would teach him to read the final third of the book? Would they have an academy? A forgotten library? Monks eager to teach the good word to those who'd come to hear? How could he hope to learn the dead language of Narashtovik and track down and kill Samarand at the same time? He didn't imagine it would be as simple as walking up behind her in the street and sticking a sword between her ribs. She was chief architect of all the chaos in the south. From what little he'd gathered, she was practically queen of a city that paid service in name only to the greater kingdom of Gask. He knew he wasn't nearly potent enough to kill her in a fair fight and wasn't nearly stupid enough to think her army of priests and retainers would let him get close enough to die that way in the first place. He wished Cally were with them. The old man would know what it would take. How had all this dropped on his shoulders? He and Blays to end a war? It had seemed far less insane back when they were nestled safely in the temple outside Whetton. Here and now, with less than a hundred miles to the end of their journey, it seemed to Dante the caprice of colossal miscalculation. This warranted armies or hardened assassins, not a pair of boys whose faces didn't even wrinkle when they smiled. They were going to die. Three days from now, perhaps a week from now, but they were going to die.

"What's so funny?" Blays asked.

"Our'plan,'" Dante said. "The brilliant part about it is we can get as drunk as we want, because if we accidentally tell someone about it they'd never believe a word."

"Hilarious. Does that mean you've been working on it, then?"

"Yes."

"Oh?" Robert said.

"I've got to the part where we get to the city."

"Ah."

It was two more days till they climbed the brown mound of a low hill and saw the dead city. It consumed an entire quadrant of their horizon, a boundless smear of black and gray buildings broken here and there by the windy spires of cathedrals and the closed fists of keeps, circumscribed by two concentric rings of walls, a bigger bulge of accumulated industry than Bressel itself, ten miles across if it were an inch. Two of its arms reached north to hold the gray waters of a bay, and beyond it the haze of the sea. Dante's face split with a smile. He'd come from shore to shore, well more than a thousand miles, a distance he'd ever only dreamed of crossing. Whatever else befell him, by noon tomorrow he'd step foot in Narashtovik, the city of the book, the city of the dead. He had dreamed it and then willed this dream to life.

Robert stopped them the following morning some ten miles from the city. He pawed through a pack and passed around meat and cheese, stabbed a knife into the cork of a wine bottle and twisted it open. He tipped it back into his waiting mouth, bubbles glugging into the bottle's upturned base, then wiped his lips and passed it to Blays. Blays chugged and passed it to Dante and Dante had a sip. Robert sighed through his nose and considered the distant lumps of the city.

"Never feels right to say goodbye without a drink of wine," he said.

"I've never liked it at all," Dante said. Robert nodded.

"Who's leaving?" Blays said, handing the bottle back to Robert. "Are we sending off the horses? Why would we send off the horses?"

Dante frowned at the ground. Robert chuckled, then went quiet when he realized Blays meant no joke.

"We're not sending off the horses."

"Then what are you talking about?"

"It's time," Robert said. He tapped his nails against the side of the bottle. "Here's where I leave you two to yourselves."

"Why?" Blays said, just the one word, and Robert had to look away.

"You two have your mission. I'd just get in the way."

"No you wouldn't! You're the best swordsman I've ever seen!"

"What you need right now's not a sword, it's a story to tell the locals why you're here. Two young men could be anything—lordlings out to see the world, a pair of hired blades, a scholar and his man-at-arms. Whatever you say, they'll never imagine the two of you could be a threat, and that's the thing that will save your asses." He took a drink and pushed his mouth against his sleeve, face red. "Some old bastard tagging along's just going to confuse them. Make them wary where you want to be a snake among the reeds."

"This whole thing seemed stupid and crazy when there were just the three of us." Blays' eyes shined with anger and some rawer hurt. "Now we're supposed to do it all with two?"

"Trust me, you'll be better off. This calls for subtlety beyond my means."

"And what if we're not enough to take her down?" Blays said, flinging his hand at the city. "What if they go and unleash Arawn? Maybe he *will* eat the world. Even if that's a steaming pile meant to rile things up, they look pretty damn safe up here. The king's not going to march an army to the ends of the world when Samarand's got mobs burning up his back yard. People are going to die!"

"Quit that," Robert barked.

"Quit what? Saying what we've all been thinking?"

"Trying to shame me into this, you whelp," he said, stepping forward and sticking his finger into Blays' chest. "If I thought for a moment you two were skipping off toward suicide I'd make you turn back right now, or at least rob you before the others could get to your corpses. First time I met you Dante was busy lighting up the entire town watch, for gods' sakes, and you killed plenty yourself as soon as your hands weren't tied. You two could set the world on fire if you wanted."

Blays snatched the bottle away from him and had a pull.

"Fine," he said, rapping the glass with his knuckles. "Run off to your whores and your booze and your brawls. If you ever had a set of balls, they're far too shriveled to help us now."

Robert started to reply, then bit his teeth together, lips curled. He looked away. When he spoke at last his voice was forcibly softened.

"Spill as many words as you want. I'm leaving. I know in my heart it's the right thing to do. Nothing can change that. The only thing left to settle is whether you'll remember me with darkness in *your* heart."

"Get out," Blays said. Nobody moved. He raised his arm and smashed the bottle against the frozen dirt. "I said get the hell out!"

"Well enough." Robert turned to Dante, face blank but eyes bright. "I think I've repaid whatever debt I owed you."

"I never held you to any debt," Dante said.

"I know." Robert grinned. "That's the only reason I stuck around at all."

Dante nodded, gazed back the way they'd come. "Where will you go?"

"Should have a few friends still kicking around these parts. Would be plain rude to come all this way and not say hello." He sniffed, wiped his nose against the cold. "I'll be there in Whetton, Blays. You know where to look."

"Passed out in your own filth behind any public house," Blays said, back turned.

"You were listening after all." Robert smiled for just a flicker, then flashed his eyebrows at Dante. He climbed into the saddle, wheeled his horse, began to backtrack the first of the miles. He halted thirty feet out and faced them. Blays turned his head at the sudden silence of the horse's hooves. "Walk with the gods, boys. Don't you dare let them get you before you get them."

Dante watched him ride away. At a hundred yards Robert dropped down a ridge and left his sight. Dante nodded to himself. He'd see Robert Hobble again, he pledged, and when he did he'd bring Blays with him.

"You don't look too surprised," Blays said, face matching the dark clouds overhead that hadn't yet decided to spill their burden.

"You saw how he was in that town. He's been saying he meant to leave us since Gabe's."

"I didn't think he meant it."

Dante shook his head, a flare of frustration budding in his chest. "He means every word he says."

"He does," Blays agreed. He kicked a stone. Dante couldn't

think of a single thing to say to soften what had happened. He stared dumbly at the dead city, thinking ten miles, ten miles, two hours if we hurry and three if we don't; ten miles, ten miles, as if all he had to do was think hard enough and they'd shrink away to none. He risked a look at Blays.

"Want to rest before we finish it?" he said.

"When we're this close? What are you, a girl? A baby? I want to see this fancy city of yours."

"It's not mine. Yet." He nudged his horse forward. A breeze followed him. He imagined he smelled the faint scent of saltwater. "Gabe told me, before the attack, you ought to name your sword."

Blays glanced at his side as if he'd forgotten it was there. "Name my sword?"

"He said it might give it power."

Blays laughed and pulled it free. Sun glinted down its steel as he waved it in front of his face.

"You believe him?"

"All the famous warriors do it," Dante said, lifting half his mouth. "They must be on to something."

Blays slitted his eyes, nodded. Air whistled over his swing. He smiled grimly.

"I dub thee Robertslayer."

"No, come on," Dante said.

"It's my sword. I can name it what I want."

"What kind of a name is 'Robertslayer'?"

"It's a vow," Blays said, brows furrowed like Dante was stupid for asking. "Next time I see him, I'm going to challenge him to a duel."

"What about all the help he gave us?" Dante said. He tried and failed to see any hint of humor in Blays' eyes.

"I'm not saying I'm going to *kill* him." Blays held the sword level with his arm and peered down its length. "Just slosh some of his blood around. Show him who's the whelp."

"All right." Dante freed his own weapon from its sheath. "I think I'll name mine Blayschopper."

"The gods will know you're copying. Your blows will land as falsely as its name."

"You've got a direct line to them, do you? You have chats?"

"I know how these things work," Blays said, cutting the air between them. "You can't just name your sword a joke."

"You named yours Robertslayer!"

"And it's going to taste his blood," Blays insisted. His lips twitched. "The only blood of mine you'll ever taste will be my skinned knuckles on your teeth."

"I'd burn you to a cinder first," Dante said, pointing to him with the first two fingers of his right hand.

"You'd set me on fire?" Blays gave him a look of mock horror. Dante laughed, looked off toward the city, for a moment felt as if things were back how they'd been before they'd ever met Cally and been so ensnared in all these problems of churches and kingdoms. Things were different now, though. They rode not solely for the lives of themselves, but for those of thousands in the southlands. They rode with the cold force of a mortal purpose. Through it all, they carried the weight of the men they'd killed on the way. The dead city took the land before them, boundless and ragged, black and ancient as the earth's first wound.

12

Narashtovik grew wider with every step, taller with every minute. Its outskirts were a tumble of old stone and moldering wood, tainted everywhere by a confusion of indistinct black smears, as if a hundred years ago an all-consuming fire had chewed the city up and left the ashy remnants to the slow erosion of time. But from the city's interior wispy columns of smoke twisted into the seaside haze of sky.

"Stay sharp," Dante said. "Someone still lives here."

"Sorry. I was lost in the rugged beauty of that giant mound of trash up there."

Once they drew nearer, Dante saw the black spaces weren't charcoal and shadow, but the deep green needles of northern pines. Thick in the streets, pushing up among tumbled stones, choking out the places where men once lived. They'd make easy firewood, but there they were, unmolested, undisturbed. Dante touched the pair of horns that hung from his neck. The tracks of others broke the crust of snow that lay on the road. From within the jumble of houses and trees he thought he could see the shadows of movement. Far too few for a city of this scope—the silhouettes he saw lived in the lawless ruins, wouldn't necessarily bear the mantle of docility that seemed to affect most men who lived in the company of thousands of others. Dante closed one eye, reached out for the nether, felt it reach back.

He led his horse around a tongue of rubble that lay in the roadway. They left the pine-specked fields and crossed into the sprawl of empty buildings. Once or twice a minute he saw a man hurrying across one of the streets ahead, heard the footfalls of inhabitants from somewhere within the alleys and cross-streets; further toward the city's heart he'd catch a shout, a bell, a few moments of breeze-scattered blacksmith's hammerblows. He slowed his horse, watching both sides of the road as they passed the moss-coated stump of a home that couldn't have stood for two hundred years; then an open patch of half-buried timbers that may once have been an innhouse but now looked one strong rain from washing down to a square of dirt no different than any of the rest; then a weed-choked foundation resting bare of walls or roof. From the distance of a mile or more an uneven line of gray stone showed behind the worn roofs of those buildings that still stood.

"Tell me why this feels wrong," Dante said.

"Where should I start?"

"I don't mean that," Dante said, jerking his chin at the detritus.

"Cally made it sound like we'd be trussed up in a net and thrown in a stew the instant we showed up." Blays chewed the inside of his lip. "I don't see a damn thing, and all I hear's one smith who can't keep time."

"That's it. There's not enough noise. You can separate one sound from another."

Blays nodded. He loosened his sword. They followed the road. Not all was empty, not all was ruin; some houses boasted all four walls and a roof without holes, and here and there wooden structures that didn't look completely decrepit shared walls with older ones. The chock of a solitary wood axe echoed from no more than a hundred yards away. Down a street where the cobbles were as gappy as the teeth of a serf Dante caught the unexpected flash of a garden, an ordered spread of green amongst the defeated crumble of housing. A man's soughing footsteps came from the other side of the street and he turned in time to see a pair of wary eyes before the figure disappeared behind a damp wall. They moved on.

Voices and the clanking of men at their labor grew thicker as they approached the city's first wall. It shared the disrepair of the lands around it, webbed with cracks, its top as jagged as the peaks they'd crossed weeks earlier. Graying, fluttery lumps dangled from spears planted in the stone. In places there was no wall at all, just a carpet of stones and beyond it a view of a city that looked half normal. The road led to a gate of sorts, or at least one space in the stonework that was intentional, though Dante saw no sign of a grille or doors to shut the twenty-foot walls against invasion. They halted a stone's throw from its base and moved off to the sod at the side of the road to dismount, stretch their legs, have a bite. Foot and carriage traffic moved on the other side of the gates. If they hadn't just crossed through a couple miles of desolation, Dante could almost imagine it was a city no different from any other.

"I don't suppose you have any idea what you're doing," Blays said.

"Not really," Dante said, and the admission lifted a weight from his shoulders. He gazed back at all the empty buildings. "At least we won't have any trouble finding a place to stay."

"Yeah." Blays flexed up on his calves and crossed his arms, watching the signs of life past the gate. "I was kind of expecting to've had to kill someone by now."

Dante nodded and chewed on a bite of bread. Dirt peppered their legs and they jumped back. Six feet in front of them, an arrow vibrated in the soil like a plucked string.

"Outstanding," Blays said. He twisted it from the dirt and gazed up at the walls, patting the arrow's head against his leg. "I believe that was a warning."

More dirt spattered them and again they heard the twang of an arrow coming to rest in the earth. The second had landed a mere cubit from Blays' boots. He gaped.

"Who shot that!"

Dante lifted an open palm and turned a slow semicircle in front of the gate. He didn't know whether Mallish customs would mean anything here, but figured if they were bright enough to know how bows worked they'd get the picture. Blays yanked out the second arrow and snapped it in half, casting the fragments into the street.

"Don't," Dante said, scanning the crest of the wall for movement.

"Tell them not to shoot at me."

"We're travelers," Dante called up to the fortifications.

"That's why I shot at you," a voice came back from up and to the right. In Mallish at that, not the barking language of this land. Dante squinted at the horizon of stone and sky.

"Stop shooting at us!" Blays said.

"State your business," the voice said.

Blays sucked air and looked at Dante. Dante pushed out his lip and shrugged.

"A critical error of preparation," Blays murmured. Dante nodded.

"Um."

Another arrow hissed over their heads and tinked off a wall somewhere behind them.

"State your business in Narashtovik or join the others on this wall!" the voice called out, and Dante took a step back as he reexamined the gray things stuck from the spears along its top. What was wrong with mankind?"

"Got it," Dante said to Blays, then raised his voice and tipped his face toward where he thought the guard was emplaced. "We're pilgrims of the south. We've come to pay homage to Arawn in the city that is his most holy."

"Arawn?" Blays hissed. "Are you trying to get us killed?"

Dante waited, sucking breath through his teeth. No more arrows creased the air. The walls stood silent.

"What should I have said?" he whispered to Blays. "We're merchants here to sell our invisible wagons of riches? I didn't hear you brimming with suggestions."

"What about all those great lies Robert came up with?"

"At least they've stopped trying to kill us."

"Unless they're on their way down so they can get their hands involved."

"What are your names?" the voice said, and the two boys jumped.

"John Girdle and Bob Oxman," Blays called before Dante could give their real ones. "Him being John, of course."

"What kind of names are those?" Dante whispered.

"What kind of names are those?" the voice shouted.

"The ones our fathers gave us!" Blays roared back.

He was met with more silence. The breeze ruffled the needles of the pines, the refuse in the streets.

"Very well, John Girdle and Bob Oxman," the voice said at last. "You may enter. The sermon of Samarand will be at noon three days from now."

The boys looked at each other. Dante cupped his hands to his mouth. "Where, exactly?"

"The Cathedral of Ivars," the voice said slowly. "Where did you say you were from?"

"The south," Blays said.

"Indeed," the voice said. "Enter, then."

They grabbed the reins of their horses and walked them forward. Dante kept his eyes on the part of the wall where the man had spoken from until the stone cast its shadow on them and they stepped into the next circle of the city. He glanced toward Blays as they made their way up the road and into the company of others. John Girdle and Bob Oxman indeed. What if the gatekeeper hadn't let them pass? What would they have done then? Would they have died in the street among the filth and the ruin? It was a strange world, he thought, a horrible world, an ongoing rush of violence and confusion where no place felt like home. The wrong words could make his stomach churn with loathing for his failure, could make others move to strike him down. Where did Blays find his bluster? For all his own mind had opened since he'd found the book, the only moments that didn't feel like a test that found him wanting were when he was reading or he'd said something to make Blays laugh. What was the rest of it? The running from those who would kill them, the riding to this city for the one they would kill? And if they managed to make that so, would anything be different once Samarand was dead? Wouldn't he always feel this way? Wouldn't he always be worried to the nub of his nerves by the memories of the foolish things he'd said, the times he'd tried and come up short, the moments he'd reached within himself and found he didn't have the strength to act at all?

"She's here," he said, staring dumbly at the space between his horse's ears.

"Where?" Blays said, hand snapping to his sword.

"I mean, in the city."

"Didn't we know that already?"

"Not for certain, did we?"

Blays screwed up his face. "I thought you and Cally were certain she was here. I thought that's why we decided to ride a million miles to get here. Are you saying we could have come all this way and had to turn right back around?"

"No," Dante said, slowing as they reached an intersection with another broad avenue. "Well, yes."

"You son of a bitch."

"All's well that ends well, right?" He was about to make fun of Blays' concerns some more but was suddenly too busy collecting his dropped jaw. "Do you see that?"

Blays followed his finger. "See what? That you haven't washed your finger in five years?"

"That's a temple of Arawn," Dante said, pointing down the street at the white tree standing in relief above the double doors on the face of a tall, spired structure missing most of its roof and pitted with wear on its walls. Fine-boned gargoyles stood watch on its eaves.

"So? I thought this was their capital."

"Out in the open like that? It looks hundreds of years old. It would have been burnt down a dozen different times back in Bressel."

Blays made a smacking sound with his lips, then just sighed instead.

"I suppose you want to look inside."

"Hells yes I do," Dante said. All the dread he'd felt toward himself and his surroundings a minute earlier lifted like a fever dream. What was this place?

"Should we just put these horses in our pockets?"

"What? Oh." Dante glanced around the square, the couple of men on about their business, the dark-windowed faces of steep-roofed buildings. "Let's just stash them behind some place empty. It still looks pretty clear."

Blays snorted. "Thieves are like roaches. Everything looks clear till the moment they're running off with your food."

"Then we'll steal someone else's horses later," Dante said. "Just carry anything you can't replace. Don't forget your blankie."

"And just leave our mounts for the first guy with an eye for easy money?"

"Yes? We're in the city now. They're practically a burden. Oh, what should we do with the horses. Should we stable them? When did we last pay the groomsman? Should we just tie them up? What if someone robs us? The horror! Oh, if only we didn't have these horses!" Dante stopped waving his hands around. "You see?"

"But I like them," Blays said, patting his horse's neck.

"There's a time to let things go," Dante said. He turned his horse down a narrow road and they wandered a while in the rows of mostly-whole buildings lined against the city wall. He chose one that looked particularly abandoned—the trash looked old and gray, no bootprints in the yard, no smoke from the chimney or any of the other holes in the roof—and they tied their horses to a pine sapling that had shot up through the front stoop. Dante led Blays back toward the temple, orienting himself by the wall behind him and the cluster of spires toward the city's center.

The door creaked like the planks of a ship but opened easily enough. Weak sunlight diffused through the broken and shutterless windows. The ground floor was filth. Apple cores and chicken bones and eye-wild potatoes and small moldering piles that may have been edible a year or five ago or, judging by smell, may already have been eaten once. Clouds of crumpled paper sat in front of the fireplace of the front hall. Dante smoothed one against his knee. The alphabet was foreign, but he knew enough to know the name of Arawn when he saw it.

They stepped carefully past the refuse to the back rooms beyond the mostly-empty great hall and found more of the same. Clearly the temple had been used more recently for the housing of the penniless than as the home of the god. A wooden staircase, missing only a few slats, rose to the second floor. Dante tested its footing, keeping close to where the steps met the wall. They squeaked like cancerous rats. Blays followed him up, face tight, spitting curses each time the boards popped or groaned.

"We could have found these same wondrous treasures out in the gutters, you know."

"But not this," Dante said, crossing the landing to a bookshelf behind some smashed-up tables. Three-quarters empty, and when he picked up what works were left most of them sloughed rotten pages over his feet or dangled as empty covers, their leaves stolen for starting fires or far less dignified ends. A handful of intact and legible volumes remained, however, and three of those were even in a language he could read. He wedged them into his pack and turned in a circle, looking out on the dust and the kipple. "Let's try the spires."

"Let's," Blays agreed much too enthusiastically, but he tailed Dante up the solid stone stairs they found at the far rear of the temple. The only things left in the upper floors were a number of plain iron candelabras and horn-hewn statuettes, a lot of wood chips, and a few axe-scarred tables which had evidently been too much trouble to haul downstairs and burn. Dante picked up a thumb-sized carved imp and handed it to Blays.

"Here. He'll ward away your troubles."

Blays held it up in Dante's face and frowned. He held it beside his ear, shook it.

"It's not working."

"Funny," Dante said. The temple had long since been scoured of nearly everything that could be sold or set on fire and they finished their search within minutes and reentered the street. The horses hadn't been stolen from where they'd tied them in front of the old house by the wall, and finding the premises no less dirty than the streets and far cleaner than the temple or either of the house's neighboring edifices, the boys settled in. The sun was just saying hello to the western horizon. Dante lit a couple candles looted from the temple and set them at either end of the house's main room, i.e. the only other room besides the one the front door opened on.

"We should find the Cathedral of Ivars tomorrow," he said, easing himself to the floor. He rocked back and forth on the hardwood. "Feels weird not to have bumps beneath your ass."

Blays gave him a look, then moved on. "Going to be a lot of people. I get the impression we weren't the first pilgrims the gatekeeper'd seen."

"I'm just saying we know she'll be there. We should see if it's an option."

"I doubt it'll be a good one."

"Thus the scouting." Dante exhaled hard. "It can't hurt to look. Maybe it'll be perfect."

Blays shrugged. "Let's not be in some big hurry to make it the first option. I'd prefer to leave here on my feet than on my back."

Dante got out one of the books he'd found in the old church. Its cover bore the inky silhouette of a man holding out his hand to a rat.

"It's going to be a risk no matter how we do it."

"There are risks and there are risks," Blays said, wandering around the far side of the room. He slipped a finger under one of the slats nailed over the window and gave an exploratory tug. "You know?"

"I know," Dante said, but three days from then they'd be looking on Samarand with their own eyes. Whatever risks it carried, whatever else it would mean for his other goal within the city of the dead, the opportunity would be there, and if it looked right, they'd be fools not to take it. "We'll see how things look tomorrow."

Through force of habit they were up well before the sun. Dante rose first and lit a candle in the other room and skimmed the new additions to his library. The first was a sort of rebuttal to the *Cycle*, fleshing out historical detail of its major figures and often diverging into windy lectures about the way its theology failed to account for the fundamental and contradictory truths of Mennok and Carvahal. Its penultimate chapter purported to examine the final third of the *Cycle of Arawn*, the part written in ancient Narashtovik, and Dante plunged into it with a pounding heart, but after a dozen-odd pages Dante found it scarce on actual references and long on opinion. Fascinating to the author's scholarly circle, Dante was certain, and would perhaps have been of interest to him if he'd first been familiar with the source material, but for the meantime infinitely boring.

The second tome, the one with the man and the rat on its cover, was, as anyone could have guessed, a slim volume devoted entirely to Jack Hand. A lucky find, but irrelevant to his present purpose. He smiled and set it aside. The third told the tale of the Two-Part War, what later became known as the Second Scour. Dante's knowledge of that time was hazy at best and he read until Blays woke, absorbing the tale of Mallon's ill-fated crusade four hundred years ago through the Dundens into Gask, where hard winters had regularly left their forces under-armed and poorly fed, weakening them until they'd been in no condition to drive out the Gaskan counter-thrust into their northeast territories, which had menaced the neighboring lands until King Sarl I had been forced to sign treaty granting Arawn's faithful in all Mallon freedom of worship, a treaty that had been broken eight years later when the other houses declared they could no longer stand for such blasphemy in their homeland. Sleep had mostly dried away the sunken mood Dante'd entered after their encounter with the arrow-firing gate-keeper, and as he read the last of his depression burned away, leaving his mind light and swift, renewed under the warm glare of written words.

But for Dante's finds, interesting as they were, he was yet no closer to understanding the remainder of the *Cycle* than when they'd left Shay. Somewhere in this city he had to find the key.

They ate a cold breakfast and decided to venture out on foot, reasoning the horses might command respect, but they'd command double that in attention. Dante was certain the Arawnites were still searching for him, but was fairly convinced they'd lost his trail and didn't know how to get it back. He doubted they had anything more than a vague description of his appearance and wanted to give no watchers any reason to look his way twice.

After twenty minutes of aimless walking and another thirty of fruitless attempts to get directions from other pedestrians, Dante was considering heading back for the horses if only so the next time his Mallish words were met with a sneer he could just trample the offender to death. Finally they lounged in an unused doorway on one of the busier streets and tried to look undisturbably dangerous till they heard words they could understand. They fell on the two men who'd spoken their language, swords swinging from their belts, maneuvering themselves between the men and the open street.

"I swear I'll run the next man through who brushes us off," Blays muttered loudly as they approached.

"Pardon me, but are you able to direct us to the Cathedral of Ivars?" Dante said to the pair, tilting back his head and shooting for an air of ironic embarrassment.

"Easily," the taller of the two said, glancing between the road-worn faces of the boys. "Follow the road through the Ingate, then make straight for the Citadel. The Cathedral will be the rather large thing across from its gates." He considered the cluster of structures toward the middle of the city. "In fact, you can see its spire there," he said, pointing over the roofs to the titanic arm of a steeple standing across from what appeared to be a single enormous block of gray stone. The structures were a couple miles away, faint through the smoke and the early morning haze of the bay, but indisputable, the clear heart of Narashtovik.

"I see," Dante said.

"Our thanks, kind sirs," Blays said.

"Right," Dante said. "We'd been warned of the aloofness of this city, but hadn't warranted it would extend to the honest faithful."

"Indeed," the shorter man said, eyes flicking down their shabby clothing and unkempt faces. "You've traveled far?"

"From Bressel by the Aster Sea," Dante said. The two men raised their eyebrows. Dante licked his lips. "But we left it months ago. And now we have a couple miles still to travel, it seems. Good day."

"I told you," Blays said once they'd headed up the street.

"We had no way to know that," Dante said.

"It's the tallest thing in town!"

"And if we'd guessed wrong we might have spent so long wandering we'd miss the sermon. That's right, we'd be wandering for two days." Dante glanced toward the Cathedral and Citadel whenever their great heights could be seen above the clutter of the streets. He had the unpleasant suspicion the clergy of Arawn didn't limit their control of the city to its finest church.

Things got louder, busier, and fouler the further they traveled toward the city center. They walked through a decent number of poorly-dressed people speaking two or three different tongues and gazing up at the ruin and age like all newcomers to a major city, but despite the pilgrims' presence and the locals hurrying on about their business it felt less alive than a place as middling as Whetton or the Gaskan town they'd stopped in along the way. They made good time through the modest traffic, reaching what the man had called the Ingate within a half hour.

Four men bearing pikes twice their height and dark-plumed helmets flanked the gate into the next ring of the city, the last set of walls besides the Citadel itself. The guards' eyes tracked the comers and goers with the alert boredom of those used to standing on the same square yard of street all day. Dante and Blays settled against a nearby building to share a drink of water and watch the people pass. For no reason they could see, half the company peeled from their post and stopped a dirt-smeared man on his way through the gate. They spoke in the garrulous local language, voices pitching up, and then the guards flung down their pikes and dropped the man in a flurry of punches. They picked up his unconscious body by the armpits and dragged him through an iron-banded door set into the stonework beside the gates.

Abrupt shifts in the gray of the stone betrayed where attackers had successfully bombarded them down, but in contrast to the earlier walls, these ones were unbroken, unadorned by the heads and quarters of criminals and the unwelcome, clean from moss and lichen. These walls looked like the rock on which the enemy waters would break. When Dante crossed beneath them, sharp eyes meeting those of the pikemen, the city within the tight circle of the Ingate looked whole, as prosperous and peopled and mighty as the noble quarters of Bressel. At its center, no more than a quarter mile distant, the sheer, smooth walls of the Citadel dwarfed all but the spire of the Cathedral. It had once been a palace, Dante knew, the ancient capital, but now it looked more like a castle. Narrow slits were spaced along its curtain walls and the towers they connected; among the crenels he saw the far-off shapes of men standing watch on what lay below.

"Now that is a big building," Blays said, letting himself look impressed.

"What do you want to bet it's where Samarand calls home?"

"I don't know. My life?"

Dante snorted. They strode down the street. Men with half a foot in height on them shuffled out of their way without seeming to know why they were moving. They turned another corner and before Dante looked up he thought he could sense the vast weight of stone pressing on him with greater force than the rocky walls of the mountains had. He lifted his eyes. They'd found it. To his right, the keep; to his left, the church.

The Cathedral of Ivars was built with clean lines and elegant swoops that made the intricate buttresses and delicate arches of the great churches of Bressel look like an unshaven man in a dress. For a full minute they gazed at the charcoal-hued stone spearing up into the sky. Two thick towers flanked a central one whose flattish face seemed sewn together by a series of vertical lines standing out from the stonework. From the gigantic block of the body of the church the main spire was stacked in three discrete levels: two of them squarish, the second somewhat narrower than the one beneath it, and crowning them, reaching so high as to stab the stars, a conical tower of dizzying steepness. At its apex Dante saw a plain ring of steel, the icon he'd come to know as Arawn's.

"I think I need to sit down," Blays said, falling back a step, arm held out behind him for balance.

"My gods," Dante said. He fought the desire to fall to his knees.

"That must be...that is really, really tall."

"Five hundred feet?" Dante guessed.

"I've got no gods damn clue."

"Higher than the Odeleon of Bressel. That's 366."

"By a lot," Blays said. He lowered his gaze and shook his head. Nobody was paying them much mind, Dante saw. A few others were standing on the far side of the street trying to catch the cathedral's full perspective. Others filed in and out from its great doors, eyes downcast, speaking softly if at all.

"Let's go inside."

"What?" Blays said. "Just walk right in?"

"I think it's okay," Dante said, jerking his chin at the others. "They don't look any cleaner than we do."

"But what if Arawn knows?"

Dante frowned at him, then led them up its steps and to the double doors. Ten feet high and five inches thick, but they swung easily, noiselessly. Dante followed a couple other pilgrims through the foyer and then they were in its main chamber.

Captured space soared above them. The ceiling arched like the keel of an upside-down boat, or like the ribcage of Phannon's leviathan. It was the single largest room Dante had ever seen. At its far end was a richly draped dais, a red pedestal and a number of metal trappings gleaming brightly in the light through the shadowcut glass windows and hundreds of candles lining each wall. The front half of the room was consumed by row on row of benches, their wood stained as dark as silt. Between where they stood and where the benches began lay a clean floor of creamy stone tiled with the twelve-part circle of the Celeset. Recessed alcoves along the walls sheltered icons and minor shrines to the prophets of Arawn. All that space looked empty as the air beyond a cliff, but there must have been eight guards and forty pilgrims in the main chamber, lighting prayer candles in the alcoves, kneeling before the altar, standing near the room's edges with their hands over their mouths and eyes drifting across the wings of the ceiling.

"Awfully wide open," Blays said. With small gestures Dante mimed sighting down an arrow shaft and letting fly toward the altar. He raised his eyebrows at Blays, who shook his head. "I don't know."

"Imagine it packed," Dante said.

"With soldiers, maybe."

Dante headed over to one of the walls. Footsteps and coughing echoed from front to back, but as long as they kept their voices to a murmur he didn't think their words would carry. He contemplated an alcove presenting a three-foot statue of a holy man he didn't recognize, a work of thickly impressionistic muscles and blunt features. Its clean lines mirrored the greater build of the cathedral.

"Could take cover in one of these," he said. "Nearer the front."

"I'm guessing those benches aren't intended for the huddled masses. Might not be able to get too close."

Dante nodded, trying to gauge the distance from alcove to altar. It was a ways. Somehow it was harder to guess indoors, inside a building where a full-grown man had no more presence than a mouse.

"How's your archery?" Dante said.

"Shitty."

"That much better than mine?" Dante sighted in on a couple of decently-dressed men standing in front of the main altar. He couldn't tell one from the other. He and Blays would have to be closer to stand any good chance of landing an arrow — if they could even get the bow through the door. If they had a straight line of sight, which was doubtful when the crowds filled the place up. And the closer they got for the purpose of improving their chances of a true strike, the further they'd be from the doors that would let them outside. "No. Won't work."

"Spell?" Blays said, catching his eye.

"Not sure my range is any better." Dante rubbed his eyes, trying to remember the furthest he'd fired the nether. The tree in the graveyard in Whetton, probably, and that had been barely half the distance they may need. They had two days yet till the sermon of Samarand. They could return to the wilds to let him test and flex the reach of his mind, but such an attack would rest on a full foundation of assumptions. Was this sanctuary warded against hostile employment of the nether? For that matter, was there any such thing as wards? Samarand's priests, would they be as wary for otherworldly assaults as her pikemen would be for those of steel? "I'm thinking this isn't the place."

"I'm rather doubting that castle outside would be any easier."

Dante bit his lips between his teeth. "She'll have to walk here and back from it."

Blays huffed, the puff of air ringing from the walls. He lifted his eyes and lowered his voice.

"From just across the street."

Dante nodded. "There'll be crowds. Confusion."

"And probably no more than a minute when she's in the open. Not much time for the right moment."

"You know, this was never that hard all the other times."

"Not counting all the times we were nearly killed," Blays said, eyes full of scorn. "Can we go back outside? Talking about this in here's creeping me out."

"Yeah. Gods, it's beautiful."

They left its hushed shelter for the bright daylight and the relative roar of the babble of pedestrians. Across the way the Citadel stood as solid as if it had been carved straight from a hillock.

"We'll get here early," Dante said. His voice wasn't yet back to a normal level. "Watch how she comes in. They'll probably follow the same route back."

Blays bit his pinky nail, spat it into the street.

"How is it," he said, staring at the battlements, the flags snapping in a wind they barely felt at ground level, "they seem to know our every move when we're 1200 miles away, but here we are close enough to piss through their bedroom window and we're free as an eagle?"

"Probably don't recognize you with your hair down in your eyes," Dante said. "Not to mention that stupid beard."

"Yours is so much better. Looks like you sewed a rat's tail to your lip."

"Rat tails are hairless."

"Well, imagine they're not."

"Two days," Dante said.

Blays bit another nail. "Only if it looks good."

"Maybe the whole city's lit up with the stuff of the book," Dante said. "It'd be like trying to find a lantern held in front of the sun."

Brays wrinkled his brow. "Are you basing that on anything at all?"

"Well, it would make sense."

"You're an idiot."

"Nobody's come through that gate the whole time we've been here," Dante said, nodding at the closed doors in the frontside of the Citadel's walls. "Do you think that's odd?"

"Oh yeah. When I was growing up in our castle back home we let people in and out all the time. The walls were just to impress the neighbors."

"I mean you don't need to keep them closed all the time when you've got all those soldiers. You'd think we'd at least have seen someone carrying food in or garbage out. Or couriers waving letters around so we can see how important they are. There hasn't been a thing. Closed in the middle of the day."

"Yeah," Blays said, folding his arms. "It is a little odd."

"I'm going to ask someone," Dante said, straining his ears for the sound of their native language.

"What? What did Robert tell you about questions?"

"Suddenly you're on his side?"

"Just because he's a prick doesn't make him wrong."

"Excuse me," Dante said, flagging down someone who wasn't dressed in fur. "Excuse me." He put a hand on the man's shoulder. The man spun, face dark, but his eyes went guarded when he met

Dante's. "Can you tell me why the Citadel's gates are closed midday?"

"No one goes in," the man said in a thick accent.

"Ever?"

"Ever."

"No one?"

The man rolled his eyes. "Priests go in. No one else. That's why they call it the *Sealed* Citadel?"

"Ah," Dante said. "I thought that was just an expression."

"No, this is an expression," the man said, following up with something obscene. He walked away.

"Did you hear that?" Dante said to Blays.

"Yes, but I think you'd break your back before you reached it."

"About the Citadel."

"Yeah." Blays tipped his head at its high walls. "So what?"

"So we can't get in. We might just have this one shot at Samarand."

"Yeah, and maybe she'll recant her wicked ways and off herself before we have to do it for her." Blays' mouth twitched. His brows drew together, creasing the skin between and above them. At that moment he no longer looked in any way young. "There's no way we can know until the moment comes. Let's not talk about it till then."

13

Instead of talking they prepared. The next day Dante sold the horses, reasoning it was better to take whatever they could get now than to get nothing when they were stolen. In his haste he received perhaps a third their worth, and in coin noticeably blacker and irregular than the Mallish chucks that had been minted within his lifetime, but to him it seemed a fortune, a rogue's retirement in the coin of the realm. They blew half of it on clothes, on fur-lined black cloaks and gloves, on unpatched trousers and padded doublets of the high-collared fashion popular in the rank of Narashtovik. Dante chose red, Blays a deep pine green. No one would mistake them for princes, but neither would they any longer be indistinguishable from the gutter-sewage. They found a barber, were shorn of their wispy beards, had their shaggy hair shortened and straightened. In the clean sunlight of the street, Blays brushed stray hair from the back of his neck, a strange smile on his face.

"I feel like a jacketed ape," he said.

"We look like traders," Dante said, feeling the weight of the coins in his pocket. "Maybe even minor nobles. They won't turn us away."

They walked around the city till long after dark, not yet ready to forfeit the long hours to sleep. At last, legs weary from the trip to market and back to the cathedral and two circles around the Sealed Citadel and a trip to a public house, they returned to the home they'd made inside the first wall and stretched out on a pile of their old clothes and blankets.

"I wonder how Gabe fared," Blays said into the quiet and the darkness.

"I bet he turned that monastery into a fortress."

"And knighted the monks?"

"Why not?"

"Picture it," Blays said. He laughed through his nose. "Those bony old men sallying forth on goatback. Waving butcher knives and rakes."

"The rebels don't stand a chance." Dante chuckled. They were silent for a while. "He'll be fine," he said, mind on all the weeks that had gone by since they'd last seen him. All the southlands had been under threat of fire when they'd left that world behind. "We'll see to that."

In the ethereal dawn hours before Samarand's sermon they walked to the bay at the north edge of the city and gazed out at the subdued waters of the northern sea. Gray, brackish on the breeze, calmed by the sandbars at the bay's mouth and the arms of land to either side.

"How many men can say they've seen both this and the Aster?" Blays said, kicking rocks through the fine dirt of the beach.

"I'm glad we came," Dante said, uncertain what he meant. The sun struggled against the mists of the waters, cloaked and concealed. He wished he could have watched it rise one last time.

They arrived some three hours before the sermon. Already the streets were thick with people. Men in rags with strips of burlap tied around their feet, men in finery to shame Dante and Blays' new clothes, passels of boisterous merchants whose rings shined in the sunlight. Norren loomed above the crowd like the Cathedral of Ivars above the dead city. Dante shifted the sword at his belt. Robert's warning about the curiosity of foreigners had cowed him into asking no questions about the legality of bearing arms in this place, but they'd seen many men in the streets who wore blades without worry, including men of obvious lowness and poverty, and this day was no different. He supposed a couple thousand years of constant invasion had made lax the laws of arms so strict in Bressel.

Dante's nerves felt as tight as the morning before the Execution That Wasn't. He sipped often from his water skin and halfway wished he had something stronger. The boys spoke little, eyes on the crowds, eyes on the men standing post on the walls above the keep's great gate. An hour before noon they entered the cathedral. Half full already and still the streets were packed. They returned outdoors, restless and beware, ambling down the broad way, then leaned against the side of the thick walls of the house of some noble estate. The shield above its gate wore the black and white of Barden and the same spiral horns Dante still wore around his neck. He'd seen other men wearing them, too, men dressed in the plain and frill-less clothes of traders who profit too little to ever stop for festivals and feasts, but he had no idea what the horns meant to those who saw them, whether they were doing him any good to wear them.

Noon came. The bells of the cathedral pealed for three full minutes. The crowd quieted, then heaved with the volatile energy of anticipation, eyes on the silent gates. The last bell rang and wavered in the cold, crisp air. One moment slipped by, then another.

The groan of ropes and clank of chains cut through the babble. They hushed as if commanded by the earth itself. Guards emerged from a small door by the gate and helped guide the huge gates apart. Behind them a grille of iron bands as thick as Dante's arm lifted a final foot and locked into place. A stream of footmen bearing swords and short pikes and dressed in the black and silver of the watch of Narashtovik marched from the walls of the Citadel to the street, carving an open lane to the doors of the church. They assembled into two solid lines, arms presented, chins lifted, heads held immobile as a small retinue of fancy-dressed men and clergy in soft, thick-folded robes entered into the open space. A chant thrummed through the silence, a foreign song shot through with grace and loss and renewal. Dante stood on his toes and at the center of the procession he saw a woman in a silver-trimmed black robe that clung to the swing of her arms and the sweep of her legs. Her open face was aged but not worn; rather than the crumbling edifice of something that had once been grand, her features looked like the accumulation of a strength that could only be built through long years, the way a cathedral as eternal as Ivars could only be built by two or three or five generations of architects devoting their lives to its completion. A single black braid ran down her back. Dante heard Blays draw in his breath. Her name rippled through the crowd.

"Straight from the keep," Blays said, low. Dante nodded.

"Right out in the open."

The men from the keep moved with formal deliberateness. None looked younger than forty; most much older, bearing varying degrees of beardedness and baldness, walking on knees and hips stiffened by the clutch of time. A single norren walked with them with ponderous strides. Ninety seconds spent crossing the street, no more, and then they walked through the same cathedral doors as everyone else would. When the last priest had disappeared from the street the castle guard turned as one and filed back through the Citadel gates, leaving behind a small detachment of troops, half of which followed the retinue of clergymen within while the other half split itself to posts on either side of the church doors. The crowd woke from the spell of having looked on something holy and piled up through the doors. Elbows jostled Dante's ribs and back. Blays clung to the back of his cloak to keep from being separated. They squeezed inside and after that crush of people the soaring interior of the cathedral felt as open as the head of a hill.

Seated to either side of the dais at the great hall's rear were the monks and priests of Samarand's detachment. She was nowhere to be seen, though through the close-pressed masses and the shaggy heads of norren and the faint smoke of candles and braziers she could have been standing at Dante's shoulder without him having the wits to notice.

By habit and instinct as deeply felt as the drive that calls sea-salmon to take to the rivers and streams of their birth, the men with fine dress and tongue-tripping titles had settled in the benches at the front, and like the striations of rock the boys had seen in the shelves of the Dunden Mountains, the men and women who filled the temple grew progressively grubbier the closer they got to the front doors. Blays said something Dante couldn't catch. He tugged Dante's cloak and they slipped off to the right, cutting through the relatively loose crowds that filled the space between the solid clumps of men lining the alcoves and the clustered masses toward the church's center. After a minute of rubbed shoulders and dirty looks their fresh clothes matched those of the men around them. They stopped roughly two-thirds of the way toward the altar, perhaps eighty feet from where Samarand would speak. It would have been impossible to fire a bow within these person-choked confines.

Blays leaned toward Dante's ear. "So this is the part where they make us wait to remind us just whom Arawn loves most, right?"

"Lots of guards out front," Dante said.

"Lot of crowd, too. That could help."

"Yeah." Dante rested his hand on the pommel of his sword and wondered how many of the priests up on that altar could channel the nether. He could sense it, he thought. Power like a gaping chasm. When he narrowed his eyes he thought he could see the shadows hovering around them. Perhaps it was just his eyelashes. He giggled, covered his mouth. Seconds birthed and died as the masses waited and he found himself strangely awed by the precision of time, ever revolving, matched with the undeviating courses of the sun and the moon and the five roving planets and the backdrop of the stars. Perhaps these believers were right; something so regular could only exist through the glory of the gods of the Celeset.

The crowd inhaled as one. There she was, alone at the center of the dais, materializing as if she'd always been there. Her hands were folded in front of her stomach. Despite her robes, Dante could tell she was a thinnish woman, possessing no more body than was necessary for the discharge of her responsibilities. He had a clearer look at her face, both plain as a farmer's wife and unadornedly magnificent as the standing stones of the long-dead people they'd seen in the hills on the northern side of the mountains. It held no arrogance, however, none of the severe lines of austerity that should come with the isolation of her holiest stature.

"Welcome, travelers," she said into the light buzz of voices. Her voice spread through the acoustics without echo. The people fell utterly silent. "Welcome to this place and to this time. Many of you have come from distant lands. Cities and hamlets I couldn't pronounce." She gave a wide smile, then let her face grow sober. "Let us first offer prayer to any who may have left this world along their way. It's a cold season. A dark time, though we see the promise of dawn and will soon feel the warmth of the sun. Not everyone who stepped out on the path toward that sliver of sunrise now plants their feet inside this cathedral. They are honored but not grieved on, for they are with Arawn now, culled back to the form from which we all sprung. Let us remember the years they spent among us in this world."

The people bowed their heads as one. A couple coughs broke the stillness, but no one spoke. Blays leaned in toward Dante again, whispered so softly he could barely hear it.

"She's speaking *Mallish*?"

Dante opened his mouth to offer some insult, then stopped. He hadn't thought about what language Samarand would choose in this swapped-up place, or how they'd hope to understand her assuming she chose Gaskan, but she spoke clearly and without accent. There had been a kind of hum to her words, though, an undertone which couldn't be explained by any special architecture of the church. It was as if she spoke through a vibrant fog that cleansed her words even as it enshrouded them. A trick of the nether, perhaps. Dante shook his head, shrugged.

"Thank you," she said softly. "May they find peace in the kingdom beyond our own." She gazed out over the crowd, letting long seconds speak of her contemplation. "These times are indeed troubled. It's easy to forget we're not alone in our strife and struggle, that our fathers and mothers and their mothers and fathers saw troubles every touch as serious as our own. It's been that way as long as our city and indeed the race of man can remember. There is a story I've heard that speaks to this, from a place very far from here, from a time that's beyond the memory of any of our long lines, about a young man named Ben."

She paced forward on the dais, gave her head a little tilt, spent a moment examining the mathematical beauty of the arch of the ceiling.

"Ben was the second of the eleven sons of an old and clearly well-loved man, a miller who'd lived on the banks of the same river all his years. For all his heart, his home was humble, and as his sons came of age he could no longer support them all in its modest walls. When the last of them reached the age of fifteen, he gathered them in the yard, for none of his simple rooms could contain them all, and said to them as follows:'I've been your father for many years, and I've done what I can to see you never want for food or shelter. But now I'm old and you are young, and it's time for you to become men of your own right. Go out into the world. Make your fortune. Return here, in seven years' time, so we may share your joys, for I know all of you will grow to be fine and honest men.'

"His sons nodded and they embraced and went their separate ways. The years passed and it was as the father had said: they prospered, found the love of wives and the respect of men. At seven years they ventured back to their home, families in tow, to rejoin their father and support him as he had once supported them.

"The father and his sons wept openly when all were back in one roof. They built a grand house around the old, one to keep them all in warmth and safety, and after the final hammer stroke they gathered in its airy kitchen to toast each other and tell the stories of their seven years apart.

"'All of you are healthy, wise, rich,' he said, though Ben, in his unclean robes, showed no wealth of coin, and possessed no more than the clothes on his back and a sad-eyed black hound.'Tell me what you have become, my sons, and how you've made your way in this world.'

"'I have become an armsman, strong of arm and stout of heart,' said the eldest.'I am a farmer, a man of wide fields and sweet grain,' said the third son.'I am a harlequin of the king's own court,' said the fourth,'and every time he calls me my tricks lift the clouds from his brow and lift his heart to rule with the wisdom of the gods.' And so they went through the line, each telling the story of his wealth and place, until at last only Ben remained, second-son Ben, swathed in his simple robes and unshod feet.'And what wealth may you share, Ben?' the father said.

"'I am a monk,' he said.'I have no temple, no mass or brotherhood to call my own, and I live only through the charity of alms. But I am at peace, and perhaps I can bring that to my brothers and my father.' The father smiled and again embraced his sons. But the others looked askance at Ben, lone among them who'd have no place in the gardens of the nobles."

Samarand paused her story and drank from a plain copper cup. She smiled out on the people. For the first time Dante thought he saw a crease of skin beneath her eyes.

"And so the brothers lived together as they'd done while young. The armsman kept their fields free of bandits, the farmer fed them each meal, the harlequin made them laugh and clap each eve. All shared their gift and talent—even Ben, silent Ben, would tell them stories of the gods and their prophets when asked. And for a time they did live in peace.

"But as with all men who don't understand those whose joy comes from a different source, in time the brothers grew resentful and jealous.'Ben swings no sword,' the armsman said.'Why should I protect him from the thieves?''Ben grinds no bread,' the farmer said.'Why should I feed him of my harvest?''Ben knows no dances,' the harlequin said.'Why should I pass his long hours with mine?' And so they decided to cast Ben from their house. The father tried to argue, saying Ben was of their blood, he was wise as any, but he was old and couldn't stand against these ten sons. And so they took Ben up, breaking his fingers when he tried to hold fast to the doorway of the house, and they cast him on the street with his dog, penniless as the day he'd returned.

"Ben grieved for the loss of his brothers and his father, but he told what he'd learned to the beggars and the vagabonds and they shared their bread. He preached in the street and the people came to hear his words until no traffic could pass that throng in the square and still the crowds grew larger. A year from when he'd been cast out the people of the town came together and built him a temple: a proud, simple shrine of stone to hold his flock and hear the things he'd learned in his years and his travels. Twice each week Ben spoke his sermons, and in those times he smiled to see the joy he brought to those who'd listen.

"The brothers heard of his temple, came to town to see it. It was simple enough, but beautiful, in its way, and when they looked on it the shame of what they'd done to Ben burned inside their hearts. Instead of coming to him with open arms, they clustered together in angry words, and that night they came upon the temple and burnt out its roof and smashed down its walls with great golden hammers in defiance of the success Ben had earned.

"When Ben saw what they'd wrought, he wept. Not for the temple: temples can be rebuilt. Nor for himself: he knew the permanence of his temple had been an illusion, and that though it had been built for him, it was in no way his.

"He wept for his brothers. He wept for the anger that had turned them from joy; he wept for what he knew was next to come. For the townsfolk came to Ben and cried out at the sight of the ruins of what they'd built.'Who did this?' they said, and Ben, who in his virtue told no lies, answered them:'My brothers.'

"He tried to salve their anger, to tell them this was an earthly matter, that more stone could always be dug from the ground and set in place. His words fell on ears deafened by righteous rage. The crowd marched upon the house of the brothers and drove them out. They put the fine house to the torch and the brothers to the sword. The flames of their destruction cast long shadows on the town. They spared the father, the old man, and with damp cheeks and beard he walked from that place forever, taking with him Ben's black dog."

Samarand paused to smile forlornly and from his distance Dante saw Ben's terrible sadness reflected in her eyes.

"In time they built a new temple. Its spire kissed the heavens. It was more beautiful than the first. They brought Ben to it, and said unto him,'We are sorry for the fate we brought your brothers, but they tore down what we put up.' Ben looked at them and nodded.'I do not condemn you,' he said.'There was no right in what they did.''Then we did right, to burn their house, to plant them in the earth?' the people said.'No,' Ben said, and he held up his hands for silence.'I do not condemn you. But do not mistake vengeance for justice. The gods look on us all with sorrow, for truly we have forgotten the harmony of their sphere.' The people bowed their heads. Ben returned to his sermons and the people returned to his temple. He spoke with joy and with righteous visage, and never again let the townsfolk see the sadness that had stolen his heart."

Samarand sighed. She stepped down from the altar and paced its steps, meeting the eyes of the barons, the ships' captains, the farmers, the docksmen, the landed gentry, the wandering vagabonds. She turned her back on the assembly and stepped back up to her place at the altar's peak. A few men coughed, muffling their weakness in their hands and cloaks. She let a minute go by before turning her plain face back toward their sight.

"The jealousy of men finds us all. The men of the south and the east, even some of our brothers and neighbors in our own land of Gask, they look on what we do and they mistake piety for threat. Who is Arawn? He takes us all, this much is true, but he does not seek nor want our end. He takes us in his time, and when he does he welcomes us to his fields in the stars.

"Still, we strive for Ben's virtue. His patience. We try to make his peaceful compassion our own. We try not to blame our brothers for the wrongs they do us. After all, they are our brothers. I've been to a dozen lands and I see the same faces here as any corner of the earth. Look around you. Go ahead." Thousands of faces turned and met each other. Samarand met men's eyes and nodded. "I see the same men and women, sons and mothers, uncles and sisters as anywhere else. Are we so fearsome? So foreign? Such a menace to the ordered world?

"Maybe we are. Our brothers think so. When they see our temples they look upon their own mortality. When they hear our scripture they hear the bells that toll for their souls. When we speak our truths, we speak of things that trivialize the weight in their purse, the bounty of their soil, the flash of their brooches and rings. Still, we want no man's death. We don't even seek to own his mind, which is more than can be said for some orders of the house of the Belt. We want nothing more than a place at the table.

"In the end," Samarand said, clasping her hands before her, her voice clear and pained in the open air of the great cathedral, "who is to be blamed for the chaos we have seen? Is it our brothers, for their failure to understand us? Is it us, for having the temerity to raise arms to reclaim those things we would build upon the face of the earth?"

She pursed her lips, shook her head.

"Let us seek to be like Ben. Let us take no pleasure in whatever we must do to keep our temples and our faith. The gods do not smile as we bury our dead. Not even Arawn wishes a man's blood to fall before his time, no matter what the men of other gods may say. We are not right to take their blood, no matter how wrong they may be to make us take it. Remember that. Whatever we must do, they are our brothers. They are our brothers. When they

die, we must weep. We must be like Ben."
"Live this earth."

"Live this earth," the crowd responded, and this time Dante heard their words in a mixture of tongues. Samarand nodded simply. She stepped down from the dais and was surrounded by her clergy. For a long while no man spoke nor moved, their minds consumed by the truth of her parable. At last the men on the benches closest to the dais stood to speak to each other or gaze longer on Samarand's face where she exchanged words with the others of her order. The standing crowd blinked away their trance and the singular acoustics of the room dissolved into babble. A general movement toward the front doors began.

"Let's get outside," Dante said. "Get a good spot for her walk back."

Blays nodded. They forced themselves into the crowd. Dante glanced over his shoulder as he shuffled forward, trying to catch sight of the woman in black and silver. She would be delayed with her duties to recognize the presence of the men of importance who'd attended her sermon and now waited for her in the first rows. The rest of the masses oozed toward the doors, a foot every couple seconds. After a few minutes the blockage gave way and the people thinned and the boys could walk at something near a normal pace.

"She tells a good story," Blays said.

"Reconsidering?"

"Pretty words don't change what she's doing down in Mallon."

Dante nodded. "No swords." He glanced around the square, shielding his eyes against the glare of the day after the dim of the church. "I may be able to do it unseen."

"Right."

They drifted a short ways from the straight line between church and keep. The square was filled with men just milling about, talking over the speech, discussing what they'd do for lunch, a confusion of Gaskan and Mallish and a couple other minor tongues Dante couldn't place. The gates to the Sealed Citadel were open, but blocked by a black mass of guards. They weren't expecting Samarand to be long, then.

"I wonder how she does that," Dante said.

"Does what?"

"Reconciles what she's saying with the burning of Whetton. All the things they're doing down there."

Blays rubbed his left eye with the back of his hand. "She probably doesn't think she's doing anything wrong. Otherwise she wouldn't be doing it, would she?"

"But it's acting more like the townsfolk than Ben."

"So? That was just a story. That's just something they say to keep everyone else in line."

"Yeah, but it doesn't bother her." Dante stared into the space above the heads of all the people. "I really think she believes it. It's so hypocritical."

"Ben's a dream, you dummy. Something to keep little people like us happy and faithful while she's off getting things done. She's not moping around worrying over the state of our souls. She's off fitting the world like a glove to her hand."

Dante looked at Blays, alarmed. He was supposed to be the clear-eyed one, not Blays. Blays was supposed to be breezily unconcerned, unflappable. Something in his speech reminded Dante of the careful parsing he imagined Samarand must do to cleave her beliefs to the things she did.

"How does someone get like that?" he said.

Blays shrugged, spat between his feet. "We've killed a lot of people to get here."

"But we *had* to!" Dante said. Blays only shrugged once more.

Dante watched a half dozen troops march with pikes on shoulders across the square. A few pilgrims continued to trickle from the church doors. No sign of the priests. He took a drink of water. Though he could feel the pressure of his blood beating in his veins, his hand was oddly calm. He smelled the stink of the city and its people, the shit and the rot and the sweat, odors his nose had ignored since the day of their arrival. If he concentrated he could isolate a score of different conversations. The sun shined from the stones of the street and the faces of the buildings. It was a nice day.

"Did I tell you," Dante said, a grin replacing the brooding on his face, "the morning they were set to hang you, I wrote a letter to be read after my death?"

Blays' face lifted with laughter. "What did it say?"

"I can't remember. Something about how I was off to save my friend and I expected to die in the doing."

"I'd have traced my middle finger."

"I wasn't in the best of moods," Dante said, shuffling his feet. "That was actually the least hysterical thing I could come up with."

Blays nodded. He rubbed his clean-shaven jaw. "What would you say now?"

Dante thought a moment, giving the question its due. "I'd say hello to Cally and Gabe and Robert."

"That's it?"

"That's it. What would you say?"

"I'd ask them to catapult my body through the roof of a nunnery."

"You wouldn't!" Dante said, wiping cold sweat from his temple.

"Why not?" Blays yawned into the sunlight. "What would you do if a body came crashing through your roof? Scream, right? Get all excited? I'd like to think my last act was to give the sisters a little fun."

"Shut up," Dante laughed.

"They spend all day reading holy mumbo-jumbo and squeezing their legs together. Don't tell me they don't deserve a good time."

"There she is," Dante said, grabbing Blays' arm. He bumped him toward the cathedral. Men clustered up around the doors and called out to Samarand from the midst of her retinue. She met their wide-eyed gazes with a look of pleased shock. Men called out for blessings, falling to their knees at her feet. She touched their hands and brows and Dante could see her lips moving. He called out to the shadows just enough to make sure they were there. They waited, restless and snapping, as if aware of his intent. Samarand waded through the penitent. A number of armed and uniformed guards followed the troop of holy men, but they cleared no path, letting Samarand mingle with the faithful. Dante grasped Blays' cloak and forced them forward, trying to guess her course. A dozen priests at her side, as many guards. Not a chance for a straight fight. He had it, then, the plan that had till that moment been so nebulous and abstract. A single dark stab at the woman when she was too close to detect it before it opened her belly—then blend off through the crowd. Simple enough. His ribs felt prickly, like a hill of ants were walking up and down his skin. Samarand made no hurry through the surge of men and women seeking her touch, her words. More pushed forward to fill up the spaces as soon as they opened.

She came closer. Men walked away dazed and smiling with parted lips. The process was orderly in a way mobs weren't. Dante pulled his lips from his teeth, turned it into a tight smile to try to match the faces of those around him. He heard the musing tones of Samarand's voice and then the laughter of men. The priests clasped hands with men in gold-threaded capes and soft-furred cloaks, leaning in to exchange counsel and well-wishes. The knot grew nearer. Thirty feet off, now. The eyes of her bodyguards were clear, casting through the men who thronged around her for the glint of daggers or the shadow of nervous faces. Someone bumped into Blays and he fastened his fist tight. The boys exchanged a look. Blays' eyes were flat, cold, ready. Dante imagined his own as their mirror. Samarand smiled, bowed her head to someone's kind words, and Dante remembered all the men she'd sent to kill him. The dragging gasps of their last breaths. The way they'd hounded him through city and forest. Letting him be baited by the book, then making him fight his way to their favor or die on their blades. Like beating a pup until it was ready to prowl the grounds with nothing but hate for any man it saw. She would deserve it, he knew. She wasn't like Ben. She treated people like tools to keep her safe behind her high walls.

Twenty feet away, ever closer. Ten. He could hear each of her words now, the thick-tongued scrape of Gaskan. He moved to put Blays to his left, between him and the Citadel. He slid his knife from his belt and sliced a shallow line over the ball of his left thumb. Blood wormed into the folds of his hand. A single bead rolled down his palm, dripped to the street. He closed his eyes to catch his breath. When he opened them she was standing in front of him. Their eyes met. Samarand's were a sky blue, airy with the peace of her fifty-odd years. He saw no violence in them. She was a good liar, then.

She murmured something in Gaskan and he steeled himself against a flinch as she reached out for his forehead. Her fingertips were warm. She looked at him again with kind creases in the corners of her eyes and he felt a yawning fear sweep through the marrow of his bones. He let the nether wait. When she moved down the line, when she turned her back. He dipped his head to mimic the gratitude of the others. He kept his left hand clenched, blood slick between his fingers. Samarand smiled at him again and turned to Blays, who doffed an imaginary hat. She laughed, took his hand. Dante held his bleeding fist against his stomach and sent for the nether. He found nothing, an emptiness he'd never before felt. His breath shuddered. At once the shadows flooded forward, filling his vision with gray. He looked down and saw a violent darkness surging around his hand. Samarand said something holy-sounding to Blays and moved along to the next man. It was time. Release it. Split her chest so no man could mend it. Use his blood to spill her own.

She shuffled along. Blays glanced at him from the corner of his eyes. Dante licked his lips. The high collar of a priest brushed his nose and he jolted back and nearly blasted the man with the shadows he intended for her. Heads craned and waggled between his and hers, now. He thought he could feel the weight of her presence, the deep substance that bulged beneath her skin. Release it, strike her down. His fingernails bit into his palm. Blays' elbow nudged his hip. He shook his head, paralyzed but quivering. She was well into the crowd now, hidden by the upraised chins of those she'd passed, by the bulky shoulders of monks and men-at-arms. Dante let the shadows fade, felt them burn along his hand as they dispersed back to the cracks of the earth.

"I couldn't," he whispered.

"I know," Blays said softly, but Dante saw the doubt in his eyes. Dante closed his own. Laughter and chatter battered his ears.

"I was waiting for the moment, but when it came I couldn't get a hold on it."

"We can find another," Blays said. "We know where she keeps herself."

They threaded their way from the square. Dante didn't reply to Blays' simple stabs at jokes and after a while of walking Blays began humming a hopeful tune he'd sounded along the river beyond the mountains. Dante let out a long breath. His feet ticked over the cobbles. He rubbed dried blood from his hand. Blays led the way;

he gave no thought to their path or the city around them and was mildly surprised some blank time later to find themselves back at the house they called theirs. She had meant to take his life: she'd tried it on four separate occasions. Yet he couldn't end her own.

"I wonder if she always travels with so many guards," Blays said. He shut the door behind them and gazed at its iron handle.

"I expect so," Dante said, the first words he could remember saying since the square.

"The priests, could you tell? Were they all swoll up with the same power you've got?"

"Some of them. There's a stillness around the ones who do. A heaviness."

"Maybe it was for the best, then," Blays said. "They probably could have told it was you."

"Probably," Dante said, and wasn't consoled.

They burned a week walking endless circles through the dead city, scouting the Sealed Citadel for ways inside, waiting for open gates, searching for tricks of passage. Every time the doors opened and the grille raised forty armed men watched the entry of the man they had parted the gates for. Wagons were searched before they were allowed through. They saw nothing more of Samarand, heard of no other sermons or appearances. They could bribe their way in, perhaps, or try to scale the towering walls by cover of night, but the keep was a city to itself, and even if they stood inside the courtyard they'd have no way to find the woman priest within its alien layers. Every measure seemed too desperate, its hopes far too trivial to risk their lives for.

They killed the rest of their long hours sifting through the rubble in the outer regions of the city, kicking around the trash of houses for anything they could use or sell. It was a tedious business, dirty and exhausting, and they did it in their rough old clothes. At four hours a day, they found more to sell than they spent on food enough to keep themselves alive. Dante rose each day feeling hollowed out, torn open. He'd missed his chance, and as time raced on, time that surely saw the spread of unrest and death in their homes in the south, he saw no way to amend his mistake. His weakness. It had been a single moment, but it had confirmed every fear and close-held hate for himself he'd ever felt.

He thought of nothing else, knew his life from now till death would be defined by the single minute when he'd thought himself strong but found himself wanting. Whatever else he'd done well or done right meant nothing. Blays' attachment to him was hollow. His skill with the nether, a talent he'd once allowed himself to think would one day enshrine him in immortal glory, that was a sham, a delusion. There was only his failure, that non-act that loomed cyclopean from his memory, sharper and more crippling than any wound to his body. He began to wish he'd never existed; he daydreamed of standing at the foot of a hill and being consumed by the damp, cool dirt, leaving no trace of himself on the stupid earth.

By night he found some small comfort losing himself in his books. Dense works, dripping with intricate thought and elevating efforts of logic, it was a week before he finished the three he'd found in that abandoned temple on their first day within Narashtovik. The day he finished the last of the tomes, he and Blays walked the roads between the two sets of walls until they found another edifice bearing the marks of Arawn and none of recent use. Dante combed its floors and shelves for more books with which to salve his mind, and there, among the rubble and the ruin, at last he found the answer.

14

"Here's your damned book," Dante said, flipping the *Cycle of Arawn* at the feet of one of the priests they'd found inside the Cathedral of Ivars. The bald man raised an eyebrow at its sprawled pages.

"A copy of the *Cycle*," he said, replying in Mallish. "Shall I add it to the hundred others in the cellars?"

"Not *a* copy," Dante smiled. "*The* copy."

The priest glanced at him, then at the book on the floor, then shot Dante a sharper look. His shoulders jerked at the cold defiance on the boy's face. The priest tripped on the skirts of his robe as he bent to snatch up the book. He cupped it with both palms, the White Tree of Barden shining up at his face. A tall, willowy priest, silent till now, leaned over his shoulder to gaze on its cover.

"Dante Galand," the bald priest said, and Dante willed his face to keep composed. "Why have you decided now to return it to its proper owners?"

"I've read it all," Dante said, tossing his head. "Besides, I'm tired of killing your men."

"It's not even sporting anymore," Blays added from his side.

"You wouldn't know a real man if you were staring straight at his kneecaps, boy," the tall priest spoke down to them.

"You think so little of Will Palomar?" Dante said through curled lips. "We slew him too, you know."

"Will's not dead," the tall man said. Blays burst into laughter. "Is he?"

"He hasn't come back yet," the bald priest said, meeting the other's eyes. They turned back to the boys. "No. Boyish fancy. What are you, twelve?"

"Almost sixteen," Blays said.

"Our friend robbed the corpse of his mailed shirt," Dante said. "We thought his cape too womanly to take."

The tall priest gasped. The bald one beetled his brows.

"I assume," he said, voice measuredly soft, "you didn't come all this way to let us know we need to order another tombstone."

Dante nodded, body as tight as a bowstring. It all hinged on their reaction to his next words.

"I can't read that gibberish in the back," he said. "I want to know what the rest says."

"There's a nice long section about the tragedy of outgrowing one's breeches," the bald priest spat.

"I don't remember that verse," the tall one said. The first priest blinked at him.

Dante folded his arms. "I'm joining your order. I want a cell in the Citadel. Access to your archives. A tutor who knows enough to be of use to me."

"We'll give you a cell." The bald priest licked his pudgy lips. "A nice dank one, with good thick walls to keep you safe."

"You'll do as I say," Dante warned, stepping forward until his nose was an inch from the priest's. "You'll give me my books. My lessons. The knowledge I still lack. And I'll release our god from his chains in the heavens."

"You're a rat's asshole," the tall man said. He splayed out his hand. In the same moment Dante met the priest's nether with his own and Blays' sword whipped up to dimple the man's throat. His adam's apple bobbed against the killing steel.

"Put your weapon down," the bald priest said, and for the first time his eyes were bright with fear. "And you step back, Paul. I've heard enough to know he's not as weak as he looks."

The priest named Paul spread his fingers in peace and lowered his hands to his waist. Blays kept the blade at his neck. He twitched his hand and a tiny rivulet of blood leaked down Paul's skin. Paul suppressed a whimper. Blays snorted, lowered his sword.

"There," the bald priest said, folding his hands below his chin.

"All right. Let's calm down and think about this for a minute."

"Think about me gutting you like a trout if you try one of your little spells again," Blays said, twitching the point of his sword at Paul's belly.

"Like a flounder for him," Dante said, pointing to the bald one. "It's fatter."

"And think about me gutting you like a flounder."

"I said let's calm down," the bald priest said, shuffling the anger from his face and waiting till Blays put away his blade. The man took a long, slow breath and gazed around the small living quarters in the back of the cathedral where the boys had ambushed them. "This is beyond my authority," he decided, nodding so the wattles on his neck ruffled like a lace sleeve. "Paul. Go see Larrimore and tell him the boy has come. Tell him he's brought us the book."

"And then what?" Dante said, pointing his chin at the bald priest's sternum.

"And then he'll figure out what to do with you," he said through his teeth. Blays' sword ground against its sheath as he worked free the first half foot. "Which I'm certain will be peaceable and amenable to both parties." He fixed Blays with a look. "They'll appreciate you've returned our property without any more bloodshed."

"What are you waiting for, Paul?" Blays said. "Move your bony ass."

The bald priest fought a smile as Paul hustled from the room. Blays glanced at Dante and bugged his eyes. Dante fought down a laugh that would have unmasked them both. They snapped their faces flat and dully contemptuous as the priest turned back to them.

"What's your name?" Dante said.

"Nak Randal," the bald priest said. He nodded to Blays. "And yours? We never learned your name. We'd taken to calling you 'The Pain.'"

Dante saw Blays swallow a grin. "Blays Buckler," he said.

Nak sucked his cheeks and darted his watery brown eyes between the two boys for any sign they were putting him on. Blays didn't need to act to make his face go red.

"Very well," Nak nodded quickly. "Dante Galand and Blays Buckler. You've come a long way."

"We heard of your city's legendary hospitality," Dante said.

"Thought we'd see it for ourselves," Blays said.

"I hope it hasn't disappointed," Nak said, wiping something from his eye and examining his nail.

"Someone shot at us on the way in," Blays shrugged. "It's been better since."

Nak nodded. "It might have helped to learn the language. Things are a bit bestirred at the moment, but some of the city's wary of foreigners."

Dante snorted. "We've been a little busy being snuck up on in the night by Samarand's hounds to work on our education."

"I suppose that's true," Nak said. He crinkled up his face and rubbed his eyes with one hand. "Things are going to get interesting a few minutes from now. Care for a seat until then?"

"Thanks," Blays said, thunking into a chair. Dante took the one beside him and Nak bent over the last one in the room and dragged it in front of them. He sighed as he sat down, then laughed, shaking his bald head.

"They're not going to like this."

"Too bad," Blays said. Nak crossed one leg over the other, wincing when his slippered toe snagged on his robe.

"Trouble with your feet?" Dante said.

"Bunions," Nak said sadly, then looked up, faintly embarrassed. He frowned hard at Dante. "Speak like that to Larrimore and he'll either kill you on the spot or take to you like a duck to water."

"Lots of non-duck fowl like the water," Dante said.

"What?"

"Who's Larrimore?" Blays said before Dante could expound.

"He's known as the Hand of Samarand," Nak said with a hint of irony around his mouth, "because he turns her will into something you can grasp."

"He's a priest, then?" Dante said, leaning forward.

"Just a man with an uncommon facility for getting things done. If he weren't so damned good at it, you can bet one of the council would have stilled his restless tongue a long time ago. Thus why he might actually like you two."

Dante cocked his head. "If he's that good, maybe his arrogance is accurate."

"Even if that were granted," Nak said, folding his robed arms, "he still lacks the wisdom to realize that fortress over there may be jammed with holy men, but it's no less a court than the palace in the capital, where respect and obedience are the highest virtues of all."

"I thought the winters up here were supposed to be cold," Blays interjected, cutting Dante off once again and refusing to return his annoyed look. Nak swiftly took this turn of the verbal crossroads, allowing it had been unseasonably warm, in fact the mildest winter he could remember from the last twenty years. He was still telling Blays about all the people who had died during last year's blizzard when the door swung open and a thin, sharp-boned man with the light brown face of one of the Marl Islanders from the sea south of Bressel strode into the room. Two guards bearing sheathed swords followed at his heels; Paul took up the rear, eyes locked straight ahead, as if he were afraid where they might land if he let them free.

"Nice of you to return our book," the sharp-boned man said, glancing between Blays and Dante as they stood. "It would have been a little less trouble if—"

"You're Larrimore, then," Dante said, taking in the man's unfashionably short black hair, the tears and stains to his thick, fine-stitched cloak. His boots looked like they had once been worth more than all Dante owned, including his life, but had since been scuffed and worn to the point where they resembled the bark of a pine. His black gloves and scabbard were the same. The only thing he wore with any hint for its care was the silver badge pinned to his collar: a gleamingly polished ring around the wide-branched image of Barden, and at the tree's center a pair of sapphires winked as richly blue as the glacier-fed lake they'd looked on with Robert. From his tight-trimmed hair to the knot-heavy laces of his boots, he gave off an air of almost willful disrepair, like it offended him to have to concern himself with anything as trivial as how he made himself not naked. Dante was thrilled in a way he couldn't explain. The man was thirty years old at the utmost and at the clear peak of his life, wholly vital but in no way boyish, and when

Dante summed him up it was like looking on the man he could become if he grew into himself without flaw or injury.

"You weren't kidding," the man who must be Larrimore said, eyebrows raised at Paul. Paul nodded, eyes still fixed rigidly across the room. The man turned to Dante and spoke in a quick tone that nearly sounded bored. "I am indeed Larrimore, the Hand of Samarand, and as an acolyte of our order you will address me with the respect my station is due."

"So you've seen reason," Dante managed, thrown by the man's use of the word "acolyte." He hadn't known what to expect—this plan, like their plan for when they'd first come to Narashtovik, had been built on the desperate premise they'd show up with a goal in mind and let no resistance stop them from reaching it—but at his most optimistic he hadn't expected such ready acceptance.

"Did you really slay Will Palomar?" Larrimore said, tilting his head.

"I smote him down with a column of flame."

"Wonderful," Larrimore said. "Nak, how would you feel about a move?"

"A move, sir?"

"Across the street. The boy will need a teacher. He hasn't slapped you around. I assume that means he likes you." He raised an eyebrow at Dante and Dante nodded. "Well?"

Nak drew back his chins. "I'd be honored for the chance."

"Then it's settled." Larrimore nodded to the guards. "Take them to the chapel. Clear a cell for Nak and one for Dante. Throw out some of the monks if you have to."

"Blays comes with me too," Dante said, struggling to keep up with all that was happening.

"Only men of cloth may live within the chapel," Larrimore said.

Dante set his jaw. "He is my hand as you are Samarand's."

"Well, I do set the rules," Larrimore said, rubbing his throat. "I suppose no one can say anything if I'm the one who breaks them." He jerked his head at the two armsmen.

"By your will," one guard said through his beard. He gestured toward the door. Dante took the lead, Blays and Nak moving to flank him. The second guard moved toward the head of their sudden formation. Their bootsteps echoed through the vast emptiness of the cathedral. Dante and Blays exchanged another look, all but jogging to keep up. The lead guard held the front door and they broke into the overcast afternoon of the square. Across the way the castle gates stood open. Motionless pikemen lined the walls that led inside. They walked across the square and the shadow of the gate's thick stone cooled their faces as they crossed from Narashtovik to the separate city of the Sealed Citadel. A small squad of guards drilled in close order in the yards. A minor market lined the wall to the right of the main gates, peopled by keepers that spoke in normal tones with the men who handled and haggled for their wares. The clink of smithies underlined the modest chatter of the market and the barked orders of the soldiers. Directly ahead, the keep jutted straight up from the ground: shorter than the church on the other side of the square, but an immense thing in its own right, a powerful block of dun stone and pure strength, like a titan's front tooth sown in the earth. Dante's eyes tracked up its neck-bending height.

"I haven't been in here in a while," Nak said, pleased. One of the guards gave him a bored look. Behind them came the clank of chains lowering the grille and pulling closed the reinforced wooden gates. Before they reached the keep they heard the boom of tons of iron-hard wood clapping together.

The guards escorting them wasted no time taking them to a small but ornate chapel that leaned against the outer wall of the keep. Its main hall, perhaps thirty feet by twenty, felt toyish in comparison to the cathedral they'd so recently left. One guard led them to the cells at the chapel's rear while the other pulled one of the curious monks aside to confer about quarters.

"Don't leave this room," one of the guards said once the monk had shown him to an empty cell. He ushered the boys inside. "Someone will see to you in time."

"Goodbye, for the moment," Nak said, offering a wave.

"See we're not kept long," Dante said. "And bring us some food."

The guard's mouth twitched. He nodded to the monk and they walked on down the hallway. Blays waited for their footfalls to recede, then closed the door and pressed his back against it, palms spread wide across the wood.

"Lyle's parboiled guts," he said, gazing stupidly at Dante, lower lip tucked between his teeth. "Did what I think just happened actually happen?"

Dante sat down on the cell's feather pallet. When they brought in another for Blays there would hardly be room to walk around. Dazedly, he pinched the bridge of his nose until his eyes watered. The last half hour had felt like a completely different life than that of the prior week.

"Ow," he said. "I think it's real."

"Well what now?"

"I don't have the faintest idea," Dante said, rubbing his finger below his nose. "Really, I didn't want to think about what would happen after we threw the book at them."

Blays nodded, still grinning. "Let's try not to get killed."

"I promise nothing." He leaned back, gazed up into the timbers of the ceiling. He felt as if he could rip the roof down with a look. Why hadn't he been like this before? Why hadn't he known that what he was depended on no more than what he willed himself to be?

It was there. It was all there. Everything he'd wanted collected within the walls of this simple temple: copies of the *Cycle*; references and interpretations; versions with the final third translated into Mallish. He reached toward the shelf of the chapel library and heard Nak, who'd been sent back to their room an hour later to settle them in and show them around, say something about reading it in the original. Dante slid free a Mallish translation and sat down in the strong sunlight of the south-facing reading room, glad to be off his feet, which had felt swimmy beneath him. He hadn't realized just how long he'd been kept from finishing the *Cycle*, just how much its version of the world had come to underpin his own.

"Much simpler than your idiotic mishmash," Nak was saying.

"What?"

"The grammar. Unlike your'tongue,' if it can be so called, ours actually follows rules." Nak scowled at him as Dante leafed through his book. "Certain subtleties are lost in the translation. Besides, you sound like a barbarian. You're in Gask now."

"Tomorrow," Dante waved.

"I've been charged with your instruction," Nak said, slipping his hand beneath its cover and folding it closed, "and if the remainder of the *Cycle of Arawn* is still beyond you, I need you reading at least as well as a child before I can direct you through the rest."

"I said tomorrow!" Dante swung to his feet, sucking air through his nose. "I'll be your student then. I'll be as diligent as the course of the sun. I just need this one day with what's eluded me for so long."

Nak ran a finger around his flabby jaw, then nodded. "Very well. This day is yours. Tomorrow is mine."

It was a translation, and for that he was wary, but the difference between the *Cycle*'s first sections and that final third were too clear to be caused by the liberties of any scribe. It felt older. Primal. They were the words not only of a different man, but of a different race of men, a men whose waking thoughts were just as much a dream as the hours they spent in sleep. As Dante read the same basic story that had begun the *Cycle*, he felt as if he'd found a cord between himself and the deepest, purest knowledge of that first and brightest spark of man—that at last, the riotous chaos of civilization might be put into some kind of sense.

> *In the days before day, in the nights before night, all things swirled, all things mixed with another, the waves broke but there was no shore, the foam foamed without light to see its crest on the waters, great Arawn and Taim fought the serpents and the dragons of the stormy north and roiled the water with their struggle, Arawn's great mill cracked and fell.*
>
> *The bodies rolled on the surface, scale and claw, eye and tooth, and from their spines Taim grasped them and formed them to the shores and the peaks, he plucked their knuckles and set them to the islands, and Arawn split the first sky from the second sky, where he left to grant the measure.*
>
> *And what of man? Carvahal said, and from the blood of the serpents and the blood of his own shining wounds Taim packed them into the mud where the river met the banks, the wind filled their lungs and they stood and saw what Taim had made.*

To the men he gave the earth, and he made the sun to warm them and coax the seeds of plant and babe. To the heavens Arawn forged the thrones of the gods and he planted the stars of his law. Carvahal left his seat, he left his house and found the northern fire where once a dragon watched its waters, he cupped that star-light in his hands and bore it down to minds of men, he showed them where the two rivers rose into the skies.

And so Taim cursed men to wither and return to mud. Arawn cried out, he cried to see the men so used: he took their dust and ground it in his mill where he ground the grist that fed all things, and there the wind would carry the last breath of men, there it would take them to the black fields, again they would mix with all that once had been.

But Arawn's mill was cracked, it had broken in the struggle with the north-laired dragon, it had fallen when that dragon fell and cracked upon the earth. And when it ground again, this broken mill, it ground no more of stars and plenty; the stars had shifted; now strife was ground with man.

"What?" Blays said, and Dante realized he'd been laughing.

"I just read how the gods made the world."

"You mean like you could have done in any temple back in Bressel?"

"Their story is like this one's shadow," Dante said. His shoulders felt like hilltops, his fists like boulders. "We didn't make the world a terrible place, like the priests of Taim say. The gods did."

Blays grunted. "I thought you didn't believe in the gods."

"I don't. But maybe they just died a long time ago, and this is what they did before they went away." His smile fell as Blays continued to watch him. Did he suspect it? The second layer of the plan that had gotten them inside? That the only way Dante could think to get close enough to Samarand to kill her would also take him to the one place he knew would have a *Cycle* he could read? It wasn't that Dante had lied. He'd gotten them inside the Sealed Citadel, meant to learn its layout well enough to figure out how they could murder her and then escape back to the south. That hadn't changed. But neither had his other need. He could do both. Learning the *Cycle*'s last secrets could only help him when it came time to snuff Samarand's candle. If suspicion tickled Blays' mind, let him hold his guesses. Dante had been the one who'd gotten them through the gates.

He read on. He heard Blays' boots knocking around the confines of the chapel, the whisper of pages as the boy pawed through the monks' stash of romances, presumably in search of saucy pictures, then more footsteps and the close of the front door. Dante read without cease, lighting a candle once he realized he'd been squinting into dusklight for the last half hour. He read without pausing to take down all the names or map out all the places like he'd done when he'd started the book. That would come later. For now he had this one night to read it through, and when he turned its last page a couple hours before dawn, he felt the breath stir in his lungs, the blood in his veins. He felt elevated, touched by a mood of lightness and wholeness. From that vantage, his worries and doubts looked like malborn vermin, things he could pick up and snap into two dead halves. He closed his eyes, pressed his palms together, felt the fiber of the shadows mingle with the flesh of his self, felt it pour into the empty places in his body, in his skin, in his blood, in his hair and eyes and heart, felt his own position as an extension of the eternal burn of the stars. He opened his eyes and the world was changed, he a part of it and it a part of him, and he knew that when he died, it would mean no more than a retreat from the isolation of this body back into the blood-warm swell of nether.

Dante woke the next morning the same way he always had—confused, vaguely angry, already weary toward whatever the next hours would bring in a way he thought unfair for any 16-year-old to feel—and it was a while before he remembered he should feel any different. But sleep had robbed him of that elevation he'd had on finishing the book, that sense of oneness and rightness, like if he had to die it would be all right if it just came then. He had its memory, though, the thirsty knowledge it was possible to feel that way, for however brief a time, and instead of feeling cheated, he lay beneath his blanket in a mood of deep removal, not at peace but too far from his worries to be hurt by them, and passed an hour coldly dissecting the facts of his life until Nak knocked on his door.

"Get teaching," Dante said once he'd let him in.

"Oh, so it turns out you've still got things to learn?" Nak said, and in the mental coldness that hadn't quite left him Dante could tell Nak's jest wasn't meant to run him down, but came from a sense of admiration the monk could never voice in plain words.

"I finished the *Cycle*," he said.

"And?"

"It felt like I'd been lifted to the moon," Dante said. He frowned. That wasn't right—it was incomplete, at least. "It felt like a foundation. Now it's time to quarry more blocks and keep building my tower."

"Ah," Nak breathed. "You felt the touch of Arawn."

"Perhaps," Dante said, not because he thought it might be true, but because he found he didn't care how Nak wanted to classify it. Nak scratched his bald pate and led Dante to the reading room. A spread of sparsely-worded primers lay in the soft winter sunlight on the desk. Dante picked one up, felt the last of his clear-eyed coldness seep away. "These look like they're made for children."

"And unfortunately you know less than a child," Nak said, "but they're as simple as we have."

Nak stepped him through the Narashtovik alphabet, which was nearly identical to Mallish but lacking three letters, and the subtleties of its pronunciation, which unlike the Mallish stew was regular and orderly as the board of a game of cotters, and which Nak claimed was close enough to Gaskan to sound like no more than a regional accent. He made Dante write it out five times, then speak each letter five more. He drilled Dante on the verb conjugations of Narashtovik and its relation to modern Gaskan. He showed him the structure of its grammar in simple sentences, taught him a handful of words, the precise laws of how a verb cycled through the tenses of the present, the past, the future, the subjunctive. He bade Dante write out a dozen verbs through each of their forms and left on some monkish errand. Busywork, Dante thought, and far too much to take in at once. That Nak wanted him to learn through rote memorization struck him as an insult. He did it anyway, writing out Nak's precise little tables. Nak returned and nodded at his work, correcting his past pluralizations, then went over it all again before leaving the boy with pages of hand-prepared vocabulary to study through the evening. The next day he had Dante write out maddeningly simple sentences about cats chasing balls and boys throwing sticks. The next day was the same, but working in the other tenses, repeating and repeating until Nak was satisfied what he'd taught had stuck.

"When are we going to read something real?" Dante asked as Nak prepared to leave him once again.

"Once we've laid a few blocks on your foundation."

Dante rolled his eyes and turned back to his lists of words.

"Learning much?" Blays asked him when he came back to their cell for the night.

"Conjugates," Dante said, staring at the shadows on the ceiling.

"How do you say to murder'?"

"Natus," Dante said. He lifted his head, stared at Blays. "We knew this wouldn't work overnight. They have to learn to trust me before I'll be able to get close."

Blays shook his head at the cold night and silent yard past the cell's small window.

"There's a world outside this keep."

"Give it time," Dante said. "I haven't forgotten why we're here. You just keep your eyes open while we wait for something to happen."

Their wait didn't last long. Nak bent over Dante's latest lesson, following his sentences with the sharp tip of his pen, striking out words and muttering corrections, when the door banged open and slammed against the wall, shuddering to a stop.

"Knuckles possess a great facility for knocking," Nak said. He looked up and his teeth clacked shut. "Uh, my lord."

"The boy," Larrimore said, beckoning with a single flick of his finger. Three guards crowded in behind him.

"I have a name," Dante said.

"That will only be an issue if we decide you're worthy of a tombstone." Samarand's Hand nodded to the guards. They grabbed Dante by the elbows and dragged him toward the door. The bluster he'd come at them with back at the cathedral and ever since crumpled into nothing. He could only gape at Nak, plead dumbly for help from the middle-aged monk.

Nak tapped his fingers together. "May I ask—"

"Their *Cycle* is a fake," Larrimore said, running his tongue along his teeth.

"Ah," Nak said. "Upsetting."

Larrimore ignored him, turning on his heel. The guards hauled Dante out the door and out the chapel. He struggled to keep his feet, toes scraping the stone yard. Blays shouted from behind them. Dante winked at him and tried not to throw up.

"I have legs," he said, boots scuffing through the dirt.

"For now," Larrimore said.

"I don't know what this is about." He wriggled his shoulders, twisting his body to find a way to meet Larrimore's eyes. "Do you hear me?"

Larrimore looked down on him, face impassive, then reached out and flicked Dante's nose hard enough to make his eyes water. They carried him up the steps and inside the keep, through its airy entrance and down a hall adorned by tapestries of Arawn and his deeds, by gray-bearded men hoisting pennants and flags over their foes. The guards slowed enough to let him catch his feet as they reached a stairwell that descended to a cool, well-lit subfloor. Larrimore took out a heavy iron key and opened the second door they reached. Dante was yanked through the doorway and heaved into a heap on the plain stone floor. Other than a single lantern by the door the room was empty, chilly, hard rock with dust on every surface.

The armsmen moved to either side of the door. Larrimore shut it and folded his arms behind his back, regarding Dante for a long minute. Dante tucked his feet beneath him and clasped his hands in his lap. Without changing his expression, Larrimore lashed out and booted him in the ribs.

"Cut that pious crap. There's no priests here."

Dante had fallen to his palms, gasping for breath, rage flashing through his skull. Pain rattled up his nerves, but he let his body hurt, knowing it wouldn't kill him.

"Tell me why I'm here," he said.

Larrimore snorted. "Don't play games. You gave us a copy."

"I gave you the same book I took from the temple."

Larrimore stepped forward and slapped him so the ends of his nails bit into Dante's cheek.

"Tell me where the real one is. Now."

Dante made his face twist with anger. It wasn't hard. "How do you know it's a fake?"

The man just laughed. Dante's heart shuddered. How did they know he'd given them the copy he'd found in one of the temples in Narashtovik? Had they found the real one? Had they dug it up from where he'd buried it in the yard of the house next to the one he and Blays had lived in just inside the city's first wall? But they couldn't have: otherwise they'd be busy killing him, not questioning him. He stayed silent.

"There are no identical copies," Larrimore said. "You idiot. Like we wouldn't look past the pretty white tree on the cover. Your attempt at deception is outrageous in its stupidity. As if we have no records. No way to check." He blinked, tightened his jaw. "You gave us a copy. An old one, but a copy nonetheless."

"It's the same one I found. Maybe you've been chasing the wrong one this whole time."

"Where is it?"

Dante rolled his eyes. "If you're so sure I've got it, why don't you just conjure it out of my pocket? Or sniff it out like you did all across Mallon?"

"Because we can't," Larrimore snapped, jerking his head back and forth with each syllable. "We're not hounds and it's not a fox. It can be lost as simply as anything else. Including lives."

"Then how do you know you *weren't* chasing a fake?"

Larrimore lashed out with his boot, aiming for Dante's side. The boy shifted at the last instant and it struck him in the hip. He sprawled out on the stone. The nether throbbed at the edges of his vision. He panted, glaring up at the other man.

"Answer me!"

Larrimore bared his teeth. He pressed his fist against his brow and shook his head.

"We followed you by the blood you left at the temple," he said, leaning forward as if preparing to kick Dante again. "We know the book there was the real one. Ergo, you had it."

"But it's fakes you plant in the temples!" Dante pushed himself back to his knees and glared up at the man. "That's right. I'm versed in your bizarre little scheme. How you leave out copies where people can find them, then if they survive your attacks you scoop them up and induct them into your order. If they break instead, you toss them away like toy soldiers. And I'm supposed to believe I somehow got my hands on the one true *Cycle*."

Larrimore had drawn up short during Dante's speech. His eyes were slits, his voice as low as the floor.

"How do you know all that?"

"You look at me and you see some boy. I've traveled a thousand miles. I've killed a dozen of your men. I've taught myself to work the nether." For a moment he forgot his bluster, was taken instead by a curiosity he'd had since Cally'd told him how they used the book. "Why do you leave it out like that? Why do you recruit people that way? Why so complicated?"

"Because it works," Larrimore said. He stood in place a moment, face frozen as he stared at Dante. "Men like you are as rare as a monk that isn't fat. Do you know how few people can work the nether? We need as many as we can find. Their strength's the only thing keeping us from being crushed." He continued to stare, like he'd forgotten this was an interrogation. "You're a strange one."

"I just want to learn."

"You still can. Just tell me where it is."

"I don't know," Dante said, though he knew the man wasn't lying, that they would still take him back if only he told them where to find the book.

"Enough. More than enough." Larrimore crouched down in front of Dante, eyes bright and hard. Again Dante had the sense he could become this man. Cunning as the animal mind of a drunk, open-eyed enough to seize the unexpected and turn it to his advantage before it could be turned against him, with a will so swift and sharp he could trust his quickest instincts to lead him where he wanted. That was the difference between them, Dante thought. Dante knew what he wanted, had the same ability to adapt rather than be caught flat-footed by the false assumption of a rigid mentality. But he didn't know how to act—or didn't trust his impulses to make his desires fact. The burn in Larrimore's eyes told him the man hadn't yet made up his mind to kill him, that there was a way to convince him he didn't have the book and still be kept as a student of the order. Yet Dante's only plan since he'd found the extra copy of the *Cycle* in the garbage of one of their old temples after Samarand's sermon was one of scorn and contempt, a whirlwind of arrogance meant to keep them so far back on their heels they wouldn't have the wits to question anything he said. It had worked till now, till they looked closely at the prize he'd tossed at their feet. And now he was snared.

Bluster and violence were all he knew. He didn't know how to convince Larrimore of a lie. They had him. This was their castle. Their city. Their army of men guarding its gates, their troop of priests hoarding its lore. If he'd been something more, he could have talked his way out. Instead he had no more than his one simple lie:

"I don't know where it is."

"The boring part, then," Larrimore said, almost sadly. "Torture. I think we'll start with Blays."

"He's got nothing to do with this!"

"Of course he doesn't."

"Then why him? Why not me?"

"Because he'll get to you better than if we put you in the boots."

"Don't," Dante said. He knew Blays would die before he gave up their secrets. He was stupid that way. "You're a reasonable man. Why don't you just believe me?"

"Because you're lying," Larrimore sighed. He got up, knees popping, and nodded at the guards. One opened the door.

"Wait," Dante said. He swallowed back his nausea. "What about the prophecy?"

Larrimore paused at the door, face unreadable. "Which prophecy might that be?"

"The one from the *Cycle*."

"It's a big book," Larrimore said, dropping his hand from the door frame.

"The south shall bear the child of flame," Dante intoned, quoting the passage he'd found in the last pages of that final third, the close of which he'd read every night since, "with bleeding hands and bleeding blade; in Millstar's skies he'll write his name and brother's treason be unmade."

"Rubbish. Just like all poetry."

"I came from the south."

"*Everyone's* from the south," Larrimore said. "There's nothing north of here but piles of rock and farmers too stupid to know you can't squeeze wheat from stone."

Dante held up his hands, showed the scars of all the times he'd cut his hands to feed the nether's hungry mouths.

"And these?"

"Every priest of worth has those. Or on the backs of his hands, or on his forearm—or his forehead, if he's given to theatrics."

Dante folded his hands in his lap. Other than attacking the man and his guards outright, it had been his last play. He might be able to kill them. He might even be able to get to Blays before the rest of the Citadel knew what was happening. He wouldn't be able to get them out, though, and would never be able to kill her. It would all be for failure. Tears stung his eyes and he closed them. He couldn't give up the book, either; he didn't know why, just that it was too important, could tip the balance so far that even Samarand's death wouldn't be enough to cease their aggression. He would do nothing, then. He wouldn't break. The least he could do was keep his silence until they stole his very voice.

"Stonewalling," he heard Larrimore mutter. "Delusions of destiny don't impress me. Your only coin's the book. If Blays doesn't give it up, we'll be back for you soon enough."

Dante snapped open his eyes and fixed them on Larrimore. "If I'm so unimportant, why are you doing everything you can not to hurt me?"

"You're overlooking the possibility that's a measure of my own stupidity rather than a measure of your own worth." Larrimore smiled, then remembered himself. "Wait here," he joked. He gestured to the guards and they stepped outside.

"What will Samarand do when she finds you've murdered the keystone of her desire?" Dante shouted after them. He heard them speak in Gaskan to each other, then the door clunked shut. A lock snapped into place and the hallway went silent.

Dante stood, wincing at his rib and hip, brushed dust from his trousers. Other than himself, the dust, and the lantern flickering by the door, the room was completely empty. At least it was clean. He felt calm, somehow, as if his few minutes with Larrimore had spent all his available emotion. Feeling stupid, he tried the door and was almost glad that it didn't budge. He had nothing in his pockets but some of Nak's papers and his torchstone. He sat back down in the middle of the room. Had anyone ever learned to teleport themselves? What was the point of all he'd learned if he couldn't use it to escape a simple dungeon?

He could probably blast down the door, he thought. Murder the guards Larrimore would have posted outside. Still, anything drastic depended on being certain they were going to kill him or Blays or both, and he had the odd conviction that wasn't the case. He'd planted the seed of doubt with Larrimore, thrown him with that crazy scripture of prophecy, if only by a little. Larrimore didn't strike him as the kind of man who put too much stock in anything—likely why Samarand had taken him as her captain—but he was the captain, and if he was off consulting with anyone it would be with her. As the holiest of their order, perhaps she would put a little more weight in the possibility of Dante's importance.

He'd wait and see, then. Doing anything rash would ruin both their chance to assassinate Samarand and his ability to learn the nether through the structured instruction of this place rather than through whatever fragments he could scrape together on his own. They'd decide either to kill him or use him. He wouldn't act until he knew which.

Time went by. Without a window on the sky he had no way to tell how much. He conjugated irregular verbs for a while. He killed some time holding his breath for as long as he could, then waited for his gasps to subside and tried it again. He made a methodic sweep of the room, poking every stone up to the eight-foot ceiling, tapping his toe against every block in the floor. None were false or loose. He hadn't expected they would be, but he liked to think someone who'd shared this room before him had made an effort to escape rather than let himself rot, clapped up and forgotten.

It wasn't until he could no longer forestall urinating that he grew angry. There were no buckets, no holes in the floor. They hadn't exactly forgotten about him in a few hours, either. It was deliberate. They wanted to reduce him to an animal. Degrade his pride. He did his business in a corner and laid down on the other side of the room, breathing through his mouth. After a while he even slept.

Dante woke to pitch darkness. He jerked upright, flinching as if he expected to bang his head. The lantern had gone out. He groped for the near wall, leaning forward until his fingers brushed stone. He let himself wake up for a minute. Torchstone in his pocket. He cocked his head, listened for the scrabbles of rats or anything else lurking in the blindness. There was no need for light, the room was practically a complete seal. Darkness couldn't hurt him. For a while longer he sat there, listening to himself breathe. Maybe it was a good thing he was still locked up. Maybe that meant they had lots of things to talk about.

His stomach gurgled. He had no way to know how long he'd slept, but from his stomach, insistent but not yet pained, he guessed it had been some twelve hours since he'd eaten lunch shortly before they'd dragged him here. He sucked on his fingers, straining his eyes against the inky darkness. He stilled his mind. A coldness like exposing wet skin to a breeze crept over his hands. He thought on the nature of the shadowsphere, the all but solid substance of its delumination, a deeper blackness even than that of this room. He bent his mind to define the sphere by what it wasn't. By its un-ducklike properties. He laughed through his nose, and as his breath touched his palm he could see the creases of his skin, white and illusory as a flash of pain. It winked out at his surprise and he cast back out for its feeling, gathering it in like rope onto a pier. First a spot: and then he saw his hand, his wrist, it expanded over his arm, the dust on his knees and the smooth stone floor. He stood slowly, willing the light to grow. His line of sight bubbled outward until all the room was lit in ghostly white. It had been so simple. What else could he do if he took the time to think about it?

Metal scraped on metal on the far side of the door. Dante started. The bolt clicked. He swept his thoughts clean and popped back into darkness in time for the light of the hall to spill into his chamber as the door swung open.

"Still alive?" Larrimore called. He walked inside, glancing idly to either side of the door, then saw Dante standing half in shadow at the far side of the room. Larrimore was silhouetted, his face unreadable. "Stinks in here."

"That's what happens when you treat a man worse than you'd care for your stock," Dante said.

"At least it hasn't dulled your tongue."

"How's Blays?"

"Untouched, despite my best counsel and his brilliant plan to try to brawl his way to wherever we might have you," Larrimore said. He raised a dark hand to his face. "How would you like to see Samarand?"

Dante snorted. "Do I have a say?"

"Of course not. But I thought you might be comforted by the illusion you did." Larrimore turned toward the door. "Come."

Dante squinted against the modest lantern-light of the hall. After a single day in the room it already felt strange to walk about relatively free — qualified only by Larrimore, the sheathed swords of the guards who followed him, the walls of the keep, the hundreds of soldiers within it, the walls around the keep, and, he supposed, his own need to stay here until Samarand lay dead at his feet. He stumbled and a guard put a hand on his back. He shrugged it away. His heart railed against his ribs. Samarand, face to face. He felt certain he could take her life if he sacrificed his own. Why had all this fallen on him?

They ascended to the entry hall and Larrimore strode straight back to the sets of doors at the far end of the room. A few soldiers and well-dressed men glanced their way. Into a hallway, through another couple doors, a tight spiral staircase. Dante stopped counting steps after a hundred.

Larrimore turned off on a landing a short distance from the top. Dante smiled at the heaving breathing of the others. He was winded, but not badly. All that running away had been good for something after all.

From there they entered a sort of fore hall, thick black rugs on the stone floor, weavings and paintings on the walls, elegant sculpture of the same make he'd seen on the temples within the city. They passed a window of purified glass and Dante stopped short. Below him lay the yard and the walls and the open street, and beyond that, across a yawning gap of empty space, the upthrust steeple of the Cathedral of Ivars soared into the sky. For all their height in the keep, a full two thirds of the church's spire towered above them. Dante was beginning to understand just how big the world was, but surely Ivars was the tallest thing man had ever built. Behind it, the dead city stretched for miles through swaths of gray and white stone, riverlike streets, black fringes of pines growing frequent between the first and second walls and thickly enough to resemble a forest in the crumbling fringes of the outermost city. To his north he could see the gray waters of the bay, the tree-painted arms of land holding it in place, the silvery line of a river feeding it and coursing off to the southeast. It was earlyish morning, he saw, eight or nine o'clock. He'd spent closer to twenty hours locked up than twelve.

"Enough goggling," Larrimore said. Dante pulled himself from the window and hurried to catch up. They drew up in front of a solid-looking set of doors and Larrimore rapped his knuckles against the wood.

A woman's voice filtered through the door and with a distant thrill Dante realized he understood the foreign words: "Come in."

The room was close, warmed and lit by a hearth at its far end. Samarand was seated in front of it, turned toward the door. She folded up the book on her lap and looked up. Her gaze caught on Dante a moment, then she smiled at Larrimore, who walked forward and bobbed his head. They exchanged a few words and Dante's comprehension of Gaskan-by-way-of-Narashtovik evaporated. He shifted his feet as their talk wore on. Samarand laughed regularly, pressing her hand to the base of her throat. His eyes settled on the hollow there, the white, fragile skin. He imagined slitting it. Gathering the nether and caving in her face. If he made the room go black first, he could probably do the same to Larrimore and the armsmen before they could stop him. He was more dangerous than they gave him credit.

"Dante Galand," Samarand said, standing and facing him. Her voice was soft but carried a current of command. Her words were Mallish, but accented with the thick consonants of Gask speech, an influence he hadn't heard when she'd given her sermon. He met her eyes. "I'm sorry you spent so long in that cell. I was out."

"My fault," Larrimore agreed, smiling. She gave him a look and he gathered his men and bowed out through the door.

"It was at least a step more civil than all those times you tried to kill me," Dante said, managing to keep his voice level.

"I've never seen you before today."

"In the fields. Coming for the book. Did I pass your test?"

"Was I ever out in those fields with you?"

"Whose men were they, then?"

She shook her head, gaze steady. "This isn't why I brought you here." She nodded to a chair across from hers. He fell into it, leaning his head against its high back.

"I bet the others were grateful for the chance to prove themselves," he said. She just smiled. He found it maddening.

"It's easy to forget," she said, "when Larrimore tells me of all the things you've done, you're still a child." He let that go. "The others were angry, too. They didn't understand at first. But the same drive that brought them to the book gave them the vision for what they could become. Two of them are present members of our council."

"Is that an offer?"

She laughed again, then touched her fingers to her lips. "You've made things difficult for me. I'd like you with us. We need talent now more than ever. But I need that book."

Dante made himself sigh. "I told Larrimore. The book I gave Nak is the same one I found in that temple."

"Indeed." She leaned back in her chair. She could have been discussing the health of a distant relative. He readied himself to reach for the nether.

"I suppose you've already made up your mind."

"Why would I have done that?" She frowned, showing the wrinkles around her mouth. "This isn't a formality. I wanted to see you for myself."

He narrowed his eyes. "Is Blays safe?"

"Your friend is fine."

"I want to see him."

She lifted one gray-flecked brow. "If it turned out I'd killed him, what would you do about it? Try to kill me?"

"That would be suicide," he said evenly.

"Here and now you and I are in this room," she said with the same easy power with which she'd given her sermon. "It's high and isolated. The doors are shut. I have one question: do you want the knowledge I can offer?"

His hands tightened on the chair's arms. "Yes."

Her blue eyes skipped between his. "Then give me the book."

"Look at these," he said, pointing his finger so close to his eyes he might poke them out, "and know I'm telling the truth when I say I've given you everything I have."

She stared at him the way you'd stare at a scorpion while deciding whether to crush it or leave it be and he felt a flickering around his mind. He jerked his head, then made his mind go as blank as when he sought to channel the nether. Burn in hell, he thought, but he saw no recognition cross her face.

"You're a snake," she said, freezing his blood, "but I see no lie in your eyes."

"Finally. Now maybe I can get back to my lessons."

"Heavens forbid I infringe on your time. Is that how you aspire to spend it? With grammar and vocabulary?"

"I need to know those things," Dante frowned. "You all speak more than one language."

"Yes, we're wise enough to know the world's a large place. And good for us. But you didn't travel all this way in hopes of learning your letters. I'm inclined to agree."

Dante leaned forward, trying to keep his eyes guarded. "Meaning?"

"If these were ideal circumstances, we'd be in no hurry to rush things along," she said, lifting the corners of her lips at what she saw in his face. "But they're not and we do. You'll continue your lessons with Nak, but we've got a lot of work and not enough hands to get it done. Larrimore will make use of you with some tasks more suitable to your skills than copying conjugation tables."

"What kind of tasks?"

She gave an ironic tilt to her head. "Trust my great wisdom will see they're matched to your ability and temperament. I'm not interested in wasting either of our time on tests."

Dante nodded, considering her placid face. He'd have training both formal and experiential. In the employ of her most trusted servant. A chance to at once realize his talents and stay close enough to find the right moment to strike her down. He couldn't have asked for more. He knew this was no fortunate turn of a die, though. He had made this thing happen. Through wit and will he'd put himself in position to receive this offer. He wouldn't squander it.

"I accept."

"Excellent," she smiled, appearing genuinely pleased. Dante still hadn't seen the violence and radicalism Cally'd claimed she'd ridden to power. For a brief moment, he wondered if the old man might have been wrong, if the Samarand he'd known years ago had let age temper her ambition with wisdom. People did change, he thought. He wasn't the boy he'd been three months ago. He'd become potent in a way he'd imagined would take years, had done things he never would have dared on his own. If he could reforge his personality so much in three months, what could Samarand have done in twenty years? Perhaps when she'd gotten the wants of her heart, she'd mellowed, satisfied with her power and her place. "You won't be seeing much of me, of course," Samarand went on. "I've got a lot to do beyond holding the hands of all those administrators who keep writing me for money and troops." She nodded at her desk, overflowing with signet-stamped letters. "Larrimore will tell you whatever we need done. Grow strong. We'll need you soon enough."

He nodded, dazed. She stood and he did too. He wondered if he was supposed to bow. He offered a kind of deep nod, and when the guards escorted him from her chambers, he knew it wasn't to control his path, but to protect him.

"Why didn't you do it then?" Blays asked when they had a moment alone. He had a bruise high on his cheek and a cut across his nose, but he looked to be in one piece.

"We'd have been killed," Dante said simply. He rubbed his eyes and looked up from a pile of Nak's notes. "We can't do this like we've done all the rest. We need a plan. A real one."

"Yeah," Blays nodded, letting his heels bounce against the side of the desk he was sitting on. "Was she as nice in person as at her sermon?"

"There's something about her. She's seductive."

"That's disgusting!"

"Not like that," Dante said, face going red. He shoved Blays.

"Wait, let's not rule this out," Blays said, righting himself on the desk. "We can use this. First, you flatter and sweet-talk your way into her confidence. Then, when the moment is right, you use that sharp tongue of yours to—"

"Shut up!" Dante shoved him again. How had they started talking about this? "I mean, she has a way with people. She's a leader of men. If she's like Cally said, then she hides it well."

"Well, I see how little it takes to win you over," Blays said, eyes lingering on Dante's neck. Dante touched the cold clasp on his collar, the badge Larrimore had given him after his talk with Samarand: a silver ring around a simple, stylized, seven-branched tree.

"This is how I'm going to keep close to her."

"Closer than a private audience?"

"This lets us choose the moment when," Dante said. "That gives us the power." He moved across the room to their one window. "They told me they'd assign you an instructor from the soldiers. You'll be with me on our assignments."

Blays tapped his finger on the desk, then leaned forward, elbows on knees.

"Just what are these errands, anyway?"

"I don't know," Dante said. "Things they need done."

They found out soon enough. Larrimore appeared the next afternoon to interrupt Nak's lesson with a tersely-worded order about a man spotted in the ruins beyond the outer wall. He wanted Dante to bring him in.

"Why?"

"Because I'm telling you to."

"A time-honored logic."

"Because," Larrimore said, tugging his collar forward, "he used to be one of our acolytes."

"Not fond of those who leave the fold?" Dante said, judging he still had some play to his rope.

"Not fond of those who leave it with their pockets sagging with our property." Larrimore tapped Dante's badge. "Nor is it particularly pleasing when they make a point of lurking about and robbing our monks when they're out on their business. Stealing from men of peace! What is this world come to?"

Dante nodded, mollified. "Should I know anything about him?"

"Dark hair. Queued. Bearded—in fact, a general mess, you'll know he's been on the streets a while. Name's Ryant Briggs."

"I meant of a less tangible nature."

Larrimore laughed, met his eyes. "Scared?"

"No," Dante said. He picked up his sword belt. "Well? What can he do?"

"Minor talents. Nothing you can't handle."

"Want him in one piece?"

"Would be nice," Larrimore shrugged. "But denial of men's desires is the gods' way of saying hello."

Dante nodded, buckling his sword around his waist. "He'll be yours by nightfall."

"I hope you're cognizant of the irony here," Blays said after Dante'd found him trading blows with one of the soldiers in the yard and explained their job.

"I'm cognizant. Remember why we're here."

"You'd do well to do the same."

Dante shook his head. They crossed the yard to the small door at the other side of the Citadel's walls, the only other exit from the place, a door far less ostentatious than the main gates but thick as his palm was wide and set in a passage too narrow to swing a sword. The sunlight flashed on the icon on his collar and the door's guards let them by. They strode east into the city, toward the fringes. Citizens' eyes lingered on Dante and the silver at his neck as he brushed by. He gazed straight ahead, a faint thrill of rank and recognition tickling his nerves.

It had snowed the night before and their boots slid on the ice-slick cobbles. They passed under the Ingate to the shabbier, less-peopled buildings between it and the gappy ring of the Pridegate, so named, Nak had told him in a brief break from the endless language lessons, because in all the times the city had been sacked no man who'd defended its outer walls had ever abandoned them except to be thrown in a coffin. Much of the city was still a mystery to Dante—he hadn't been outside the Citadel since the day he'd given them the fake copy of the *Cycle*—but the keep and the church were landmark enough to keep his direction even with the sun hidden behind a screen of clouds. The ground sloped down between the two sets of walls before leveling out in front of the Pridegate, threatening to yank itself from under their feet with every step into the snow.

It was easy to forget, behind the thick stone of the Sealed Citadel and among the bustling crowds behind the Ingate, that so much of the city was wrecked, forgotten, neglected, peopled by the lost and the landless and the outcast—when it was peopled at all. Dante paused in the street just past the outer walls. Birdsong and single footsteps trickled through the rubble and the pines. Behind him, far-carrying notes of shopmen crying prices, hammers shaping steel.

"We were rats recently enough," Dante said, gazing over the houses in their various states of decay. "Larrimore said he'd been seen in this quarter. If you were a rat, where would you hide from our soldiers?"

"A basement, to hide my light," Blays said. He sucked his teeth. "Or the second floor of a place where the stairs had caved in. If someone came for me in my sleep I'd hear them scrabbling around before they could get up to me."

Dante nodded, impressed, but didn't say so. They made a few circles of the weed-choked streets, examining the houses with fresh litter or footprints in the yellowed grass and snow-patched dirt, spooking a few grimy men ensconced in their filth in single underfurnished rooms. In the sixth or seventh house of their search they saw a tuft of long black hair beneath a blanket. Dante called their quarry's name, got no response. He walked toward the man and nudged him with his boot. Stiff. Blays took out his sword. Dante knelt and pulled back the blanket. The body's cheek looked bruised where it rested on the dirt floor, its open eyes dull and glassy. Dante shook his head.

When twilight came, the hour of roaming, they returned to the gateless gap in the wall and sank down against the stone, watching the shadowy figures of men in the distance. Footsteps echoed from the other side of the walls and they put their hands on their weapons. A blond man walked through, eyes darting to the scrape of swords being put away. He hurried into the growing gloom.

"Are they going to string you up if you don't find the guy?"

"They'll probably start with you," Dante said. "Give me something to think about for next time."

"I'd give *them* something to think about," Blays said. He picked up a stick and flipped his wrist in a tight circle, stabbing at the air.

"Been learning much?"

"A bit," Blays said. "They don't fight as dirty as Robert showed me."

Dante grinned. He hadn't thought of Robert in days. "Then they won't be expecting it when we make our move."

"Nor will I, at this rate."

Dante put a finger to his lips. More bootsteps, slowing as they approached the walls, as if their wearer were nearing the end of his journey. The man began whistling. In the day's last light Dante saw a bristle-bearded man emerge from the wall into the dirty street. A light, steady wind tossed locks of black hair over his eyes and nose. Dante let him get a ways down the street, then stood and moved to cut off the way back inside the gates, Blays half a step behind him.

"Ryant Briggs!" he called in the husky, cheerful voice Larrimore liked to use when he was delivering bad news. The man spun, his smile freezing on his lips.

"Who are you?" he said in Mallish, which came as only a mild surprise. His name was southern. He squinted at the pair. Dante edged forward, falling out of the long shadow of the wall and into the soft light of dusk. Ryant's gaze dropped to his neck. "A trained dog? Can you play dead?"

"My name is Dante Galand. You're to come with me."

"And you're to kiss my puckered ass," Ryant said, face gone tight. His left hand lowered to the short sword on his right hip.

"I wouldn't," Blays said.

"They'll give me much worse at the Citadel."

"You've been robbing monks," Dante said. He took another step.

"I had a brother in Bressel," Ryant said, and Dante stopped short to hear the city's name. "I say 'had' because I heard he died on the road a few weeks ago. Killed in a skirmish." He glanced beyond the wall to the hulking mass of Cathedral and Citadel miles deeper into the city. "Surely you've read the scriptures," he said, returning his eyes to Dante's. "Do you remember the part where they compel the church to drag the innocent into its squabbles?"

"What's happening in Bressel?" Blays said. His hands hung at his sides, empty for the moment.

"For all their talk, these people can't take the city," Ryant spat. It was like he'd been waiting for them, Dante saw, had been stewing in his reasons with no audience to which he could explain them. "So they camp in the woods and ambush the nobles and guildsmen and clergy and soldiers whenever they leave the walls. The sure sign a god's on your side, when you're forced to squat in the woods like a cur. They say the people are remembering the old ways, though, that they're joining the fight. For all I know Bressel's burnt by now."

The boys looked at each other for a long moment. They'd speculated sometimes on how things were going in the south, but no one had been able to give them any real news. Dante wanted to press for more, but Ryant would be in the hands of the Citadel soon, might say anything to ease his time if he were put to the knife or the boots—could even, unlikely as it may seem, speak about the boys' unnatural interest in the events of their homeland.

"Unbuckle your blade and come with us," Dante said to Ryant. "They may find mercy when they hear your story, but if you try to run or resist, I'll grant you none.

"Yeah, go on. Do as you're told."

"You don't know a thing about why I'm here," Dante said. He tensed himself. Ryant smiled with half his mouth.

"I know enough," the man said. He pinched his fingers together and the boys were swallowed in pure blackness. Blays' sword rang out from somewhere beside Dante. He drew his own and heard boots pounding away from them.

"Careful," Dante said, then ran after the sound of the man's feet, clenching his teeth at the blind plunge over uneven ground. He managed not to trip and dashed free of the shadowsphere and into the sudden brightness of twilight. Ryant disappeared around the rough-edge corner of a house a score of yards ahead. The boys sprinted after him, making a wide turn around the house in case he'd planted himself against its wall in waiting. Up ahead Ryant glanced over his shoulder and slipped in the snow, cursing as he bounced against the ground. He hauled himself up before he'd finished falling, faltered on his right ankle, then cursed again and ran on with little drop in speed. Dante closed to twenty feet. Ryant weaved through pines, ducking branches. A foot-high fragment of what had once been a full wall sprawled out in front of him and he vaulted it, crying out as his feet hit frozen dirt. He popped up, jogging backwards, and waved a hand at Dante. Fire whoomped up and Dante bent double, hand trailing the ground to steady himself. A strange anger took him—as if it were somehow offensive this man should try to kill him in order to save his own life—and Dante blanked his thoughts and wrapped the nether around Ryant's body in the opposite trick of what Gabe had shown him. Ryant's legs froze up and he toppled forward, sliding facefirst through the snow. Dante approached quickly, Blays circling to his right.

Dante dug his knee into the man's back and yanked his arms behind him. He bound his hands and elbows tight with the rope he'd taken for his task, leaving Ryant's legs unsecured. Let him walk his own self all that way. He gave the knots at the man's wrists another tug.

"I'm going to let you up now," Dante panted, "and if you try anything other than walking exactly where I tell you I'll reduce you to a fine red mist."

Ryant only gurgled in reply, his throat caught by Dante's shadowy grip. Dante let the nether fall away, feeling its reluctance to part, its primal urge to clench Ryant's throat until his breath stopped. Freed, the man gagged, gasped, curled up as his body rediscovered it could move. Dante gave him a moment to regain his wind, then grabbed the ropes around his arms and, with Blays' help, hauled him to his feet.

"I'm going to curse your name the instant before they trim my thread," Ryant said, still half-choked. "One morning you'll wake up dead and never live again. Or maybe your arm will go black and drop off. Or maybe it won't be your arm, it'll be—"

"Get moving," Dante said, shoving him in the back.

Ryant had twisted his ankle in his first fall and their progress was slow. Blays took point, cloak thrown back over his left shoulder to keep his sword visible. Dante walked behind Ryant, eyes on anyone who drew too close while he kept his mind open to any surge of shadow from their prisoner.

"You can still let me go," Ryant said when they were waved through the Ingate after Dante'd shown the wall-guard his badge. The city lay under full dark by then, lit by sporadic lanterns outside public houses and at the more major street corners and by the weak aid of the moon through an overcast sky.

"Be quiet," Dante said.

"Look in your heart. I haven't hurt a soul. That's more than can be said for them."

"Boo hoo," Blays said from over his shoulder.

"It isn't a matter of justice," Dante said.

"What, then?" Ryant pressed, trying to catch Dante's eye. Dante shoved him forward again. "Do you like to hear men beg? Is that what tightens your trousers? The sound of a man's voice who knows he's at your power?"

"Shut up," Dante said. He grabbed the knots at Ryant's wrists and twisted them so the ropes cut into his skin. Ryant cried out softly. "You don't know a damned thing."

The man went quiet. From there, like the prisoners Dante'd seen brought up to the Crooked Tree outside Whetton, even Blays and Robert themselves, Ryant was docile, following their course without speaking, accepting orders of movement with a downturned face. Why did they do that? Why didn't Ryant try to kill him? Did the man's dead brother mean so little to him? For that matter, how was robbing monks supposed to honor his memory? It made as little sense as whatever divine scheme had necessitated his brother's death in the first place, or why the house of Arawn had ever had to face the Third Scour, or why Dante had been chosen to stop a war he couldn't be certain was unjust. He felt no pity for Ryant. So the man had snapped awake enough to see something was wrong. Bully for him. All he'd done with that fresh vision was skulk around the ruins taking pennies from those who'd wronged him. Dante's own ambition was no less than the killing of the order's head. If, as Gabe believed, even that was no guarantee for any kind of change, what chance did a man like Ryant have to make some sense of his life? No wonder he didn't struggle when it came time to give it up.

Dante bore his prisoner to the eastern door from which he and Blays had set out and hailed the guards with his name. They opened it and led Dante's troop single-file down the dark passage through the Citadel's walls, the entry being too narrow to comfortably walk shoulder to shoulder; not content with that precaution, the passage's interior was lined with holes meant for firing arrows and stabbing pikes at anyone with the right combination of strength and stupidity to try to force their way through it. Perhaps they could kill her, Dante thought, and then just walk on out under color of Larrimore's errands. On the other hand, what was the hurry? Who said killing her would solve anything? Couldn't he see a while longer to his training with Nak while he worked out a safer route to the process of transmuting Samarand's living body into a rotting corpse?

"Excellent," Larrimore said when he saw the three waiting for him inside the keep's main hall. He tucked his lower lip beneath his upper teeth and grinned, nose sticking out like a fox's. "That room downstairs has been feeling a touch empty since you left it. It'll be glad to once more be a home."

"He tried to set me on fire," Dante said.

Larrimore's eyes flicked up and down his form. "You don't smell burnt." He spoke orders in Gaskan to a pair of guards and they led silent Ryant away. He turned back to Dante, who lingered in the hall, uncertain what he was expecting. "Well done. If only we'd had you to send after yourself."

"We'd still have gotten away," Blays said.

"Probably," Larrimore said. He raised an eyebrow their way. "What are you waiting for? A knighthood? Get off to sleep. Busy days ahead."

He strode away into the belly of the keep. Probably to let Samarand know of the capture. A strange pride crept across Dante's chest as he exited to the yard. He'd done the service of the enemy, but he *had* done it well. An average man-at-arms would have died to Ryant's simple sorcery. In his brief time in the Citadel Dante had vaulted from a life of self-education and fleeing for his life to one of formal, rigorous instruction and meaningful work. He could be important here, he knew. He was already useful in a manner he'd never been. Nak thought he was bright, if occasionally too aware of it. Already Larrimore trusted him enough to give him tasks beyond the grasp of 99 men out of 100. With no other obligations splitting his focus and loyalty, Dante felt certain he could one day have been one of the twelve men on the council. But he would have to give that up for the well-being of his homeland, a place that banned the light of Arawn and had recently tried to execute Blays and Robert, two of his only friends. He could see no way in which that was fair.

For all those thoughts, as he returned to his cell in the chapel he could see nothing more than the slump of Ryant's shoulders, his slack face, the hollows of his eyes as he disappeared into the dungeons. Ryant probably thought the wrong done onto him was the rightful price of his resistance. He was probably even so vain as to think there was some meaning to whatever would be done to him next—whether it was torture and execution or no more than interminable imprisonment. Well, Ryant was an idiot. Either way he'd be forgotten, just one more body in a city already choked with the yards of the dead. His brother was gone and now he would be too. That was the way of things, Dante decided. With the gods and the stars so far removed from human matters, the only justice to be found was what you took for yourself.

15

By morning he learned language with Nak and by evening they trained with the nether. Dante's methods were undisciplined, Nak noted, crude if effective, and the monk showed him cleaner paths to channel the nether and more closely bend it to his thoughts.

"Most men have to struggle with every step of this, you know," Nak said in mild confusion after Dante had mastered another lesson on his third attempt. "You fly through it like a bolt. It's less like I'm teaching than that I'm revealing things your mind already knows."

They worked in the cold of the open yard beside the chapel, filling the space with shadows and light, with bursts of flame that melted the snows on the grounds and spikes of force that could crack small rocks. When soldiers suffered injuries in training or in scuffles in the streets, they were brought to the chapel and Nak showed him the proper methods of mending flesh and bone. Through all his education, the bald priest made no mention of the peculiar talents of Jack Hand and the few men like him mentioned in the *Cycle*. It was as if death, for as much as the prayers and studies of the priests and acolytes of Arawn centered on the life after life, were a thing beyond them, the one depth forbidden to be plumbed. It was a blind spot, Dante saw. A thing he could exploit.

Larrimore came to him with a new task most every day and Dante'd cease his lessons with Nak to deliver sealed letters across town and wait for a hastily-scribbled reply; to place orders with smiths and tailors; to escort priests and monks and nobles and ambassadors through the danger of the city to the relative peace of the wilds; to tail emissaries and messengers from other cities and lands and see to whom they spoke away from the eyes of the Sealed Citadel. Once he was sent to capture another man, and when the man drew his blade instead of letting himself be tied, Dante struck open his guts with a thrust of his hand. He left the body where it fell and went back to the keep to let them know to send a team if they wanted to pick it up.

A week into this routine, Blays asked again about Samarand, about their true purpose, and Dante answered him like before: in time. He kept his eyes and ears open as he did Larrimore's bidding, and between gossip at the keep and the fragments of conversation he could understand from the well-dressed men bearing the colors of lords and territories all throughout Gask and beyond, he began to piece together that something was coming to a head. The council factored heavily in this intrigue, meeting frequently behind closed doors high up in the keep. More doors opened to Dante by the day—he'd had a reputation before he'd arrived at the Citadel, he discovered, based on the gruesome tendency for none of the men dispatched to kill him to ever be heard from again, and as he carried out Larrimore's will in the field it only grew: he was grimly efficient, they said, already more talented than half the priests who weren't on the council, cold and harsh as sunlight glinting from snow. He was on the rise. Nothing was shut to his blend of ambition and ability.

Nothing, for now, but the doors to the council.

He learned the Citadel's regular orders for weapons were being sent to the city smiths rather than their own forges, which were busy dealing with the bricks of silver as big as his forearm that disappeared behind their walls each day. Dante explored and lingered as much as he dared, intentionally losing himself in the twisting halls of the keep so that, when the time came to still Samarand's heart, he could flee the halls without a wasted step. Priests and guards sometimes caught him in places he had no strict business to be in and he'd lie about an errand of Samarand's Hand or walk on by without a word, as if he were too wrapped up in his latest responsibilities to even notice their questions and turned faces. Once he'd learned the general lay of the keep he started waking earlier, finding excuses to slip away from Nak and walk alone in its halls in the hopes of at last hearing the details of whatever they prepared for—and perhaps, though Dante didn't think it outright, to hear something that would push him into completing the task Cally had sent him here for. When he delivered letters he crowded close to their recipients, daring glances at their responses as they wrote them. He was cutting it close, he knew. He was earning their trust, but he was still an outsider. He wasn't certain they'd believed him about the book, and if they hadn't, why they were giving him so much rope. Sometimes when he heard Larrimore's laughter it no longer sounded innocent (at least, as innocent as Larrimore could claim to be), but scored with an undercurrent of scorn, as if the man could see the treachery hidden in Dante's heart. The slightest noise could make him start like a rabbit. His nerves were getting too frayed to maintain his double purpose.

If he couldn't breach the council doors in person, perhaps he could do it by proxy. The Sealed Citadel was secured against the intrusion of men, but wasn't meant to keep out rats. The night before the next council was scheduled he lay awake in bed until the chapel was long silent, then crept out to the pantry. He waited no more than a minute before the dark blot of a rat wiggled across the floor in search of crumbs. Dante snapped its neck with a brief flicker of nether, then surrounded it with a stronger hand of shadows and reanimated it as he'd done in the past. He closed his eyes and saw the pantry from its alien perspective so near to the ground. Heart racing, he opened the front door of the chapel and sent the beast scurrying toward the keep. Its doors were shut firm and Dante had to wait for half an hour before someone opened them on a midnight errand. He made the rat run inside, head swimming as the ground rushed past its nose.

He kept it tight to the walls of the main hall, eyes out for guards. A few stood watch, faces hooded by gloom, but either they had no interest in vermin or were sleeping on their feet, for his rat made it to the corridors beyond the hall without drawing their attention. He sent it down the passages he'd memorized in his wanderings, running from doorway to doorway, pausing to listen for the sound of footfalls—would the priests be able to sense its intrusion?—but saw no more than one stock-still guard before it reached the stairwell to the upper floors. The dead rat leapt tirelessly from one step to the next, clambering ever upward, until at last it reached the seventh-floor landing where they held their counsel. The hallway was silent, still, lit by a single lantern. The doors of their chamber were open. Dante willed the rat inside, then sent it snuffling around the room's edges until he found a crack in the stone just wide enough to lodge its body and look out on the dark blurs of the great table and its chairs. The task had taken no more than an hour, but he was exhausted, and despite his pulsing nerves he fell asleep within minutes of hitting the bed.

Dante woke an hour after dawn and drew breath so sharply he choked on his own spit. He sat upright, muffling his cough to keep from disturbing Blays, then closed his eyes and sought the sight of the rat. Sunlight diffused through a north-facing window, illuminating the same furniture he'd seen by the darkness of the previous night. It remained empty of people, but as Dante went about his breakfast and then his morning grammar lessons with Nak, he'd briefly shut his eyes and catch glimpses of servants sweeping the room, straightening the sashes on the windows, lighting candles along the walls. In still-framed flashes he watched the council chamber grow tidied for its use.

Nak was grilling him on Narashtovik verb tenses he hadn't yet mastered and in his frustration Dante let twenty minutes pass without checking on his spy. He rubbed his eyes and with a shock to his heart saw robed men seated at the table, heard tense voices arguing their points.

"This isn't something we should be trying to hasten," he heard Samarand say in her lightly accented Mallish. "I'm not going to risk a false step for the sake of shaving off a few days."

"But every day we spend on our haunches is one more day we give them to prepare," a man's voice said in an accent so thick it was a moment before Dante could make sense of his words.

"And what are you doing about them? How is it they're able to prepare so close to our city?" a third voice said.

"Enough, Tarkon," Samarand put in. "You know we're spread too thin to root them out right now. We'll lure them to us in the open field, then break their spine then."

Dante heard Nak clear his throat and he scrambled to reply to the priest's obscure linguistic query only to get it wrong. Nak threw up his hands and sighed, and as he repeated his lesson for the third or fourth time Dante divided his attention between his bald teacher and the conversation high up in the keep, only to find it had turned to an overspecific discussion of payments due for the maintenance of their soldiers.

"What's going on in that head of yours?" Nak snapped, leaning in so his nose was six inches from Dante's. "This may not be so exciting as Larrimore's little ventures, but it's just as important to your education, damn it."

"I know," Dante said, rubbing his eyes again. "It just feels like I'm making so little progress."

"You're doing fine," Nak said. "Better than fine. Your fundamentals are sound. No one can learn a new language overnight."

"All this waiting is killing me," Dante said. Nak furrowed his brow at the boy, lifted himself from his seat.

"Tell you what," he said. "Take a break while I go fetch us some tea."

"Okay," Dante said. Without pausing to wonder what tea was he plunged back into the vision of the rat. The council was still going on about the finances of the soldiers. Did they usually talk about things like that? Or was it the prelude to military action? From the rat's vantage in the crack in the wall he could see no more than a few slippered feet and the hunched backs of old men. He leaned his senses forward, as if that would somehow shine light on everything that was now obscured. Why were such important people talking about such trivial things?

"I sense—" he heard Samarand say, then cut herself short. There was a shuffling of robes, a moment of silence.

"What is it?" one of the men said.

"Nothing. Pardon my interruption, Baxter." Their conversation resumed. Dante slapped absently at the back of his neck, thinking he felt a fly. A hot prickle ran across his scalp and he realized it wasn't his nerves he felt, but the rat's on the other end of the connection. At once he could sense her the way you can sense the presence of a person in an unlit room. She had found the rat, felt the nether that kept it on its feet, was now tracing whatever line tied it to Dante as delicately as a spider climbs down its web when it knows there's something large stuck in the far end. Dante jerked himself away from the rat—some part of him registering he'd also jerked his back against his chair—but that cord held fast. Samarand's presence surged forward. Dante stood and cast about the chapel reading room as if looking for a physical axe with which to cut the connection, feeling her cold intelligence dropping down the line, ever closer, then with an exertion of will so forceful it made sweat stand up on his forehead, he took a breath, cleared his mind, gazed on that needle-thin shadow that bound him to the rat. He severed it quickly and cleanly, heard a sharp question from Samarand's consciousness: then darkness and softness, nothing more than his own five senses. He stood there a while, half dazed, trying not to move for fear it would somehow draw her back to him and this time identify him. He couldn't remember a time he'd tried anything more stupid.

"What's the matter?" Nak said, returning to the room with a copper tray bearing a kettle of something that smelled like lan leaves. "You have the look of a man who just tried to puke up a live horse."

"What?" Dante said. "Maybe. I mean, maybe it was something I ate."

"Well, sit down and have some tea." Nak gave him a doubting glance. "Grammar isn't that upsetting."

After they'd drank a bit they returned to their lessons, but Dante was too busy trying to convince himself he hadn't been caught to pay any more attention than he had before, and Nak dismissed him less than an hour later. Dante wandered to his cell, napped fitfully through the afternoon, rose and reread the translation of the *Cycle* until Blays returned from his training with the soldiers. Blays unbuckled his sword and threw himself down on his pallet, sighing into his pillow.

"I feel the way a club must feel," he said muffledly. "Everything hurts."

"I'm losing my grip," Dante said, double-checking the lock on the door.

"How do you mean?"

"They're up to something big. I can't find out what. They almost caught me today."

"Then regrasp it," Blays said, wriggling onto his back. "Make a plan already."

"The time isn't right."

He heard Blays snapping straw in the dark. "And why does it matter what she's up to, exactly?"

"Whatever it is, it's going to distract her," Dante said slowly. He hadn't tried to explain to himself just why the council's plans were relevant to their own, but he couldn't shake the need to know. "I think if we take her out then and she fails, this whole thing might fall apart. Break into too many pieces for someone else to put back together."

"Can you find out what it is?"

"Not unless it's dropped in my lap. I can't do any more snooping. It feels like I'm being quartered by my own cross purposes."

Blays hmm'd. "Why don't you just ask them what they're up to?"

"What?"

"For some reason they think you're arrogant and ambitious, right?"

"They do appear to be under that impression," Dante said. Blays tapped his chin, then went on.

"A man like that wouldn't like feeling left out of the loop, right? You'd *demand* to know what's going on. You'd say 'Larrimore, tell me what you're up to before I smash this castle down around your head.'"

"And he'd say 'Dante, grow the hell up.'"

Blays shook his head in the gloom of their single candle. "And you go on to tell him you're being wasted as his errand-boy. Delivering letters? Guarding ambassadors? That's for servants, not Arawn's chosen. Ask him if they'd have left Will Palomar in the dark."

Dante licked his lips. "And when he says no, remind him who killed him."

"Exactly!"

"I wonder who Will Palomar was."

"Who cares? He was somebody around here, that's clear enough. And you can be damn sure they wouldn't be treating *him* like a trained bear."

"Just ask them," Dante repeated.

"Really, it'd be suspicious if you didn't. How's this look right now? The first day you barge in here and throw their most prized possession in the dirt like it's a used whorerag, all the while threatening their lives, and two weeks later you're bumbling around saying yessir no sir? You've got to act like a prick again! For the good of the land!"

Dante laughed, buried his face in his rough cotton bedclothes. "If this gets us killed tomorrow, I'm blaming you."

Blays snorted. "Then when it goes off like a dream, I get all the credit."

"No way. I'll be the one that got it done."

"Based on my brilliant idea."

"I could have thought of that."

"But you didn't," Blays said, lobbing straw at him. Dante grabbed some from beneath his pallet and threw it back. "You were over there, woe is me, I'm adrift in a cruel sea. Blays, won't you be my anchor? Bring me back to shore, Blays!"

"That's not what I sounded like," Dante said.

"Maybe not to your ears," Blays said. "To mine it was all I could do to keep from slapping you."

"I'd have turned you into a toad first. Then chopped you in half with your own sword."

"You'd have to turn yourself into a man first so you could actually lift it."

Dante had no answer to that. He closed his eyes and swiftly fell asleep. He brushed Nak off the following morning, and before Larrimore could find him and make him play sheepdog to letters and people for another day, he found Larrimore. He was in the room of the keep he considered to be his business quarters, drilling a bevy of servants in Gaskan. Dinner. They were talking about dinner, Dante understood. The particulars of this dinner remained obscure, but Dante felt a faint thrill to know Nak's lessons hadn't been a waste.

"I need to talk to you," he called from the doorway to Larrimore.

"Do you want our guests to starve?" the man tossed before turning back to his orders. Dante waited in the frame until Larrimore dismissed the servants and waved the boy over. Dante closed the door and took up a chair.

"There shall be no mistakes regarding the gravy tonight," Dante said, trying to remember how he'd acted that first day.

"Indeed not. I presume you came here for higher reason than mocking the skillful administration of a home this large."

Dante steeled himself. "What's going on here?"

"Yet another banquet," Larrimore said, waving a hand. "Fine fare is terribly important when you're a man of noble concerns."

"I don't mean dinner, you oaf. What's Samarand preparing for? What's gotten the Citadel so busy?"

"Oh, that."

"Yes, that." Dante said.

Larrimore clasped his hands beneath his nose and regarded Dante for a moment. "I wondered when you'd stop skulking around and come see me. I thought, Why the secrets? Why is the boy of infinite hubris creeping around like a mouse in the larder?"

"None of that is any kind of answer."

"Well, it's no great secret," Larrimore said.

"Yes, I know." Dante leaned back in his chair. "You wish to release Arawn."

"You see?" Larrimore said, tipping back his head. "Everyone knows."

"And rather than involving me in what must be the most important moment in the history of the house of Arawn, you believe my time's best spent toting letters and playing wet nurse to fat idiots from faraway lands."

Larrimore pressed his hands to his face and chuckled into them, his whole body bobbing with laughter.

"Anyone else would have you whipped for that," he smiled.

Dante rolled his eyes. "Do you have any explanations for anything? Or does your existence consist entirely of sitting around approving the chef's plans for supper?"

"I should be so lucky. All right. What is it you wish to do, exactly?"

"Be involved!" Dante yelled, long past the need to pretend to be frustrated and scornful. "I'm not even in the same sphere as the other students I've seen here. I can help if you'd let me."

Larrimore laughed happily. "You really believe you're a boy of destiny, don't you? You think you're the one in that prophecy you quoted me."

"I've made no such claims."

"You certainly hinted, implied, and danced around them."

"Only to keep the Hand of Samarand from strangling me prematurely," Dante said. He and Larrimore looked at each other, surprised, then exchanged a chuckle. Dante rubbed his nose and let the new thought he'd had take its course. "What's so important about the original copy of the *Cycle*, anyway? Aren't the others just as good?"

"Look," Larrimore said, flexing his fingers against each other until they popped. "There's no guide written for what we're trying to do. At best, we've got a rough idea of the procedures involved. It's important to reduce uncertainties wherever possible."

"Then why did you leave the book lying around in the first place?"

Larrimore sighed. "We didn't."

"Yes, but you thought you had. You locked me up over it. Or don't you remember that time you locked me in a cell and didn't feed me for a day?"

"Oh please. You can't blame us for being suspicious. We weren't about to take a chance on that."

Dante bit back his question about why they'd believed him about the fake. Or, he thought queasily, why they'd pretended to. There was something else he needed to know first, something he hadn't expected to find an answer for when he first sought out Larrimore this day.

"Then how did you lose it in the first place?" he said.

"We didn't *lose* it. Someone stole it."

"How?"

"Because he was technically its owner," Larrimore said, folding his arms and glaring across the room. "A couple decades back, there came a time when the old head of the order was supposed to step down. He didn't much like that idea, despite his obvious frailty and probable senility, and was even less fond of the idea of Samarand taking his place. After the council forced his ouster, it was found he'd absconded with the book."

Dante pinched the bridge of his nose. "What was his name?"

"Callimandicus," Larrimore said. He rolled his eyes. "Needless to say, that's caused us no end of trouble between then and now."

"I read somewhere Samarand killed the previous head of the order." Dante felt as if he were speaking from a point a few feet distant from his body. "That she usurped the position."

"Hardly. His time was up, figuratively speaking. Though surely he's with Arawn now. The old bastard had actually fought during the Third Scour."

"But that would mean even twenty years ago he'd have been a century old!"

"95ish, I think." Larrimore shrugged, gave Dante an odd look. "This was all before my time, in any event."

"So what did he do after he left?"

Larrimore laughed to himself. "A lot of intricate but ultimately failed scheming, for the most part. About a year after he ran away he made a rather pathetic attempt to retake control. When that didn't work, he spent the next four or five years in petty vengeance. Did manage to kill a few of our men, including one who meant something. He disappeared after that last fight. He's dust and bones by now. If he were still breathing, he'd be trying something even now."

"I see," Dante said, groping mentally for the top of his head, which felt like it had floated free at some point in their conversation.

"What's wrong? You have the look of a drunk lord who's just discovered he's shat himself."

"Perhaps it was something I ate," Dante said numbly.

"Shall we go for a walk? Cleanse out the blood?"

"Let's."

Larrimore was a lively man and he didn't so much rise from his chair as spring from it. He strolled in the direction of the main hall, passing servants and soldiers rushing about on their business of keeping the castle together, brushing by acolytes and students off on some duty for their instructors. Dante felt their eyes tracking him and Larrimore through the hallways.

"You already have more responsibilities than some men who've been with us a year or more, you know," Larrimore said in a normal tone, not caring who heard.

"I've earned it, haven't I?" Dante said through the screech of his thoughts. Had anything Cally told him been true? How much could he question Larrimore before he betrayed his split interest? What should he be asking now if he were here for no other reason than worshipping Arawn and culling his own power? Did Samarand deserve to die?

"I suppose," Larrimore said. "You haven't failed us yet, anyway. I suppose you're of the school of thought that young men should be allowed to rise until they falter? To ascend like a hawk on an updraft until they can naturally go no higher?"

"That seems fair."

"Seems fair," Larrimore laughed. "Then it would be no stretch to assume you think a measured education, promotion through experience rather than raw potential, those are no more than meaningless hoops you have to jump through for the amusement of powerful men."

"Aren't they?" Dante said, and he sensed they stood on a peak, that his answers now would determine which way everything else fell. "How close are you to your goal? How badly do you need strong backs to help shoulder the load?"

"We're close. Very close. Do we really need one more hand to help us shape the nether? Who knows? It would help more to have the book. Failing that, we're going to need all the aid we can muster."

"Then stop throwing hoops at me and make me into something that can tip the balance."

"Indeed." Larrimore snapped his fingers, looked surprised. "Oh, it didn't work!" He snapped again, then a third time. He shook his hand at the wrist, scowling at it. "Damn thing seems to have given out."

Dante stopped mid-stride. He bit his lip, oblivious to the self-inflicted pain, until the metallic taste of blood filled his mouth. He opened the channels of his mind and let the shadows flock through them, calling out through the clear, open pathways Nak had showed him until he could actually see black streaks shooting from the dark places in the room to gather around his hands and at the trail of blood that leaked past his lips. So Cally too had used him and now Larrimore mocked him. Were all men treated this way? Or was it because when they looked on him they still couldn't see past his unlined, beardless face? They pretended to be wise, but none of these self-important men knew a gods-damned thing. Let Larrimore, at least, look on the full reach of his power.

For a moment Dante didn't know how he'd make it manifest, simply letting the forces grow until his limbs shook and his blood burnt with a sheer energy he hadn't felt since he'd strained all his body in the battle to free Blays from the lawmen of Whetton. He saw Larrimore's natural state of ironic glee melt away, his smile recede until his lips were a taught line, the light of his eyes shift from amusement to alertness, and perhaps to alarm. Dante's throat felt too tight to swallow. His vision grayed at the edges. *Release it*, Cally would say, *for the love of the gods let it go*. Dante let it burn on until his skin felt ready to peel from his flesh, enjoying every hot second of the pain that held him in its palm. He spread out his arms, as much for the spectacle as for the need, and then he nodded, once, and set the shadows free, not in a focused fire or the bleeding edge that cut people's flesh, but in a pure sphere of unfiltered force.

It expanded from his body so fast Larrimore was knocked down before he could cry out. It whipped the dust on the floor into billowing clouds. Rugs flapped and spun into the walls. Vases and statues flew sideways from tables like an invisible tablecloth had been yanked from beneath them, smashing on walls, clattering on the ground. Servants and students spun from their feet to land on hands and knees or hard on their backs. The sphere met the walls then, striking so hard it boomed like cliffside surf, like a battering ram swung into a great gate. Dante sunk to his knees, seeing black and white through the slits of his eyes. Then the crash of the nether was gone, replaced by a silence interrupted by the clinks of glass and pottery ringing to rest on the ground, by the slow crackle of stone flaking from the nearest wall, by the light sobbing of the servants and his own ragged breathing.

"How insightful," he heard Larrimore say, distant as a cloud. The man rolled to his feet and brushed dust from his worn clothes. Around them, the other men who'd been knocked down dragged themselves up and suddenly remembered tasks of calamitous importance, disappearing through doors and around corners. Dante made no move to get up. His whole body tingled as if it were no longer just his but belonged to all the world. His mouth was a loose O of dumb shock and simple exaltation. Larrimore toed a broken shard of glass. "As if we didn't have enough work already."

"I don't need you," Dante slurred, dreamlike. He laughed, the low, breathy laugh of an idiot.

"Shut up, you clown," Larrimore muttered. He crossed to the wall and fingered the cracks that had appeared in the stone. "I want you to go to your room and think about what you've done. Tomorrow your true purpose begins."

He'd walked back to his cell in a daze. The world felt as close and translucent as the time he'd been drunk back in Bressel. He lowered himself to his pallet, heavy as a boulder. It was a long time before his thoughts became shapes he could understand or control.

"Cally lied," he said when Blays showed up after night had fallen.

"He's pretty old," Blays said, turning his back and hanging his sword from a peg on the wall. "Maybe he just forgot the truth."

"Gabe, too. He said Samarand led a coup, killed the old priest. *Cally* was the leader, and the council forced him out, not her. And obviously she didn't kill him."

Blays frowned down on him, noncommittal. "Were they both lying? Or was Gabe just repeating the lies Cally'd told him?"

"I don't know," Dante said. He stared at the ceiling. "I don't suppose it matters."

"What do you mean?"

"Did Cally send us here to exact justice, or to execute a personal vendetta that's twenty years old?"

Blays' face clouded up. He shuffled his feet around the straw and dirty stone of their cell.

"You're thinking maybe it's a good thing it's taken so long to get things in place."

"I no longer have any idea what the good thing may be."

"Whenever I have that feeling, I try to go with whatever I haven't tried before." Blays sighed through his nose, ruffled his hair. His eyes shifted to Dante's prone form. "When did you learn all this, anyway?"

"Today."

"Not a week ago? Not a month ago? You haven't just been sitting on this while you let them teach you all their fancy tricks, have you?"

"No."

Blays stuck out his jaw. "I'm not stupid. I know you pretty well. You've been enjoying this. Playing them with one hand and me with the other."

Dante sat upright. "That's not true!"

"Isn't it? You're not putting off what we have to do so you can puff yourself up with power?"

"Blays! I'm not using you here." Dante told him about his conversation with Larrimore, how he'd asked the man what the order of Arawn was up to and how it had led to their talk of the history between Samarand and Callimandicus. He left out the part at the end, when he'd blown up the keep, and Larrimore's promise about his "true purpose," whatever that meant. "I didn't know," Dante said, clasping his hands in his lap. "You see? I'd been looking for a way to get to her. I had. And now it's all been swept away."

Blays blew up his cheeks and knocked his knuckles on his forehead.

"I'm going to ask a question," he said carefully. "It's going to sound crazy, but I want you to think about it before you answer. Okay?"

"Okay," Dante said.

Blays raised his brows. "Does this change anything?"

"That's crazy!" Dante said. Blays sighed again. Dante bit his lip, wincing when his teeth found the raw split where he'd bitten it open hours earlier. He lowered his voice. "We came here thinking she's a usurper. That if she died, reason would take her place. If her place in the council's legitimate, how can we expect things will be any different just because she's gone?"

"I don't know!" Blays hissed. "Gask seems peaceful enough. There's no more murder out there than in any other city. No towns were burning on our way through. But they *are* burning down in Mallon. If we can do something about that, how can we hold back?"

Dante looked down. Whetton, Bressel, the village he'd left the year before, they were just places he'd once drifted through for no reason more special than that they were near where he'd been born. He didn't miss any of the people he'd known from those times. Who were they? Faces, fragments of memory. That was all. Did the fact he had once known them somehow make them more important than the people in this city, in this kingdom? There were people in Mallon who wanted to worship Arawn shoulder to shoulder with the devotees of Gashen or Lia or Carvahal or Mennok. That was somehow a crime? Who'd made that decision? He shook his head at Blays.

"Killing her won't change a thing. It'll be like Gabe said. Someone else will take her place and the wheels of history will roll right on."

"Not if you're the one who takes it," Blays said. Dante squinted at him until he was certain the boy was serious.

"Did someone hit you on the head while you were sparring today? Let me see," Dante said. He stood and reached for Blays' head. Blays wrestled him away.

"I'm serious."

"So am I. Let me see your skull. I bet it's got a big fat crack."

"What's stopping you?" Blays said, shoving Dante back again.

"An army of men and an order of priests."

"Then here's what you do." Blays narrowed his eyes and tipped back his head in an owlish expression. "Get Larrimore or someone from the council to back you. Divide them up against each other and promise your supporter you'll be their cat's-paw, that you'll do the thing they wouldn't dare and so claim her seat in their name. Even if they throw you out right after, they'll be too busy squabbling to keep screwing up the south. And if they leave you in her seat, then you can rule like a king and end it all yourself."

Dante sat down and chortled into his hands. "You're right. Your question wasn't crazy. *That's* crazy."

"Only if you lack the vision to see it through."

"Let's suppose I give it a shot," Dante said, exaggeratedly stroking his chin. "I'll have to expose my plan to off Samarand to whoever I want to back me. What if they don't go for it? How well do you think that's going to fly?"

"Like a cat in a trebuchet?" Blays shrugged. "Someone's got to hate her. Just figure out who."

"Good gods. Sometimes I think we should just sneak into her chambers in the dead of night and fight our way outside."

Blays' brows knit together. "Do you think that would work?"

"I have the strange suspicion the high priest of Arawn is smart and strong enough to use her eerie powers to make sure nobody just stabs her in her sleep."

"So that's a no."

Dante squeezed his eyes shut. "You're supposed to be the reasonable one. This is going to be a disaster."

"You're going to do it!" Blays said, looking as if he couldn't decide whether to be enthralled or horrified.

"No. Maybe. Larrimore's got something in store for me tomorrow. Something important. I want to see what it is before striking down the road to madness."

"Ah! Cowardice."

"Cowardice! You're right," Dante said. "I'll have the whole place taken over by tomorrow, then. I'm naming you my Secretary of Parades. It had better be grand, or I'll redub you Secretary of Getting Eaten to Death by Rats."

They argued nonsense until Blays claimed exhaustion. Dante lay in bed for a while after Blays had fallen asleep, laughing softly at Blays' plan, its tempting confusion of absurdity and daring and total stupidity, until the darkness of the night and the talk he'd had with Larrimore bubbled back into the fore. Why hadn't Cally just told him the truth? Why send him all this way on a false story of Samarand's treachery? Didn't the old man know Dante would have thought the way Blays did now—that it didn't matter how she'd gained her power, that legitimate or not, the things she was doing with it were wrong?

But he knew why the old man had lied, of course. Because Cally didn't trust him to make the right decision. And so he'd used him in a way he knew would get the results he desired. Dante wanted to feel angry, to rage at the fact he'd once again been used as a piece on someone else's board, but all he felt was tired. For the first time since he'd touched the book, he wanted it to stop. He wanted a moment to catch his breath, perhaps to run away from all these schemes and live for himself, free from the snares of the ambition of other men and himself.

He knew that want was nothing more than fantasy. He was caught up in something that would only get bigger before it went away. All he could do now was ride it out until it came to rest.

"No lessons today, Nak," Larrimore said as he spilled into the chapel. "We've got more important work for our little scholar."

Nak rolled his eyes over his papers. "I don't see how you expect me to teach him two languages as well as refine his more ethereal talents when you're always dragging him off on your chores."

"I'm learning," Dante said in Gaskan. "Make me some lessons. I will go over them tonight."

"We'll start with clauses," Nak muttered. He waved his fingers, dismissing the boy. Larrimore led Dante into the keep and immediately made a left turn for the stairwell into the dungeons.

"What are we going down here for?" Dante said, peering into the dim torchlight. He had a sudden vision of being forced to torture Ryant Briggs for answers.

"Nothing!" Larrimore said. "How cunningly I've tricked you back into prison. You thought you'd get away with your insolence?"

"You could use a dose of sobriety," Dante said.

"Wrong. In time you'll learn the value of running your fool mouth until no one can tell when you're serious. Only then can you get away with saying anything to anyone."

"What does that even mean?" he said, but Larrimore didn't seem inclined to explain. The air of the lower levels rose up to meet them. Cool but sturdy, the faint whiff of human filth and things that may once have been rotten but had since turned to dust. Larrimore opened the door to the corridor where they'd hauled Dante not so long ago. Dante skipped his gaze over the thick door behind which he'd been imprisoned, straining his ears for sounds of Ryant. Was he still alive? Alone in the darkness of that empty room? He glanced at Larrimore. The man was smiling.

The hallway terminated in another door that opened onto a second stairwell. Larrimore grabbed a lit torch from a sconce in the wall and they continued down into the darkness. The walls weighed on Dante's shoulders. The stones seemed to move beneath the shadows thrown by the flickering torch, as if the walls weren't mortared in place but were in the process of a silent and half-stalled avalanche. Dante stared hard at his feet until they hit the landing of the lower level and the walls widened out into an unlit corridor.

"Here we are," Larrimore said, stopping at the hall's first door. He fit a key to the lock and leaned into the door as it opened, pouring himself into the room. From behind him, Dante saw black shadows, gray stones, the dull white of a floor full of bones.

"What—?"

"It's not as bad as it looks," Larrimore said. "Do you have any idea how many people have died in this city over the years? Sometimes after the larger sieges they had to sort of dig up the old to make way for the new."

"That's barbaric!"

"Pragmatic," Larrimore corrected. "Egalitarian, even. This way everyone gets a turn in the earth." He stepped forward into the mess, shuffling his feet against the floor. Bones rattled away from his boots. Dante followed in the path he cleared.

"What do you want me to do with them?" Dante said, shrinking back from the top half of a skull that had rolled within an inch of his foot. "Tidy up?"

"I said you'd be doing something important, didn't I?" Larrimore bent at the waist and knocked away a few random bones. He made a satisfied grunt, then plucked one up and displayed Dante the jawbone in his palm. "Weird looking, isn't it? Strange to think your teeth are the same substance as the jaw they're embedded in. Yet they're exposed, naked to the air and the eye, while the rest of our bones are buried under all that flesh."

"Truly a marvel of nature," Dante said. It was a large room, perhaps forty feet deep and just as far across, and except for a small space around the door, the carpet of bones lay ankle-deep from wall to wall. In the corners they were piled to the knee, gathered in drifts like snow in the wind.

"We've got a few mirrors around the place. You should look at your teeth some day. Quite frankly it's scary when you think about them like that."

"Is this some kind of lesson on the virtue of looking closely at the things we take for granted?"

"No, it's a lesson on how disgusting our bodies are." Larrimore tossed the jawbone at Dante. It bounced from his chest and he puckered his face. Larrimore laughed through his nose. "Jawbones, ribs, and thighs. One of each in sets of three. Write Arawn's name in blood upon the bone—in Narashtovik, not this decadent Mallish—and soak it through with nether until the whole thing's bound up tight. Repeat. Gain my eternal praise."

"What?"

"'What' as in you didn't hear me, or you don't understand?"

Dante kicked the nearest skull away from him. "Why?"

"Because Samarand's children are bored with their old toys."

"Samarand has kids?"

Larrimore's face bent with a shocking flash of anger. "What are you, some kind of idiot? They have vows of chastity."

"I thought I was going to be doing something important," Dante said. "You want me to bleed on some bones in a room so low it's under the dungeon?"

"This *is* important! Before you volunteered, the council was drawing lots to see who'd have to do it."

"This is asinine."

Larrimore plowed his feet through the debris, sending bones clattering over each other. He chuckled without humor, then fixed Dante with a stare emptied of any patience.

"When the time comes for all the excitement, the council's going to need all the power they can find. Sources they can depend on other than their own frail bodies. These bones? The bones you're going to bleed on? They'll be the fuel for their deeds."

Dante frowned up at the man. "Are you putting me on?"

"Big events are always preceded by countless hours of tedious preparation. Like the good book says, proper preparation is the difference between celestial glory and standing around in a field with our dicks in our hands."

"I don't remember that verse."

"Obviously you haven't been studying hard enough." Larrimore dug into his pocket and removed a small, thin knife, more of a pick than a blade, and a delicate black quill covered in intricate silver Narashtovik words. He handed them to Dante. "Any questions?"

"Yes," Dante said, holding the knife in one hand and the quill in the other. "How do I do the things you told me to do?"

"Lyle's flayed balls." Larrimore rubbed his face in his hands. "Ribs of the watchdog, jaws of the dragon, thighs of the lion. Just like Mommy used to sing about when she'd point out the stars. Give yourself a good nick and write Arawn's name on each. In Narashtovik. Bind blood to bone with nether—I'm not sure how that part's done, but you're a smart lad, figure it out." He sucked in his cheeks. "Don't kill yourself or anything, but we need a lot."

"Define'a lot,'" Dante said, gazing out on the thousands of bones.

"Drink plenty of water," Larrimore winked. He used his torch to light another by the door. "Don't shut this door, either. We've only got the one key, and sometimes I lose things. Got a lot of responsibilities for one man, you see." He flashed his eyebrows, then picked his way out into the corridor. Dante heard him whistling on his way through the gloom.

He turned around. Bones from wall to wall. Was this another test? Larrimore had barely told him what to do. The man gave the impression he didn't care about anything, but somehow he was the one who kept the wheels of the Citadel greased and turning. Dante swept an open circle with his feet and sat down. Larrimore wanted bones, did he? He took up a rib, grasping the natural handle where the bone would meet the spine. This bone had once been a part of someone, he thought, then realized he didn't give a damn. That man had been dead for decades. Whoever he'd been, he hadn't even had the simple courtesy not to get dug up and stored in a forgotten basement until his remains could be involved in some morbid ritual.

Dante set the quill in his lap and with the knife he drew a light incision below his left thumb. His blood gleamed a blackish red in the uneven light from the torch ensconced beside the door. He picked up the quill, glad for the small favor that no one was here to see this bizarre melodrama, then dipped it in the blood in his hand and held the rib close to his face. He painted the letters delicately, one stroke at a time, adding a flourish to their ends. He held out the rib, eyeing it critically. Bind it? With the nether? He blinked back the frustration that was crowding his mind. Shadows sucked up from under the piles of bones, coursing up his arm and wrapping themselves around the rib's white surface. He let his desire become a semiconscious thing, felt rather than verbalized, the way he recognized he was hungry without thinking "apple" or "roast chicken," and smoothed the shadows over the length of the rib. Become one, he thought, and twitched back as the shadows pulsed and then sunk into the bone like water spilled on hot sand. The formerly creamy rib had grown gray, lined with the red-brown letters of Arawn's name, and when he set it aside he had a creeping sense of energy—not warm, not motile, certainly not conscious, but far sharper than the bland feel of the bones around him or the still air or the stones of the wall. He grunted and placed it gently on the floor.

The second bone was easier. He misspelled Arawn's name on the third and lobbed the thighbone into a far corner. After that first mistake he moved quickly, pinching the skin around the cut on his hand to keep it from clotting. Each bone was the work of no more than five minutes, and within half an hour he had the start of a pile lying beside his knee.

Last night's talk with Blays felt impossibly distant. He no longer had any way to deny he was doing the work of the Arawnites. Delivering letters was reasonably harmless; no doubt 90% of them said nothing but empty chatter. Bodyguarding men who couldn't help themselves was a respectable enough position, Blays' similar occupation notwithstanding. Capturing criminals was no more wrong than when the watch did it in every city on the planet. But this—painting bones with blood and locking them up with nether for use in what could only be their attempt to unleash Arawn—there was no defense of that. Mercenaries and men off the street couldn't do what Dante was doing now. If they succeeded in releasing the old god—not that he thought such a being even existed—Dante would be in part responsible for that success; and if he failed again when it came time to kill Samarand, perhaps that too would have its roots in what he was doing down in this neglected ossuary.

He grasped a jawbone, tensed his arm to hurl it against the opposite wall. All at once his feelings broke, his conflict left him like a hulled boat slipping beneath calm waters. Let him do Samarand's work with one hand while with the other he honed the knife meant for her heart. Let him tell Blays he was biding his time even while he used Nak to learn everything the monk could teach. Uncertainty and self-doubt wouldn't help him. No army was going to smash down the Citadel's gates, no heavenly hand was going to guide him through his trials and lead him to justice. He had nothing and no one but himself, the strength of his hands and his head and his will. If he was going to become the kind of man he intended to be, that would be enough.

The wound on his palm had scabbed as he brooded and he cut a parallel beside it. He worked without thinking, adding to the pile near his knee. He broke for lunch and wandered upstairs, wanting beef, red meat and fruit and a barrel full of water. Servants and guards watched him walk by the way he'd watch a wolf pad through the brush of the open woods. He ate by himself and returned downstairs without a word more than what he'd needed to get his meal. Once more the logic of the nether took his mind. He knew his part. One bone at a time, he created order from the decay.

"Make any progress?" Larrimore called to Dante when he'd halted for the evening and was making his way through the keep.

"See for yourself," he said, ignoring whatever the man said next as he stepped into the yard. Back at his room, Nak had prepared a thick sheaf of notes and lessons. He paged through them, recognizing more of the words than he would have expected, then set the papers aside. Too much lust for knowledge was the trappings and vanity of an unreal world.

He spent the next day with the bones, seeing others only at meals. Scabbed lines lay across his palm like tallies on a prison wall. Midway through his third day in the sub-basement he heard footsteps, the first that weren't his own. He didn't turn away from his work.

"Impressive," Larrimore said.

"I'm busy."

"That's enough for now. I've got something else for you."

"More important than laying the foundation of our finest

hour?"

"Oh, be quiet." Larrimore walked around in front of Dante. He pursed his mouth at the boy's blank expression. "The council's meeting in an hour. I want you cleaned up by then. You look like you haven't bathed in a week."

"I haven't." Dante blinked up at him. "What does the council want with me?"

"It's not what they want, it's what you want. Up with you. Time for a lesson in politics."

Dante snorted and finished up the summons for the rib bone he was still holding. "Sounds enlightening."

"Stop sulking like a child or you'll miss the self-important men puffing their throats and preening their tails." Larrimore beckoned. "Come. Take a bath, for the gods' sakes. Samarand's Hand's Hand will never be of any use if he doesn't understand how the council works."

"Awful lot left," Dante said, nodding to the numberless bones, then the few score he'd prepared.

"That's enough. I told you the council'd been working on this before you. Come and see the court before I punch you in your gross little teeth."

It wasn't the threat that stirred Dante, it was the life behind it. He stood, knees and ankles popping. Larrimore stepped forward and patted him on the cheek hard enough to sting.

"There's some fire for your eyes. The way you carry yourself in that chamber will reflect on me, you know. The only way to keep those old bastards in line is to remind them just how old they are."

"Shall I dance for them?" Dante pulled out the collar of his doublet, tipped back his chin. "Where's my fancy jacket? Don't trained apes wear fancy jackets?"

"Better." Larrimore gave him a self-satisfied smile and led him back upstairs, leaving the stacks of bones behind. In the main hall he found a young man in a black cassock and dispatched him to gather the fruit of Dante's basement labor. Larrimore summoned a gaggle of servants and rattled off a line of orders in Gaskan. Dante could follow enough to pick out the words "bath" and "dress" and how the price of sloth would be a word he hadn't learned, but whose etymology meant "the breaking of limbs from the body."

"Go make yourself presentable," Larrimore said to Dante. "I'll send for you in forty minutes."

Before Dante could smart off the man strode off for other business in the deeper rooms of the keep. Dante turned to the servants with something close to guilt. They ducked their heads and gestured him upstairs, where a steaming bath had already been drawn. He barked at the pair of servants who'd stayed with him to turn away as he undressed, then allowed himself a brief soak. They waited with fresh clothes when he climbed out and he accepted their finery, slapping away their hands when they attempted to help him put them on. This was how royalty lived? For two full minutes Dante fumbled with the ends of a sash apparently meant for his middle, then sighed, looked up at the ceiling, and let the servants' swift hands secure it around his waist. He suffered them to dose him with perfume, waving them off after the first application.

"I'm a man, not a tulip garden," he mumbled in Mallish, then ordered them away before they could convince him it was the way of court. He brushed his hair, which had grown back out a bit since he'd had it trimmed before Samarand's sermon on Ben, then paced around the cushy quarters until Larrimore showed up. The man's mouth was tight, but his eyes danced with mirth as they jumped down Dante's laundered frame. Dante scowled at him. "You people are ridiculous."

"Deal with it like a man." Larrimore gave him a closer once-over, from his combed black hair to the fine silver trim on his cape and doublet and breeches, eyes coming to rest on the scuffed and scarred leather of his boots. "Where are the shoes? What's that garbage wrapped around your feet?"

"The boots stay."

"Fine. Look like a peasant who tripped over his hog and fell into a rich man's closet."

"You dress like you lost a fight with a wildcat!"

"And I've earned that right. All right, Little Lord Spitpolish, let's be on our way." Larrimore turned on his heel and took them to a staircase leading to the upper floors. "I'm guessing you're going to think the old men are stupid. You might even be tempted to try to educate them to the specific nature of their idiocy."

"Surely an idiot could never attain a position as lofty as theirs," Dante said, suspicious he was about to be told what to do.

"Indeed. So I'm going to entrust you with your toughest challenge yet: keeping your damn mouth shut. If you try to toss your pair of pennies into the hat, they're just going to laugh at you. Have you ever heard the sound of eleven corpses laughing? It isn't pretty."

"I've been writing on bones with my own blood for the last three days."

"And that will seem like a beautiful dream."

"I'll be good," Dante promised.

"Good. I don't like making threats."

Dante fell silent, pensive rather than with the moodiness that had consumed him for the last few days. What was Larrimore doing? Was he grooming him for leadership? No doubt he thought this was funny, in his perverse way, but the man's eyes sparked with something more. Dante'd gotten the impression no one around the keep really liked Larrimore. They feared him more than they derided him, granting a grudging respect to the undeniable efficacy of Samarand's Hand, no matter how slapdash a demeanor he wore on his cool brown face while executing his many charges. But they did laugh behind his back, imitating the sharp tone of his words, perhaps thinking he used too many or thought himself too clever; they muttered obscenities and the kind of mild threats that carried no weight. They did what he said, but they didn't like him. Perhaps the only one who did was Samarand, and she was so busy handing down orders from on high Larrimore was all but autonomous. As far as Dante knew the man had no pull with the council—clearly he hated them, resented them for his own obscure reasons. His lot was wholly thrown in with Samarand, and if for any reason she lost her seat, he would lose his as well. Was that it, then? He was snagging up Dante before anyone else noticed his potential? Shaping him up into an ally to help Larrimore carve out his own tiny piece of the empire inside the Citadel's gates?

Dante thought so. Larrimore had kept a close eye on the long leash he gave his pupil. His attention had gone beyond the way all adults had of trying to turn the younger people they had influence over into shorter versions of themselves, that strange instinct they had to stamp any sign of youth into their own mold, as if the existence of different opinions and methods threatened their very lives. It was like old people were terrified of dying without duplicating their minds on those who would replace them.

That instinct, too, was in the things Larrimore did. But unlike most men, it wasn't his driving force. He had other intentions for Dante. He wanted the boy to be able to hold his own. Perhaps, in time, to be able to watch Larrimore's back. That's what this sit-in with the council was about, Dante decided. The council was his weak point. He wished he had a little more time to build Larrimore's loyalty to him. There would come a time when it would be tested against the man's ties to Samarand. Maybe with another couple months, half a year, Dante would pull harder than her. He hoped when that moment did come it would at least cause Larrimore to hesitate long enough to lend Dante the advantage.

"Care to share the thoughts twisting your face up like that?" Larrimore said, spitting Dante with a severe look.

"What insults an old man most? Calling him withered, weak, or impotent?"

"Why not try all three?" Larrimore said. They reached the landing to the floor of the council chambers and he took Dante aside before they went into the hall. "I want you to pay close attention to the individuals," he said, voice low. "It would be a huge mistake to think their minds are united. The most important thing you can learn is what divides them. Pay special heed to the oldest man there—Tarkon Vastav. He's the nominal voice of what you might call the men of moderation. Doesn't speak his mind as freely as he once did, but perhaps that's a sign he's starting to lose it. This meeting might rouse him."

"Are you expecting a fight?"

"Not from him. I expect more trouble from Olivander. Brown-haired, ogrish-looking, ten or twelve years my senior. You'll know him by the way he fawns on Sama's every word."

Dante filed away the nickname. "If he's so taken by her, why would he be causing trouble?"

"Because she plans to leave him behind while she's off earning the glory."

"What? Why would she do that?"

"You'll see," Larrimore said, and would say no more. He opened the dark-stained door and took them down the corridor that led to the chambers, brushing past servants too busy with preparations to give him and his protege a second glance. Larrimore paused outside the council's double doors, the ones imprinted with the stylized tree of Barden, then cleared his throat and straightened his collar. He opened the door, revealing the long, simple table Dante had seen through the eyes of his rat. Sunlight spilled through the north-facing window. A half mile distant, the gray waters of the bay foamed against the shore. Dante counted eleven taken seats: ten men and one norren, enormous as a rampart, his brows and hair and thick gauzy beard looking white and tempestuous as a storm around a peak. The seat at the head of the table was empty. Servants stood frozen against the walls, eyes and ears trained on the deep, deliberate chatter of the assembled council. Dante looked at Larrimore for help and the man jerked his head and circled around the table to stand behind and to the right of the empty chair. Dante moved to take his left, and with a discreet tug of the boy's cloak Larrimore shifted him behind and to his own right.

About half of the council were white-haired and in varying degrees of personal antiquity, but from the look of resigned martyrdom on one of the old men's unbearded face Dante took him to be Tarkon, dissenter. He sat silent, unheeded. Olivander was one of if not the youngest, a bare hint of gray in his well-trimmed brown beard, and when he spoke the men around him turned their heads to listen. A few of the council cast glances Dante's way, examining this novelty in their cloisters—the norren, Tarkon, a middle-aged man with a long nose and his hair in a queue. All outsiders in their way, Dante guessed. Before he could parse out any more details the talk died off and Samarand emerged into the airy chamber. Larrimore stood straighter, tilted his chin. By reflex Dante did the same. She made her way to the head of the table, giving Dante a distracted look as Larrimore pulled out her chair.

"Anything new about the rebels, Olivander?" she said, and already Dante was lost. He'd expected a prayer or something to start it off. They were priests, right? She did speak in Mallish, at least, and he didn't have to trust his spotty Gaskan. He'd come to learn almost every man of means in the dead city was bilingual while many men of the south never bothered to learn the tongue of the north, with the result being most conversation in mixed company took place in Mallish. It was almost a point of pride among the Mallish men to speak no other language but that of their birth.

"Our scouts are nipping around their heels," Olivander said in a steady baritone. "They have a few hundred, four at the utmost. Good men, but they've been living in the wilds for weeks. No official backers, from what I've seen. Just rabble."

"Do they look especially schemish?"

Olivander frowned, as if he didn't recognize the word. "I don't expect they've come all this way to shake their fists at us. Best prepare for something."

"Right." Samarand put her hands flat on the table and met the eyes of each man in turn. "I'm not going to waste words. I'm only taking six of you."

"Six?" the old norren rumbled after a general exchange of looks.

"That's all we need. I'm not going to triumph in the field and then return here to find a smoking crater."

"We do have a few soldiers," the norren said. "Not to mention a tall set of walls."

"Look," Samarand said, and pressed her lips together. "We need seven. Anyone else would be lace frills. Nice to look at, not terribly functional."

"And wearing all your lace at once doesn't usually leave you open to invasion," Olivander added. Dante watched Samarand smile with half her mouth.

"Who's to come?" said the man with the long nose and longer brown hair.

"Walter, Baxter, Vannigan, Vaksho, Fanshen, and Pioter," Samarand ticked off on her fingers. None of the men Larrimore'd named for him.

Olivander's nostrils flared. He pinched his brows together. "My lady—"

"Stow it," she said. "I need you here overseeing the Citadel. Take pride in that responsibility."

The men who'd been named exchanged smug looks while those

left off struggled with their shock. After a few moments a general babble arose as they marshaled their arguments and Samarand held up her hands for peace.

"I know this must feel arbitrary to some of you. Try to remember we're not here for individual glory. Arawn knows your hearts and minds. He'll know those who ensure the safety of this keep are no more important than those who'll be with me at Barden. Can you understand that?"

"And how did you decide who goes and who stays?" said the long-haired man.

"With great trouble, Jackson, and anticipating all the arguments." Samarand leaned back in her seat and touched her braid at the back of her neck. "Don't take that to mean I just dismissed them. You know I'm anything but unreasonable."

"Granted, but neither infallible."

"I'll assume you wish to argue why your presence at the tree will be necessary. Let's hear it, then."

Jackson didn't hesitate. "I've spent less time in service than most of the men here. Maybe that should count against me. But if this truly isn't about rewarding service or whatever other favor with glory, and is instead a matter of who's most vital to which limb of the body, I'd argue my grasp of the nether is second to yours alone. To leave me behind, then, when it's uncertain how much skill we'll require, and would thus be safer to err on the side of abundance, appears to me as an oversight."

"Perhaps," Samarand said slowly. She cocked her head and stared at Jackson a few moments the way Dante imagined she'd stared when she felt the presence of his rat. "I'll give that its due consideration."

"Samarand—" Jackson started.

"Are you about to forward another argument, or just repeat the first in different words?"

Jackson's face darkened, then he nodded. "Well enough."

"Anyone else want to educate me on the unfairness of my decision?" she said, raising her brows at the others.

"I assume the wisdom of my long years isn't considered crucial," old Tarkon said.

"Honestly, I don't dissemble when I say I'd prefer to have it with us, Tarkon. My fear's you may falter on the way. It's even colder that far north. The trek will take days. If we leave you here, we risk missing out on some knowledge that could help us, but I've judged it a smaller risk than that of your health if you went. We can't stand before the White Tree with a gap in our seven."

He nodded, some of the resigned irony gone from his face.

"Anyone else?" No one spoke up, perhaps knowing she'd handle them as swiftly as she had the others. She pushed out her lips, impressed. "Good. Don't try to assign any slights or whimsical boons to my selections. We're all working toward the same end. Those of you I named, be ready to leave on the morning of the eighth day. Everyone else, you've got your duties here, and they'll be doubled with the rest of us out. Make sure you're prepared." She waited to see them nod their understanding, then set her elbows on the table. "Loath though I am to get ahead of ourselves, what's the latest from the south, Jackson?"

"Whetton's still the only city in Mallon where we might be said to have gained a lasting toehold," he said. He reached up for his chin and seemed surprised to find it beardless. "Fewer have come back to the old ways than we'd wished. The less said about Bressel the better. The devotion of our loyalists can't be questioned, but their ability is another matter—though nor can it be said they face no obstacles."

"And the Collen Basin?"

"There we may safely forecast a more optimistic outcome," Jackson said. "We've taken a number of the outlands and negotiated a treaty that will hold for the rest of the winter. That should leave them free to aid us with direct action elsewhere in Mallon, should that be our course. Olivander would know more about that than I."

Samarand nodded his way, and Olivander, who'd been lost in his own thoughts since he'd heard he'd be left behind, creased his brow and leaned one elbow on the table.

"Won't be easy," he said. "Still, with support from Collen, and if Hart's got the sway he says he does with the norren"—here he nodded at the norren priest—"I think a late spring strike through the pass at Riverway would work. It would certainly hearten the locals to know they've got our support."

"Especially if it comes on the heels of our success at Barden,"

Samarand mused. "Set it in motion. Prepare for a mid-March march."

"You're going to invade Mallon?" Dante blurted. A few of the priests gave him dubious glances. Larrimore elbowed him in the ribs amidst the awkward silence. Dante ignored him. "What about the Parable of Ben?"

"From the mouths of babes," Tarkon chuckled.

"Oh, that's not even relevant," Samarand said.

The old man twisted his mouth at her. "Is he wrong, then? Raising an army hardly suits your delicate words about the wrongs of vengeance."

"We're not talking about revenge, we're talking about liberation," Samarand said, meeting his gaze. "This has nothing to do with the Third Scour."

"You say that with almost enough conviction for me to believe it."

"Tarkon. You're old enough to remember when those people would kill you if you dared worship Arawn. Burnings, hangings—that sits fine with you?"

"Of course not," Tarkon said. He cleared some phlegm from his throat. "The physicians have an oath about not applying the cure when it would be worse than the disease. Surely in our wisdom, deriving as it does from a far higher source, we're able to apply that credo here."

Samarand touched her lips. "Unfortunately, we don't have the physician's experience to know when that cure would be worse. All I know is what I see."

"What I see's a woman more driven by her own vision of justice than what we're given by the heavens," Tarkon said. The table was still and silent as Dante's days below the dungeons. Olivander coughed into his fist, as if that would be enough to make the moment pass.

"We've been through this," said another graybeard who'd kept his peace so far. "This argument was old when I was still shitting myself."

"You say that as if you ever stopped," said a third elderly man. The table dissolved into laughter, and Tarkon's momentum dissolved with it.

"Indeed," Samarand said once they'd quieted down. "Olivander, get word to the smiths. Start drawing up estimates for what else we'll need and much it's liable to cost. Hart, speak to your people. Drop a hint I'm considering their request for a free principality at the fringe of the Dundens."

"Are you?" the norren asked levelly.

"I am *considering* it," she said. "Their actions between now and our hour of need may help their case." Tarkon chuckled, shaking his head. She ignored him. "That's it for now, then. Keep me apprised of your business. We move for Barden in eight days."

She got up, nodding absently at Larrimore as she left the room. Some of the council filtered out as others stayed to rehash what had just happened. Larrimore stepped around Dante and the boy had to hurry to catch him in the hall.

"Did you see that?" Dante said, glancing around to make sure she was gone.

"Masterful," Larrimore said, shaking his head. "Throwing them off with who was going and who was staying, then bowling them over one by one."

"Masterful? She started a war!"

"While they were all too stunned to react. They respect her, though—she gives them just enough rope to think there's no leash at all. She may even grant Jackson's request to come along."

Dante yanked on Larrimore's sleeve. "Did you hear what I just said?"

"Yeah. War. What about it?"

"Well, is that all it takes?"

"What did you expect?" Larrimore frowned down on him, twice as far away as his normal ironic distance. "Inspiring speeches? Duty and honor? They've been working toward this or something like it since the day she took power twenty years ago. The only issue for the last ten was how they were going to get it done.'

"What about Tarkon? He thinks it's a bad idea."

"She was just letting him vent some of his more noxious vapors. You could tell by looking he didn't expect to sway anyone to his side." He glanced down at Dante again and frowned harder. "You have family there? In Mallon?"

"No," Dante said quickly. He made himself cough to buy a moment and almost missed a step on the steep stairwell that led down to the ground floor. He caught himself, pressed his back against the solid stone. "It's about time they did something about the situation down there," he said before Larrimore could ask if he was all right, or any less convenient questions than that. "I just thought there would be more to the declaration."

"Nope. You were just there to see how she kept the old bastards in line. She's the only one who can be that bold with them, of course, but the same tricks would apply for you or me."

"It was eye-opening."

"Well, get ready for a lot more of it. Later, of course. I've got too many tasks for you between now and when we ride out to spare another meeting."

"So I am coming with you," Dante said. He allowed himself a long breath. In the headlong rush of the conversation around the table, he hadn't had the time to work out what he'd do if they meant to leave him behind. All his other ambitions had withered the moment he'd heard Samarand's nonchalant decree of war. He now had no other intent than killing her somewhere on the trail between the Citadel and Barden. He had to be there.

"Of course," Larrimore said. "It pains me to risk swelling your fat head any further, but the others still underestimate you. You're my hidden trump if anything goes wrong."

"I'll need Blays with us."

"Whatever helps you do the things I need you to do."

They reached the ground floor and parted ways. Eight days, Dante thought. Eight days before the beginning of the end. He was sent off with an order for a local merchant and returned to the Citadel to find three wounded watchmen being carted through the gates. Nak's fat belly jostled as he rushed across the yard to meet them. Dante joined the monk, saving two of the three and then all four of the others who arrived bleeding a few minutes later, the casualties of a small ambush on the fringes of the city. By the time a pair of acolytes came to relieve him should any other wounded arrive, Dante went to his cell and tumbled asleep.

He awoke feeling cold and sore. Weak moonlight flashed on metal near the foot of his bed and he made out the dim silhouette of a man standing over him.

"Blays?" he said softly.

The sword snapped back. Dante rolled off his bed, heart jolting, and scrabbled back as the blade slashed down into the pallet. His own sword was on the wall across the room. He readied himself to die, finding it much easier than the last times he'd so resigned himself, then his half-awake brain shouted through the din of his pulse and the chorus of his nerves. He twisted away from a short sword-thrust and reached out to the nether. It came at once, enveloping his hands, and Dante blasted the shadows forward in the next instant.

He heard a deep grunt and a wet splatter like someone pouring stew out on the ground. The silvery line of the sword dangled in the man's hand. Weirdly, his belly seemed to be bisected by a faintly incandescent line. The man wavered on his feet and Dante realized the light was the outline of the bottom edge of the door, visible through the huge hole in the man's stomach. Dante's own convulsed, and he had to jump aside as the man fell onto his knees and then his face.

"What are you doing?" Blays croaked from his bed.

"Killing someone."

"Ah. That again," Blays said in a dream-distant voice, then rolled over to face the wall.

"Someone just tried to kill me, Blays. Blays. There's a dead man on our floor. He tried to kill me." Dante leaned over Blays' slumbering form and located his ear. "Blays!"

Blays twitched his head up and conked it into Dante's. Dante fell back, bare heels bumping into warm skin. He skipped forward involuntarily. Blays squinted into the darkness, his body an indistinct blob in the middle of his bed, then all at once flailed all four limbs like he'd just been shot by an arrow.

"There's a dead man on our floor!"

"What should we do about that?" Dante said.

Blays rubbed his face with both hands. "Who is he?"

Dante knelt beside the corpse, inching away from the pooling blood that lay black in the moonlight. He grabbed the dead man's chin and stared into his face.

"I don't know. I've never seen him."

"You never called him the son of a whore? Spat on his boots?

Gave him that look where you look like you think he's a fresh pile of crap?"

"No," Dante said, in a light state of shock that made him feel this close to laughing. "I've never seen him."

"We know he's from the keep, don't we?" Blays refolded his blanket over his shoulders. "I mean, you don't just wander in here off the street."

"There are hundreds of men who live inside it."

"Go get Larrimore. He knows everyone."

"I can't," Dante said. "He'll start asking questions. Why would someone want to kill me? Am I up to anything he doesn't know about? He'll smell a rat. He's too smart. I already feel like I'm treading a knife's edge with him."

"Well they're going to have a few questions when they find a *body* in our room."

"We've only got one option." Dante swallowed. "We've got to eat him."

"*What?*"

Dante laughed like an idiot. Some part of him knew how serious this was, but at the same time it felt completely unreal. Bodies were ceasing to have any meaning to him. No matter what he did, they kept appearing at his feet, limp and useless. He snapped his mouth shut.

"We've got to get it out of here," he said. Blays got up, blanket draped down his body to his bare shins. He circled the corpse.

"Yeah, we'll just drag him out the front door," Blays said. "What the hell did you do to him? How much blood can one man bleed, anyway? Look at that. It's everywhere."

"Don't worry about that. Get the window open."

"Good idea. Bodies smell terrible when they're all opened up like that." He threw off his blanket and swung the bubbly glass window open. He leaned out it to get a breath, shoulders nearly brushing each side. "This isn't going to work."

"Just get out there," Dante said, crouching hesitantly beside the body. How could he get a grip when it was so blood-slick? "Make sure no one's outside. I'll sort of hand him to you."

"And then what? We heave him into someone else's back yard? Those walls are forty feet tall. You're not even going to be able to lift him."

"Stop naysaying. We'll just drag him off somewhere that isn't here."

Blays swore through his teeth. He planted his hands on the windowsill and wiggled his hips up on the ledge. He leaned the top half of his body through and paused there to consider the physics of his next move, ass and legs dangling back into the room. Dante swatted his legs. Blays kicked at him blindly, then wriggled forward into a controlled fall into the yard. Dante heard a soft whap of flesh on stone and more cursing. A moment later Blays' angry face appeared in the window.

"Okay, genius. Hand him over."

Dante grappled the man under his armpits and lifted from the knees, staggering back under the dead weight. He'd put on some muscle over the weeks of riding, running, and fighting, but he was still small, not yet grown into his full size, and the corpse, though not overly large, surely had outweighed him by thirty pounds before it had been drained of a few pints of blood. Dante's back thumped against the sill and he grunted. He regained his footing and strained upwards, thighs and back quivering, but somehow he lifted the body enough to get its head into the windowframe.

"Give me a hand, damn it," he panted, hot with sweat and sticky with blood. Blays' arms snaked through the window and grasped two thick handfuls of the man's cloak. "Got him?"

"I guess," Blays whispered. Dante stood there a moment, pinning the body to the wall with the weight of his chest, blinking and breathing until he didn't feel so weak, then he lowered himself and wedged his shoulder under the corpse's legs. Warm fluids soaked through his single plain shirt. He straightened his legs as hard as he could and Blays heaved from his side and the body scraped over the sill. All at once the man's gravity reached its tipping point and his loose legs kicked up as he fell into the yard, catching Dante on the chin hard enough to make him bite his own tongue.

"Get out here," Blays called inside. Dante planted a palm on the wall, giving himself a moment—already he was exhausted, flushed and wheezing—then hoisted himself into the sill and wormed his way through the window. Halfway out, he realized there would be no graceful exit. Blays held out his arms like the walking dead and Dante sighed and let himself fall into them. They crumpled to the ground.

"Now what?" Blays said from the bottom of their two-person heap. Dante untangled himself and glanced around the yard. They were in the dark corner where the chapel met the keep. A few outbuildings stood against the outer ring of wall across one hundred-plus feet of open space. There were no lights in the chapel other than the lantern that was always lit in its hall, at least, and he saw no guards patrolling the grounds at that moment. Just a few motionless bumps of men high and far on the outer walls. There was one other building further along the side of the keep, a simple wooden barracks where some of the pages and stableboys slept. Straw was mounded waist-high against its wall.

"Dump it in that straw," Dante pointed. Blays shook his head but he grabbed one arm and Dante took the other and they leaned into it, one step at a time. The corpse whispered against the stone. They had to cross a full sixty feet, but they moved in the shadow of the keep, and he heard no shocked cries, saw no guards turn a corner and gasp at murderous intrigue. At last they reached the housing and heaved the man into the snow-damp pile.

"Make it look half-assed," Dante whispered, shoveling some straw over the man's body.

"That won't be hard." Blays circled it, kicking straw on the man's glaze-eyed face. They shifted enough around to hide the body from casual inspection, then stepped back and glanced throughout the silent yard. Blays' eyes followed the foot-wide track of blood between the pile of straw and the window to their cell. "And that? Shall I fetch a mop?"

"Only if you're going to stuff it in your mouth," Dante said. He beckoned to the shadows and knelt alongside the gleaming trail. Nether poured from his hands and onto the smeared stones, whirling down it like the rapids of a stream. Where it passed the ground was left bare. Dante tugged Blays' sleeve and they hurried back to the window and stuffed themselves through, waiting in the middle of the original puddle for the nether to finish its business. It poured over the sill, cleansing the floor, then pooled around their feet, seeking what was caking on their skin. It rushed up their limbs, black and noiseless as empty space. When it had finished its cleaning he summoned it to the window and gazed up on the star-pricked sky, then sent it hurtling straight up in as fine a point as it could make. It streaked away without a sound.

The boys faced each other in the room, breathing heavily, laughing nervously. A few drops of blood congealed here and there, but it no longer looked like the obvious murder it had a minute before. Blays picked up the man's sword off the ground and tucked it under his pallet.

"Do you have any idea why he was here? Who could have sent him?"

Dante shook his head. "Another initiate, maybe, jealous of my progress. One of Larrimore's other agents, for the same reason." He shrugged, baffled. "Maybe someone discovered my true purpose and thought he'd win Samarand's favor taking care of it himself."

"How could they have done that? What have you been telling Larrimore?"

"I don't know. It's impossible to keep it all straight." Dante thumped down on his bed. Something twinged in chest and he hugged his arms to each other. "I'm always lying, always bluffing to hide what little I do know. I couldn't tell you a tenth of what I've said." He could feel Blays' eyes on him, but he couldn't make himself meet them. The humor that had sustained him all this way, his own private Pridegate, felt shattered and mossed-over as the outer stretches of this thousand-year-old city. "Most of the time I'm all right with it, but sometimes my stomach feels like it's bleeding from the inside. Do you have any idea what it's like? I'm on my guard every second of every day. I just want it to be over."

"I had no idea. You always look the same, you know." Blays sat down across from him. "We've been here too long."

"I know. You're right. I should never have let it go this far." He closed his eyes, shivered. "They're moving out in a week. We'll do it then. No matter what."

"No matter what." He heard Blays resettling himself among his blankets. "Get some sleep. It helps."

He tried, but was still awake by dawn. No one else came in the night to strike him dead. In the morning he heard exclamations from the yard, but when he saw Larrimore for the day's errands the man was inscrutable. Despite the monks' best efforts to heal them, men did die with some frequency within the walls of the Sealed Citadel, lapsing into drunken squabbles and the long-boiling bitterness that grows among men in cramped quarters. It was possible they thought nothing of finding one more body buried in the straw. Dante was too tired to try to sound out if anyone was suspicious of the man's death or even who he'd been; he was too tired to be affected any more by that helpless feeling that had taken him after the attempt on his life.

It was almost a blessing when Larrimore ordered him to fill his day informing the priests of a few of the city's minor temples about a general prayer in the Cathedral of Ivars six nights hence. On his way back to the Citadel, he detoured to the sad wreck of a ruined house. Among the splintery timbers he killed three rats with a flick of nether. There he raised them, hid them in his clothes. By night he set one outside his window, one outside his door, and one inside his room, bidding them to watch from the nooks for anyone who tried to enter. He woke often, gasping and half-panicked from dreams he couldn't remember, but he saw no silhouettes through the eyes of the rats, heard no furtive footsteps with their ears or his own. He thought the days of the remaining week would drag as long as the endless grammar lessons with Nak, but between his duties and his sleepless haze the hours clipped along like the now-blurred years of his early childhood. Like that, they were gone.

16

With each gate he left he felt a weight lift from his feet. He hadn't realized, leading his two lives in the keep, how deeply it had marked him, how each false word and fresh lie had lain on his shoulders like a stone. The attempted assassination had nearly broken his nerve; he'd maintained himself only through insomnia and the knowledge his goal had grown definite, that he'd still Samarand's heart somewhere along the path to the White Tree of Barden. Though he rode at Larrimore's left at the head of a column of a couple hundred men, Blays was at his side, they were in the saddle, and the cold air hit him with the full freedom of the first moments after a bad dream. The muscle of the horse beneath him. The chill nip of the wind on his unhooded ears and nose. The sword tugging on his left hip when he moved, the mass of the true book in his pack from when he'd slipped out the night before and dug it from the silent yard of the crumbling house just past the near side of the Pridegate. These too weighed on him, but they were a comfort rather than a burden. He'd worn them many miles before whatever was to come in the next few days. Blays, his sword, his book. He didn't think he'd be coming back, but he took with him everything he'd need.

"You look jolly enough," Larrimore remarked, gazing out at the battle between city and forest taking place at its forgotten fringes.

"I've been cooped up too long. It's good to be back in the open air."

"Well, eyes sharp. We're expecting attack."

"From who?"

"Who can keep up?" Larrimore shrugged. "Regional rebels. You heard a little about them at the council. No doubt they know Samarand herself is leading this troop."

"Why do they care?" Dante said, eyes darting among the wreckage of buildings.

"They think Samarand's ignoring the will of the king and dragging all of Gask to war. Which is sort of true. But the palace leaving Narashtovik didn't mean they took all its power with them."

"I don't follow."

"The priesthood stayed put. With the kingdom's power scattered hither and yon, everything got all swapped up. These days it's almost more like a score of baronies than a kingdom. About the only thing they all agree on is they don't like Mallon telling them what to do and the norren should shut up and do as they're told." He scratched his cheek, regarding Dante. "You should ask Nak about these things, he doesn't have anything better to do than read about why things happened. Point is, they're out there, they'll take their chance, and they'll die for it."

Dante nodded. "You're so certain they'll fail?"

"Those old men are an army unto themselves," he said, glancing toward the carriages bearing Samarand and the six other men of the council, one of whom was Jackson. Dante had been surprised to see he'd talked his way on the mission. Samarand's will had seemed made of iron.

"I suppose the soldiers are no slouch, either," Dante said. Larrimore grunted agreement. "Well, good. Glad to know we're not on a suicide mission."

Most of the soldiers were on foot and after they'd left the Pridegate it was the better part of half an hour before they'd crossed the bridge over the river and left the last mossy vestiges of the city behind. The lead riders took them down a road that ran north-northeast, roughly parallel to the coastline a couple miles distant. The land between them and ocean was spotty with scrubby pines, as if the thick forest to their right couldn't make the hop across the rutted dirt trail. Ten or fifteen miles deep into those woods the land cranked up into a range of tall hills or short mountains. Either way, they were heavily snowcapped. It had snowed again in the city and its surroundings a couple days previously, but that had melted in the not-quite-freezing breeze that blew in off the seas each evening. Riders came and went to Larrimore and the carriages that traveled in the caravan's center. Dante caught fragments of intelligence about the state of the road and the signs of enemy scouts in the mud of the woods. Larrimore murmured orders and rode on, uncharacteristically subdued. Dante kept his eyes roving. Sweat built up beneath his arms.

"Quiet enough out there," he said to Blays after a time.

"Yep."

"What's wrong with them? Are they scared?"

Blays drew back his chin. "You almost sound like you want to be ambushed."

"I just don't like waiting." Dante lowered his hand to the haft of his sword. He remembered how it had felt to wield it in battle, the sense of oneness that came from the timing of a perfect parry, as if his body were in tune with a deep note of the song of the world. The silent potency that took him when he drove the blade home in another man's ribs. The rush of the nether thrumming in his heart and through his arms to spill the blood of those who'd see him dead. "So what if I am? You're not?"

"A little, maybe." Blays sniffed, rubbed his nose. "With all the drilling I've been doing it would almost be a waste not to use it."

The attack came at dusk, when they were some twenty miles from the dead city, too far to be reinforced before the battle was decided. One of their mounted scouts galloped from the woods, wide-eyed and panting, and pulled up before Larrimore.

"They're coming," he said, clutching his chest. "Just a few minutes out."

"That's all the warning you've brought me?"

The rider tossed his head back at the woods. "They concealed themselves well. I could have stepped on them and never known it."

Larrimore swore thoughtfully. He glanced at Dante, who'd already loosened his sword in its scabbard.

"Stay with the cavalry. Prepare yourselves."

The column of soldiers had grown irregular with the passage of miles and Larrimore pounded down its length, calling out formations and orders to his captains. Their force made a general shift off the left side of the road, opening perhaps forty yards of clear ground between them and the woods. The carriages were drawn in tight and buffered by a thicket of pikemen. To the pikemen's front, forming a chevron back along the flanks of the carriage, the swordsmen formed a loose line, letting the two score archers mingle at their front. The cavalry were but a score in number, captained by a dark-bearded man named Rettinger who barked orders in Gaskan to his men.

"We're to hold at the top of the column," Dante translated to Blays, "then sweep across their second line once they rush the archers."

"Not many men for a charge."

"No time for more complicated maneuvers," Dante said, and the roar of men's voices pitched up through the pines to their east. His skin prickled from ears to toes. Larrimore's voice piped out and the chevron begin to swing so its point faced the bulk of the battle cry. A husky voice rang out and the archers let fly. Dante still couldn't see anything but shadows of movement among the trees and the first volley provoked no more than a handful of screams. A couple dozen points of light flashed from the edges of the wood, catching the harsh slant of the last rays of the sun, and he saw arrows lancing almost without arc into the front lines of Samarand's soldiers.

"Can't let that hold up, we've got no cover," Rettinger said, glancing toward Larrimore. He growled. "Cut across."

His horsemen followed him across the road and they lingered just before the pines began. The woods weren't overly dense so close to the road, but it was a forest nonetheless, full of shrubs and cut trunks and rocks half-buried in leaves. More than enough to negate the speed of their horses. Another volley swished from both sides and again the screaming was louder from their own force. Dante gripped his blade. How long would Rettinger let the footmen get shot to pieces?

"Hell with it," Rettinger said, as if reading the boy's thoughts, and he whipped out his sword and pointed it forward as he brought his mount to a trot. "In and out. Cut down any man with a bow and get the hell out."

His men drew arms and fell into a ragged skirmish line.

Hooves thunked hard earth. A battle cry ripped up from the bottom point of the column and through the screen of trees Dante saw a mass of footmen charging the force concealed in the wood. Arrows swished over their heads from the archers by the carriages and then more pelted them from the safety of the pines. Men spun in their tracks and thumped against the ground. Then the footmen filtered into the woods and as Rettinger's men burst upon the front line of archers the music of meeting steel exploded from the southern edge of the battle.

Dante set his eyes on one man as he'd been taught and cocked his arm. An arrow thrummed past his ear and hot rage burned between his eyes. He gasped, nostrils flaring, then the man was before him and he wheeled his blade and screamed and lashed the archer across the face. He glanced toward Blays a couple lengths ahead and saw him knock aside the blade of a pike. To Blays' left, at their outer flank, an arrow hammered into a rider's chest and he flopped in the saddle, horse veering left into the lines of enemy footmen. Dante compensated right without thinking and turned in time to duck beneath a pike being jammed at his face. He made a quick stab at an archer diving behind a tree and then bore right to follow Rettinger's curve back into the open. Swordsmen exchanged blows and shouts. Rettinger called out as the cavalry passed. They broke back into the field and cut back toward the caravan.

Rettinger pulled up and counted off his men. They were missing two. Dante breathed heavily, relishing the air in his lungs, the air that dozens of men had suddenly ceased to taste.

"We're in reserve for the moment." Rettinger nodded toward the battle in the woods. "Be ready for another pass if they don't bring them into the open."

"Why wait?" said a man with sweat-streaked blond hair.

"Need them in the open so the priests can do their thing."

Calls of "Retreat!" hued up from the forest. Over the next minute Samarand's footmen fell back in a scattered mass, backs turned to their pursuers.

"That's organized," Dante said to Blays, pointing at the lines visible in their retreating ranks.

"See if they bite," Blays nodded. The footmen reassembled to the far side of the road. The enemy gushed from the woods and took another volley to their face. Arrows flew irregularly from the cover of the trees. Some of the riders grumbled, pointing to the other flank of footmen holding around the carriages. They were holding fast to the fire of the enemy archers, dragging the dead and wounded behind cover of the coaches and the handful of trees. The retreating forces regrouped and turned to meet their pursuers. Shouts and clanging metal filled the field. Swordsmen continued to rush from the woods. Already the numbers of the two armies looked equal and still the enemy emerged from the wilds.

"Get your men out there!" Larrimore shouted toward Rettinger.

"Let's cause some chaos," Rettinger said, lifting his sword, and Dante aped him. He took them wide around the fury of the melee and back into the woods. Long shadows striped the ground. The trees were of decent age and few had branches low enough to interfere with their immediate lines of sight. Rettinger whooped and shouted taunts. The other men bellowed along a split second later, Dante's young voice mingling with those of the men. They trampled through a loose fringe of stragglers, slowing enough to aim their blows for the softness of the neck. Dante cocked his arm, laughing at the panicked face of an unmounted soldier before he split it in half with his sword. He understood now they weren't meant to ride down the entire enemy troop. They were the dogs of the hunt, meant to bay, meant to hound, meant to cause panic in the larger animal. He put those thoughts away and cleaved someone's skull.

Up ahead a wedge of pikemen scrambled to intercept their course. The riders veered right, deeper into the woods, away from all that hard steel. Blays had raced ahead and Dante spurred his horse to catch pace. He threaded through the trees, keeping one eye on the mass of men rushing off to lay waste to each other, running through the woods, shadows banding their bodies, then emerging for a brief moment to be speared with the glittering dust in an unbroken beam of sunlight. The drumbeat of their hooves drowned out the jangle of swords. They'd been riding for some seconds in a recently-abandoned stretch of wood, circumscribing a wide arc around the battle, and Rettinger made a sharp turn, driving them to the northeast. Dante was so close on Blays' heels the churned turf of his horse dashed against his face. Within moments they were skimming along the rear guard, lashing out with their simple straight cavalry blades into the dispersed ranks of the rebels, cutting raised arms between elbow and wrist, the sweat and thunder and howls forcing back the dirty-faced men of the opposition. They rode as an ancient law of the world, as destruction on horseback, as the right arm of an angry god. Like that they were in the midst of a sizable troop, up near the front of the forest, slashing archers in their turned backs. Cries rang out and arrows creased the air around their heads. At the head of the charge, Rettinger broke right, straight north away from arrows and swords and pikes. Dante's horse jerked and uttered a choked whinny. Then his level, speeding world of half-glimpsed faces and whipping branches was replaced by a sudden rush of earth and fallen tree limbs and he felt his legs part from the horse as it went down and his momentum went on. He skidded facefirst through dry pine needles and wet dirt. Some small part of his mind was happy he'd been thrown clear of the wounded horse. Then he rolled to his feet and found himself alone, surrounded by archers and men with hostile swords, the rear of the cavalry hurtling away into the safety of the woods, the drum of their hoofs already obscured by the shouts of men.

"Blays!" he cried. His sword had buried itself in the ground a couple feet away and he yanked it up and beat back the first thrust of a swordsman. Most of the soldiers around him were occupied with their own troubles, be they plunking arrows at the men in the open road or rushing to the side of their friends just cut down by the screaming horde of Rettinger's charge, but he was there, alone, with too many alien faces to make it out alive. He parried another blow and riposted, as Robert Hobble had shown him an eternity ago on their long march, a wild swing that nonetheless slashed across his opponent's chest and felled him. He heard the shifting of the carpet of needles and spun to meet a sword meant for his spine. His senses felt like living things. The scent of blood and sap. The power of the weight of the blade in his hand. The mixed anger and fear of this new swordsman bringing his weapon back around. Dante punched out his left hand and the nether knocked a hole in the man's neck. His eyes bugged and he too went down, painting the forest floor with his blood. An arrow ripped past Dante's ear and he felt a stinging numbness where it clipped his cartilage. Blood trickled down his forehead and cheeks where he'd slammed into the dirt. Two more swordsmen popped up from tending the wounded to meet this new threat and Dante backpedaled, resisting every urge to throw down his weapon and run till his legs gave out. He swept his free hand through the blood at his ear and face. When the two men stood shoulder to shoulder in front of him he sprung forward, arm held straight as the arrows hissing through the woods, and white fire belched from a foot in front of his hand to sear past the two soldiers. Its pure heat wrenched the screams from their throats.

Others fell back, shielding their faces with their forearms. The flash of flame and the whump of igniting air drew a glance from a dozen other men. Dante had slung the nether like a limb of his own body, trusting blank terror to keep him safe, but from the depths of his fugue he knew if he stayed here he might take a few more with him out to Arawn's indifferent arms, but it would end with his unblinking eyes staring up through the wind-shook needles of the pines.

He turned and ran what he thought was north—away from the loudest sounds of fighting, at least; the sun was down too far to judge by it in the middle of all those trees—zigzagging through trunks, meaning to confuse any archers drawing a bead, to string out any pursuing swordsmen. He risked a glance. A half dozen giving chase, maybe more. They'd seen one of the riders unhorsed and wanted to cut out a nobleman's heart and see it bleed the same as theirs. Maybe work up the courage to join the main fray. He knocked down the lead man with a bolt of shadow. Shouts to his immediate north. They were cutting him off. Time nearly at a stop. Watching the shadow-struck man's feet slide up in front of him as he slipped in the needles. Blood wobbling away from the wound on the man's forehead. The world was nightmare, choked gasps and blood gurgling in punctured throats, blind rage in the eyes of all the men who were about to kill him as the agent of a woman he hated here near the ends of the world.

"Blays!" he screamed. Chill fingers wrapped around his spine as he reached out again to the dead man's corpse now slamming to a final rest. Would it be no different than with the rats? Would the effort tear Dante apart like a storm-swollen stream? His body shuddered as the nether left him and darted over to the body. The next swordsmen rushed by, a couple seconds away. He turned his gaze to them and from the corner of his vision saw the dead man stand and raise his sword. Dante tasted bile. Just like the rats. He imagined the dead man's sword splitting the neck of the man running past him and the corpse swiped out and removed a head from a set of shoulders. Then the closest pair was on him.

His back bumped into a trunk and he rolled alongside it. The sword of a man with a black beard and dirty buckskin clothes whacked into the trunk, spitting bark over Dante's face. Dante leaned forward to stab his guts while his sword was stuck but his partner cut a quick downward stroke and Dante had to lean back and twist his body just to get his sword up enough to escape with a gashed shoulder rather than a severed arm. He wanted to scream. He grimaced and punched the man in the jaw with the pommel of his sword, knocking him back a couple steps to spit gobs of blood and teeth. The other dislodged his blade from the tree and, being right-handed, stabbed around it. Dante jumped to put the full trunk between them and beat down with his sword, pinning the attacker's against the tree. He ripped up the point of his blade, just a quick flip of the wrists, but it cut across the man's chest, sending him sprawling, guts open to the air.

To his left, toward where the other men had been chasing him, the animated corpse was laying into three swordsmen. Three other bodies sprawled at its feet where it had caught them unaware. There was no grace in the swings of its sword, just a tireless, painless strength, a stroke as ponderous and inevitable as the turning of the stars. It didn't try to dodge or block when one of the men stepped in and hacked through its left arm. Instead it raised its blade and buried it in the man's ribs. The other two fell on it, chopping wildly, knocking it to its knees.

The man he'd punched had recovered and circled around the tree. The man was young, his beard patchy and his hair stringy, blood dribbling past his lips to catch in the hairs of his chin, and as they exchanged strikes and parries Dante found he could hold his own. A one-man cheer came up from the left and the sliver of second awareness he'd felt since returning the corpse to its feet blanked out. They'd be on him in a second. He reached out for the shadows, expecting hesitation after all his exertions, resistance, but found them ready. In his surprise he nearly lost hold of his simple intentions but maintained his grasp and formed a ball of black around the man's head. The man gasped and Dante had to duck his blind swing. The sword whooshed over his head. He poked the man in the ribs, then the gut, and at the sight of two more men running toward him he took off like a jackrabbit, straight west toward the road and all the clamor of a full battle. He weaved through trees, boots slipping on the pine needles. He held his sword with both hands and chopped the back of an archer taking sight through the thinning trees. His cut shoulder flared with pain. Bootsteps thudded behind him. He ran straight through a line of archers at the edge of the woods and then he was clear and saw the raging anarchy of the fight along the open ground around the road.

Swordsmen lashed at each other, the fine black cloaks of Samarand's men mingling with the tanned leather dress and time-thinned furs of the rebels. Pikes waved over their heads, descending in awkward slashes through the crush of men. Men died on their blades and were held on their feet by the pressure of the surging troops. Others tripped on corpses, then lunged to meet the enemy's swords. Shrieks of wrath and pain and steel deafened him to everything but the pulse in his ears. Six hundred soldiers or more all told, he guessed, the men of Arawn outnumbered and with more ready to meet them in the woods—how would real war look if it came to Mallon, tens of thousands clashing in a single battle? Wounded men retreated back to the cover of the treeline, soaked in the blood of their own mangled flesh, pointing and shouting when they saw the flap of Dante's black cloak. He struck one down with a spear of nether. Archers behind him, a war to his front and to his left. The field to the right was mostly empty but if he went that way the archers could fire on him without worry of hitting their comrades. He clenched his teeth. Everything was ruin. He'd die here. He'd fall in the field and become lost to the dirt. Another man closed on him, right arm dangling useless, blood dripping from the torn sleeve around his elbow, sword held in his left. The man swung with strength but no precision and Dante deflected it from his body and swung a forehand counter that took the man's throat.

A keening bloom of fire flared from the middle of the battle around the carriages, followed in the same instant by a second and a third. Screams dominated the crash of weapons. Dante started forward to make use of the confusion, meaning to lose himself to any watching archers in the mixed-up outskirts of the fight, but before he'd crossed the open ground the tide of men began to turn back toward him, driven by the tongues of flame and the terror of the men at the front. Dante backed up toward the woods, readying the shadows. The first of the enemy reached him as he heard the pounding of hooves approaching from his right.

The cavalry smashed into the scattered lines. Hands and swords and strings of blood flew into the air. The enemy men stopped short to meet this new threat, caught between the anvil of the council priests laying waste at their front and the hammer of mounted men cutting them apart at their rear. Dante stumbled backwards, seeing the faces of the riders whip past, their expressions fusions of glee and rage.

"Blays!" he called out. "Blays!"

A handful of rebel footmen had been cut off from the lines by the swift strike of the cavalry. Their eyes turned to Dante's shouts, saw him alone and unhorsed. He sobbed, then tightened his throat and shook his sword and made white fire slither around its length. He held his left hand aloft and swathed it in a hazy sphere of darkness, bellowing for all his worth. His voice cracked. The men hesitated, a couple actually stepping back in the face of his demonry, then saw they were many and he was one and continued toward him. He could run back toward the woods, but that would just delay this fight to put him into an even more lopsided match. He tensed his arms, heart rebelling against what the next moments would bring.

Two riders peeled from the rear of the cavalry while the others, too few to risk getting mired down in the throngs of men, continued the charge to Dante's left. One of the riders stomped down a footman and cut across the back of a second. The other leaned down in the saddle and with a smooth stroke sent a man's head tumbling. The first horseman swung away to hurry after the rest of the cavalry, leaving Dante and Blays—for it *was* Blays, his blond head bobbing with the motion of his horse, blood splashed on his sword arm and face so his eyes stood out bright as beacons—alone to face the remaining men who hadn't turned back to the main fight at the departure of the cavalry. They stood alone, detached in the open ground between woods and the full-out battle at the carriages.

Blays tried to turn his horse for another pass, but saw the men would be on Dante before he could complete the maneuver. He drew up his legs in a crouch and hurled himself into the mass of men as they converged on their target. Two fell beneath his tackle and only one got back up with him. Dante whirled his fiery blade in front of him, drawing no blood but lending his own discord to all the violent babel. He swept his shadowed hand in a broader arc and the nether cut a line across the veins of the lead man's neck. Blood jetted away from him and he fell to his knees, clutching his mortal wound. Still the warriors didn't break. Blays had freed his sword from the man he'd plunged it in during his leaping dismount and was fighting in a way Dante had never seen him do before: fists held steady at a point just above his waist, he twisted his wrists and elbows to swing the sword's tip in front of his body with little strength but great precision and speed. In no time at all he opened a hole in his opponent's defense and lashed the blade back and forth across his body.

Dante sidled to his left as they fell in around him, hacking out at one man, forcing him back enough to keep the ones on his right out of arm's reach. He flat-out charged then, the bright lance of his sword held out before him. His target sidestepped and Dante spun right to block his strike. Blays came at him from his flank and the man pivoted to prevent being skewered. Blays had already moved on to the next man coming their way as Dante sunk his sword to the hilt in the man's side. He thought he could feel the steel sliding through the separate organs of the man's gut.

Their foes fanned out around them. Blays and Dante fought shoulder to shoulder, a two-man line against the number and determination of the enemy. The soldiers' eyes swirled with hate for

Dante and the uniform he wore, oblivious to the true nature of his presence, how he would land the blow at Samarand's neck the rebels would fail at here. Sick laughter bubbled in his throat. None of them had to die, but they'd be killed in this battle by the score. Whose justice was that? Surely not the gods'. This was no reflection of the heavens. This was the law of the soiled earth, a place of angry confusion and mewling deaths. This was the edifice of man, this blood-watered field, where they fought and fell cold for a joke of fate.

He snapped his head away from a whistling sword. Blays was fighting two men at once, wrists flicking so fast his blade blurred in the afterglow of the sunset. Dante kept his own, and for half a minute of ringing swords he was too busy keeping himself alive to reach out to the nether. He landed a deep cut to a man's thigh and the attacker fell back to be replaced by another. In the open moment Dante took a clumsy grasp on the shadows and rather than a stab of force released it in a blunt wave that knocked away the next man's breath. He pressed his advantage, battering away the man's sword and gutting him. He glanced at a grunt to his side and saw Blays lean into a killing strike and immediately pull back to parry his other foe's reach. He turned back. The sword of the man whose leg he'd cut was sweeping in a level plane toward his ribs. Dante tossed up a half-strength block and sucked air through his teeth as he felt the steel parting his skin. He skipped back a step, stomach soured with nausea. The shadows swept through him—too much this time, an itchy tingle beneath his skin that flared into a burst of pain before he went numb. His assailant fell, but his vision grayed, his sword arm lowered to his side. The shouts and screams and pounding of steel met his ears as if he were underwater. He blinked, turned to watch Blays hack it out with one last man. Everyone else around them appeared to have either retreated into the woods, rejoined the fighting around the carriages and priests or further down the road where footmen battled footmen, or been struck down in the field. Amazingly—though in his lightheaded state everything seemed at least mildly surprising—Blays' horse stood a few yards off, tossing its head at the noise and the scents of blood and bile and scorched air, but there it was, standing its ground.

"Your horse is good," he said to Blays, who offered no reply. Down to a single opponent, Blays' swings had become less defensive, wider arcs meant to take advantage of the strength his arms had gained these last few months. "Hey. I said your horse is good."

"I heard," Blays said through his teeth. He countered a few blows then leaned into an offensive of his own. He struck successively higher, and on the fourth swing he twisted his wrist, giving it an upstroke, knocking his opponent's sword up over his head. The man regained enough balance to start a cut aimed at Blays' neck, but by then Blays' own blade had passed back down and opened his throat. The man dropped away. Blays spun in a quick circle and saw the only men near them were corpses. He ran past Dante to the horse and wriggled his way up into the saddle. Dante gazed dumbly at the blood that covered his hands and sword. He wiped his weapon on the coat of a dead man, then brushed his hands in the wet grass.

"Come on!" Blays shouted.

"What, both of us?" Dante said, wandering up beside the beast. It smelled like sweat and dust and hair.

"Now, you god damn dunce!"

"Right." Dante got a foot in the stirrup and swung himself up behind Blays. "Sorry. I'm a little—" He tapped the side of his head.

"What's new," he heard Blays mutter. Blays wheeled the horse around and spurred it north along the right-hand side of the road. A couple arrows whisked past their head. Dante twisted around and gave the forest the finger. They swung around the top edge of the battle, giving it wide berth, working their way toward the rear. After a few moments the cold air filling his lungs and rushing over his skin began to clear his head.

"You're pretty good," he said.

"Shut up," Blays said, glancing quickly between the ground ahead and the slaughter at the carriages. As they curved around the lines of combat Dante saw streaks of fire lancing out from the hands of council men who'd looked too old to walk without a staff. He laughed, then fell silent at the scent of scorched flesh. Samarand's men had repelled another surge and were slowly driving the rebels back. Blays cut across the road and through a makeshift camp of wounded men. As they approached the rear of the caravan two horsemen rode out and hailed them.

"It's Blays! I've got Dante Galand with me!"

"Alive?" one of them asked with professional interest. Blays reined in the horse and dropped down to the ground.

"Takes more than that rabble to kill me," Dante said. He hopped down and staggered to one side, arms wheeling. "I'm all right."

"What's been going on?" Blays said to one of the riders, a man whose thick black hair was clipped short.

"Looked bad until the priests come into it," the man said in halting Mallish.

"And now?"

"Not so bad."

"We need to go help them," Dante said. He took a step forward. Blays planted a hand on his chest, unbalancing him again.

"No we don't. Look at you, you're like a drunk two-year-old." He glanced over at the sounds of battle, then at the rider, then finally back to Dante. His mouth worked over itself. "What if..?"

Dante frowned, confused. Then he caught the glint in Blays' eyes and shook his head.

"Not until the Tree!" he whispered loudly.

"But it's so mixed up right now. No one could tell."

"I don't even know what's going on," Dante said. He walked around the caravan to get a view of the fight, letting his hand trail along the side of one of the wagons. Blays' feet crunched through leaves and dirt behind him. Dante turned a corner and gazed out at the swarms of men, swords and pikes flashing in the dim light. He wondered vaguely if Larrimore were still alive. He could make out Samarand, her thick black braid swinging behind her head as she called out orders and weaved her hands to form the nether before unleashing it in a booming flare amongst the enemy ranks, and after a moment he'd counted all six priests of the council on their feet and lobbing death before them, but he didn't see Samarand's Hand.

It wasn't long before the rebels began to retreat. Once it had begun, any meaningful points of battle were over in seconds. Men turned to see open gaps in their lines and the backs of the men who'd just been beside them. Before them, the priests blasted fire and chaos. They fell back swiftly, dropping weapons, stumbling over the wounded and the dead, a motion that began with a handful and ended in a total retreat. Samarand's forces gave chase for a few yards, hacking down anyone within range, then pulled up and cheered. The fighting on their southern flank followed suit within half a minute. The rebels disappeared into the lines of trees and the air stilled to the rustle of pines and the groans of the dying.

Dante sighed and as he felt the air streaming through his nostrils he realized he hadn't been thinking clearly since he'd last drawn the nether. His senses crept back to him like dogs frightened off by the shouts of their master. He saw soldiers put away blades and sink to their knees, huffing for breath, faces spattered with mud and blood, eyes shadowed in the twilight. Others prodded among the prone bodies, hauling off the conscious ones to the carriages, where the priests did what they could to stabilize their wounds. The stink of spilled stomachs clung to the air. The wounded rolled in the grass, sobbing, voices choked with snot. Bodies carpeted the field between the road and the forest. He'd never seen so many. All the men he'd killed along the way to Narashtovik suddenly swum before his eyes: the two at the temple, the neeling, the three in the alley in Bressel, the tracker by the river, the two in Whetton, the uncounted watchmen at the hanging, Will Palomar and his men in the woods, Hansteen and his rebels at Gabe's monastery in Shay, the assassin in his cell in the Citadel. A few dozen—and every one after his own life, he reminded himself—but a fraction of those dead and dying in this place. A drop in an ocean to all who must fall in the real wars. However high his count might be, it wouldn't fill a single row in any of the endless cemeteries of Narashtovik. Dante shuddered, not for what he looked upon so much as how he'd come to see it. He tried to rise and didn't trust his knees to hold him up. He lowered himself back to the dirt and for a long time felt nothing but the hollow ringing of his body.

Larrimore appeared after a few minutes, blood running freely down his face from a wound on his scalp, but Dante knew head wounds always looked worse than they were. He touched the scrapes on his own face, the nick in his ear, the cuts to his shoulder and ribs. The shoulder was tender to the touch, still leaking blood.

He shook his head, gazing out at the triage.

"Hard to tell who won," he said to no one in particular. He cleared his throat against the catch he'd felt. Scores of bodies tamped down the grass every way he looked. A full third of their force was dead or would die from their injuries, he'd bet; others would be left without arms or legs or would spool out the rest of their days hobbling, unable to move any faster than a jerky walk.

"Do you feel that?" Blays said.

"What?" Dante perked up his ears, strained for whatever Blays was lifting his head toward. Out on the fields, men with naked blades stalked among the bodies, pausing here and there to hack once or twice at the fallen. Not all of their targets wore the irregular clothes of the rebels.

"The clarity. Like my dad said." Blays held his hand before his face and stretched out his fingers as if to touch something only he could see. "Everything is closer. Don't you feel it?"

"I feel tired," Dante said. "Is that a revelation?"

Blays gave him a sharp look. "I'm not kidding."

Neither am I, Dante didn't say. He drew a deep breath and tried to ignore the throbs of pain throughout his body. After a moment he understood the pain was a part of whatever Blays was talking about and he stopped trying anything at all, letting his eyes see the men gathering bodies, his ears hear the murmur of their low voices and the weeping of the dying, letting his nerves feel the shell of his body telling him the pulse of its pain. Everything about the battle had been so fast. Where was the glory? Before, at the end of things, he'd often felt a thrill so deep it was like being touched by the hand of the god. It was as if something had been proven. If a god touched him now, he thought his bones would crumble. The wind picked up, hissing through the pines, tousling the grasses. In fifty years, no one would remember this. The earth had forgotten it already.

"Your father was right," he said.

"He died, you know. A few years ago. Hired for border work in one of the baronies. He just didn't come back."

"I didn't know that," Dante said.

Blays nodded. He unsheathed his sword and planted it point-first in the ground. He leaned on it, watching the men stack the bodies.

"It was odd, with all the fights he'd been in, he'd die in one of those jokes they called a war."

"Someone shot my horse from under me today. I should have died."

"Why do you think you didn't?" Blays smiled with half his mouth. "Fate?" He glanced to where Samarand was ordering men around. "Destiny?"

"I taught myself to do things other men can't," Dante said. Blays' smile faded and Dante reached into his pocket and touched the torchstone he'd had since he was a kid. "My dad died when I was young, too."

"That's too bad. He must have been something."

Larrimore bounded up to them out of the gloom. He had a handkerchief pressed against the still-leaking wound on his forehead, but he smiled at them through the blood drying on his face.

"Oh good," he said. "I'd heard you were dead."

"Wouldn't want to trouble your sleep," Dante said.

"Why so glum? Did you have to kill someone?"

"I lost count."

Larrimore chuckled, then stepped closer and bent to examine Dante's face.

"You're all torn up! Go and see a priest, will you?"

Dante waved a hand. "They've got bigger problems."

"I don't want your humors all corrupted by some little stab. You already seem to have a preponderance of bile."

"I can take care of myself," Dante said. Larrimore looked skeptical. "How'd the battle go?"

"They had numbers and terrain, so I'd call it a success," he said, shrugging at the bodies being dragged into piles. He considered Blays. "Rettinger says you did all right."

"All right? I saved your pet's life here," Blays said, tipping his head at Dante.

"We'll get you a medal."

"I'd prefer some whiskey."

"Whiskey's fleeting. Badges of honor last until you have to pawn them." Larrimore removed the handkerchief from his wound and turned a critical eye on whatever it had sopped up.

"What am I talking to you two for? I've got things to do. If you're not too busy sitting on your asses, you could lend a hand out there."

"Sorry," Dante said, stretching out his legs. "Single-handedly winning the battle is exhausting work."

Larrimore snorted and left them to go confer with Samarand over in the road. They spoke and nodded at each other for a minute and a minute after that a rider trotted south back toward the dead city. An hour later the troops had finished gathering the corpses. The field stunk with the dizzying smell of oil. They laid a torch to the bodies and the smell got much worse. Samarand marched them a couple miles north, just enough to get upwind and find a decent hill to camp on if the rebels surprised them with another attack. Behind them, the fires kept burning, spitting greasy smoke into the night, clogging the skies between them and the lights of Narashtovik. Like that they were gone, the ashes of their bodies mingled with the ashes of the earth. Were their spirits with Arawn? Dante stretched out beneath his cloak, watched the columns of smoke cast a haze over the stars, dulling their bright points to dying embers. How old was the world? How many men had fed it with their bones in hopes their children wouldn't have to do the same? He meant to stay up till the fires burnt themselves to darkness, but sleep slapped him down like a rogue wave. For the first night since he'd killed the assassin, he didn't wake once before it was time to move on.

17

The northern road stretched on. Mounted scouts came and went and exchanged words with Samarand and Larrimore and Rettinger. They'd scared up a new horse for Dante and he and Blays rode a few yards off the road on the right edge of the column. Other than a sporadic breeze, the woods were silent. The surviving soldiers joked in low tones, but the proud sense of purpose that had filled their spirits the day they'd left the city had been replaced by something more somber, a humorless wariness. Dante's entire body ached like he'd been sewn in a bag and rolled down a mountain. He checked the cuts on his shoulder and ribs for excessive redness, but other than some dried blood and angry bruising they looked all right. He touched the nether, meaning to soothe his wounds, but the powers felt stirred-up, fickle, and he let them be. Best to be rested, if another attack came.

It started to snow late that morning, at first with a few small flakes no more likely to accumulate than the ash drifting around a campfire. Within minutes fat, amorphous bits were dashing against Dante's face. He pulled up his hood. It was a wonder (or maybe just a tendency of coasts, for Bressel's weather was just as weird) it had held off that long. By the afternoon two inches coated the ground. He heard a scout tell Larrimore they'd found a few tracks a couple miles east, but nothing indicative of the remaining rebel troops, and when they encamped on a small hill that night they slept without interruption.

The land swelled and dipped in old, gentle hills, masking the riders that trailed them until the foreign troops crested a ridge less than a mile behind Samarand's force. Dante freed his blade. Larrimore rode up and down the column, loosing orders like arrows; the pikemen dropped to the rear, but the procession marched on. The riders advanced with no apparent haste and it was the better part of an hour until Dante could make out the white icons of Barden stitched into their cloaks. He let his horse plod on while he counted men. Forty more riders, hoods raised against the snow that continued to spit from the low clouds. The foot soldiers saw their colors and smiled, some for the first time since the battle. The riders caught up before noon and Rettinger dropped back to exchange greetings and news. Not many men at all, in the scheme of things, but enough, Dante would wager, to hush the schemes of any enemy scouts.

They paused that afternoon to hack a shallow grave from the frozen dirt for the dozen-odd men who'd died of their wounds during the day's march. Once the grave was refilled, Samarand stood at its edge and cast a plain iron ring on the upturned earth.

"Don't weep for these men," she said, voice carrying through the assembled troop. "There can be no higher glory than to die in the service of Arawn. We should someday be so lucky to have our names written in the same stars as theirs."

She said more in that vein, but Dante had heard similar sentiments plenty of times before, and as with all conventional wisdom he couldn't be certain whether he'd once believed it because it were true or simply because he'd heard it so often it had driven all other thoughts from his head. He tried to think how a eulogy should sound, but was able to draw no truths. They were dead. What was there to say?

By the end of the fourth day from the city Dante could see snowcapped peaks peeping through the fog of cloud and snow that shrouded their path to the north. It was almost improper that they hadn't been attacked again, he thought. They marched with no less a purpose than to unlock a god. Where was the conspiracy of the world to stop them? Were he and Blays its last weapon? It was like the southlands were slumbering, waiting for spring thaws to sniff out the roots of the recent unrest—either that or were simply too stupid and disorganized to do anything at all. It was obscene to think that for all Mallon's strength, the king and his many lords hadn't sent a single man to stop the Arawnites—didn't even know, perhaps, the scope of their intent.

On the other hand, Dante himself considered this whole trip to be nothing more than an impressive example of the insanity of crowds. He expected they'd find a warped old tree clinging to life on some ice-swept hillside and start bowing down and chanting. Once their ritual was complete, how would they even know whether they'd freed their lord? Would Arawn appear in a poof of smoke and brimstone, twenty feet tall with a blade as long as a man's full height? Ready to scourge all Mallon for its hubris? Or would Samarand be infused with his essence, be able to stretch out her hand and see her will be done from sea to sea? Most likely, they'd make a lot of noise and fire and become so excited by their own power they'd convince themselves they felt Arawn's celestial touch. These people put an awful lot of stock in things they'd never seen. Lyle was the last man to have claimed to speak to a god (excluding the rum-drunk ravings of the lunatics that camped out on the corners of every decent city around the globe), and now he rotted in the ground while men invoked his name as a joke. "By Samarand's snowy tits!" they'd swear a century from now. "By the whiskers of Samarand's moles!" Dante snorted, glanced over at the carriages.

"What?" Blays said.

"What do you think's going to happen when we get there?"

"Weirdness," Blays said. "And lots of it."

"An almost demonic insight. What else do you foresee, o great prophet?"

"Well what about you, Holy Man?"

Dante smirked in the direction of the deluded priests. "Sound and fury. I don't think we're in any danger of a starry-eyed god with a beard as great and white as the ocean's foam showing up and laying waste to us heretics."

"That's what Arawn's supposed to look like?"

"Don't they all look like that?"

"Well, then no wonder everyone's so impressed with him."

Dante woke the next morning to find his blankets thick with snow. The road continued straight ahead, but the land to their west began to fall away until they traveled no more than a hundred feet parallel to sheer cliffs, and below that the gray sweep of the ocean. To their east the forest fell back until it was a smudge of dark green behind a veil of falling snow, leaving them to travel on through open hills. Ahead, the mountains were a wall of white and blue, too close to disappear from sight no matter how thick the weather got. They were running out of room, Dante thought; surely the land would end with those peaks. They trudged on. The snow crested the ankles of the men on foot. He pulled his cowl tighter.

Shortly before noon, as best as he could judge it through the clouds, the leading edge of the column reached the top of a hill and drew up short. Those at the front pointed to something blocked to Dante by the hill's white mass. Talk rippled back through the men; he could hear their voices but couldn't make out the words. He glanced at Blays. They swung up the side of the hill, halting on its flat head, a few feet away from the line of men, who themselves were leaving the orderly column to bunch up and lean their ears together and murmur in tense tones. Below them lay a broad, treeless valley, blank with drifted snow, the faint outlines of the road tracing ever to the north. A great snow-streaked peak rose up behind the hill at the far end of the valley. White-capped waves tossed the waters to the west. For a moment Dante couldn't see whatever the men were straining their fingers toward. He looked at Blays again, saw him frowning at something on the far hill. He followed the boy's gaze and saw it, then, the obscure outlines of a white, branched object just below the crown of the opposite ridge.

"What does that look like to you?" Blays said.

"It could be a snowy tree." Dante bit his lip and strained his eyes into the snowfields. It was a tree, he thought, the only one he could see between them and the mountains. Rather than the lumpy cones of the pines they'd been riding alongside for days, it had the wide, globular boughs of an oak, which spread away from its trunk like outstretched hands. Leafless—he thought he could see the hill behind it through its limbs—though that was hardly a surprise given that it was midwinter in the furthest north of the continent. Solid white. A shade duller than the snows everywhere else in sight. Dante dropped his hood to his shoulders, as if that would help him see.

"That doesn't look right," Blays said distractedly. Dante nodded. A call cut through the cluster of men and they began to shift back to their lines. Larrimore rode along the broken column, insulting those he deemed too slow in the same tone he gave encouragement to others. After a minute they were moving again, beginning the slippery descent into the featureless valley. The tree loomed larger as they went down. With no points of reference to provide a scale, Dante could tell no more than that it was very tall.

At the low point of the long saddle between the hill they'd left and the one they were about to climb, Dante's horse balked, stamping its hooves into the snow. He gave it a tap on the flank and it tossed its head. Blays' mount stuttered to a stop, too, snorting mist from its nostrils. To his left he saw other horses halting and the glowering faces of their riders as they tossed helplessly at their reins. The footmen went on a short ways before realizing what was happening behind them, then turned around with questions stamped on their faces. Dante led his horse crossways to a handful of mounted men talking and nodding to each other.

"Good a place as any," Rettinger said. "They're not going another step."

"All right," Larrimore nodded. "Post a couple riders back up on the hill. This would be a bad time for someone to sneak up on us while we're gawking."

Rettinger nodded and pointed a couple of his cavalry back up the road. He sent three others east, into the open land, in the general direction of the woods that began five or six miles out.

"We'll bivouac here," Larrimore called out to the men. "Tie the horses to the wagons. They're too smart to go any further."

The mounted men hopped down, passed their reins to pages. Dante dropped out of the saddle and wandered over to the body of action. The doors of the carriages swung open and old men in thick robes eased their way down into the snow. Samarand got down from her private conveyance and engaged Larrimore's attention. Dante set his mouth and gazed out at the sea, where the horizon met the water in a blur of gray clouds and gray waves. It looked, he imagined, like what the gods had seen before they'd separated one from another and put order to the elements of the world. In all his travels, he'd never been able to escape a vague sense of disappointment that even the farthest-flung lands, exotic and mysterious on the clean lines of a map, turned out to be peopled with the same general range of nobility and serf, of merchant and armsman and farmer and wife, as he'd seen growing up. They might dress a little oddly, or look a shade lighter or darker, or speak a little funny, or in another tongue altogether, but Dante could never shake the idea he could find a scene just like it if he turned the right (or wrong) corner in Bressel. In all the miles he'd traveled, through all the walking and running and riding he'd done in the past couple months, the only moment that had hit him with any kind of real wonder or sublimity had been the bright green waters of the glacial lake in the mountains between Mallon and Gask.

But this moment here, the raw wind off the ocean, the spine of mountains ahead, the silent valley and its skin of snow, it finally felt like something wondrous, like the true end of the world; he knew if he tried to walk past the hill ahead and up into the mountains he'd always find himself in the gentle rise and fall of a white field, never a foot closer no matter how long he walked. The northern mountains, as real as they looked, would come no nearer than the seven moving heavenly bodies, or perhaps the fixed stars themselves: things you could look on with awe, could hope to calculate and understand given patience and discipline, but bodies that would forever be beyond the touch.

He paced around the snow. He felt small things snapping and crumbling under his boots, buried branches or hardened dirt. They rolled like stones, though, and he knelt and brushed away the snow and picked up a white pebble. One end was knobbed, the other cracked. The broken end was filled with a spongy weave of marrow. He kicked away more snow. The bones were scattered, far too few to make a second carpet over the dead grass, yet there were far too many for these open meadows, which to his eyes looked barren, trackless, lifeless. Blays came up to join him and saw what he was holding and gave him a weird look.

"It was just lying on the ground," Dante told him. He dropped the finger-sized bone back into the snow.

"That sounds like a fine reason to pick it up."

"Oh, like you're so much cleaner," Dante said. He glanced back toward the road where priests flapped their cloaks and bunched their fists against their chest. Blays grunted. They stood in silence.

"Come on, pups," Larrimore called to them after a few minutes had gone by. They rejoined the group. Samarand took the lead, the six other priests at her heels, followed by a small hand-drawn wagon bearing sacks of food and a few rattling bags. A dozen soldiers took up the rear.

"That's it, isn't it?" Dante said to Larrimore in the kind of voice people use in airy, echoing cathedrals. "Barden."

"Unless they swapped it out since the last time I saw it," Larrimore said, unable to keep the reverence from his voice. "Why? Do you see any other immortal trees of life and death around here?"

"Maybe."

"Move your ass. The council's going to need us to watch their backs while they're indisposed."

Wind gusted over the clear ground, driving dust-like snow into their faces. Less than a mile to the top of the hill. By the time they'd climbed halfway up Dante could tell the branches weren't snowy, they were actually white. A slight nausea perched in his stomach. The older council members picked a careful path through the squeaking snow and blustery wind and the upward slant of the ground. Dante tried to match their pace, but found himself constantly moving ahead. He dropped his eyes to his feet and made a game of trying to plant his feet in the exact steps the swordsman ahead of him had made. He thought for a while of Fanna, a pretty, dark-haired girl from the village who had a bright, friendly way that used to seem like encouragement. For months she consumed his every thought with the clever things he might say to her. She'd thought him quick and funny, but had broken things off before they'd really started, saying there was something dark about him that she'd never be able to heal even if they were one day married. He still hadn't understood what she meant or what had happened by the time he'd left the village for Bressel and the book.

Fanna might be engaged to another boy by now, even dead. Dante knew that thought should make him sad, but he doubted if she ever thought of him anymore; leaving people behind and forgetting them piece by piece was just the way life worked. His past fixation on her struck him now as almost pathetic. He was glad to be gone from her, glad to be older, but he wished he could have met her all over again now that he'd begun to grow into his age — or that she could see him here for just a moment, compare what he'd become to the odd, nervous boy she'd known. He thought she'd like what she saw.

Dante bumped into the back of the man whose footsteps he'd followed and saw they were nearly at the top of the hill. Without warning, someone vomited noisily to his right. Before he had time to laugh his eyes fell on the trunk of the tree that stood a mere thirty yards away and his mind went empty as it struggled to categorize the thing he saw.

The trunk was wider than his arm was long. White and gnarled, it looked at first glance like a rope of spines twisted around each other. He thought it might be one of those tricks of nature where a fly paints its wings to look like a wasp, or a harmless plant grows its leaves in the pattern of the poisonous one, but there were no leaves on this tree, none of its branches swayed in the winds. Instead it was starkly empty, horribly motionless in a way every other tree he'd ever seen wasn't.

The main branches appeared composed of ribs and humeri and femurs — not as if they were each a single big bone, but rather a fused line of thousands, like a hundred corpses had been forged into the curve of a single limb; the branches forked into smaller versions of themselves like a normal tree, terminating in willowy fibulas and ulnas and radii and individual ribs, and sticking out from those delineated bones were the prongs of tarsals and metacarpals and knuckles and toes and teeth, looking like twigs and pale blooms. Barden stood a hundred feet high or more and every inch as wide across its branches, casting still, sharp-edged shadows on the snow. Dante fell back a step, struck by a guts-deep revulsion. His boot caught against a rock-hard root, a jumble of jawbones and backbones.

At first glance Barden looked like it might have been built by someone's hands rather than coaxed from the soil, but for all its stillness he had the sense it was alive, not artifice. It wasn't inert in the same way that bones in a grave were inert, or like the stones in a fieldstone wall were no more than stones. But if it had been built, who could it have been built by? Some insane person who'd hauled a caravan of countless dead to this desolate spot and spent a year nailing together the bones? When he looked closer, he could see no sign of craft in its branches. Where one bone met another they blended till the seam was nearly invisible. They had grown that way. Some time ago, a very long time ago, the seed of the White Tree of Barden had been planted in the dirt, had risen as a sapling and raised its bleached arms to the heavens, and grown and grown and grown until it filled the sky.

Blays' hand clamped on his shoulder. Around him men muttered oaths or said nothing at all. Three of the six priests dropped to their knees, arms held out from their sides. Samarand took a slow step forward, neck tilted, and for the first time Dante saw her eyes humbled. Even Larrimore looked put out of sorts—chewing and chewing a splinter of wood he'd picked from the handcart, running his fingers down his face and scratching the stubble on his neck till his skin turned red. A gust of wind screeched through the branches like something living being torn and the man who'd vomited let loose a fresh stream.

"Barden," Samarand breathed. "I've never been this close," she said, as if she had to explain her awe. But for an occasional retch, every man went silent. "This is where Eric Draconat spilled the blood of Taim in the first days of earth," she said in quiet tones as she turned to face the small group of men. "This is where the birth of man began, where Arawn and Carvahal plotted to hand the fire of the heavens to the low reach of our race. It's only fitting it will be the place where we restore Arawn to his seat in the stars."

"Live this earth," one of the priests replied, and was echoed by the others.

"Bring the treated bones," Samarand said. She walked toward the bleached bole of the tree. A few of the armsmen reached into the wagon and hoisted rattling bags and Dante darted to grab one as well. The priests leaned into the wind and snow and continued up what was left of the hill between themselves and Samarand and Dante followed, the hard ends of the bones in the sack battering against his back. Overcast shadows of the White Tree fell on his face, striping his skin more coldly than the northerly gusts of wind. His toes stubbed against roots concealed in the snow, but he kept his eyes fixed on the branches, making sure they weren't about to snatch him up and patch his frame into the greater body of the tree. The branches stayed as immobile as the flanks of the mountains many miles away.

He stopped ten feet from the sinuous trunk. Samarand stretched out an unsteady hand and laid it on the smooth bone, ran her fingers over the bumps of its vertebrae. One of the armsmen set his bag by her feet and Dante did the same, daring himself to touch the trunk. Samarand took a long breath, then drew away her hand and picked up one of the bags, scooping out a handful of bones scripted with Arawn's name. Dante recognized his handwriting on a few of the pieces. She scattered ribs and jaws and thighs around Barden's gnarled roots like a fowl farmer tosses seed to his flocks. The bones sank into the snow, gray on white. Samarand circled the putrid trunk, throwing bones, and when her bag ran out one of the priests hurried to hand her another. Scores of bones, clattering heaps, each one holding a speck of the same shadowy force Dante felt rolling off the White Tree in waves. She made seven circuits in all, then paused where the road ran up to meet the trunk, considering the rings she'd made around it.

"It's time to begin," she said. She met the eyes of each man in turn. Dante squirmed. "I don't know what will come of this," she went on. "Perhaps nothing. Perhaps three hours from now we'll stop our work, exhausted and defeated, and everything will be the same as it is now. There are no guarantees we know the steps as well as we need. There are no guarantees we possess the power to do what no one before us has been able to accomplish." She paused in the manner she'd done while giving her sermon. "Yet I have no doubts we'll succeed. Why? Is it simple faith? I feel it's something deeper than when we tell our parishioners or each other to place our trust in the hands of the gods. Perhaps it has something to do with standing in the shadow of a thing from another age and knowing at least some of the old stories must be true."

She drew back her lips in something close to a smile and gazed up at the many arms of Barden.

"Perhaps it has to do with you, the men who've come here with me, and our purpose, which defines justice. If, some time from now, we cry the final word and the heavens crack apart and we look upon the face of Arawn, know we still live in and of this earth — that this will be but a beginning to restoring his place in the hearts of men. Rejoice, but be resolute. Remember also that a god may take a form we can't understand.

"I need everyone not of the council to leave me now. Our concentration can't be disturbed."

"Even me?" Larrimore said, eyebrows scooting up his forehead.

"Even you, my Hand."

He frowned but nodded. "May your will be done where I can't follow."

Larrimore started back down the hill and Dante and Blays and the armsmen who'd carried the sacks fell in behind him. They reached the wagon with the other men and looked on the seven priests some twenty yards away. Samarand stood at their center, three of them to both her sides, all heads bowed. They were silent.

"What now?" Blays whispered at Larrimore.

"Now you keep your damned mouth shut and hope against hope we have nothing more to do than stand around."

"For how long?"

"For however long it takes," Larrimore said, leaning toward the boy so intently Dante felt sure he'd punch Blays in the face.

After a few minutes of silent prayer Samarand's clear voice pitched into a droning chant of ancient Narashtovik and the men of the council joined her. The wind tried to drag away her words, and for all Dante's lessons with Nak much of its meaning remained foreign, but he made out something about star-touched blessings, verses about the cycle of the twelve months of Earth and the twelve houses of the heavens, how the lives of men had been warped by Arawn's missing seat in the house of the gods and how that balance must be rebuilt. It was an eerie tune, harmonious but as fundamentally wrong to Dante's ears as the leafless limbs of the White Tree were to his eyes. At times the pitch of their notes seemed to match that of the wind in the ragged branches. The council ceased singing, their last word hanging in the air.

They bowed their heads again. Other than a few oblique references in the *Cycle*, Dante didn't know a thing about what they were doing. He couldn't even tell if they were actively shaping the nether at the moment or just praying. He reached out for the shadows, meaning no more than a touch to try and see what they were up to, but the energy lurched up in him so fast he gasped. The White Tree was a nexus so potent that any tap into its pool shot up like a geyser. He sent the nether away and held perfectly still. Nobody had seemed to notice his intrusion. He supposed they had their own concerns.

For a long time the priests didn't move. Men leaned against the cart or quietly took a seat on it, brushing snow from their trousers and watching the scouts coming and going on the crest of the hill across the valley. Samarand lifted her head and bent down in front of Barden. She picked up one of the bones she'd thrown down and turned it in her hands. For no obvious reason, she dropped it and picked up another instead. Dante made a face. None of it made any sense to him.

"Come with me," he said softly to Blays after another while had gone by with no evidence of progress. Blays blinked at him, then got up, snow falling from his hood and shoulders. Dante wandered left toward the cliffs.

"What's up?" Blays said once they were a short distance away.

"I get the idea they're going to be a while."

"Yeah." Blays glanced back toward the tree. "How will you know when it's time?"

"Samarand will give up her last ounce of strength before it's over," Dante said, just above a whisper. "I'll be able to tell when they're drained."

Blays ticked his nail against the hilt of his sword. "What do you think we should do after? Fight off all her men, or leap off the cliff and take our chances in the ocean?"

"I think we're doomed, whatever we do." Dante laughed through his nose. His breath steamed.

"Oh, that's funny to you?"

"There's this story in the *Cycle of Arawn*," he said. "It's about a man named Kiel."

"Sounds fascinating," Blays whispered.

"It is," Dante said. He took a moment to remember the important parts of what he was about to tell. "Kiel was an average man. A follower of Arawn, but not of the clergy. He was a farmer. For many years he and his neighbor Harron had feuded. It had gone on so long they no longer remembered how it had begun or who was in the right—one night Harron would open Kiel's goat pen and make him spend all day recapturing them, so Kiel would dump old grain in Harron's troughs and make his swine sick before market. That sort of thing. Angry as they were with each other, neither considered actually taking up arms. This was, excuse the pun, a domestic matter."

"That's not a pun."

"Shut up. And so on it went. Harron impregnated Kiel's prized mare with his spavined nag, Kiel sowed one of Harron's barley fields with batweed, and so passed the years. One night Harron tried to burn the sign of Simm's hare into the Arawn-fearing Kiel's yard—I don't think I need to explain the blasphemy—but a wind picked up his fire and spread it to burn down Kiel's barn instead."

"Tough break," Blays said. The aggressive disinterest had faded from his face as Dante went on.

"Indeed, tougher yet when the townspeople saw the fire and came to see what had happened. Harron, guilt-stricken over the consequences of his prank, told them what he'd meant to do and that he'd accidentally started the fire. As it is now, burning someone's land was a serious crime, but rather than our humane hanging, the people of that time punished arson with death in a fashion similar to the crime, and the townspeople grabbed Harron up and carried him into the city to be burnt on a pyre.

"For a brief moment, Kiel was grateful as he thought on what a nuisance Harron had been. And the loss of his barn was no mean price. However, as he saw them stacking up the cordwood for the fire, he realized that, if justice were to be done, it couldn't come from the hands of these intrusive men who'd had nothing to do with he and Harron's squabbles—for justice isn't earthly, it's handed down from the stars of the heavens, and must be seen by their silvery light. Neither, he realized, did he want Harron to die, for Harron was a part of his life. So he put himself in front of the stake where they'd tied Harron up and spoke to the men who were preparing to burn him.

"'I know it is our law to burn those who'd burn our houses and lands,' he said.'But I know Harron, and I know he didn't mean to do the thing he did.'"What you think doesn't matter,' the townspeople said.'The law is the law. Justice must be done.' But Kiel didn't move.'He harmed me and me alone,' he said.'Let him free, and I will decide how he may repay me for his unintended crime.''We cannot do that, Kiel,' they said back.'Now stand aside.' Again Kiel refused:'Let him go, for I will not budge.' The townspeople gathered around him.'Stand aside, or we will tie you with him to the flames.'"

"Kiel sounds like a hardass," Blays said.

"He does. And Kiel saw they meant what they said. He also knew they deserved no role in the punishment, that their lust for blood and vengeance was driving them rather than a natural hunger for justice. Harron was, Kiel knew, his friend, and he wouldn't let his friend be burnt as Harron had burnt his barn.

"'I see I cannot stop so many of you from killing him,' Kiel said, leaning on the barley-scythe he'd carried into town.'But I am this man's friend, and if it is his time to be rejoined with Arawn in the black skies, I will send him there in the manner I deem just.' Before the townspeople could stop him, Kiel swung his scythe and cut out Harron's throat.

"'You fool!' the townspeople cried.'You've murdered, and so stolen our justice! You will take his place on the pyre.' Kiel only shook his head. He could not fight them all, and so he let them take him and lash him beside the corpse of Harron. They lit the pyre. Kiel closed his eyes and even as his skin crackled and his fat popped he made no sound but to thank Arawn for giving him the strength to send his friend to that great place with the peace Harron deserved. The men were humbled then, and slit his throat with his own scythe before the fires could roast him. They carried his scythe to the altar of Arawn, where it has stood ever since."

Blays shuffled snow with his feet. "I'd have swung that scythe at the mob till my arms dropped off." He stole a look at the priests, who were again bowing their heads beneath the tree. "Did that really happen?"

"I don't know," Dante said. "It's a story from the book. One of the Mallish parts. It's too old to know which parts were true."

"Do you think anyone will know?" Blays said, squinting into the snow. "The whole town saw the good thing Kiel did. Then they told his story till we heard it now. Will anyone know what we've done here?"

"Cally might," Dante said. "He'll be able to figure it out, at least."

"And probably claim credit for himself."

"The people will know someone did something right when there's no war in the spring."

Blays shuffled the snow with his toes some more. "But they won't know our names."

The priests started another chant, saving Dante from trying to answer that. He made the faintest touch to the nether and saw Barden's skeletal canopy go dark with the shadows of unseen leaves. Around its roots bright black rings marked where Samarand had scattered the bones. Each of the priests was enveloped by a hazy nimbus; a gray umbilicus traced from their chests to Samarand's. Their auras pulsed with the tune of their words. Dante looked on a power he'd never imagined possible, and still they added to it.

"Larrimore's going to try to protect her," Dante said softly.

"I'll see to him, then. You stay with Samarand."

"Thanks."

Dante had never seen the nether in any form but small, swift parts that sometimes gathered in swirling orbs or shifting planes. It was ever moving, amorphous and unbounded as water. As he watched, the priests ceased their chant and held up their hands and the disordered shadows snapped into a stark geometry of lines between them and Samarand and the White Tree: she at its nexus, six dark lines converging from the priests to a single point at the middle of her back and emerging from her front to meet six equally-spaced points on the branches of the tree. Samarand held her arms perpendicular to her body and dipped her fingers in the slow currents passing from priests to her to Barden, as if it were bathwater in need of testing. Minutes went by that way, the silence broken by the splitting of the wind through the bony branches, by the cough of one of the men at the wagon, by taut, whispered words among a couple of the soldiers. Dante began to feel a tension in his nerves, almost like an all-over sting, but it was never quite enough to hurt—more of a constant vibration, like the strings of his body were being plucked by the forces being summoned to the tree. A high whine sounded in his ears. He fought the urge to slap at a bug that wasn't there.

"How about this," Blays mused. "Take her down, then run away from the priests and back toward the troop. Steal a couple horses. Ride hell bent for leather."

"Sounds dubious," Dante said.

"Can you make us fly?"

"No."

"Teleport us back to snug beds in Bressel?"

"No."

"Conjure up a giant mole that can dig our way to freedom?"

Dante looked up into the clouds. "I could always try."

"Then we'll steal some horses and run," Blays shrugged. "Who knows what happens after that."

Dante laughed. "Try to shout something confusing when we're running up to grab their horses."

"I'll tell them the whole hill's about to explode and it's every man for himself."

Dante clasped his hands over his mouth so his laughter wouldn't be heard by the others. It was a strange thing, talking about their death in this way. He didn't think he could have faced it with a too-serious mind and he didn't think he could be anything but serious without Blays to ease his thoughts. It made him mad to think it would all be over soon: but that, too, was foolish. He was beginning to learn how little it meant to be angry.

The rites went on. Samarand reached into a satchel at her side and drew out an age-weathered copy of the *Cycle*. She spread the book's broad pages and read aloud from the verses of prophecy and malediction. Black sparks crackled and spritzed from her hands, visible to Dante without any help from the nether. His ribs thudded like when a door was slammed in his face or the wall of a building crumbled down in one big boom and a vague rectangle coalesced at Barden's foot, ten feet high and half as wide, hazy as a twilight fog. Some of the soldiers gasped. One of the priests took a half-step back, then forced himself back into place.

"Did they do that?" Blays whispered. "Or did the tree?"

Dante shook his head, equally ignorant. The blue shadows of the snowfield flocked to the doorway. After five minutes he could no longer see the part of the tree that stood behind it. After ten it had darkened to the pitch of a moonless night. Samarand turned pages as she read on, dividing her gaze between the darkening rectangle and the words she invoked. The priests began to repeat her sentences, parroting the harsh consonants of Narashtovik. The wind faltered and blew itself out and the still-falling snowflakes settled into a lazy drift groundwards. After another ten minutes points of light brightened within the black frame, faintly at first, slowly hardening into icy white points that winked like the stars. In time, Dante could see they made all the designs of the Belt of the Celeset as arrayed to their opposite: the two rivers and the golden hammer, the hourglass and watchdog, the lion and the hare, maiden and cicada, fox and ship, the snake and the dragon. The constellations burned with fierce white purity, brighter in that doorway than he'd seen in the sky on the clearest nights of silent winter. Dante's head swam with vertigo. Looking into the door was like standing on a roof and pretending your feet were stuck to the bottom of the world and the night sky was the ground beneath you, vast as the ocean, deep as an eternity of unbroken sleep. Samarand's voice softened in the doorway's presence. The words of the priests dropped to a rustle just above a whisper. The air felt charged, pregnant with a mutable power.

Something passed over the stars in the door like a face upon the waters, blacker, if possible, than the portal of sky behind it. Blays' hand jumped out and gripped Dante's shoulder. Dante hesitated, then put his hand on top of Blays'. His thoughts circled and bit each other's tails: this was a mirage, a show; it was the touch of something greater, the sign he'd been waiting to see; it was as false and empty as all the world's other so-called miracles. How could he tell the difference between the work of godlike men and the work of true deities? The stars flared brighter, as if Samarand's words were breath blown on smoking embers.

A white-haired priest began to waver, his head tracing a wobbly circle in the air. He dropped to one knee and knelt there, shivering. The stars within the doorway dimmed. With a strength of will Dante could almost taste, the old man planted his hands in the snow and pushed himself back to his feet, his thin chest heaving. The man inhaled deeply and then his voice joined the others in the repetition of Samarand's speech. The stars glared with all their former intensity, and as if lit by their newfound blaze the rings of bones around the White Tree erupted into pale fire, shimmering tongues of white and blue that reflected the snowscape and the skies and seas and mountains to the north. Samarand tipped back her head and shouted out the text of the *Cycle of Arawn* and the whole world seemed to go dark. A great black halo formed around the crown of Barden's bone branches. Dante felt light and insubstantial as ether. The string-like vibration in his body increased until he thought he could predict Samarand's words before she spoke them. That sense of connection extended to the priests, to the doorway they faced, to the constellations that shined from within it: Dante felt so close to the order of their revolution he could touch it if he reached out his hand, could hold in his palm the nature of existence.

"It's almost time," he whispered to Blays.

"I'm ready," Blays said.

"Why did you come with me all this time? All those miles?" Dante no longer felt the need to cloak himself, to arrange his words like pinned insects before he let himself speak them. Arawn was about to appear from that door to the stars—he had no other way to explain what he was feeling, that sensation of attunement to the world—and as the god clambered free Dante would strike down the woman who'd freed him. Dante had no illusions of survival after that. He wanted one clear answer before whatever he was became parted from the meat of his body. "You could have left at any time, you know. They were only ever after me." He felt the weight of the book in the pack on his back. "Me and this book."

Blays let his hand rest on the haft of his sword and gazed on the motions around the tree.

"I wanted to do something important with my life," he said. "Back when you insulted me in that square in Bressel, I knew if I followed you, you'd lead me to it."

"Did you think it would be anything like this?"

"No," Blays said, eyes fast on the tree, on the halo at its head, the rings of white fire at its feet, at the starry door and the dark auras around the six priests and Samarand. She lifted an open hand above her head and held the book before her with the other.

Blays shook his head and smiled crookedly. "I thought we'd make some money, maybe. Overthrow a baron and marry his daughters, if we got really ambitious."

"I'm glad I met you," Dante said.

"Yeah."

The nether surged and tossed. A subverbal hum quivered on the air. Samarand shouted what Dante recognized as the last passage of the Prophecy of the Three-Tailed Beast, the one he'd quoted in part to Larrimore when he was trying to keep from being tortured and killed down in the dungeon.

"Let the prison of the heavens be unmade," Samarand said. She closed the book and faced the door.

Dante drifted toward her up the hill. Blays crunched through the snow at his side. Samarand waited, oblivious, arms dangling at her sides, transfixed by the black portal. One of the burning bones flamed out in a wiggle of gray smoke. The sense of a presence grew excruciating, maddening Dante's mind like all the things he'd ever been unable to recall, like the panicked eyes of a birthing mother whose child won't come, as chthonic as the fires of the earth forging the scaled body of a dragon. Samarand glanced over her shoulder at the priests, eyes wild, and Dante slowed his pace.

"Something's wrong," she said.

"There was no error," Jackson said quickly.

"I don't understand," a balding priest said.

"I can feel him waiting," said another.

"There is a flaw," Samarand said. Her face was creased with an animal dread. Another bone burnt out, then a third. The halo around Barden was growing indistinct, muffled by the falling snow. Tears of exhaustion and frustration slid down Samarand's cheeks.

"We don't have the time or strength for a second attempt any time soon," a dark-haired, middle-aged priest said, face blank with fear.

"No," Samarand said.

"What are you saying?" the balding priest said. "What does this mean?"

"Nothing," Samarand said. She gazed into the void of the doorway. "We've failed."

"Then we're lost!" the middle-aged priest said.

"We're the only ones who know that right now." Samarand drew a ragged breath. Some of her old sternness returned to her eyes. "It makes no difference. We'll tell the people we have restored Arawn to his seat at the heaven's twin rivers and they must do the same for him on this earth. Perhaps their faith will succeed where we have faltered. Perhaps we will find the true *Cycle*, and on that day we will try again."

"Wait!" Dante blurted, reaching into his pack. He drew out the first copy of the *Cycle of Arawn* to ever be written and held it over his head. The white tree on its cover mirrored the bone oak that dwarfed them there on the plains of snow. "I have the true book!"

"You could have warned me this was your plan," Blays hissed in his ear.

The eyes of Samarand and all six priests snapped to Dante's face and the book in his hand. All the strings of his body hummed like a living chord. He gestured to the vault of stars shining through the doorway, as if that would explain to Blays what he felt lurking within the constellations. What if he held the key that would turn the final tumbler? Arawn, the god who'd made order of the mixed waters of the heavens, he who'd set the order of time from his seat in the light of the furthest roaming planet-star — in Arawn's presence, would Whetton hold the trials that had condemned Blays to die? Would he allow the meaningless slaughter of the rebels outside Narashtovik? What other power could make the laws of nature sing in tune with what Dante felt in his bones? If he had the ability to bring that god to life, how could he prevent such justice for the world?

Destiny, perhaps, had guided Dante to steal the book, and through its subtle machinations, inevitable as the revolution of the Belt, had put him here to complete what the council had begun. Samarand could complete the rites, but none could deny she'd done so only by Dante's mercy. If he cut her throat in that final moment, in the weakness of her effort, he could seize the reins of the order, ensure peace for the southlands as Arawn made for the earth what he'd set right in the skies.

This was the moment he'd been born for. This was the moment that would test his will to its limit.

"Give me the book," Samarand said. She stepped forward and extended her hand. Dante held out the impossible weight of the *Cycle of Arawn*.

"You mewling *worm!*" Jackson thundered. He leapt forward and slapped the book from Dante's hand. It sunk into the snow.

"What is this?" Samarand said, whirling to face him.

"Old debts repaid," Jackson said. "I told you I'd come back for it, Sama."

Samarand's eyes widened, then narrowed to fearful slits. "*You.*"

"Me," Jackson said in a nasally, clipped voice that wasn't his own. He laughed unevenly, then swept a hand down his middle-aged face and body and became a skinny old man with a fiercely curled beard and sharp blue eyes that burned with their own ageless fire.

"When did you replace him? How?" Samarand said. Dante felt her clutching at the nether.

"I know things you couldn't dream, you usurperous hag," Cally said. "You've let your dream of conquest blind you. Your monstrous, braying ego. Let me remind you the look of righteous power."

He thrust out with the shadows. Samarand jerked up her hands and their two forces met with an inhuman scream. Blackness burst over her and she was knocked to the ground.

Shouts hied up from behind them. Dreamlike, Dante turned to see Larrimore and his soldiers racing up the snow. The oldest of the priests flung his arm at Cally and Blays cleaved it off at the elbow.

"Who do we kill?" he yelled at Dante.

"Everyone!" Dante said, mind splintered. The cogs had turned again and yanked him from his solid ground. He didn't know whether to help Cally or kill him. The old man had sent the assassin to the chapel, he knew at once, having seen Dante at Larrimore's command and assuming he'd turned to their side, ignorant that Dante held fast to his first purpose. But the moment was too desperate for fine distinctions. For the moment Cally was on the side trying to kill Samarand. That was all that mattered. If it came down to it, Dante would deal with him once all the men who were about to try to kill them were dead themselves.

Samarand was scrabbling to her feet away from Cally. She curled her fingers and a ghostly blade spun for his face. He cursed and whacked it aside with a hastily-formed shadow sword of his own, then swung his bony arm and slung the weapon at her body. She twisted and it clipped her right arm. Blood pattered into the snow.

Around them, Dante felt the priests beginning to open their own overused channels to the nether that saturated the grounds. Blays crouched like a cat, then slashed his sword across the gut of the middle-aged dark-haired priest when the man made his move at Cally, dropping him without a word. A tall, stout priest clenched his fist and blue fire rushed at Blays. He yelped and threw himself into the snow. Dante flicked his wrist and sent all the snow between he and Blays to bury the boy in cold white and smother the remaining flames. He whipped out his sword and met the tall priest's next assault with a wave of pure energy. The man had been weakened in the hours he'd spent in the ritual and when Dante tapped into the primal river flowing around Barden's roots it roared past him and charred the tall priest on the spot.

"Is it really you, Cally?" the balding priest called out as Blays dug himself out of the snow and hunted for a victim.

"It's really me, Baxter," Cally said, then grunted as Samarand lunged forward and punched him in the ribs. The priest called Baxter chuckled wildly and turned on the last remaining man of his order, a fat man of some sixty years with a gray beard in place of his chin. If the fat man died, none but Samarand would be left to oppose them, and for a careering moment Dante thought they might actually win. Then Larrimore and his soldiers closed the distance between them, and Dante remembered the small army across the valley, and why he had resolved to die.

"Arawn's come loose and is killing everyone!" Blays screamed, dropping into his defensive posture, fists holding his sword tight at his waist. He cut at the calf of the lone soldier who'd broken ranks to face him. "Head for the hills!"

"What's going on here?" Larrimore shouted, sword in hand. Before his eyes Baxter grappled nether with the fat priest.

"Kill them, Larrimore!" Samarand commanded, dipping her hand in the wound on her shoulder and tossing burning drops of blood at Cally. "Baxter and the children! They're traitors!"

Larrimore's long face went blank. He stuck his sword through Baxter's back and blood jetted where its point emerged from his chest. The fat priest fell back, wiping blood from his eyes. Dante ran him through before he could recover, and like that half the council of Arawn would be dead once Samarand and Cally's fight was concluded. Blays finished carving up his soldier and then he and Dante stood to face Larrimore and his men.

"Dante! What are you doing?"

"She's going to burn our home," he said, sword arm quaking. "I have to stop her!"

Larrimore shook his head, squeezed his eyes shut.

"I'm sorry," he said, then hurried uphill to the duel between Samarand and Cally, a couple armed men crunching along behind him. The remaining ten-odd soldiers and armed servants turned on the boys, swords out. One took a quick swipe at Dante and he jumped back, meaning to give the man's blade a mere nick of his left arm, but his timing was off and he felt the steel bite deep, bringing with it far more blood than he needed for his next summons.

"Get down!" Dante shouted, planting his hand on Blays' neck and stuffing his face toward the ground. Blays fell into the snow with a sigh and Dante punched out with all the force he could draw from the White Tree.

Blood spurted from Dante's ears and nose as the shockwave hammered outward from his body. Already he'd pushed it too far, drank too greedily of the bottomless energy drawn by the tree, but he had no intention to hold back at any stage of this fight. The men were blasted head over heels. He heard bones snapping, then the muffled thuds of their bodies bouncing in the snow. He lunged forward and hacked at the man who'd laid open his left arm. Blays staggered to his feet, half stunned. Six armsmen struggled and swayed upright. One had lost his sword and scuffled to find it in the churned-up snow. From over their heads, Barden groaned with an earsplitting shriek, and as the first man closed on the boys a two-foot rib fell free from the White Tree's branches and pinned him to the earth. By instinct Dante grabbed the rib's rounded end and his left arm went numb to the shoulder. He tugged it loose and snarled at the survivors. Shockingly, they fell back.

"Any other tricks?" Blays breathed, glancing between the five opponents that still faced them and the crackle of nether from further uphill where Cally fended off four of his own.

"A few," Dante said, and his eyesight blurred and the world went mute as he poured the shadows into the veins of the recently slain. Three of the ruined bodies retook their feet, broken limbs dangling, blood still oozing from their wounds. Within a second the dead's oafish blows had struck down one of their living comrades. A soldier swung at Dante and he brought up the rib to block it. The man's sword shattered like an icicle, raining shards of steel into the snow. Dante stuck him in the gut with his sword. He swung the rib and it passed cleanly through the man's trunk.

The walking dead overwhelmed another while Blays charged one of the remaining armsmen, who could do nothing more than fend off his wild blows. Blays drove him back and the man tripped on a corpse, arms flying out to break his fall, leaving his body exposed. Blays stabbed him in the neck and whooped.

A calmness had taken Dante, a stage beyond confidence. The shaking nausea that had hit him when he'd revived the dead flesh of the soldiers washed from him like it had never been there. He walked through the falling snow toward the last man standing.

"Please," the man said, his face a rictus of terror. He let his blade hang loose from his grasp. Then the dead took him and pounded him into the earth.

"To Cally," Dante said, sprinting up the hill. Cally had retreated steadily, outnumbered. One of the two men Larrimore had taken with him lay in a reddish heap in the snow, but blood flowed freely from Cally's left hand, now missing a couple fingers, and from a gash on his thin chest. Nether sputtered from his fingers and Samarand wrestled up the strength to turn it aside. They were both near the end of their limits. Soon they'd simply be an old man and a middle-aged woman, no more potent than a beggar and a fishwife. Dante put himself between Cally and the others and brandished the fallen rib of Barden. Everyone stopped in their tracks.

"You don't have to die," Dante told Larrimore, meeting the man's eyes.

"Don't you ever get tired of being so cocky?"

"What's this about?" Samarand said, blinking at the blood trickling from her split eyebrow. "Has Cally promised you a seat on his council? One you couldn't wait for under my rule?"

"He's promised me nothing," Dante spat. "He's told me nothing but lies since the day I met him."

"I told you what you needed to hear to stop a war," Cally said from behind him.

"And then you tried to kill me!"

"I thought you'd thrown in your lot with these vermin. Look at it from my perspective. You'd have tried to kill you, too."

"You've cut enough holes in my order to make killing me moot," Samarand said. "We can't risk war with so few priests to lead it."

"Shut up!" Dante shouted, chest heaving.

"What *have* you gotten yourself into," Larrimore said softly. The man tightened his grip on his sword.

"More than these lordly figures ever intended," Dante said.

"I gave you every opportunity under the sun," Samarand said. "I let you study in the Citadel. I let you replace Will Palomar as Larrimore's right hand. I even brought you here!"

"I taught you enough to save your friend," Cally said. "You let me send you here through your own ambition."

"Oh yes, everyone's innocent!" Dante cried out, unable to tell if his face was wet from snow, tears, or laughter. "You'd use me as a tool in your harmless plot to kill thousands in my homeland," he said, waving the rib at Samarand, "while you'd angelically send two boys to kill the political rival who cast you down," he finished, poking his sword at Cally.

Cally raised his brambly brows and laughed. Larrimore gave him an odd look.

"You have to admit it was a keen enough plan," the old man said. "What are you going to do about it, then? Kill us all?"

"Don't tempt us," Blays said.

"We couldn't go to war now if we wanted to," Samarand said. She flipped her battle-frayed black braid over her shoulder, gestured at the corpses of the priests melting the snow with body heat and blood, pointed at the hulking mass of the White Tree. "You have the book. You know how close we came today. We can try again."

"Heaven must be a place where other people shut up," Dante said.

"You know it can be done," she said, locking eyes with him. "With your help and a few years."

Dante sighed through his nose. He felt cold and bleak as November rain. They could come back and try again, but they didn't need Samarand's hard ambition for that. It seemed laughably cruel that Cally's clear-eyed lies would be preferable to anything, but if one object of value remained in the ruin of Dante's beliefs, it was the knowledge that killing her would guarantee Mallon's safety. With Samarand's death, they could start over. Perhaps whoever took her seat as lord of the dead city would come closer to the pattern of the heavens than she.

"Stand aside, Larrimore," the boy said in an unsteady voice. "It's time."

Larrimore shook his head at the ground. He smiled then, a wan thing that marred his eyes with the first sadness Dante'd ever seen on his face.

"You know I can't do that," Samarand's Hand said. "I'd have died a hundred times without her. Whatever conflict I may feel can't erase that past."

Dante nodded. His throat was dry. "I liked you better than any of them."

"Considering you want them all dead, I think you damn me with faint praise," Larrimore said, finding himself again. Dante's spirit faltered. How could he kill the one man he'd met other than Robert who understood his place in the world so well? And not just understood it, but seized it, knew by instinct which things he could control and which he could only defy by mocking them? Of all Dante's crimes, he knew killing Larrimore would wear on him the hardest. In time he might forget the rest, but Larrimore's burden would weigh on him till the end of his days.

"I'll do it." Blays stepped forward, hand on hilt, sensing Dante's hesitation. "You deal with her."

"He's my burden," Dante said, seeing the face of a farmer through a sheet of flames. "I'll be the one to send him to the banks of the two rivers." He called over his shoulder to Cally. "Samarand's yours. I never wanted her in the first place."

"Oh good," Cally said weakly.

"If you get a moment, you might think about what we're going to say to them," Blays said, jerking his chin toward the scores of men who'd left the encampment a mile down valley and were dashing through the snow toward the battle under the tree. Dante laughed tonelessly and lifted his weapons. Larrimore brought up the point of his blade. He winked.

"I'll save you a room in that place behind the stars, you little bastard."

He made a quick swipe for Dante's throat and Dante turned it with the flat of the rib. Larrimore's sword rang but stayed intact. To his right he heard Cally advance on Samarand and then the whisper of nether called and discharged. Blays headed for the last remaining soldier and, wisely, the man turned tail and ran downhill.

"I should have stomped your wrinkled ass twenty years ago," Samarand said.

"Then good for me you're such an idiot," Cally laughed.

Larrimore struck again and if the two said anything else Dante didn't hear it. He parried and stabbed for Larrimore's stomach and Larrimore twisted his wrist to turn Dante's blade. He swung the rib for the meat of Larrimore's torso. The man sucked in his gut and swung back his hips and the rib tore through his cloak and cut a shallow crease across his stomach. Larrimore smiled harder and pressed the attack, blade flashing. With both his weapons Dante barely held him back. Blays grunted and tensed, but Dante waved him back. He lashed out with the rib and Larrimore spun away and slashed across Dante's extended arm. He bled freely from both wounds to his left arm, grip unsteady on the bone's natural handle. He felt himself nearing the end of his endurance.

Samarand screamed from off to their right, a bright note against the clash of weapons and the frazzled pop of spent nether. Larrimore's smile broke. He glanced her way and in that brief moment Dante clamped the man's sword between blade and rib and wrenched it from his grasp. It spun away and disappeared into the snow. Dante placed the point of his sword over Larrimore's heart, willing himself to steady the quiver in his arm.

"Don't make me do this," he whispered.

Larrimore leaned into the blade. Dante's wrist twitched as he felt the skin parting. Then he cried out and drove his arm forward, eyes closed to the steel burying itself in the man's chest. He felt his sword tug from his hand as Larrimore slumped to his knees.

"One last thing, boy," the man whispered. Dante's eyes shot open and he knelt across from Larrimore's strained face.

"What is it?"

"My gravestone," Larrimore gasped. "Make sure it describes me as I was."

"Anything."

"'He died plucking the queen from the jaws of a dragon,'" Larrimore said. He smiled at the boy and slumped into the snow, breath rattling past his lips. Dante sat down beside the body and gently freed his sword. He wiped it clean on the white snow and put his hand on Larrimore's still shoulder. For all the years he lived Dante could recall that moment as if living it for the first time: Larrimore's prone form, warm but vacant, his empty hand stretched out in the snow, oblivious to the freezing cold, droplets of water melting on his fingers; his open-eyed face showing no pain or agony, just an enigmatic twist to his lips, a budding surprise in his eyes, as if he'd looked on the order that underpinned the turning of time. Dante's eyes stung. An emotion as heavy as the hand of gravity pushed him against the earth. That Larrimore, a man of wit and action and utter disregard for the fearful opinions of the lesser men around him, that he had died in defense of a woman like Samarand—Dante wiped his eyes, so consumed by injustice he felt nothing but absurdity. He stood, sniffling, to see Cally thrashing around in the snow, strangling away Samarand's final seconds.

Dante sheathed his sword, slid the rib down the right side of his belt. He drew a shuddering breath.

"You're keeping that?" Blays said, scrunching up his face. "Why?"

He shrugged. "I'll have a sword made from it."

"That's sick."

"What isn't," Dante said, then felt dumb, however true it may be. Cally leaned back on his knees, chest heaving, scraggly white hair plastered to his brow. He scowled down at Samarand's red, bug-eyed face and slapped her across her dead cheek.

"Look what you made me do," Cally said. He clambered to his feet and kicked snow over her body. "If you'd known your place you could have been indispensable to me. Idiot pride!" He kicked more snow, stumbled forward.

"I don't think she can hear you," Blays said.

"If there's any justice in the world a passing spirit will give her my message." The old man's green eyes gleamed in the glare of the snow. His gaze shifted to Dante and some of the wildness faded from his wrinkled face. "He's dead, isn't he." Dante didn't reply. "Larrimore was a good man, from what I saw of him."

"You don't know anything about it," Dante said.

"No, I don't."

"Then don't speak as if you do."

"Right," Cally said. His eyes drifted downhill and he frowned at the walking dead standing rock-still a short ways down where Dante'd left them. "You're dealing with dangerous forces."

Dante shrugged, severed the bonds that kept them upright. They dropped like cut puppets.

"I'm not the only one," he said.

"I'm starting to see that." Cally ran his fingers through his beard. "So. Going to add me to the pile of bodies fertilizing this tree?"

Dante snorted, wanting nothing more. It wasn't Cally's assassin that tempted him to strike down the old man; that he could forgive. It was everything else that he couldn't: betrayal and lies, the false friendship he'd let Dante believe so long as it would benefit him, the empty ache he felt to the marrow of his bones. Dante shook his head, sickness curdling his heart.

"I need you to tell that army down there they serve you now. They'd never follow me."

"Wise beyond your years." The old man considered the few dozen men running up the hill toward them, no more than a minute away. "It could work, though some of them probably weren't even born the last time I ruled the order."

"Deal with it."

Cally chuckled to himself, brightening by degrees. He smoothed his hair away from his brow and looked shocked to see he was missing most of the bottom two fingers of his left hand.

"That's unfortunate," he said, watching blood pulse from the stumps with the beating of his heart. He shook his hand, like two new fingers might pop out, then sighed wearily. "Shit."

He spent the minute before the troop arrived binding the wounds with a strip of his black doublet. The sixty-odd men who'd come slowed as they approached the otherworldly spread of the White Tree and the fresh carnage beneath its boughs. Rettinger separated himself from the pack and looked between the old man and the two boys, eyes thick with confusion.

"Tell me why I'm not about to cut you three down as traitors," he said, voice trembling with an indecipherable mix of emotion.

"Because that would make you a traitor, too," Cally said, "and then some bright young man would have to kill you. Where does it end?" He smiled vaguely at the waiting men. Dante felt him gather a trickle of shadow and lend it to his words so they'd boom down the slope of the valley. "I am Callimandicus. Years ago I led this order until Samarand stole it from me. I've just now reclaimed it."

"He killed her! He admits it!" someone shouted from the crowd. There was a general shift of cold steel. Dante clenched his jaw and readied the nether, wondering if he killed a few of them suddenly and brutally enough whether the rest would flee. He doubted that. Somehow his fate again rested in Cally's too-clever hands.

"Do you serve an all too mortal woman, or do you serve Arawn?" Cally barked, sweeping his eyes over the ranks. A few swords faltered.

"We serve the pleasure of the Sealed Citadel," Rettinger said slowly. "All I see is a few outsiders with the blood of good men on their hands."

"He is who he says." A middle-aged man with a scar-creased face stepped forth from the line of soldiers, nodding at Cally.

"Hello, Vlemk," Cally waved. A couple other time-weathered soldiers spoke Cally's full name. Rettinger sucked his teeth and rested his hand on his sword. Snow fell on their faces. Cally lifted his unwounded hand. "I know it hits your hearts as false. But don't act in haste. The rest of the council will know my claim. Let them accept or reject it as they will."

Rettinger's expression flickered as he gazed on the wreckage of the woman and men he'd so recently followed. He shook his head. But he was a born lieutenant, Dante knew, had seen it in the course of the battle with the rebels.

"That's the only smart course," Rettinger said. "I won't risk adding to this tragedy, no matter how hard I might wish to." He turned around to face his men. "Gather up the bodies. It's time to go home."

Dante let the nether bleed away from his grasp. Blays bent over Larrimore's body and plucked at his cloak. Dante dropped his jaw to see his friend looting the body of the only other man he trusted in the entire kingdom, but before he could upbraid Blays or punch him in the face the boy stood and held out Larrimore's badge. It was nearly the same as Dante's own, the outline of the tree surrounded by a silver ring, but at the center of the tree two blue sapphires glittered in the overcast light.

"I think he'd want you to have it," Blays said.

Dante nodded, unable to speak. The twin sapphires winked up at him from his palm. He turned away and wiped his eyes and shuffled around the snow until he found the *Cycle of Arawn*, the book that had been used to cause so much hurt. He brushed away the snow, held it to his chest. The soldiers piled the bodies on the wagon, wrapping loose limbs in the cloth of the slain. Hundreds had died on the journey to Barden and all that had changed was the position of power from an old woman to an older man. A hundred miles lay between them and the dead city. Dante closed his eyes and took the first step.

18

Cally led the soldiers through the empty miles of the road, encountering no one till they reached the fringes of the dead city. He took them over the river and through the outer sprawl, past the silent guards atop the Pridegate and Ingate and finally to the gates of the Citadel itself. Without attacks, with significantly fewer men to slow them down, it took them under four full days. The guards of the Citadel saw the colors of the order and the faces of their fellow armsmen and swung open the doors to let them through.

"What are you going to tell them?" Dante said to Cally as they approached the keep. The remaining members of the council stood on the keep's front steps, awaiting them in the dull afternoon sunlight. Over the last few days, Dante's anger toward Cally had sunk from the base of his skull to the pit of his stomach, leaving his mood sour but his mind clear. He'd resolved to use the old bastard. The council would never allow Dante as its leader, but with Cally seated at its head, he'd have a straight line to its decisions—perhaps a seat for himself. Whichever, he'd no longer be a pawn to any other man.

"I'll tell them the truth," Cally said. He scowled at Dante. "It's not funny."

Cally had sent no riders ahead of their march and they'd made no stops once they'd hit the city. The members of the council spilled down the keep stairs and as they saw how few had come back from Barden their faces switched from anxious expectation to wavering shock.

"*Callimandicus?*" Tarkon said as they drew up. The priest's face wrinkled double as he squinted through the gleaming snow in the yard to look on Cally's face. Cally waved at him.

"Where's Samarand?" Olivander demanded.

"Dead," Cally said.

"Dead?"

Cally nodded. "Very unfortunate."

"And the others?"

"Check that corpse wagon back there," Blays said, jerking his thumb behind him.

Olivander struggled for control of his face. "What about Arawn? Did they release him?"

The four other priests drew themselves as straight as their old backs would allow. Cally combed his beard with his hand.

"That," he said, doling out the words syllable by syllable, "is the reason she's dead."

Olivander gaped. "Arawn slew her?"

"No, you halfwit, Arawn didn't slay Samarand," Cally said, giving Dante a look that suggested how little he'd missed some parts of this place. "She failed. She failed and she decided to lie to you and the people of Gask and say she'd brought him forth. We disagreed on the wisdom of such a plan."

"How were you there to disagree with her in the first place, Callimandicus?" Hart said, looking down on Cally with all the height of the keep's front stairs and his own seven-foot frame. "We thought you've been dead for fifteen years."

"A very good question," Cally said, tapping his chin. He thought for a moment, then laughed and gave them a bony-shouldered shrug. "No more lies. We've had too many already. Why don't we try the truth for once?"

"Which is?" Olivander said.

"I killed Jackson when he was down in Mallon. Couple months ago now. Isn't hard to duplicate a man's appearance if you know what you're doing. You probably won't believe this, but I meant no more harm than to be a voice of moderation on the council. I was of the mind Samarand's warmongering would set us back another hundred years." He glanced between the remaining members of the council. "I know I'm not the only one."

"That's a convenient enough story, considering you ended up

killing her," Hart said.

Cally shrugged. "Well, it happens to be true. Things disintegrated at a regrettable pace when I revealed myself and questioned her intent to deceive you."

Olivander stared hard at the old man. "So you say."

"It's true," Dante said to bolster Cally's lie. "Blays and I were there at the foot of the White Tree. Some of the council agreed with Cally, others with Samarand. When they attacked him, everyone else was killed."

"Larrimore's boy," Olivander said, cocking his head at Dante. "So why didn't you kill the old man when it started? Surely Larrimore went to her aid."

"He also once told me this man had led the council. I hesitated. It all happened so fast. Most of them were dead before I knew what was going on."

"Say I take this at face value," Olivander said, shifting his gaze to Cally. "It sounds enough like her. You've had a few days to think about what the rest of us should do."

"That is a delicate subject," Cally said.

"I was next in line."

Cally's face grew guarded. "It was never Samarand's to take."

"I thought you weren't here to take back your old chair," Olivander said. His hands drifted toward his belt.

"You were here when she stole it from me, weren't you? Botching your lessons in that little chapel while she and the others conspired?"

"I've been defending this city for thirty years," Olivander said, dropping down a step. "I've been on this council for fourteen. Where have you been all that time? Hiding in a cave a thousand miles away? It seems to me it was the will of the council that you should step down, not an act of treason."

Cally thrust out his chin and paced forward and Dante felt the nether shrouding the old man's form. He clamped his lips between his teeth, ready to bite until he bled. If there was to be one more battle, he'd hit as hard as he could. He'd leave it all in rubble.

"I was driven out by treachery," Cally said in a voice that wasn't yet a shout. "She turned them against me, bent the laws to her advantage. The passage of time doesn't make it any less a betrayal."

"Things kept going while you were gone, old man. This isn't the same order you left behind."

"I'm here now."

"So am I," Olivander said. He wrapped his fingers around the hilt of his sword.

"Stop!" Tarkon said, putting himself between Cally and Olivander. "You weren't yet in a position to see how it happened, Olivander. All you know about why Cally left is what Samarand told you. Well, now she's dead. So are five of our brothers. You want to see the rest of us killed over a dispute that was never right in the first place? You want to take your vengeance till there's none of us left at all? Then time can finish turning our city into ruin."

"You're on his side?" Olivander said, flinging a hand at Cally.

"I'm on the side of our order," Tarkon said. "All of us are. I won't see any more of our blood spilled."

Olivander glanced between Cally and Tarkon and the three other living priests. No one spoke.

"Perhaps," Hart said, breaking the long silence, "the full council should be given a say in who's to replace the fallen."

Cally opened his mouth, then clicked his teeth together and nodded. Dante wished Larrimore were here. He could hardly grasp the layers of politics flying between these old men.

"I'd ask it anyway," Cally said. "I have been away too long to know who's worthy to appoint."

Olivander met eyes with Hart. He dropped his hand from his sword. "It's been a long time since the laws of the Citadel were amended. Perhaps we should learn from Samarand's death. Perhaps it's a dangerous thing to collect too much power in the hands of a single man."

"I thought so even when I had it," Cally said.

"We could shift more responsibilities to the council," Tarkon said. He smiled wryly at the few who remained. "If it's time to make changes, the time won't get any righter than this."

"We'll have open discussions on the council's new structure," Olivander stated more than asked.

"It will all be open," Cally said. Olivander looked for a moment like he were trying to swallow a stone the size of his fist. At last he nodded.

"Then let it be remembered I laid down my claim in the name of rebuilding."

Relief washed the faces of the council. Again it had all gone too fast for Dante to fully follow. He felt the nether the priests had held ready soak back into the substance from where it had come. They turned to smaller details: the horses of the troop were led away to stables, the armsmen dispersed to meals and barracks. Rettinger made orders for the storage of the corpses until they could be properly buried. Cally and the boys followed the council priests out of the cold and into the keep.

"Well done out there," Cally told Dante once they'd freed themselves from the others; Blays, sensing he wanted a moment alone with the old man, had run off in search of real food. Cally smoothed his long, stringy hair back from his brow. "That could have turned ugly."

"Shut up," Dante said. "You're naming me to the council."

Cally scratched one of his brambly eyebrows. "Why am I doing that?"

"Because I'll kill you in your sleep if you don't. Olivander will back me."

"Not if I kill you in your sleep first," Cally chuckled. His face froze when he met Dante's eyes. "You're not joking."

"Not at all."

"Then what if I do get to you first?"

"Old men take five naps a day," Dante said. A tendril of nether curled around his finger.

"They're not going to like it," Cally muttered. He grinned, then, as if acknowledging the weakness of that argument. "But what would be the fun in ruling if you never make men do things they don't want to."

Dante tightened his jaw. "I'm glad you're so reasonable."

"Don't take that tone. I don't need to be threatened to do what's right. I'm not a recalcitrant child." Cally tugged on the end of his beard. "You've earned your seat. All you had to do was ask."

Dante said nothing, just stared at the old man who'd once given him safety in the maelstrom of the world. At one time Cally had looked to him like a font of wisdom. Dante had thought the old man could teach him not just to wield the nether, but how to live easily, to use his knowledge to rise above the petty concerns and emotions that threatened to drive him mad. Cally taught him how to use his blood to fuel the shadows, but the only thing he'd taught Dante's heart was a hopeless bitterness he feared he could never escape.

"Do better with your rule than you did with me," Dante said. He turned and left the old man alone in his chambers, the room that had once been Samarand's. Blays was waiting for him in the hall.

"All finished?" he said.

"Yeah."

"Let's go get drunk," Blays said. He clapped Dante on the shoulder and led the way down the stairs. At last Dante saw its appeal.

At first the council resisted, citing Dante's youth and his newness to their order, but Cally held fast and in the end Dante was named to their ranks, by far the youngest to have ever held a seat. They promoted two monks of long standing and left the other three seats vacant for the time being, reasoning it was better to wait until they had worthy candidates than to fill them in haste and risk erring. After two days of discussion, the council agreed now was not the time for open war with Mallon, and Cally sent riders for points across the south. Their agents were to be recalled, asylum granted to any Mallish rebels who may have lost their homes and families in the struggle. The orders with the smiths were canceled. It was a time to rebuild, the council declared, to restore their strength and study what may have gone wrong with the rites to free the vaulted god. For the time being, the business of the southlands was beyond their scope.

The funerals were to be held the day after that decision. Dante ran down the keep's stairs the minute the council concluded and galloped through town to the stoneworker they hired for their markers. He paid the craftsman three times the worth of the work and told him to put all his others on hold.

"But we don't even have a queen right now," the stoneworker said when Dante explained his order.

"That's what makes it so impressive," Dante said.

It was delivered to the Citadel the next morning in time to join the wains headed for the hill overlooking the bay. The stone was simple, but then so had been Larrimore's looks. The procession of council and monks and an honor guard of soldiers walked quietly from the Citadel to the top of the hill where the order kept its vaults. The bodies were laid at rest in the walls of the current sepulcher. Those who still lived stood on the hill, gazing at the gray, white-capped waters of the bay to their north and west, the city spread out behind them, buried in white; the same snows covered the ruins of the outer housing, the age-spotted buildings past the first wall, the well-kept temples and manors and business-houses inside the second; the same white snows draped the black spires of the Cathedral of Ivars, lay on the gray stone walls of the Citadel, the roof of the keep. Now and then a single shout from down in the city caught a freak gust and reached their ears atop the hill, but mostly they stood in a soft breeze that blew unabated over the shin-deep snows.

"These bodies, they're just things," Cally said once he'd readied himself to address the few score men and women who gathered outside the simple columns and cuts of the vault. He had actually combed his beard for the occasion, had switched his torn clothes for the elegant wear of his station. He looked old but ageless, thin but potent, as if he weren't a man but a marble statue of himself. He moved his blue eyes over the waiting crowd. "The people they were, the people we knew, they're not what's turning into dirt in that tomb behind his." He narrowed his eyes until the folds of his skin threatened to squeeze out his sight entirely. "No," he said. "We're here for a while, in these fleshy shells, and all the while we ask Why? What's this pain I feel? Why do I feel so cut off from the men around me, from the skies above? I don't think any of us ever receives the answers to those questions. Have any of you?" He raised his eyebrows at the men. A few of them cleared their throats and murmured soft negatives that could be mistaken for coughs. "Neither have I. And I've lived a very long time!"

He looked out on all that snow, the silent violence of the cold-torn sea, the banks of clouds that hung over the land from one horizon to another. It was threatening to snow again.

"The people that wore those fading cases in there no longer have to face those questions. They've found their answers. Don't let's feel sorry for the dead! Perhaps they've moved on to paradise at the right arm of Arawn. Perhaps they howl into the oblivion of the starless void. Hard to say. Hard to know. One thing of which we may be certain is they're no longer alone. In some form, they're reunited with Arawn and all those he's culled from this earth through all the long ages. I imagine that's an awful lot of people. As many as the flakes of snow that look like one big sheet from our position way up here. It stretches as far as we can see; who knows how much further it goes beyond our sight."

He paused, frowned at himself. Wind blew strings of his gray hair into his eyes. He brushed them away, then rubbed his hands together against the cold. Someone coughed.

"We all want to be back there," he said, nodding at the cloud-covered skies. "Well, now a few more of us are. The rest of us aren't yet ready. We must still live this earth."

"Live this earth," the men sighed.

The priests spoke long, generous words about Samarand, about Baxter and Pioter and the other dead members of the council Dante couldn't remember. He wondered if he should feel something for his part in putting them in their vault, for causing the grief that lined the faces of the men on the hill. Did it mean anything that every man who died had those who wept for his passing? How many had mourned for all the soldiers and trackers and hired blades he'd killed along the way? He found he didn't care, and not just because they'd all been trying to kill him as well. The gods didn't oversee justice in this lowly place, or if they did, it was a godly brand no human could understand. No one could be surprised when the living became the departed, no matter how young they may be, no matter how abruptly it had caught them.

He heard words about Samarand's iron will but fair heart, about some old man's thoughtful wisdom, about a less-older man's noble spirit. They droned on for a long time. When the last man wrapped it up, they looked to Cally, who stepped forward and cleared his throat.

"Since no one else has," Dante said before the old man could conclude things, "I'd like to speak a few words about Larrimore." Cally quirked his brow, then gave him a nod. Dante wandered from the safety of the crowd to where those who'd spoken had faced the mourners alone. His heart railed against his ribs. How could he find any words that weren't hollow? How did a eulogy become anything more than simple-minded words meant to comfort those who went on?

"Larrimore was a good man," he started. His voice sounded thin, false. The eyes of all the men who watched him were already glazed. His cheeks burned. He thrust out his chin and looked past them all, past the condolences and aphorisms he'd heard repeated here and at a half dozen other funerals, stared through the poets' words for dead lords and ladies and all the singers' sad songs until all that was left was a burn beneath his sternum and a cold anger behind his eyes and then he was speaking before he had a chance to weigh his words inside his head.

"I think he'd laugh at us here," he said, glaring over the heads of the crowd. "Make sport of our sober words and somber faces. He was fearless in that way. Unstained by the harsh opinion of others. Yet he treated every man as his equal, even when they were just a boy. Perhaps if we had more like him the judgments we pass would be more aligned with the stars where he now rests." Dante stared at the snow at his feet, searching for more words, but realized that was enough. "Goodbye, Larrimore."

A few of the men uttered agreements. Cally said a few standard words of closure and then the men dispersed from the mass to smaller groups, talking and laughing in quiet, gentle voices.

"He'd have liked that," Blays said, coming up to Dante's side.

"He'd have made fun of me for it." Dante walked to the wagon that carried Larrimore's stone and spoke for a while with the men who'd borne it. They found a clear patch beside the sepulcher where his body lay with the others and hacked at the hard ground with spades until they could lower in the marker's broad base. They firmed it in place with the overturned dirt, stamping the soil flat. By the time they'd finished most of the mourners had started back down the hill toward the Citadel. Cally stood beside Dante and gazed down with him at the gravestone.

"That's disrespectful," he said softly. "The jaws of a dragon?"

Dante smiled tightly. "Only if you didn't know him."

"Hm. I suppose I'll trust your judgment."

Snowflakes began to coast down through the sky. Blays pulled his cloak tighter around his body. He put his hand on Dante's shoulder. He smiled at the marker, then they too turned and started back toward their home, leaving the dead to theirs.

Dante turned seventeen. He sat through meetings of policy and doctrine, met with Nak to resume his language lessons, attended the fortnightly sermons Cally'd made himself responsible for giving at the cathedral across the street from their closed gates. Winter carried on. Dante hadn't realized how much administration went into running the place and had to fight to keep up with all the communiques with distant monks and their tangled questions of scripture, the delicate politics of the courtiers from the capital, the ambassadors from small-fish baronies and earldoms looking for support from the ancient authority of the dead city. Days spun by. Sometimes Dante went sunup to sundown without seeing Blays, who spent equal time investigating Narashtovik's pubs as he did drilling with the soldiers.

After six weeks the first of the rebels and refugees began to trickle in from the lands they'd left in Mallon. Dante, as a southlander, was assigned to clear their passage with the guards of the Pridegate and establish their housing in the more recently abandoned quarters therein. They arrived with dirt-streaked faces and travel-torn clothes, some with the stumps of their limbs hanging in slings, others bearing illness and disease their war-weakened bodies had been unable to resist, or blue-black toes suffered in the frosts of the mountains. He asked Nak's aid and requisitioned some of the younger initiates to help him, overseeing their treatment of the wounded and the infirm. Two dozen or more arrived each day and he called out to the nether to heal what he could. Those he and his aides couldn't make whole were deposited in a new cemetery cleared at the edge of the woods on the southern border of the city. They weren't happy times, but for once they weren't bitter times, either. In some small way, Dante thought, he was making up for all the things he'd done between Bressel and Barden.

Blays started to go along with him, speaking to those refugees strong and willing enough to swap stories and news of their homeland. Whetton had been retaken by King Charles, they told him; the renegades had deserted the forests outside Bressel; a lasting treaty had been established in the Collen Basin between the Arawnites and the clergy of the other sects. The dead had been buried and a few new temples bearing the symbol of Barden had been burnt to cinders. Those who arrived a month after the first refugees spoke of a lasting peace, a return to the relative order of the political jockeying between the aging nobles and the growing guilds of Bressel, to the same minor sparks and threats that had always existed between the wide kingdom of Mallon and the lesser-settled territories in its west and south. Blays began to wander off when Dante attended to the ceaseless treatment of the ill, staying gone until the evening, sometimes not returning till the next day's noon. As time softened Dante's mood, it seemed to stir up Blays' in a way that was too active for melancholy and too pensive for wanderlust. He talked little, even when they found the time to drink together. Dante didn't know what to do. If it were him, he'd want the space to work it out for himself. He let Blays be. The sick kept coming, scores per day, and he lost himself restoring them to health, countering the name of the dead city one man at a time.

"Let's go up top," Blays said to Dante at the conclusion of a council session concerning the feelers toward independence that kept arriving from the norren territories around the foothills of the Dundens. Being recognized by Narashtovik would all but guarantee their freedom in the capital.

"There were more refugees this morning," Dante said, tugging the collar of his cloak straight. "They need me."

"Just for a moment. The city doesn't look so nasty from up there."

"Fine. Just for a moment."

Dante left the council chambers and walked with Blays down the hall to the cramped stairway that led to the peak of the keep. The stairs spiraled so tightly he always feared he'd get halfway up and meet someone on their way down, then have to find a way to turn himself around, climb back down to the landing, and start all over again. They met no one else, though, and emerged into the wood-roofed battlement alone. Blays walked past where the roofing stopped, out into the open wind, and leaned himself against a crenel. The city spread out beneath them.

"Snow's starting to melt," Blays said.

"I think we're going to send a force to guard the passes soon," Dante said. "King Charles must know this city played some part in everything that's happened."

Blays nodded absently. "I've been thinking," he said. "I want to go back to Bressel."

"That's not a bad idea, either. We should probably try to reestablish diplomatic channels before anything else can start up."

"Not like that."

"What, suddenly you can read the king's mind?"

"That's not what I mean." Blays stared down hard on the rooftops: black on the south faces, where the sun hit all day, and white on the north faces, where the snow lay in shadow. "I mean, I want to live there again."

"What?"

"It's something about this place," Blays said, gesturing at the walled yard of the Citadel, then the disrepair of the buildings in the outer half of the city. "I just want to leave it for a while."

"Okay," Dante said. His brain felt numb. He rested his elbows in the gap between two merlons and blinked down at Narashtovik. "When?"

"Soon. Two weeks at most."

"I thought you meant months from now, at least." Dante stared at his own hands. He'd only known Blays a few months, but he couldn't imagine one of them traveling somewhere without the other. Blays wanted to leave? "We've got wealth here," he said. "Respect. We're doing good things—saving the casualties of Samarand's war. The city's starting to come back to life."

"They don't need us for that."

"People would die without us!"

"No they wouldn't," Blays said. "You and Nak have trained enough acolytes to do the job. They wouldn't miss you if you left for Bressel for a while. They certainly don't need me."

"Do you even remember what Bressel was like?"

"I lived there all my life."

"Well, did I ever tell you about the time I tried to talk myself into eating rats?" Dante said in a tone that reminded himself of

Larrimore's. "The only thing that stopped me was the shame of being seen roasting them in the common room."

Blays snorted. "It was never like that for me."

"And what will it be like now? What's so great about Bressel?"

"I don't know!" Blays shook his head. He dislodged himself from the wall and glared past Dante's shoulder. "I just want to live for a while in a place where people aren't always looking at me like I might kill them for jostling me. I want to go to a public house where I still have to buy my own drinks. Meet a few women who won't make puns about 'unbuckling' me. The people here don't treat us like men, they treat us like caged tigers—they all want to get close to us, to touch us to prove to their friends that they're not afraid. Maybe that's all right with you, but I'm sick of it."

"They're just grateful," Dante said. "When they hear 'Blays Buckler and Dante Galand,' they're not expecting we're a couple of kids."

"I don't care what they're expecting. Whatever they think I am, I'm not." Blays turned back to the crenels and gazed down into the narrow streets. "I'm leaving, Dante. I've meant to for a long time. I just hadn't figured it out yet."

"Fine. Leave, then." Dante shoved Blays in the shoulder. "Did you hear me?"

"Yeah." Blays met his eyes and for the first time in weeks Dante saw nothing of the malaise that had dwelled in them for so long. He meant it. He didn't want to leave Dante behind, but he would if he had to. What was making Dante so adamant to stay, then? Being recognized for once? Feared, even? In part, maybe. But while he hadn't yet mastered Larrimore's total disdain for the opinions of his peers, nor was Dante ruled by them. Blays was right about the refugees, too—the monks and acolytes were enough to save those able to be saved. But it wasn't just that Dante wanted to make some kind of repentance, either. At heart, knowing only what he had at the time, he wouldn't have undone any of the choices he'd made along the way.

It was much deeper than that. Narashtovik remained the one place in the world that could teach him all the things he still didn't know. In a flash of instinct he would have overruled with logic a few months earlier, he realized if he let that need keep him here while he let Blays wander his own path, he'd be no different than Cally, no better than the motives that had led Samarand to cause so much confusion in the south. If he spent a year or three off in the world, he'd still have decades in which to hone his power.

"You really want to go?" Dante said.

"I have to."

"All right," Dante said. "Maybe it's time for me to follow you for a while."

Blays' eyebrows flickered. "You mean that?"

"I'll ask Cally to sanction the trip. Send us as delegates to the halls of Bressel."

"I don't want to just say some pretty words to princes and then come right back."

"We've done enough for now, haven't we?" Dante shrugged. "Isn't it time we dissipated for a while?"

"Long past, I think," Blays said. He grinned slowly, as if he didn't trust himself to rediscover the expression. Dante laughed through his nose.

"No changing your mind. Once I ask Cally, there's no turning back."

"You just worry about what you'll tell him."

"I'll tell him whatever I please," Dante said. "He knows I'll kill him if he ever tries to control me again."

"Yeah right," Blays said. "He probably makes you change his diapers. That's how you got on the council, isn't it?"

"You're the one who needs them," Dante said. He lunged at Blays, faking like he were going to knock him off the roof. Blays gasped, then tackled him to the stones. Below them, the city continued to unthaw.

Cally nodded when Dante made his case for the trip to Bressel. He leaned back in his chair and considered the boy.

"I've been meaning to send someone official. I suppose you'd do better at it than someone who can't speak the language without sounding like they're coughing up a cat. Let me scare up an escort."

"No," Dante said. "Just me and Blays."

Cally closed one eye. "Without a lot of retainers around to make you look important, they might not take you as seriously as you deserve."

"Going without guards and circumstance will just be the better to convince them we mean what we say."

Cally started to say something else, then sighed instead. "How long do you plan to be gone?"

"I don't know. A while."

"Even a leisurely pace and a few weeks indulging in the largesse of the courts should have you back here by summer's end."

"We'll be there longer than that. Maybe we'll head back before the passes grow treacherous. I can't say right now."

"Why don't we drop the pretense this is a negotiation," Cally said, rolling his eyes. "Yes. Fine. Do as you please. Maybe you'll take all the pandemonium with you. If you do down there what you did up here, a year from now we could all be feasting in the palace of Bressel."

"Yeah." Dante gazed on the old man and found he didn't fear him. His anger and hatred had burned down, too, become cold things, some of which looked solid but would fall apart at a touch, like charred-out logs the morning after a bonfire. "I know why you lied to me. You wanted to be important again. You wanted to have men have to listen to you again."

"I had some notion about stopping a war as well. Try to remember to include that part when you write the history."

"Why did Gabe repeat your little story, though?" Dante said, ignoring the rest. "Did you trick him, too? Gabe wouldn't care who was leading the council. He was above that."

Cally snorted. His brows lifted and pinched together, as if Dante were making a joke, then he leaned back in his chair and stared at the boy for a long time.

"We're going to win norren independence," Cally said. "When I plotted out that angle for Gabe's eyes, he snapped from his brooding with a speed that approached the alarming."

Dante blinked. "The capital isn't going to like that."

"Yes, but if you take a moment to consider the matter closely, you might see the capital's divine wisdom is a bit clouded by the belief the norren should do what they say because they can kill them if they don't." Cally waved a hand at him. "Head back to Bressel, then. Stay a while. But try to spare a moment between now and your return to think about how on earth we're going to fulfill our promise to our good friend Gabe."

Dante and Blays left alone on horseback two weeks later to the day, packs full, affairs ordered, details of the diplomatic end resolved. Dante had been burdened down with letters of introduction and various hints toward treaties written in Cally's hand. He'd left the rib of Barden with Cally for study—he hadn't thought of it in weeks, busy as he was—with orders to forge it into a sword, if at all possible, which Cally denounced as perverse and ostentatious but said he'd see to all the same. Cally made no mention of the book Dante never let from his sight and so he'd decided to take it with him once more. Other than essentials, Blays carried little more than his sword, his single-sapphired badge that marked him as Dante's second, and an empty flask which he claimed would never pass in sight of a settlement without being filled.

Larrimore's old badge winked at the throat of Dante's cloak as they emerged from the shadow of the keep. The streets were slushy, muddy at the edges. Water trickled between the cobbles. The guard at the Pridegate waved to them as they walked through. Dante waved back, then turned his face to the tumbled blocks of the city fringes. It would take the arrival of ten times as many refugees as had arrived so far to run out of space in the vacant houses between Ingate and Pridegate. Tens of thousands could come before the slums beyond the Pridegate got filled.

The scent of pines began to overwhelm those of human waste. It was early spring. Cool breezes had started to thaw the lowlands, but fresh snow appeared once or twice a week before shrinking back each afternoon. They took an unhurried route along the main roads to the Riverway, the lowest pass through the Dundens. It would add a hundred miles to their journey, but for once, neither of them cared about their speed. Blays grinned as the city disappeared behind them and the dark woods rose up around them.

"Careful," he warned. "There may be bad men about."

"Whatever will we do?" Dante said. He drew his sword and pointed it down the road. "Perhaps Blayschopper will defend us from those miserable souls."

"And Robertslayer beside it."

They laughed, slashing the air a few times, then put the weapons away, embarrassed somehow, almost guilty, as if the blades had seen too many dead men to be waved as a joke. The road rolled before them. They began to remember the prevalence of birdsong, the rhythm of clomping hooves, the rush of wind in waist-high grass and pines unbent by snow. They joked a little, talked of what they'd do in Bressel once they'd had their talks with the local officials, but mostly they rode in silence, drifting in their own thoughts.

They had stopped a war—delayed it, more likely, to another age—and that had cost lives of its own, a few of whom Dante'd even liked. To his eyes, the Arawnites were no different or more dangerous than any other sect. Back in Mallon, they would worship in secret again, or be maimed and killed for their heresy. At the foot of the White Tree, he'd been convinced they'd been one right word away from looking on the god's face, but his certainty had dimmed in the passing of days, a feeling as lost as a spent breath.

Barden itself was no proof. Sown from a god's knuckle; the creation of a human power Dante someday hoped to match; a mystery from before the memory of man. Each seemed equally likely and equally impossible.

The woods gave way to plains and they stopped in a town for a day for fresh food and a soft bed and rum for Blays' flask. The plains gave way to hills and for two days they rode in a sun so warm they were able to shed their cloaks. The following afternoon a bitter wind blew in a storm of hail and Dante raised his hood and heard it pocking from his cowl. Icy white pebbles bounced on the trail, dashing into quickly-melted splinters. Blays laughed, turned up his face to the light stings of the changed weather. Dante followed suit and took a hailstone to the eye.

He could build a Barden some day. He knew it in his bones. He knew it the way he knew water would feel wet or that he could pick up a stone and throw it. At times he felt he could plunge both hands into the pale shell of reality and strip it away like sand. It wasn't arrogance. It wasn't destiny. It simply was. If he could stay alive—he tried to tally, briefly, how many had died in the last few months (most of them faceless; a few, like Larrimore, never to be equaled again), but at last it would be a guess, and he wouldn't do the dead the final dishonor of lumping them into a single number, as if, in the end, all that mattered were the quantity—if he could stay alive where so many others hadn't, he knew he would one day peer into those powers behind the hills and the streams, and where he looked, the shadows would move.

Snow infiltrated the high hills surrounding the Dundens. The horses plodded on. They lit fires by night, cooked the rabbits Dante killed with a simple flash of nether each dusk. He prodded up the meat-flecked skeletons and set them out on watch while they slept under the burning eyes of the stars and whatever gods might call them home. They passed refugees and tradesmen and vagabonds on the roads, but by night his rabbit-guard stood sentry and was not disturbed.

The hills banked down to the roaring mountain-fed river and they followed its narrow gorge through the mountains. The snow was wet and heavy, but no more than a couple inches deep. The river flowed down to meet the wide calm waters of the Chanset and they descended into bony trees studded with the green buds of fresh growth. The horses churned the mud of the thaw and the wind-tossed rain showers.

Perhaps Blays had it right. Let the world turn on its own for a while. It had done so before they were born and it would do so after they were gone. For whatever ills it caused, the ambition of the men within it was no less natural then the nether itself. Whatever it was that drove them to do harm was the same need that compelled them to build sky-scratching cathedrals and castle walls twice as thick as a man was tall, to tramp down the roads that spoked through a thousand miles of farmland and wilderness, to gather in villages and towns and cities in the planet-hugging reach of conquest and commerce; the same need that made them grow mile on mile of wind-ruffled wheat, that made men fill libraries with books and books with words, that made them fill their lungs with air and their stomachs with beer; that peopled a poor woman's home with bright-eyed, soot-streaked children who would one day travel from one coast to another, or launch across the shuddering waves far from sight of land, or die before they knew what surrounded them, or rob an ancient temple in the dead of night and pry its secrets from the rubbly stone.

Trees thrust up around Dante, blotting out the sun. Grass sighed at his ankles and thighs whenever he stepped off the road. Hundreds of pounds of horse rose and fell beneath him. Crows spat at each other in the boughs and were chased away by nattering squirrels. In the undergrowth, mice and rabbits and wolves stirred ankle-deep leaves. Spooked deer caught the boys' scent and crashed away through the brambles. And above them, by day or by night, the wind breathed in the trees. If there had ever been gods in this place, they'd been driven out by the crush of their own creations a long time ago. Arawn, he knew, had not been at the Tree. The *Cycle of Arawn* had led him through unknown years of man's knowledge. He had thought it would show him its very roots. Instead, in following it to its end, to the endless snowfield beneath the White Tree where he believed he would find a god — an order and a meaning and a hold on this world — he had found himself simply trapped among mad people doing mad things, had killed one friend and been betrayed by another, one more mote in a blind storm of ash, alone except for Blays, vulnerable except the wrath he'd found in the nether. His silence deepened. Possibly, that was enough.

After weeks of travel the smoke of Whetton mingled with the dusky sky. Red clouds piled up to the west. The road forked, one branch east toward town, another to the south and Bressel. Dante led his horse east.

"Where are you going?" Blays said, jerking his head at the other path.

"Whetton."

"We're only a couple days out from Bressel."

"There's no hurry," Dante said. "I want to see what's become of the city."

Blays bit the skin around his thumbnail. "What if they recognize what's become of us? You do remember our last visit? The local hospitality of rope and high branches?"

"Last time we were here you looked like a rag wrapped around a stick," Dante said. "Look at you now in your fancy clothes, your hair cut straight."

Blays eyed him. "There were an awful lot of people in that field. Thousands, if I recall."

"If anyone gives us any trouble," Dante said, nudging his horse forward, "we'll just point them at our badges. They'll be in no rush to invite more trouble from the north. If that doesn't do it, we'll tell them about how, at great personal risk, we saved their stupid town from war."

"This will end badly," Blays declared, then rallied to catch up.

They headed down the road where months ago thousands of citizens had fled fire and battle. Today a shepherd was driving his flock to market and the pair skirted around the grungy blobs of walking wool. The outskirts of the city were hewn in fresh blond wood, offset here and there by the charred-out husks of what remained. The streets were thick with sodden ash and charcoal. The rap of hammers smacked on all sides. Masons and carpenters shouted from scaffolds wrapped around the sharp corners of damaged temples and half-constructed manors, squeezing out a few last minutes of work in the waning daylight. Men and women hurried home from market or the docks, or left the quiet warmth of their hearths for the clamor and company of a public house. Blays' mouth twitched at the signs above the pubs, the painted heads of stags or owls or an anchor tilted on its side.

"Pint?" Dante said, gazing down the street.

"As long as we're here," Blays grinned. They found a public stable and parted with some silver as their horses were led away to be groomed and fed. Blays elbowed Dante in the ribs and raced ahead through the damp chill of the early night. A fat turtle was printed above the doors of the first place he chose.

Blays flagged down a servant and they were brought mugs and ale. Dante drank slowly, pleasantly surprised to find he liked the taste. Perhaps he was getting older. When Blays wandered off to the latrine, Dante made a round of the room, holding a few brief conversations with any man or woman who looked at home.

"Drink up," he said when Blays got back.

"Suddenly there's a hurry again?"

"I have a terrible urge to go see if the inn where they arrested you was burnt down."

"If it hasn't, mind if we finish the job?"

"Let's see where the night takes us," Dante said. Blays drained his ale and they hit the street again. The laughter of men echoed through the alleys. They wandered the city, half-remembering streets they'd last seen half a year ago, their direction sense aided by a couple pints apiece. Dante kept an eye out for the boys who'd helped them then—he couldn't remember their names—but didn't see either. Probably, they hadn't made it through the upheaval; they'd had nothing to protect them even in times of peace. But they had had their wits. Maybe they lived yet, hiding under the docks, peering down from the roofs on the men who owned the streets, waiting to descend till they could take a piece for themselves.

Finally Dante and Blays came to the corner near the north end of town where they'd slept a single night. The building was gone, torn down, replaced by a few tents and a small shack. Blays spat on the dirt.

"Too bad buildings don't have tombstones," he said, giving the grounds the finger. "I have a sudden urge to urinate."

Dante peered down the street, knowing the pub the man in the Fat Turtle had directed him to had to be near. Blays finished his business and Dante headed down a cross street. Just when he thought he'd gone too far his eyes seized on the image of a four-fingered hand painted above a pub door.

"This looks as good as any," Dante said, swinging through the door. He glanced through the room, then sighed and took a seat. After an hour and two pints for him and four for Blays he was ready to try their luck somewhere else. Blays was rambling on about how they should try to get arrested again just to see if the watch had the guts when the door banged open.

"Be right back," Dante said, threading past tables and outstretched legs to intercept the man who'd just entered. He stood behind the brown-bearded figure and tapped him on the shoulder. "Time to meet your maker, you villain."

Robert Hobble turned and punched blindly for Dante's head. Dante sidestepped the blow, then jumped forward and grabbed the man's collar. Robert screwed up his face, eyes leaping between Dante's.

"Lyle's soiled drawers," he said with beer-thick breath. "You made it? Did you really do it?"

"It's done." Dante heard bootsteps behind him. He stepped aside.

"No thanks to you, you cowardly son of a bitch," Blays said. He brushed past Dante to face the old friend Dante'd been hunting since they stepped foot in Whetton.

"You'll understand some day, you filth-mouthed pup," Robert said, lips and eyes creased with a smile. He staggered forward and crushed Blays up in a hug. Blays' chin rested on the man's shoulder and he gave Dante a strange, knowing look he'd remember years after Blays had gone but would never be able to understand. At times he thought he saw gratitude in that look, but at others it could have been betrayal. Sometimes he saw nothing in it but a confusion so faint it was barely there at all, like the face of a man who's forgotten how it had ever felt to be young.

Robert unclinched, laughing and clapping his hands. "This calls for a round. Many rounds. Rounds until they get the picture and roll the keg right up to our table."

Dante hunted down a servant and let her know she had some lively stepping in her future. When he returned to the table Robert was already yammering on at Blays.

"So much has happened, boys," he said, draping one hand over the back of a chair and pointing at them with the other. "Came back and the place was a battlefield. I rallied a few of the fellows I knew to help retake the town and what do you know, they made me a captain!" He flicked a tri-colored badge on his chest. "How long are you here? Got time to hear a few of my stories before you start boring me with your own?"

"I think I know how all of yours start," Blays said. "'There I was, rum-soaked as the bottom of the barrel, when all of a sudden—'"

"It's like you were there!" Robert said, reaching across the table and giving him a knock on the shoulder.

"We'll be here for a while," Dante said. "For the moment there's nothing more."

They settled in to the warm smoke of the hearth, the earthy smell of simmering stew, the stinging taste of bitter ale. Around them men came and went and argued and joked. Dante bent down to his pack and made sure the book was still there. He was a young man in a strange world. Some day he would take his place among the black, but for now the book was his. Just as much, Robert would be there whenever he took the time to find him; for Blays, he couldn't imagine what could drive them apart. Dante leaned back on the solid wood of his chair, listening to the raucous calls of the crowd, to Robert's beery words and Blays' guarded laughter. His ears soared with the sounds of all those who still lived.

ABOUT THE AUTHOR

Along with *The Cycle of Arawn*, Ed is the author of the post-apocalyptic *Breakers* series. Born in the deserts of Eastern Washington, he's since lived in New York, Idaho, Los Angeles, and Hawaii, all of which have been thoroughly destroyed in one of his books.

He lives with his fiancée and spends most of his time writing on the couch and overseeing the uneasy truce between two dogs and two cats.

He blogs at http://www.edwardwrobertson.com

Printed in Great Britain
by Amazon